SECRETS IN THE ATTIC

Virginia Andrews® Books

The Dollanganger Family Series
Flowers in the Attic
Petals on the Wind
If There Be Thorns
Seeds of Yesterday
Garden of Shadows

The Casteel Family Series
Heaven
Dark Angel
Fallen Hearts
Gates of Paradise
Web of Dreams

The Cutler Family Series
Dawn
Secrets of the Morning
Twilight's Child
Midnight Whispers
Darkest Hour

The Landry Family Series
Ruby
Pearl in the Mist
All That Glitters
Hidden Jewel
Tarnished Gold

The Logan Family Series
Melody
Heart Song
Unfinished Symphony
Music in the Night
Olivia

The Orphans Miniseries
Butterfly
Crystal
Brooke
Raven
Runaways (full-length novel)

My Sweet Audrina
(does not belong to a series)

The Wildflowers Miniseries
Misty
Star
Jade
Cat
Into the Garden (full-length novel)

The Hudson Family Series
Rain
Lightning Strikes
Eye of the Storm
The End of the Rainbow

The Shooting Stars Series
Cinnamon
Ice
Rose
Honey
Falling Stars

The De Beers Family Series
Willow
Wicked Forest
Twisted Roots
Into the Woods
Hidden Leaves

The Broken Wings Series
Broken Wings
Midnight Flight

The Gemini Series
Celeste
Black Cat
Child of Darkness

The Shadows Series
April Shadows
Girl in the Shadows

The Early Spring Series
Broken Flower
Scattered Leaves

The Secret Series
Secrets in the Attic

VIRGINIA ANDREWS®
SECRETS IN THE ATTIC

**SIMON &
SCHUSTER**

London · New York · Sydney · Toronto

A CBS COMPANY

First published in the US by Pocket Books, 2007
A division of Simon and Schuster Inc.
First published in Great Britain by Simon & Schuster UK Ltd, 2009
A CBS COMPANY

1 3 5 7 9 10 8 6 4 2

Simon & Schuster UK Ltd
1st Floor
222 Gray's Inn Road
London WC1X 8HB

www.simonsays.co.uk

Simon & Schuster Australia
Sydney

A CIP catalogue record for this book is available
from the British Library

Trade paperback ISBN: 978-1-84737-202-4
Hardback ISBN: 978-1-84737-201-7

Printed in the UK by CPI Mackays, Chatham ME5 8TD

SECRETS IN
THE ATTIC

Prologue

As young girls living in a peaceful and relatively crime-free community, Karen Stoker and I should have had an adolescence full of hope, an adolescence of bright colors, sweet things, and upbeat music. No one season should have looked drearier than another. Winter should have been dazzlingly white, with icicles resembling strings of diamonds and the air jingling with our laughter at the crunch of snow beneath our boots. Spring, summer, and fall would each have its own magic. In fact, our lives should have been one long and forever special day protected by loving parents and family.

Ghosts and goblins, creatures from below or out of the darkness, were to be nothing more than movie and comic-book creations to make us scream with delight in the same way we might scream sitting on a roller coaster plunging through an illusion of disaster. Afterward we would gasp and hug each other in utter joy that we were still alive. Our excited eyes would look as if tiny diamonds floated around our pupils. Our feet would look as if we had springs in them when we walked, and all the adults in our families would cry for mercy and ask us to take our boundless energy outside so they could catch their breath.

That was the way it should have been; it could have been, but there was something dark and evil incubating just under the surface of the world in which we lived, in which I, especially, lived. I was in a protective rose-colored bubble, oblivious and happy, pirouetting like a ballerina on ice, unaware of the rumbling below and never dreaming that I could fall through into the freezing waters of sorrow and horror, the parents of our worst nightmares.

It was Karen who showed me all this, Karen who pointed it out, lifted the shade, and had me look through the window into the shadows that loitered ominously just beyond our imaginary safe havens. I thought Karen was like Superwoman with X-ray eyes, who could see through false faces and through false promises.

I wanted to be Karen's best friend the first moment I set eyes on her after we had moved into the Doral house, a house made infamous by its original owners, because the wife, Lucy Doral, was said to have murdered her husband, Brendon, and buried him somewhere on the property. His body was never found, and she was never charged with any crime, because she claimed he had run off, and back in the nineteenth century, it was much more difficult to track people. No one could prove or disprove what she had said. However, the house had a stigma attached to it, and it remained abandoned for many years before it was bought and sold three times during the past eighty-five years. Each owner made some necessary upgrade in plumbing and electricity, as well as expanding the building.

My brother, Jesse, saw the house briefly when my father took a second look at it and brought him along, but Jesse went off for his college orientation in Michigan a week before we moved, so he didn't spend any real time in our new home until his holiday break at Thanksgiving, and he was too excited about going to college to really think about where we were going to live. Later, when he did spend time in it, I found him surprisingly aloof and disinterested. It was as if he was already on his way toward his independent life and we were now merely a way station along that journey.

Karen claimed she understood his attitude.

She and I often sat upstairs in the attic of my house to carry on our little talks, because it was such a private place away from the newer, expanded kitchen and living room below that had been part of an add-on. There was a short stairway on the south end of the upstairs landing leading up to the attic door. It had no banister, and the old wooden steps moaned like babies with bellyaches when we walked up. For me, and even more for Karen, the most interesting thing about our house was exploring it and the grounds around it.

"Maybe we'll discover the remains of Mr. Doral," she said, "or at least some important evidence. She could have sealed him in a wall as the character did in Edgar Allan Poe's 'The Cask of Amontillado,' " she whispered, and put her ear to walls as if she could still hear the poor man moaning and begging to be freed.

As soon as she laid eyes on the attic, she declared it was the most fascinating part of the house, because it was large and contained so many old things, furnishing, boxes filled with old sepia pictures, dust-coated lamps, a few bed mattresses and some pots and dishware that previous owners didn't care to take with them. There was even some costume jewelry. Karen thought they might have forgotten they had put it all there. She said everything looked as if it had been deserted. She almost made me cry with the way she embraced a pillow or caressed an old dresser, claiming all were on the verge of disappearing and were so grateful we had come up to befriend and claim them. She said it was a nest of orphans, and then she clapped her hands and declared that we would adopt them all and make them all feel wanted again.

"I know just what your brother is feeling about this place, this town," she told me after he had returned to college at the end of his Christmas holiday recess and I had complained to her about how indifferent he seemed to be the whole time he was home. He didn't care that we had to drive miles and miles to go to a movie or that there were no fancy restaurants in our village. He didn't care that there were no streetlights on our road or that our nearest neighbor was a half-mile away.

Karen and I were sitting on an old leather settee that had wrinkled and cracked cushions reminding us of an aged face dried close to parchment by Father Time. After only our second time up there, Karen christened the attic "our nest." Neither the stale, hot trapped air nor the cobwebs in the corners bothered her. We aired it out and dusted as best we could, but it never seemed that clean. She told me we shouldn't care, because clubhouses, secret places, were supposed to look and be like this and we were lucky to have it.

The day we talked about Jesse, we both had put on old-fashioned dresses with ankle-length skirts and lots of lace, wide-brimmed flowery hats, and imitation diamond and emerald earrings we had found in an old black trunk that Karen said were like those that had gone down with the *Titanic*. I wore an ostentatious fake pearl necklace that had turned a shade of pale yellow. Karen wore a pair of black old-fashioned clodhopper shoes, too, and a pair of those thick nylon stockings we saw elderly women wear, the kind that fell in ripples down their calves and around their ankles.

"Oh, really? What's my brother feeling?" I asked, a little annoyed that she thought she could interpret him better than I could.

"It's simple. Don't be thick. You think I'd be here if I didn't have to?" she asked. "If I were in college like your brother, I wouldn't come back even on holidays. Not me. I want to live in a big, exciting city that never sleeps, a city with grand lights and continuous parties, traffic and noise and people, a city with so much happening you can't decide whether to go uptown or downtown. Don't you?"

Her eyes filled with such exhilaration it was as if she had the power to lift us and carry us off on a flying carpet to her magical metropolis. She held out her arms and spun around so hard she nearly fell over from dizziness, making me laugh. I had lived in Yonkers, which was very close to New York City, and didn't think big-city life held all the enchantment she thought it did, but I agreed with everything she said, because I wanted so to be her dearest friend and I enjoyed listening to her fantasies and dreams.

I was ever so grateful that I had this house, this attic, this stage where we could act out our imaginings or look at the faded sepia pictures of young men and women and make up romantic stories about them. This one died in childbirth; that one took her own life when her lover betrayed her or her father forbade her to marry him. Karen never failed to come up with a plot or a name. All her stories were romantic but sad. She seemed capable of drawing these tales and the characters out of the very attic walls.

I did come to believe there was something magical about being in our nest, something that helped us mine our imaginations with ease. There were only two naked light fixtures dangling from the attic ceiling, casting uneven illumination, but Karen didn't complain about it. She said she rather liked the eerie and mysterious atmosphere it created, and I tried hard to feel the same way. Putting on the old clothes, sitting among the antiques, gave us the inspiration to fantasize and plan, she more than I, but I was learning fast to be more like her and let my imagination roam.

I told her so.

"Yes, why not?" she asked, lifting her eyes and looking as if she were standing on a stage. "After all, it's our imagination that frees us from the chains and weight of our dull reality. Come dreams and fantasies. Overwhelm me."

She could make statements and gesture with such dramatic flair that I could only stare and smile with amazement. I told her she should go out for the school plays. She grimaced.

"And be confined by someone else's vision, plot, characters? Never," she said. "We must remain always free spirits. Your house, our nest, is the only stage I want to be on."

Our new home was on Church Road in Sandburg, New York, a hamlet that Karen claimed gave credence to the theory that some form of sedative had seeped into the groundwater. Karen said there was a picture of Sandburg next to the word *sleepy* in the dictionary.

"People here have to be woken up to be told they've woken up," she told me.

"Maybe that's why it's called Sandburg. They named it after the Sandman," I added, always trying to keep up with her wit.

"No, no one was that creative. It's named after the nearby creek. Speaking of names, I like yours," she told me.

"My name? Why?"

"I envy people with unusual names. Zipporah. It shows your parents weren't lazy when it came to naming you. My name is so common, my parents could have imitated Tarzan and Jane and called me Girl, and it wouldn't have made all that much difference," she said, the corners of her mouth turning down and looking as if they dripped disgust. I couldn't imagine how someone like her could be unhappy with herself in any way.

"It's not so common. I like your name. It takes too long to say mine."

"It does not. Don't let anyone call you Zip," she warned. "It sounds too much like the slang for zero, and you're no zero."

"What makes you so sure?" I asked. How had she come to that conclusion so quickly? I wasn't exactly Miss Popularity with either the girls or the boys at my last school. In fact, I had yet to receive a single letter or phone call from a single old friend.

"Don't worry. I have a built-in zero detector. I'll

point out the zeros in our school, and you'll clearly see that I know a zero from a nonzero."

It didn't take long for me to believe she could do that. Anyone she disliked, I disliked; anyone she thought was a phony, I did as well.

Both Karen and I were fifteen at the time, less than a year away from getting our junior driver's licenses. She was two months older. With passing grades in the high school driver's education class, we could get our senior licenses at seventeen, which meant we would be able to drive after dark. We would also get a discount on auto insurance. This was all more important to me than to her, because I was confident I could eventually have a car of my own. Jesse had his own car, a graduation present, so I assumed I would, too.

We talked about getting our licenses and a car all the time, dreaming of the places we would visit and the fun we would have. Sometimes, up in the nest, we pretended we were in my car driving along. We'd sit on the old sofa, and as I simulated driving, she pointed out the scenery in Boston or New Orleans and especially California, shouting out the names of famous buildings, bridges, and statues. We used travel brochures and pretended we were actually plotting out an impending vacation.

We considered a driver's license to be our passport to adulthood. As soon as you got your license, your image among your peers and even adults changed. You had control of a metallic monster, the power to move over significant distances at will, and you could grant a seat on the journey with a nod and make someone, even someone older, beholden.

"Of course, it's obvious we don't need a car to get

around Sandburg," Karen said. "It's so small the sign that says 'Leaving Sandburg, Come Visit Us Again,' is on the back of the sign that says 'Entering Sandburg, Welcome.'"

When I told Jesse what Karen had said, he laughed hysterically and said he was going to try to get a sign made up like that and put it on his dorm-room wall. He was so excited about the idea that I wished I had been the one to say it, especially after he remarked, "Your girlfriend is pretty clever and not just pretty."

The imaginary sign wasn't all that much of an exaggeration. There was only one traffic light in the whole hamlet. It was at the center where the two main streets joined to form a T, and because this was a summer resort community, during the fall, winter, and spring, the traffic light was turned into a blinker, more often ignored than obeyed. If Sparky—the five-year-old cross between a German shepherd and a collie owned by Ron Black, the owner of Black's Café—could speak, he would bear witness against three-quarters of the so-called upstanding citizens who ignored the light. Whenever he was sprawled on the sidewalk, Karen and I noticed that Sparky always raised his head from his paws each time a car drove through the red without stopping. He looked as if he was making a mental note of the license plate.

We laughed about it. Oh, how we laughed at ourselves, our community, our neighbors, back then. There seemed to be so much that provided for our amusement, such as the way Al Peron, the village's biggest landlord, strutted atop the roof of one of his buildings with his arms folded across his chest, his chin up, as if he were the lord of the manor, looking over his possessions. We called him Our Own Mussolini, because he resembled the Italian dictator as pictured in our history textbook. We giggled at the way Mrs. Krass, whose husband owned the fish market, swayed like a fish swimming when she walked. Stray cats followed cautiously behind her as if they expected some fresh tuna to fall out of her pockets.

We laughed about Mr. Buster, the postal clerk, whose Adam's apple moved like a yo-yo when he repeated your order for stamps and wrote it down on a small pad before giving them to you, and we shook our heads at the way the Langer Dairy building leaned to the left, a building Karen called the Leaning Tower of Sandburg.

"If too many customers stand on one side, it might just topple," she declared. Mrs. Langer wondered why Karen and I shrieked and then hurried from one side to the other when people came in behind us.

Karen and I observed so many little things about our community, things that no one else seemed to notice or care to notice. I began to wonder if we indeed had a bird's-eye view of everything and floated far above our world. Whenever I mentioned something Karen and I had noted, my mother or my father would say, "Oh, really? I never thought of that," or, "I never realized it." Maybe adults see things too deeply, I thought, and miss what's on the surface. They were once like us and saw what we saw, but they forget.

Karen agreed.

"Time is like a big eraser," she said.

It was Karen's idea that we should write down all these insights and discoveries someday, because it was a form of history, our personal history, and we would become like our parents, oblivious, distracted.

"Years and years from now, when we're both married and have clumps of children pulling on our skirts wailing and demanding, and we look like hags with cigarettes drooping from the corners of our mouths, we'll remember all this fondly, even though we make fun of it now," she said. "That's why it's so important."

It did sound important enough to write down, but we never created that book together. We often talked about doing it. Later, when we had little else to do, we passed some of our time remembering this and that as if we were both already in our late seventies, reminiscing about our youth, looking back with nostalgia and regret.

It was lost for both of us just that quickly.

1

Living in a Fantasy

My mother, my father, and I moved into the Doral house in mid-August 1962. Jesse had left for his college orientation the day before, and I was so envious I nearly cried. I think that was why he put me in charge of his things. Unlike so many of my girlfriends who had brothers, I didn't fight with mine. He teased me whenever he could, but he was never mean to me, and he was always very protective. He was an honor society student and a baseball star for our high school. The college in Michigan awarded him a scholarship to play for the college team, in fact.

He didn't care so much about which room he would have in our new house, but he did take the one across from mine. It was about the same size. He told me to look after his precious stamp collection, which consisted of almost a dozen thick albums. He kept them in a carton on the floor in his closet.

"If the house catches on fire or there is a roof leak," he said, "go for it before you go for anything else. Someday it will be worth the house and more."

I asked my father if that was true, and he said, "Could be. He's done a great deal of research on it, and he's been into collecting stamps ever since he could lick one."

My respect for Jesse grew instantly. How could someone his age collect something that would be worth more than our whole house? Surely, that took great insight, great intelligence. I wondered how we could come from the same parents and yet he could be so much more intelligent than I was.

On the other hand, according to my mother, we hadn't paid all that much for the house. She said it was a "steal," and I wondered if that was why my father said what he had about Jesse's stamp collection. The house was a sprawling, two-story Queen Anne with a wraparound porch, a fieldstone foundation, a basement with a dirt floor, and an attic that ran almost the entire width of the main house. The add-ons that came over the last forty or so years made the house look as if it were expanding on its own. I called it "a house with a gut." My parents fell in love with it despite its eerie history and sprawling layout.

"It has character," my father said. He saw the house as masculine, aging but distinguished with wisdom in its cladding and its walls, as if it had absorbed the most important things about the world and on quiet nights would transfer it all to us while we slept. After all, it stood boldly on a small knoll just off the road, making it seem as if whoever lived in it lorded over all around it. My father even liked the cracked macadam driveway, because the lines were "like character lines in an old man's face." He vowed he would never pave it over.

My mother saw the house as feminine, full of charm, the eclectic Queen Anne architecture reminding her of a woman who flitted from one style or fashion to another, wanting a little of this and a little of that. To her, the shutters over the panel windows resembled "eyebrows," and she swore she had seen the windows "wink" at her when the sun slipped behind the heavy leafed oak, hickory, and maple trees that bordered the property on three sides. She fell instantly in love with the sitting room, because it was distinguished from the living room. She said it was a place where the various mistresses of the house had come to rock and crochet while their friends visited to weave gossip through one another's heads.

"Think of all the wonderful chatter these walls heard," she told me. The way she said it gave me the feeling she believed she could somehow hear the whispered echoes of the tittle-tattle late at night. She vowed to make it so feminine that my father or my brother would feel he had stepped into the woman's powder room if either dared enter.

My mother saw all sorts of possibilities in renovations, despite having no background in decorating, design, or architecture. That didn't discourage her from going full throttle at new window treatments, flooring, and wallpaper. I always admired her for her self-confidence and courage. I hoped I would take after her. She was a registered nurse, specializing in cardiac care before most hospitals had specific cardiac care units. She never had a problem getting a job.

My mother took great pains to effect our move to Sandburg in time for me to get set up in a new school. It was one of the conditions she threw down like a gauntlet when my father told her about his opportunity in a growing law firm in the Catskills resort area and his desire for us to pull up anchor and settle in Sandburg because the real estate was so reasonable. Disrupting her and their social and professional lives was one thing, but tinkering with my education was another. She didn't have to worry about Jesse, since he was on his way, but she was very concerned about me.

My father anticipated her reaction. It was his way to pretend he didn't think of those things and then quickly acquiesce. That was a game they played with each other, a sort of loving sparring over everything from a new appliance to clothes to a new automobile to visiting family. My mother presented her arguments, and he put up his token resistance, only later to reveal that he had already taken steps to do just what she wanted. He knew her that well, and I think she knew him, too, but was smart enough to permit him the facade of having made the decision.

None of this was really deception or conniving. It was all done out of a deep love and respect that they had for each other. I was aware of it but not as appreciative of it as Karen was when she observed them and contrasted them with her own parents. My parents were affectionate, always ending an argument or a spirited discussion with a kiss to reassure each other and, if Jesse or I were there, to reassure us that all was well.

"I wish I were your sister," Karen told me more than once. "I wish your parents were mine."

In the early days of our relationship, I would say, "So do I," even though I really would rather have her as a friend. Sisters get compared too much, and I didn't think I matched up to her in looks. To me, my eyes were too far apart, my nose was too large, and my lips were a little crooked. Of course, my mother thought I was just a nutty teenager when I complained.

"You're as cute as a button," she would tell me.

Karen was the sort of girl who was as cute as a button until she was fourteen or fifteen and then suddenly began to blossom into a beautiful young woman, her body obediently following the commands of our sex seemingly overnight. Her jeans became tighter around her rear, and her bosom filled out, became rounder. I will always remember that afternoon at school just before the Thanksgiving holidays when she slowed down as she passed me in the hallway to whisper, "Guess what I noticed this morning?"

"What?" I asked. We both continued to walk. I smiled to myself but kept my eyes fixed ahead of me. We passed words between us the way good relay racers passed the baton.

"My cleavage. I have a distinctly deeper cleavage," she said, and sped up.

I remember feeling lighter instantly. It was as if I were filling with helium and about to rise to the ceiling. She walked on ahead of me, her head slightly down, but I hesitated to catch up, because I didn't know what to say.

Congratulations? That's nice?

Or lucky you? When would I see more of a distinctly deeper cleavage, if ever?

I didn't want to sound envious, even though that was exactly what I was. Just recently we had been talking more about our bodies and our looks. I was terrified of fading into the background like someone in the chorus while Karen moved downstage and became the star spotlighted in every boy's eyes. It was already happening as far as I was concerned.

She turned into our classroom, paused, and smiled back at me, drawing her shoulders toward each other to flash that cleavage. Some of the senior boys noticed and popped their eyes.

"Venez, mon animal de compagnie," she called to me, which meant, "Come, my pet."

We were both taking French as our language elective. It all came much easier to her than it did to me. In those days, the public schools still offered language study and we could choose between Spanish and French. It was, in fact, a requirement for graduation. Jesse had taken French and could read it well, and whenever he was home, he practiced with Karen, the two of them speaking so quickly I felt like a foreigner. Eventually, the schools dropped the requirement and cut back on their language teachers to trim budgets when we discovered that everyone in the world, even the French, wanted to learn English, so we didn't have to bother. At least, that's what my father says.

"Bonjour, mon jolie," Karen would say every morning when we greeted each other on the school bus.

"Bonjour, Mademoiselle Amerique," I would respond, which meant, "Good morning, Miss America."

The others riding the bus would think us mad because of how we giggled afterward or how we strutted like peacocks down the aisle to exit, practicing some new French phrase. Wherever we were, we performed a duet.

Right from the beginning, Karen and I gravitated to each other like two birds of a feather uncomfortable with the variety of flocks gathering in our school and community. I noticed rather quickly that she wasn't a favorite among the girls at school. That puzzled me, because she seemed perfect to me. Certainly, no one appreciated her as much as I did. She had some acquaintances here and there but no close heart-to-heart relationships, the sort that made some pairs of girls look like conjoined twins, laughing at the same things, hating the same things and people, and falling in love with the same boy from week to week, depending, as Karen would say, "on the phase of the moon." We were almost like that, but there was always something different about us, and as Karen was fond of saying, *"Vive la difference."*

I guess we were both a little weird, leaning just enough toward the unexpected and unusual for our peers to distrust us. It was important for us to be original. Karen came up with the idea of our being two parts of the same person.

"What we'll do is share things in ways other girls would never think of sharing," she told me.

"Like what?"

"Like earrings, for example. Here," she said, taking off one of hers. "You wear this one on your right ear. I'll wear this one on my left."

It seemed amusing to do, but no one really noticed, so she came up with sharing shoes, since we had the same size. I'd wear her left shoe, and she'd wear my left shoe. We traded every morning on the bus. That caught everyone's attention, and when we were asked about it, Karen would say, "We are becoming spiritual sisters, two bodies, one heart."

There were lots of puzzled expressions punctuated with "Huh?" or "What?" and then the shaking of heads.

Every other day, Karen would come up with a new idea to illustrate what she was telling them. We shared the tops and bottoms of skirt-and-blouse outfits, socks, halves of sandwiches, anything, in fact, that we could divide in two. We even practiced finishing each other's answers in class. I'd start, stop, and look at her and if she winked, I would smile, and she would deliver the remaining part of the response. Some of our teachers were annoyed, but most thought it was amusing. They didn't take our antics half as seriously as our fellow students.

"Maybe these two will start a new fad," Mrs. Cohen remarked in math class one day, when we came to school with her right eye made up and my left and everyone was making fun of us.

Of course, I felt everyone should be more tolerant about our being different, especially in relation to me. I was insecure about myself, still trapped in that place between unisex, even boyishness, and emerging femininity. My menarche came late. I was like a runner who had missed the sound of the starting gun and had to run harder to catch up to the pack. I would stay up at night waiting for the girl in me to emerge, almost like a creature hovering under my skin. I willed it. Closing my eyes, I would chant, "Grow a bigger bosom. Lose all the baby fat. Soften and get more curvy." In my eyes, I wasn't enough of a woman yet but certainly no longer just a girl. What was I? When would I know it, feel it as confidently as Karen did?

I was actually envious of the girls Karen despised, because they seemed so secure about who they were.

I did my best to keep that from her. She would have none of their world and quickly picked up on the French phrase *petite bourgeoise,* which meant a petty woman belonging to the middle class, the middle class being something undesirable.

She wouldn't gossip and giggle or betray someone's confidence. She wouldn't agree with a group condemnation of another girl just to be one of the girls. She never shared her lipstick or admitted to a crush on any boy, at least to anyone else but me. Consequently, she wasn't invited to parties or group dates for movies and pizza. So it was just natural for us to pal around together, and I wasn't invited to most of these things, either.

"Don't worry about it," Karen would tell me before I could utter a complaint or regret about our social isolation. "You're known more by the enemies you make than the friends you keep. The truth is, they all envy us. They wish they were half as creative and had half as much fun. They're eating their hearts out with jealousy."

Were they? I wondered. In my mind, it was certainly true that Karen was growing more and more beautiful by the hour, and she was bright and funny, but did any of the other girls really want to be her, to trade places with her, to have her life?

Karen's real father had suffered a massive heart attack and died in his early thirties and had left her and her mother with insufficient life insurance and income. Unlike my mother, her mother had not attended college. She had worked as a secretary for a lumber company, where she had met Karen's father, Dave Stoker. He was working at building his own construction company, but at the time, he was a contracted laborer and didn't even have a regular job. He never put away enough money or built enough of a reputation to realize his goal. Karen was only ten at the time of his death. For two years afterward, her mother and she struggled with their finances. Finally, her mother took a job working in Pearson's Pharmacy and a year later married Harry Pearson, Aaron Pearson's son, who had graduated from Fordham University as a pharmacist and had taken over his father's drugstore after his father died.

Karen told me, "All the ducks quacked and quacked in a line, because my mother was almost seven years older than Harry. They all thought she plotted and planned to trap him. In fact, his mother went into a deep depression that was like quicksand. She never pulled herself out of it and died two years later from a stroke. Everyone blamed my mother. Even Harry blamed her."

"How could he do that?" I asked.

"Simple," she replied. "He decided maybe the gossips were right. She was a witch at heart, and she had put a spell over him."

"You don't really mean that. A witch?"

"Yes, I do. You know why, too," she reminded me. She paused to swallow the stone of sorrow caught in her throat and then added, "He blamed her for everything unpleasant in his life, especially me. Right from the beginning, I told him I was on his mother's side and didn't think he should marry my mother. I didn't say it with her present, but I said it, and he knew it, knew I would never accept him as a father, no matter how hard he tried."

Karen had refused to permit him to adopt her, so her name remained Karen Stoker, even though her mother's name had become Darlene Pearson. If a teacher or anyone else made a mistake and called her, Karen Pearson, she would immediately correct him or her with enough vigor to cause them to say, "Well, excuse me for living," or something similar.

"Some people should be excused for living," Karen said.

I agreed. We most always agreed. We had come to that comfortable place where we could drop all our self-defenses and let our souls stand naked without fear or embarrassment. We teased each other, but we never insulted each other, and if we stumbled and did something that upset each other, we usually blathered apology after apology until the other would cry for mercy. At least, that was the way we were before our world turned topsy-turvy.

The journey that would take us there began with the simplest of gestures and smiles when we were in the same places, be they classrooms, the lunchroom, hallways, or the streets of Sandburg. We would both hear something or see something and then look at each other and shrug, smile, swing our eyes, or simply stare blankly, which made a statement, too.

It was truly as if we were prodding each other's inner self to see where the similarities and sympathies lay. We needed to know how alike we were and how much of it we would care to admit to each other. Trust came to us through simple ways then. We laughed in chorus, echoed each other's wishful thinking, and mirrored each other's feelings.

I knew that boys were always suspicious of Karen. I

also knew most of them harbored a secret crush on her as well but were afraid to admit it, because she would make them feel so inferior if they approached her at school. They would be wounded in their male egos, perhaps beyond repair. I thought that to compensate, they made up stories about her promiscuity, this one claiming that and another claiming something more. There was always some undertone of gossip running like a sewer under our feet.

After school one day only a few months after I had arrived, Alice Bucci took me into the boys' room when no one else was around to show me some of the dirty things boys had written about Karen on the walls of the stalls. Her brother was one of the authors.

"They're all lies," I told her immediately. I tried to hide how shocked I was at the descriptions and claims.

"How do you know? You haven't been here long enough, and you don't live with her," she countered. "Lots of people do lots of things secretly. Even their parents don't know. You'd better dump her before you get a reputation, too."

Everyone was always trying to get me to stop being Karen's friend.

"As long as you're with her, you're nobody," Alice told me.

"I'd rather be nobody with Karen than somebody with you," I replied.

"Suit yourself," she said, and reported our conversation to the others.

"Zipporah Nobody," they labeled me, and then pretended I was invisible by walking into me.

Ironically, that would all change. I would wake up

one morning and find myself the most sought-after girl in school.

"Tell me about her," they would plead.

But that wouldn't happen until the sleepy hamlet was jerked awake to face the most startling and shocking scandal in its modern history. Things like this happened only outside the walls of the idyllic community, only to urban people. It was like living on an island. Why, in our little town in the early sixties, even divorce was a rarity. Adultery was known only through whispers. The worst things teenagers did were still called pranks. A psychiatrist was as rare as an albino. Schools had guidance counselors mainly involved with scheduling classes and suggesting colleges rather than psychological counseling.

People didn't lock their front doors or their cars. Anyone who tried to make a living owning a home security company was on the verge of bankruptcy. Town policemen often held second jobs. Sophisticated detectives came only from the state. There were no radar traps. We could walk about unafraid on dark streets at night. Kids my age still hitchhiked and took rides with strangers. Smiles and invitations were still largely innocent and true.

When I tell my grandchildren today about that world, they think I'm fantasizing.

Maybe I am.

Maybe that's why we got into so much trouble. We were living in a fantasy and never really understood that we were.

2

A Minute Lost

Karen and I and the other kids in Sandburg went to high school on the bus unless we had a friend with a license and a car or unless my parents took us. Karen's stepfather never seemed to be able to do it, and her mother either never volunteered or Karen never wanted her to drive her.

Where we had lived before, I could walk to school. Riding a bus was new to me, but after the novelty wore off, I wasn't crazy about it. Karen didn't mind riding the bus, even though we had the noisy junior high kids riding along with us to be dropped off after we were. Their building was in a different town within the school district, and ours was the next stop after Sandburg. The ride from the center of Sandburg took us all of twenty odd minutes, but it always seemed much longer to me.

"Don't think of it as a bus," Karen told me when I complained. "Consider it our personal limousine. The bus driver is our chauffeur, and we live in Paris."

When she boarded the bus, she would look at Mr. Tooey, the sixty-year-old baldheaded driver, and say, *"Bonjour, Pierre."* Mr. Tooey would just shake his head.

Karen always wanted to sit in the last seat at the rear, which was the most undesirable, because it would take longer to get off the bus. She liked to curl up as if she were at home on her sofa or up in our nest and look out the window the whole trip there and back. She had a way of shutting out the noise and ignoring the spit balls.

Because of her, I sat back there, too. Sometimes we talked, and sometimes we made the whole journey without saying a word. I could tell when she had shut herself down. I knew it usually meant it had been a bad morning at her house or a bad evening. Usually, she was just as quiet at school those days. Like a snail, Karen could crawl into herself and practically disappear. I learned to respect her need for silence and just wait for her to resurface. Sometimes, she would just burst out with a stream of thoughts as if she had broken the surface of water in a pool, and, voilà, we'd be chattering like two mad squirrels.

Karen didn't easily tell me about all the trouble in her home. She disclosed it in little ways, sometimes not even in words. She would have a look on her face that revealed she and her mother had been arguing, usually, according to her, because of the way she had treated Harry, whom she even refused to refer to as her stepfather. He was just Harry. Those arguments grew worse as time went by, but in those days, everyone kept his or her home life and intimate information behind closed doors, so no one but me really knew the extent of them. That wasn't unusual. There were no shows like *Oprah* and *Jerry Springer*. People were ashamed of their difficulties and not willing to share them. I'm not sure if that was better or worse. It is probably true that holding it all in made for little explosions that became bigger and bigger ones.

Through her fantasies, Karen started to drop little hints that things were not just getting worse, they were getting impossible.

"Last night, they locked me in the tower," she would say. "I was given only bread and water, and the bread was moldy, too."

Or, "My mother had a tantrum last night and sliced up the mattress with a meat cleaver."

Her tidbits seemed to grow more and more violent, even though she always followed her statements with a laugh.

The first black-and-blue mark I saw on Karen was on her upper left arm. It looked like the imprint of a thick thumb, as if she had been grabbed and held until the capillaries broke and there was trauma. I knew all about that medical stuff because of my mother being a nurse. Karen covered it with her long-sleeved shirt, but she kept the shirt unbuttoned, and when she was curling like a caterpillar in the back of the bus, the shirt slipped off her shoulder and fell down enough on her arm for me to see it.

"What's this?" I asked, pointing at her black-and-blue mark.

She turned, realized what had happened, and quickly pulled her shirt back up and over her shoulder.

"Nothing. I bumped into something while I was sleepwalking last night," she said. "And lucky, too, because if I hadn't, I might have fallen down the stairs."

"You never told me you sleepwalk," I said, smirking.

"Didn't I? I must be forcing myself to ignore it," she said, but she didn't sound truthful at all.

By now, if we cast a lie at each other, it flew for a second and then fell like a bird with heart failure. She glanced back at me, her eyes flickering and her expression pleading with me not to ask anything else. I folded my hands on my books and stared ahead.

At the time, I didn't have enough of a diabolical mind. I thought it was possible she had been in some altercation with one of the other girls and I just hadn't heard about it yet. When we arrived at school, I listened to see if anyone was talking about a fight between Karen and someone, maybe in the girls' bathroom, but no one was. Of course, I became even more curious.

On the way home that day, I nodded at her arm and asked, "That still hurt?"

"Never did. It looks worse than it really is," she told me, and again turned away to signal that this was not a topic for discussion.

And so I put it back into my log of things I would rather forget. I didn't think of it again until I saw her walking alone one early evening soon after and realized she was crying. I had come into the village on my bike to get myself a chocolate marshmallow ice cream cone at George's Ice Cream Parlor. It was a reward I was giving myself for finishing all my homework early, including reading all four assigned chapters of *Huckleberry Finn* and answering the study guide questions. Lately, I had become a very good student, and my father took another look at me and decided I would be as much college material as Jesse was, after all. It came under the heading "Some Take Longer to Grow Up."

"Finally," he said, "you have your priorities straight. There is hope for you yet, Zipporah."

I didn't say anything. In my mind, it didn't require a thank you. I never thought there wasn't hope for me, and I doubted my father ever thought that, either, even though I was never on the honor roll. I never failed anything. True, I swam in the pool of the average or just above, but there was nothing about me that would bring my parents any shame. The worst crime I had committed to date was talking too much in class and serving two days' detention.

I saw Karen walking toward the east side of town, her head down, her right hand periodically moving across her cheeks to flick off tears like a human windshield wiper. I decided to forgo my ice cream reward and pedal on after her. George's was dangerously near closing anyway, since it was the off-season, and by this time in the evening, most people had retreated to their homes and wrapped themselves in the glow of their television sets. The streets were deserted, and the periods between some automobile traffic and none were longer and longer. I didn't want to scare her, so I called out while I was still a little behind her. She walked on as if she hadn't heard me. I drew closer and called out louder.

She stopped but didn't turn. I saw her shoulders rise as if she were anticipating a blow or a shout or simply wanted to hide inside herself more. It put some hesitation in my excited approach, and I slowed my pedaling.

"Hey," I said when I drew up to her.

She took a deep breath and turned. She didn't say anything.

"What are you doing? I mean, where are you going?" I asked.

"For a walk. Just for a walk."

"Oh. I came into town for an ice cream. You want an ice cream cone?" I asked, even though I was nearly certain that by the time we would get to George's now, the lights would be out.

She shook her head.

"So, how come you're just taking a walk?"

She didn't answer.

"Karen?"

"Leave me alone," she replied, and walked on.

I felt as if she had slapped my face. I remember the blood rushing into my cheeks.

"Sure, I'll leave you alone," I said indignantly. I watched her for a moment and then turned and pedaled back, now annoyed that I wouldn't get my ice cream cone.

I pedaled harder and faster in frustration and had worked up a good sweat by the time I arrived at my house. I put my bike away in the garage and tried to get up to my bedroom without my parents noticing. My mother was off for two days, and my father had just finished a case and was taking a breather. They sat in the living room watching television, although I knew my father would have a book opened as well and would read during the commercials. He hated wasting time.

"A minute lost is a minute gone forever," he told me repeatedly.

I conjured up some great lost-and-found department with the shelves weighed down by seconds, minutes, and hours. There was a meek little bald man with thick eyeglasses, clicking a stopwatch and waving his long, bony right forefinger in my face as he chanted, "Lost and forgotten, lost and forgotten."

The steps of the stairway betrayed me with their gleeful creaks and squeaks.

"Zipporah?" my mother called. "Where were you? Why didn't you tell us you were going out? Where could you go this time of night, anyway?" She rattled off her questions as if she thought she might forget one.

I turned slowly and walked to the living room. My father looked up from his book. It was always a matter of great interest to me to see how my father considered me. Sometimes he looked genuinely confused and gave me the feeling he was wondering how someone like me could be born of his seed, and sometimes he looked delightfully amused and gave me the feeling he saw something of himself at my age, just as he often saw in Jesse. Right now, he looked vaguely annoyed, because I had caused an interruption in either his reading or his relaxation.

My mother just looked curious.

"Well?" she asked.

"I went to get an ice cream at George's, but the store was already closed," I said. It was half true, and half-truths were not officially lies. I was still at the age when lying to my parents flooded me with guilt. When you're very young, you're filled more with fear, because you actually believe parents can see lies. If they don't contradict you, it's because they're being generous and permitting you an escape.

"I could have told you it would be," my father said, and returned to his book.

"You should at least tell us when you leave the house, Zipporah."

"That's right," my father seconded.

"I'm sorry."

"You do all your homework?" my mother asked.

"Yep."

"Try *yes* and not *yep,*" my father said, not taking his eyes off the page.

"Yes," I said. What was wrong with *yep?* Jesse sometimes said *yep.*

"I'm sure you did all your homework," he muttered.

"Yes, I did. Why don't you believe me?" I cried, with as much passion as if I were denying I had murdered someone.

He looked up, his face pained.

"Okay," he said. "Sorry. Don't have a nervous breakdown."

"Don't forget we're heading up to Grandmother Stein's this Saturday, Zipporah," my mother said. She already had told me twice that we were visiting my father's mother at the adult residence in Liberty, New York. She had been moved there when it became clear that she couldn't look after herself. Since both my parents worked, it would have been impossible to have her live with us. At least the Liberty residence was close.

"Okay," I said, and started to leave the living room.

"Don't you want to watch Ed Sullivan?" my mother asked.

I shook my head. I was still very disturbed about the way Karen had blown me off, and I wanted to go upstairs to the sanctity of my own room to think about it. There I could talk to myself in a full-blown split-personality mode, actually looking at myself as if I were a different person. I could ask myself questions, answer them, and criticize myself. I was confident that everyone, even my parents and Jesse, did the same things in the privacy of their rooms.

I was sure that from time to time, everyone thinks of himself or herself as weird. Keeping your sanity was truly like walking a tightrope. No matter what age, how successful, how happy you were, you could easily slip too far to the right or left and fall. Everything about us was so fragile. We spent most of our lives pretending we were too strong to be defeated by disappointments or disillusioned by anything that happened to us. It was like admitting we were mortal. Who would want to do that? Instead, we kept looking straight ahead and ignoring all that indicated we would get old, sicken, and die someday.

There was no place like your own room for such reassurance. Familiar places nourished the growth of hope. Your own room was a garden in which to plant secret thoughts and dreams that would grow into full-fledged ambitions.

I closed the door and flopped onto my bed to look up at the ceiling and let my thoughts spin out of control.

Why was Karen crying?

Why wouldn't she talk to me? I thought I was her best friend. We were supposed to be birds of a feather. We had already translated it into French, *les oiseaux d'une plume,* and Karen thought we should print it on T-shirts that we would wear to school. Surely, all the other girls would be jealous once they found out what it meant. We even created the Bird Oath, which we recited in unison often: "We'll be friends forever and ever, and we swear to protect and help each other as much as we would ourselves."

"We're so close not only can we finish each other's sentences like we do in class, but we can finish each other's thoughts," she said, and we hugged.

But if that were really true, why did she lie to me about her bruise? Why did she suddenly have to make up story after story with me or change the subject quickly? I never did that with her. Come to think of it, I thought, I never even sulked or pulled the silent act on her, either.

Seeing her crying and having her be so indifferent to me was very troubling. What would she be like tomorrow? I wondered. Was our friendship about to die? Had I done something I was unaware of doing? Did something I said to my parents get back to her mother? I couldn't think of a thing for which she could blame me, but what if she was so angry at me she would no longer want me to be her friend? Even Jesse would think it was somehow my fault. We had swum too far out to sea together. I thought I would be lost without her.

I fell asleep with my clothes on and woke up when I heard my parents coming up the stairs. After undressing for bed, I looked out my window at the dark forest that surrounded our property. The woods were deep, and one could walk for hours north and not come upon another house or road. To the south, one would eventually reach the highway that connected to busier streets and roads.

It didn't bother me or frighten me that we lived in

so isolated a place and that nearly a hundred years ago, someone might have been murdered here, and his bones might still be hidden on the property. I rarely thought about it, even after seeing a scary movie, unless Karen brought it up, of course. Most of the time, I rode my bike through the darkness unafraid. I was still at the age when I thought I was invincible, anyway. I couldn't even imagine myself terminally ill, chronically sick, or disabled. I never thought about being in an accident.

In effect, I was still living in that world of fantasy that we have to slip out of the way snakes slip out of old skin. We look back at it when we're older, and we long for the time when we didn't have many serious responsibilities, when someone took care of us and protected us. We walked on a shelf of self-confidence that would be harder and harder to find as we grew older. We would realize that we were blessed then but never knew it. Whoever dared harm us risked the wrath of the Almighty.

Karen surely knew this, too, I told my image in the mirror. And then, I thought, if that was so true, then why was she crying?

And why did she seem so terribly afraid?

What did she know about the future that I didn't?

3

Head in the Sand

The next morning on the bus, Karen said nothing about the way she had treated me or why she was so upset. I didn't know what to make of it. She was quieter than usual, but she wasn't especially unfriendly. She gazed out the window and, as she usually did, made comments about places we passed. This house looked like a house made of gingerbread, that one looked as if it was leaning worse than the Langer Dairy building and could be blown over in a strong wind, or that side road looked as if it led to a secret lake where frogs waited to be turned into princes. We were soon in a contest to outdo each other with fantastic possibilities.

Whatever had been bothering her had passed, I thought, and decided to let it go.

"I'm going to see my grandmother on Saturday," I told her, "but I'll be back by four. My mother is on duty, and it's my father's poker night. You want to come over? We can try to make a good pizza again."

She didn't answer immediately, so I held my breath. In fact, she acted as if she hadn't heard me. I was about to repeat it, when she turned and nodded. She said nothing more about it, and I didn't see much of her in school, because toward the end of the third period, she went up to our teacher and asked to go to the nurse's office. She didn't look at me when she walked out with her pass. She remained at the nurse's office through lunch. Usually, when a girl did that, it was because she was having bad cramps, but later, when the school day ended, Karen told me she had gone to the nurse because she had a terrible headache.

"She wanted to send me home, but I begged her not to," Karen told me.

"Why?"

She didn't reply. I could see from the way she frowned that she still had the headache.

"Maybe you should go to the doctor," I suggested.

She shook her head.

"No doctor can cure this," she told me, which was very cryptic and mysterious.

"Why not?"

"Take my word for it, Zipporah," she replied, and pressed her lips together firmly, which was usually what she did when she wanted to stop talking about something.

She frightened me, because I thought she might be talking about something terminal, like a brain tumor. Maybe that was what had happened the night before. She had gotten terrible news. I told my mother about it later that day, and she tilted her head to the side as she often did when something puzzled or interested her. When I was little, I believed some thoughts weighed more than others and shifted in your head to make it tilt. I told my father, and he went into hysterical laughter, which brought tears to his eyes. From that time on, he would kid my mother about her having heavy thoughts.

"I doubt it's something like that," she told me. "There would be other symptoms, Zipporah."

I breathed with relief.

"I'm sure it's just something emotional. Part of growing up," she said.

Adults were often saying that to us: "It's part of growing up."

When are you grown up? I wondered. When do all these parts come together and form you?

"I don't understand how that could be part of growing up," I told my mother. I knew some young people had pain in the legs from growing so tall so quickly, but a headache?

She looked at me with more concern than usual and said, "Come with me a moment."

I followed her into the sitting room, that special feminine place in our house.

"Sit," she said, nodding at the small settee with the light pink flowery design.

"Why do we have to come in here to talk?"

"It's long past the time when you and I should have a mother-daughter talk," she said, and sat in her rocker. "I should have done it the first time you had a period, but these days, girls are having periods so young, it seems."

"How can that change from when you were young?"

"Wouldn't we all like to know," she said. "Anyway, Zipporah, these hormonal changes that are taking place in your body and Karen's have emotional effects, too. You have feelings that you don't understand, feelings that even disturb you and can cause all sorts

of reactions, headaches included. Don't you find yourself confused by your feelings?"

I shook my head, but reluctantly. It was as if I were
confessing to a failure.

"You will," she said. "My guess is Karen already is.
I know you spend a lot of time with each other. Does
she bring up sexual things?"

"No!" I said. What an embarrassing question to ask
me. Of course, we had some conversations about it,
but I didn't want to describe that to my mother.

She smiled. She knew I wasn't telling the truth.

"I'm sure you two talk about boys. Don't worry
about that. It's normal."

"She doesn't like anyone at school, and neither do
I," I said sharply, hoping that might end it, even though
it didn't mean we refrained from talking about boys.

"You will," she said, with that adult confidence I
despised because I didn't yet have it. "Some boy will
suddenly look . . . interesting. Maybe it will be in his
smile or in his voice or just the way he walks. You'll
find yourself vying for his attention, blushing when
you least expect it, and hoping he sees you as special,
too." She smiled at me. "Are you sure that hasn't happened yet?"

"Yes, I'm sure. Why does all that have to happen
now, anyway?" I asked. "Maybe I'm different."

"I hope not!" she said, laughing. "Girls who are
that different when it comes to boys are persona non
grata."

I had only a vague idea of what she meant. Back
then, we were ages away from openly confronting ho-
mosexuality, especially in our small community. I had
really heard about it only in reference to boys, anyway,

who were derided as fairies, which made no sense to me, because fairies were magical.

"Maybe it won't happen to me for a much, much longer time," I suggested, only because I was telling the truth. It really hadn't yet, and I was afraid it never would.

"Not much longer," she said. "You're sculpturing," she added.

"Huh?"

"Your body is changing, Zipporah. We're not so unlike caterpillars and butterflies. You're emerging."

Was I? Was I finally emerging? Maybe she could see more than I could because she was a trained nurse, I thought.

"I've been watching Karen, and I can tell you she's becoming a beautiful young woman. Don't be disappointed if she suddenly pushes you aside or ignores you to spend more time with a boy. The same thing will happen to you, and you'll grow closer when you two can share that, but until then, she might be more secretive, more withdrawn. She's developing desire. When that happens to our daughters, we mothers can only hope we've given them enough common sense to protect themselves from getting into bad trouble."

"You mean getting pregnant, don't you?"

"I do. I don't want you to become the Ice Queen, but I do want you to think about the consequences of every action. Promise me you'll do that."

"Mama, I don't even have a boyfriend!" I protested.

"I told you, you will, and sooner than you think. You know," she continued, "that there are times of the month when a woman is more likely to get pregnant if she doesn't take precautions."

"Yes, I know," I said. "We learned all about that in biology class."

"There are things you just can't learn in a formal classroom setting, Zipporah. All this can happen so fast your head spins. A boy attracts your attention. You can't help wanting to be with him. You just naturally explore, push yourself toward your limits. Sometimes it all happens literally overnight."

I sat back. Was she right? Would it all just happen one day as she said, unexpected, sudden, like a bolt of lightning? Is that what had happened to Karen, and because it happened just out of the blue, I didn't notice? Who could she be with or care about without my knowing?

I thought back to my conversation with Alice Bucci in the boys' room when she took me in to see what had been written about Karen on the stalls. "You don't live with her," she had said. "Lots of people do lots of things secretly. Even their parents don't know."

Didn't I have to admit that I had secret thoughts I had never shared with Karen? Why couldn't the same be true for her?

"I hope Karen's mother has had a conversation like this with her," my mother said. "Has she?"

What if she hadn't? I thought. Was she in danger? Did I dare ask?

"I don't know."

"I want you to feel that you can come to me with any questions, any problems, Zipporah, anytime, okay?"

I nodded.

"Your grandmother was not as forthcoming. We

never had talks like this. She was old school, embarrassed by any references to sex or her own body. How
she and her generation expected us to learn everything
properly is a mystery. They simply had blind faith,
which we know does not work. There have already
been four teenage pregnancies in our township," she
said, and my eyes nearly popped.

"Four? In our school?"

"I can't tell you any more about it than that. It's
privileged medical information."

"How can they keep it a secret?"

"Some women don't show until their fourth or fifth
month. I didn't show with you until almost my sixth.
Unless you're a bad girl, you don't have to think about
it, the symptoms, I mean. There are other problems,
however, like sexually transmitted diseases. I don't
want to make it all sound unpleasant. It's not, but it
only takes a little carelessness to make it so. Understand?"

"Yes," I said. I was still uncomfortable talking
about it. I hadn't even been out on a formal date. I
felt as if I were being inoculated against a disease that
didn't exist.

"Don't bury your head in the sand, Zipporah," she
warned. "That's the way you get into trouble."

"I'm not! I said I understand!"

"Okay, okay." She thought a moment and then
leaned toward me. "There's no chance Karen's already been with a boy like that, is there, Zipporah?
No chance she's done something she now regrets, is
there?"

"No," I said, but not with enough confidence to satisfy myself, much less her.

"All right. If you need anything, let me know," she said. I knew she meant if Karen needed anything.

I nodded, and she smiled and rose.

"I love my sitting room," she said, looking around. "It feels cozy, doesn't it?"

"Yes."

"We all need our special places," she said, running her hand over my hair. "You're going to be a pretty young woman. Don't you worry. They'll be taking numbers at the door just like at the bakery."

"Oh, Mama," I said.

She laughed and returned to the kitchen to prepare dinner. I ran upstairs to my room to think about everything she had told me. I was okay with it for myself, but she really put the worries in me when it came to Karen. I was the one who had the mother who was a nurse. I had an obligation to share my good fortune, I thought. Surely, she would appreciate it.

And it would be a good way to get her to tell me what was bothering her and what secret things had happened.

It was early enough for me to get on my bike, ride into town, see Karen, and come home before dinner. I was bursting with the need to tell her some of this, to warn her. I charged down the stairs.

"I'll be back in a while," I called out, and before my mother could object, I was out the door.

Karen and her mother had moved into Karen's stepfather's house soon after the wedding. She had told me how her stepfather's mother resented them so much she would keep herself in her own little apartment at the rear of the house and wouldn't take meals with them. She did practically nothing with them as a family.

"We really didn't see much of a change after she had her stroke and died," Karen had told me. "It was as if she wasn't there before, anyway. Harry still hasn't gotten rid of all her things. My mother tells him to give them to the Angel View Thrift Store that sells stuff for charity. He says he will, but he hasn't. He hasn't done much with the apartment, either, even though he said he would fix it up and rent it out someday."

The Pearson house was one of the few brick-fronted homes in Sandburg. It had a pretty lawn with waist-high hedges and a sidewalk that curved up to the stone steps in front and the veranda. Druggists, it seemed, were only a few levels down from doctors when it came to making money. Pearson's Pharmacy was the only drugstore in the village, and people who lived in the outlying areas came to it rather than travel another five miles or so to another drugstore. They also sold toys, candy, and ice cream, but they didn't have as big a fountain as George's, and the ice cream was prepackaged and not nearly as good.

Like me, Karen had her own room upstairs. From the way she talked, once she got home, if she didn't have any chores to do, she went to her room and remained there. Unlike me, she didn't spend much time with her mother and stepfather watching television or even just talking, and she had no brother or sister to talk to or write to. She was alone much more than I was or would ever be, I thought.

Her mother had continued to work at the drugstore after she married Harry and was gone most of the day. Harry was the only pharmacist, so he had to be there almost all the time. They rarely had dinner together, because Harry always had to stay behind to close up or do inventory or prepare prescriptions for the morning. Because her mother waited for him, Karen usually ate by herself. Sometimes she even ate in her room. I felt sorry for her and wished Harry were more considerate.

Karen told me he was strict about the hours the store opened and closed. If someone needed a prescription after seven p.m., he or she would have to travel twenty miles. Occasionally, Karen said, the doctors would plead with Harry to go back and prepare a prescription, but he was never happy about it and always made it clear he was doing someone a big favor. That surprised me, because in his drugstore, Mr. Pearson was always quite pleasant and seemingly concerned about the illnesses his customers had. At least to the public, he was a jovial man with a soft round face my mother said looked like a bowl of vanilla pudding with two plums for eyes, a walnut for a nose, and a banana for a mouth. He was stout, with all of his weight going to his upper torso. Karen revealed that his legs were bony and hairy.

"They look like they had stopped growing years before the rest of him," she told me once after we had left the drugstore together.

Later, in the attic, when I asked her why her mother had married him, she told me her mother had decided to choose security over romance.

"Besides," she added, "my mother said she made love only in the dark so she could imagine him to be anyone she wanted."

"Made love in the dark? Don't you have to see a little to know what you're doing?" I asked, and she laughed, thinking I was joking. I wasn't. Karen knew much more about it all than I did, but I didn't think that was because she had the same sort of conversations with her mother that I had with mine. "Then she didn't fall in love with him?"

"No. When I asked her about that once, she said we couldn't afford it."

"Huh? What a funny thing to say."

"No, it wasn't," Karen said. Almost overnight, she had become so much older and more serious. "When you're younger and you don't have children or responsibilities, you can be carefree and adventurous. You can have twenty dollars in your pocket and elope and worry about everything else later. But my mother had me, a teenager, and she was barely making enough to give us food and shelter. We didn't have health insurance. We had nothing extra that was really important. Harry was a solution, so I don't blame her. I don't!"

She was contradicting herself.

She blamed her mother. She would always blame her mother for bringing Harry into their lives.

I pedaled to her house in record time. After my discussion with my mother, I was driven to delve deeper into Karen's problems, and I was just dying to know whether or not she had fallen in love with a boy in our school without my knowing. Was she pining over him because he had rejected her? Was that why she was crying the other night?

I dropped my bike on the Pearson lawn and hurried up the steps to ring the doorbell. I waited, but no one came to the door, so I went over to the living-room window. I saw a small lamp lit by the sofa, but no one was there. I returned to the front door and rang again and waited, the disappointment dripping through me. Where was Karen? Like me, she had no after-school activities. She hadn't mentioned meeting anyone or going anywhere that day. We had come home together on the bus as usual, and she had left saying, "Talk to you later." Had she gone off to have some rendezvous with this mysterious boyfriend I was imagining?

We spoke to each other on the phone at night, but not that often. She told me her stepfather wouldn't put in another phone line for her and forbade her to tie up their line for longer than two minutes. She said he would actually time it by calling the house periodically to check, and if she violated the rule, he would forbid her ever to use the phone, even for a minute, and would permit no incoming calls for her.

Discouraged now, I turned and walked slowly back to my bike. Just as I picked it up, however, Karen's mother drove in. She rolled down her car window and called out to me.

"Hi, Zipporah."

"Hi," I said, and before she could continue into the garage, I asked, "Where's Karen?"

"Karen? She should be home," she said. "Why? She didn't answer the door?"

"No."

"Just a moment," she said.

She looked upset, parked the car, and came out of the garage quickly.

"She didn't tell me she had anything to do after school. Is she in detention or something like that?" she asked, the fury coming into her eyes in preparation.

"No, Mrs. Pearson. We came home on the bus together."

"You did? Oh. Well, let's see what's going on," she said, and went to the front door, dug the key out of her purse, and opened it.

I wasn't sure what I should do but decided to put my bike down again and follow her.

"Karen!" she called from the entryway. "Karen, are you here?"

She looked back at me and smirked, but then we heard Karen's voice.

"Yes, I'm here."

"Well, what are you doing? Zipporah has been ringing the doorbell."

"I didn't hear it," Karen said, but she didn't come down the stairs to greet me.

"Well, do you want your friend to go up to see you or not?" her mother asked.

"Not now," Karen said.

Mrs. Pearson turned to me and shrugged.

"You heard her. Sorry. You teenage girls are a different species these days, Zipporah. I can't keep up with the mood changes. Talk to her tomorrow."

"Thanks, Mrs. Pearson," I said. I tried to get a glimpse of Karen, but she was already back in her room.

"Say hello to your parents for me," Karen's mother called as I walked back to my bike.

I turned and saw her smile and close the door.

She was a pretty woman, who, despite being older than Mr. Pearson, looked younger.

"Darlene Pearson is the sort of woman who will never look her age," my mother once told me. I could hear the underlying tone of jealousy. "She doesn't have to do anything but get up in the morning. Her skin will look like the skin of a teenager right into her sixties and seventies, and her hair will be thick and rich no matter what. The genetic pool," she added.

"What's that?"

"She inherited everything."

"Everything but good luck," my father commented. He often would sit and look as if he was reading a brief or a book and suddenly raise his eyes and reveal he was listening closely to everything my mother had been saying. "Don't forget she lost her husband."

"And don't forget she married a mama's boy with money," my mother countered. "She has him wrapped around her pinky by now, I'm sure."

Just like that, they were off to play ping-pong with words and arguments.

"How can that possibly compensate for the loss? She has a daughter without her real father."

"She'll spend her way out of unhappiness."

"Would you? Could you?"

"I am not Darlene Pearson."

My father turned to me.

"Your Honor, would you please instruct the witness to answer the question."

"What?"

"You're such an idiot, Michael," my mother told my father. He lowered his eyes to his reading.

But I couldn't forget what she had said about Karen's mother. Every time I looked at her now, I looked at her more closely. Karen had her soft blue eyes and small nose. They both had perfectly shaped full lips. Karen's face was more angular, more like her father's, from the pictures of him I had seen. Both she and her mother had a similar shade of light brown hair. Her mother wore hers short, not quite to the bottoms of her ears. Karen, like me, had hair that reached her shoulders.

Her mother was what women called a full-figured woman with long enough legs to be a Rockette dancer at Radio City Music Hall. She didn't dance and was never in show business, but no one had any difficulty figuring out why Harry Pearson would walk over his mother to marry Karen's mother. Most men in the village envied him for that. I could see it in their eyes whenever Karen, her mother, and I were in the drug-store. They stood off to the side, watching and listen-ing and smiling at one another, all probably thinking the same thing: *Harry Pearson couldn't satisfy a woman like that, but I could.*

I looked back at the Pearson house and then up at the window I knew to be Karen's. I thought I saw her peering out at me between the curtains, but I couldn't be sure. There was too much of a glare.

This wasn't like her at all, I thought. She probably did get involved with a boy. Who knows? Maybe he was upstairs with her right this moment. Maybe he had snuck in, and she didn't want her mother to know. All sorts of scenarios and explanations stampeded through my brain and bounced about all during my much slower ride home.

I said nothing to my mother, whom I caught taking secret glances at me from time to time. I guess it was because I was unusually quiet at dinner. Mothers, I was told and now can confirm, have a special sensi-tivity when it comes to their children, because their children were once part of their bodies. It was always easier to hide my feelings from my father, and I imag-ined it was easier for Jesse as well.

After dinner and cleanup, I retreated to my room. My mother stopped by only once, knocking on the door. I couldn't remember exactly when she and my father had started doing that, but one day, they just stopped barging right in and always knocked to get permission first. Something had happened to tell them that they should respect my privacy. It worked both ways. I no longer barged in on them, either. I recognized that this was one of many things telling me I was no longer a child, not in their eyes and not in my own.

"Yes?"

She poked her head in and asked, "Everything all right, Zipporah?"

"Yes," I said. The weight of the lie was so great that it almost didn't escape my lips and barely made it to her ears.

She just looked at me a moment, decided not to pursue, smiled, and closed the door.

Suddenly, my worry and concern, all my curiosity, turned to anger.

What had I done to deserve to be pushed away like this?

If Karen and I were best friends, why wouldn't she share whatever it was that bothered her?

Now I resented all the secret and intimate things I had revealed to her lately. I had even told her things about Jesse that Jesse wouldn't have liked me telling. Where was her reciprocation? She was taking and not giving, and I felt the fool because of it.

I made up my mind that the next day, I wouldn't be so forgiving, and I certainly wouldn't be as friendly.

I pouted and had trouble falling asleep thinking about it all. I had, after all, invested everything in this friendship, sacrificed many others, made myself as much of an outcast as Karen was, and denied myself all the social activities I could be enjoying. Soon, if not already, my name and all sorts of profanities would be written on the walls of stalls in the boys' bathroom.

I fell asleep feeling certain I had been betrayed.

I didn't feel much different in the morning. Luckily, it was Tuesday, and my mother had an early shift at the hospital, so she was on her way out by the time I went down to breakfast; otherwise, she would have been full of questions. My father was scurrying about, because he had to be in court in Kingston, a good hour and a half away. He barely noticed I was there. Before I was finished having breakfast, I was all alone.

I went out to wait for the school bus. Although it was late April, the mornings were still quite brisk, so I kept my scarf wrapped around my neck and wore gloves. After the snows of March melted, weeks of rain injected the trees and bushes with what my mother called a growth hormone. One morning, we awoke to see the forest thickened, the skeletonlike trees filling out with green. The very ground unfroze and came out of hibernation. It was easy to imagine the earth itself yawning and stretching and smiling up at the warmer sun.

I heard the bus rattle around the turn and saw it approaching my house. It slowed to a stop, and the doors opened. There were only a half dozen students on it, mostly junior high kids. I nodded at the bus driver and made my way toward the rear to plop down and wait for Karen so I could be dramatic and sulk.

My friendship wasn't going to be taken for granted, I thought as I hardened myself all the way into town.

Lots of other girls would like to be my friend, I told myself, especially if I stopped being Karen's best friend. I was so angry I even considered being friends with Alice Bucci.

I glanced at the students waiting for the bus in the village. I didn't want Karen to see me searching for her in the crowd, so I turned quickly and sat looking out of the opposite side. I wanted to be just like that, with my back to her, when Karen got on the bus and sat beside me. I'd wait for her to say good morning, and then I'd grunt or something. If she didn't apologize, I would pout the entire way to school.

I didn't look at the kids boarding. I waited until I heard the bus door close and the driver shift and start away. Then I turned and looked and saw that Karen wasn't sitting beside me. I searched the bus quickly and realized she wasn't sitting anywhere else, either.

She wasn't going to school, at least not on the bus.

My anger deflated like a balloon with a pinhole and was quickly replaced by frustration. I couldn't even show her I was angry at her.

She was staying home just so I couldn't, I decided. She was avoiding me before I could avoid her, I concluded, which brought back my anger.

I wore it all day, moping, keeping to myself, chiding myself until it exhausted me. Very few of the other kids even asked about her, and when any did, I just shrugged and said, "I don't know. How would I know?" They looked as if they resented my not knowing more than I did.

Despite myself, despite my wounded ego and sensitivity, at the end of the school day, I got off the bus in town and reluctantly walked to Karen's house to see why she hadn't attended school. My curiosity over-powered my indignation. I was disappointed in myself for needing her so much while she obviously didn't need me half as much.

I'm just a weak puppy, I thought, and chided myself all the way to her front door.

Little did I know how much she would come to need me and how much stronger than she was I would have to be.

4

Pretend Central

She's doing it again, I thought after pressing the doorbell and waiting and waiting.

I pressed it again.

And again.

And then I shouted. "I'm not leaving until you answer the door, Karen Stoker!"

Nothing stirred inside. The spring afternoon breeze made the weeping willow tree on the north side of the house nod. Behind me, a few cars went by on Main Street, and down the block, the four-year-old Lohan twins chased their puppy on the lawn, their squeals of laughter carried off in the breeze.

Where was she? Why hadn't she come to school? Why had she ignored me? The lazy sound of a lawn mower nearly drowned out my indignation. The scent of cut grass filled my nostrils. Even the birds on the telephone wires looked lazy and content. Right in the middle of a Norman Rockwell painting, I was falling into a panic.

I cupped my hands around my face to block out the glare and looked through the living-room window, through the living-room door, and into the hallway.

It was dark, and I saw no one, but I returned to the doorbell anyway. This time, I kept my finger on it and heard it ringing and ringing. I began to think she wasn't home. No matter how she felt, she couldn't possibly tolerate someone being this insistent.

With my arms folded at my chest, I stood there glaring at the closed door as if it were someone preventing me from speaking or seeing Karen. I felt like kicking it. I was that frustrated.

Suddenly, the door opened, and she stood there in a nightgown looking out at me, her eyes blinking madly because of the bright afternoon sunshine. Her hair was down but unbrushed, and she was barefoot. Creases from a deep sleep were carved on the right side of her face along her temples and cheek.

"What do you want?" she demanded in a cranky voice.

"What's wrong with you? Why weren't you in school? Why wouldn't you see me last night?"

"I don't feel well," she said. "I still have a bad headache."

"Still? So what's wrong? Did you go to a doctor?"

"I don't have to go to a doctor, Zipporah. Just leave me alone for now," she said, and started to close the door.

I put my foot in the way.

"I won't, Karen. I'm your best friend, whether you like it or not," I said, which sounded stupid the moment I said it.

She paused and stared at me.

"You don't want to be my best friend," she said, in a voice that sounded as if she were talking in her sleep.

"Why not? Why shouldn't I want to be your best

friend? Well?" I demanded. I still had my foot in her doorway.

She looked at it and then at me again.

"When you're someone's best friend, you have to share their pain and suffering and all their mistakes as well as their happiness, Zipporah, and you don't want to do that when it comes to me."

"How do you know what I want to do?"

"I know what you can do. Take my word for it, Zipporah. If I were in your shoes, that's the way I would be."

"Well, you're not in my shoes." I looked at her feet. "You're not even wearing shoes."

She tried to remain serious and firm, but when I said that, she just couldn't help smiling. She turned away to hide it and took a deep breath.

"Look, because I am your best friend, I won't let you be mine. Can you understand that?"

"No, Karen. I'm too stupid. Enlighten me."

She shook her head.

"Go home, Zipporah."

"I'll camp out right here until your mother comes home," I warned, and saw that got to her. Her eyes widened, and she pressed her lips together hard.

"Okay," she said, lowering her shoulders. "You asked for it. Come on."

She turned and walked toward the stairway. I hesitated. Now that I had gotten what I wanted, did I want it? I had put on a brave face, but I was trembling. Without turning back, she silently continued up the stairs and into her room. I entered the house, closed the front door, and followed, my heartbeat quickening with each step.

"Close the door," she said when I stepped into her bedroom.

Why close the door? There's no one else home. I did it anyway and stood there, waiting. The curtains were still drawn closed, and there were no lights on.

"Can I put on the light?"

She nodded, and I did so.

She had a bedroom as large and as nice as mine, maybe even nicer, because her bathroom was what we learned the French called *en suite,* whereas I had to go out and down the hallway to get to the bathroom that my parents designated as mine. The fixtures in our house had more style but were older. Sometimes the pipes knocked, and since we had been living in the Doral house, we'd had plumbers come out to repair things at least six times. One time, because of a lightning storm, we lost the submersible pump that produced our water. We were too far from the village to have municipal water and sewer. We had a septic tank, and my father was always worrying about it.

In my bathroom, I had a combination tub and shower, and if I forgot to turn the knob after I had taken a shower, I'd get soaked leaning over to turn the water on for a bath. Karen had a stall shower and a tub.

The one thing I liked better in my room was my wooden floor. It was thick, rich wood that could take on a sheen when polished. Karen had a beaten-down, knotty-looking shag rug she said was probably full of mold, because it always felt damp beneath her feet. It was stained before she and her mother had moved into the Pearson house. Her closets were bigger, but I had more to hang up than she did, and I had nicer furnishings—a canopy bed with pink swirls in the headboard that made it look like cherry vanilla ice cream, two matching dressers, and a marble vanity table, as well as a bleached oak desk. Also, I had my own television set in my room now, and we seemed to get better reception than the people in the village, because we were on higher ground.

Karen didn't say anything else. She returned to her bed and sat with her back against the propped-up pillows, her hands folded in her lap. She stared down at her hands. I remained there, feeling foolish.

"So?" I finally said. "I asked for it, so tell me. What's wrong?"

She lifted her head slowly and looked at me with such pain in her eyes I thought whatever it was, it was surely my fault. What could I have possibly done?

"My mother is deathly afraid that Harry will divorce her and we'll be thrown out on the street."

"What? Why?" I asked.

"He's very unhappy."

"Unhappy? With your mother? How could he do any better?"

"Harry doesn't worry about doing better. He thinks he's God's gift to women or something. He takes my mother for granted."

"But why would he divorce your mother?"

"I told you. He's unhappy. Don't get thick on me."

I shook my head. How could Harry Pearson be unhappy with Darlene Pearson? She worked well with him in the drugstore. People liked her. She was beautiful, too beautiful for a man who looked like Harry Pearson. She kept their house well. No one would or could believe he was unhappy.

"I don't believe it."

"Believe it," she said. "You don't live here. You don't know what goes on in this house. You don't know anything about us," she added, practically shouting.

I quickly looked away and then back at her.

"I'm sorry. I don't mean I don't believe you. I just mean it's hard to believe. That's all. So, do you know why Harry is unhappy?"

"My mother says it's because of me."

"You? Why?"

"Because I'm too unfriendly, because I don't like Harry, and I don't hide it from him or from her. I am not being cooperative," she added. "She thinks I'm selfish, spoiled, petulant. She has a whole list of words to use whenever she needs them, and that's usually daily."

"Maybe you should just let them change your name," I said, shrugging.

"It's got to do with a lot more than just a name, Zipporah. Jesus."

She looked away.

"I'm sorry. I'm trying to understand. I want to understand. I don't want you to be unhappy and sick over it."

"It's too late."

"Too late for what?"

"For me not being sick over it. I was sick over it the day they got married."

"But you told me you thought she had little choice. He could provide and . . ."

"She had little choice, not me."

"Can't you pretend to like him? I've seen you put on an act when you want to, and you're good at it.

You're much better than I am. Jesse says I have a face like a window pane, and anyone can tell what I'm really thinking or feeling."

"No, I can't fake it, Zipporah. When he comes near me, I cringe inside. I can feel my intestines go into knots and my heart tighten into a lump as hard as coal. He smells," she added.

"Smells? I never knew that."

"You don't get close enough to him to know."

"Why would he smell? He sells men's cologne and after-shave in the drugstore."

"He never wore any of that, because his mother was allergic to practically everything, even air."

"Well, he can wear it now. She's gone."

"Tell him she's gone. That's another thing, Zipporah," she said in almost a whisper. "He doesn't act like she's gone. He acts like she's still living in the back of the house in her apartment. Why do you think he's never rented it out?

"What do you mean, he acts like she's there? What does he do?"

"He goes back there at night and talks to her."

"How do you know that?" I asked.

"I followed him, and I listened at the door. I told my mother, but she doesn't want to hear about it. She was furious at me for spying on him and was terrified he would find out."

"Maybe . . ."

"Maybe what, Zipporah?"

"Maybe he just misses her so much he can't stand it," I suggested. "Lots of people talk to their dead relatives. My mother sometimes says things like, 'Ma, where are you when I need you?' Stuff like that."

"This is very different, Zipporah. He talks to her as if he believes she's right there. And he hears her talk back to him, too. I know he does. I hear him answering her questions. He whines and pleads with her."

"So he's pretending," I said, still trying to make it sound like something not so unusual.

"He's a man in his forties, Zipporah. He should have a grip on reality, don't you think?"

"Yes, of course."

"He's not normal. Take my word for it." She looked away for a moment and then turned back to me. "I actually know more about him than my mother does."

"You do? How come?"

"Because of what I hear him say in that apartment. My mother doesn't know half the things his mother did to him when he was little. She had a nice variation on confining him to his room. Instead, she tied his hands behind his back for hours and hours, sometimes most of the day. You want to hear something disgusting? She didn't even untie him when he had to go to the bathroom, and he was no infant, either."

"That *is* disgusting."

"I heard lots of disgusting things," she said.

"Why did his father let her do those things to him?"

"His father was as afraid of Harry's mother as Harry was, from what I understand, and he wasn't around all that often. There's a lot more, a lot I can't even talk about without getting nauseated myself."

I sat there a little stunned and unsure of what to say next. Now I was the one looking down at my hands in my lap. She was suffering, but she couldn't tell her mother, and her mother didn't know what Karen knew about her mother's own husband? She was making it all sound very confusing, but I was afraid to show it, afraid she would only get mad at me. Then I thought of something.

"That time I saw you had a bruise on your arm. Did Harry do it to you?"

She looked as if she wasn't going to answer, and then she nodded.

"He explodes. He'll get angry and just pout or something, which makes you think that's it, and then all of a sudden, when you least expect it, he does something mean and vicious like grab my arm and shake me or slap me. Once, he nearly pushed me down the stairs."

"What does your mother say about that?"

"She doesn't know about it."

"Didn't you tell her?"

"No. It would only make things worse. She says I'm just acting spoiled or whining whenever I do complain about anything, and she gets as angry as he does. My mother never really wanted me, you know."

"What do you mean?"

"I was a sexual accident. She's told me that a hundred times if she's told it to me once. Why do you think I never had a brother or a sister? She's not cut out to be the motherly type."

"That's terrible, Karen. You never said anything."

"I don't tell you half of it."

"I'm sorry," I said. I couldn't imagine having a mother who admitted to not wanting you born. She saw the look of pity and pain on my face.

"Actually, it's gotten worse recently," she said.

"Worse? How?"

Her eyes filled with tears, and she pressed her lips together. I waited, holding my breath. What could possibly be worse than what I had already heard?

"If you tell anyone, especially your parents, I'll kill myself," she said. "I will," she emphasized when I looked at her.

Then, to illustrate that she wasn't just talking, she leaned over, opened her night-table drawer, and took out a very sharp kitchen knife. "I'll cut my wrists so fast and so deep there'll be no chance of saving me."

I couldn't speak. It felt as if someone were squeezing my neck. She put the blade against her skin.

"Okay, okay. I believe you. I swear, I won't say a word to anyone."

She studied my face until she was confident I meant it, put the knife back, and closed the drawer. Why was she keeping such a knife in her night-table drawer? She sat back again. I saw how hard it was for her to tell me why it was worse, so I just sat quietly and waited. She took a deep breath, sounding like someone who was about to go underwater.

"He comes into my room at night," she said.

"At night? You mean, after you go to sleep?"

"Yes."

"What does he do?"

"What do you think?"

It suddenly felt as though we were sitting in an oven. I shook my head. I was afraid to think, to imagine. The expression on my face made that clear. I could feel the heat in my cheeks as my blood rose through my neck.

"What?" I managed.

"See? It's upsetting you. I told you not to come in.

I told you to go home. You should have listened to me and stopped being my best friend. I wasn't being snotty. I was only thinking of you."

"I'm all right. Just tell me, and don't worry about me or my feelings or anything," I said firmly.

"Is that right?"

"Yes. Don't leave out a detail."

"Okay, big shot," she said, as though I had challenged her. "I won't. He opens the door very slowly and comes in so quietly it's more like a dream—a nightmare, I should say. First, he gracefully peels the blanket off me. Then he sits beside me and he puts one hand gently over my mouth and his other hand under my nightgown. The first time he did it, I was so shocked and frightened I couldn't speak, much less yell, so don't ask me if I did. The first time, that was all he did. Then he took deep breaths, put the blanket back, and left the room as quietly as he had come in."

"You didn't tell your mother about that?" I asked incredulously.

"No."

"Why not? Karen!"

"You don't understand how it is. I already explained how it is when I complain about anything. I was afraid she just would accuse me of lying because I didn't like him. She would have said I dreamed the whole thing. I was afraid she would accuse me of making trouble for her and for us, and so I hoped it would never happen again."

"How can she not know herself, especially since he's doing something like that at night?"

"I guess I have to tell you, now that you've made me tell you this."

"What?"

"They don't sleep together anymore," she said.

"Don't sleep together? What do you mean?"

"It's not brain surgery, Zipporah. They don't sleep in the same bed."

"Then . . . where does he sleep?" I asked, terrified that she was going to say he slept with her.

"At first, I think he just slept on the sofa in the living room. Lately, he's been sleeping in the apartment."

"Oh." That answer brought some relief. "I can't imagine my father leaving my mother at night and her not becoming very disturbed about it. Your mother hasn't said anything?"

"Not to me. Maybe she is happy about it. I can understand it if she is. I pretend I don't know. That's another reason it's so hard to talk to her about it all."

"You can't lock your door?"

"He's the only one with keys to doors other than the front door in this house."

"That night I saw you walking in the village, crying. Was it because of this?"

"Yes. I knew he would be coming to my room later. I was thinking of just walking forever, but I had no place to go, and it got cold."

"You could have come to my house."

"And then everyone would know, Zipporah. How would you like people to know that was happening to you?"

"Well, he should be arrested or something!"

"Oh, that would be just great. That would solve everything. The drugstore would go out of business, and we'd definitely be out on the street. Besides, how do you think people would treat me, look at me? I can tell you. Remember when we all learned that Paula Loomis's brother might have raped her? Remember how everyone treated Paula, stayed away from her? It was as if it was all her fault and she was dirty or something. It's why she dropped out and went to live with her aunt in New York City. Not that I really care what people here think of me," she said. "It's what would happen to my mother here. She would only blame me and hate me."

"Well, what are you going to do, Karen?"

"I don't know. Most nights, I lie here terrified and can't sleep. It upsets my stomach and gives me headaches."

"How many times has he come into your room?"

"Enough."

"Did he do anything else?"

"What do you think?"

I shook my head. Dared I ask more, pursue, force her to give me the grisly details?

"I'll draw a picture for you. He comes in here with just his bathrobe on. He's naked beneath it."

"Oh," I said. Actually, it was more like a sigh of horror coming up out of my lungs. "I'm sorry," I said.

"Forget it. I don't want to talk about it. Don't ask me anything else. I'm getting sick again just telling you about it, and it's making my headache even worse."

"Doesn't your mother want to know why you're not feeling well?"

"She thinks it's just my time of the month. It's never been easy for me to have a period. She knows that, so she accepts that excuse."

I nodded.

"Are you going to go to school tomorrow?"

"Probably."

A multitude of things ran through my mind, especially when I recalled my conversation with my mother. Karen could get pregnant. What should I do, say?

"And you still don't want to tell your mother about Harry and what he's doing?"

She looked away.

"Karen?"

"I said I was finished talking about it! I told you, it's making me sick to my stomach."

"Okay, okay. Do you want to know the homework assignments for tomorrow?"

I felt silly even mentioning it, but it was the fastest way to change the topic.

"Yeah, I'm dying to know," she said.

I looked down at my hands again.

"I wish I could help you," I said. "I really do. I wish there was something I could do."

"Well, there isn't, so stop thinking about it. Okay, what were the homework assignments for tomorrow?" she asked, and got up to get her notebook.

None of it seemed very important now, but I rattled it all off for her.

"I can help you with anything."

"I'll do it later," she said.

"You want to come over to do it? Ride your bike? Maybe you can come to dinner."

"No. My mother thinks I'm still not feeling well. I'll have to stay here tonight. Maybe tomorrow night," she added.

"Okay. Great."

I stood up and looked at her bedroom door.

"Why don't you put a chair up against it?" I suggested. "You know, brace it under the doorknob and . . ."

"Just go home, Zipporah," she said, and sighed as if I were a child. "I'll see you on the bus in the morning."

"Right," I said. I started out.

"Thanks for insisting on being my best friend," she said when I opened the door.

"You don't have to thank me."

"Okay, so I take it back," she said, and laughed.

Just like that, we were back to being who we were. It was as if we had both detoured through a nightmare and awoken together.

"Mindy Sages has a pimple the size of a pebble on the tip of her nose. You should see her. She walks around like this," I said, putting my hand over my face.

"She oughtta get one of those face masks that Arab women wear."

"Or just wear a bag over her head."

"Or wrap herself like the Invisible Man."

"Right. When you see her, you can ask her who's her friend."

We laughed. Mindy Sages was one of the zeros Karen had identified from day one. She was always very snobby, especially to us.

"I'll walk you to the door," she said, suddenly full of happy energy. She followed me down the stairs.

Just as we opened the front door and I stepped out, her mother drove in.

"If you're sick, Karen, why are you having friends

over?" she demanded after she rolled down her window.

"She brought me the homework, Mother. Is that all right?"

"Oh," her mother said, and rolled her window up before driving the car into the garage.

"See what I mean?" Karen said. "She would have had a fit if I even mentioned going to your house tonight. We all have to play our parts here," she said. "This is the Pretend Central System, WPCS. See you," she said, and closed the door.

I felt as if she had died. Now I was the one who felt sick to her stomach. I couldn't look at her mother. Why didn't she have the same built-in sensitivity to Karen that my mother had to me? Why didn't she realize something terrible was happening in her own house to her own daughter? And then I had a more terrifying thought: What if she did, and she didn't care?

I hurried down the walk to start my trek home.

What would I do about all this now? If I didn't keep her secret, do what I promised, she might just kill herself as she had threatened to do. On the other hand, I hated not being able to help her. How easy it would be for me to go to my mother and tell her and get her to do something. My father was a lawyer. He could get Mr. Pearson put away, I thought. That was where he belonged.

But then, what if Karen was right, and things became impossible for her at school and in the community? All I would have succeeded in doing would be to drive her and her mother away. She'd hate me forever.

I was so frustrated and angry I wished Mr. Pearson

was dead, and then I immediately felt guilty for wishing that on someone, even someone like him.

Another thing worried me. My mother was liable to look at me and know something terrible was wrong. She was already suspicious about Karen because of the things I had told her. How could I carry such a dark secret inside myself and not show it on my face? I would fail. I would let Karen down because I couldn't help it, and she would hate me anyway.

It all buzzed around in my head, and I didn't realize where I was walking or how long I had been walking. Suddenly, I heard a very loud horn and nearly jumped out of my skin at the metallic scream of automobile brakes. Mr. Bedick, who owned an egg farm down the road from us, was waving his fist angrily at me. He looked as if he had been standing on his head. That's how red his face was. I glanced down and saw that the bumper of his car was only inches from me.

"I'm sorry!" I cried. "I'm sorry."

I had stepped too far to the left and put myself right in his path.

"Your parents are going to hear about this," he threatened, and drove away.

"Great," I muttered. "I'm already in trouble."

I hurried home so I could get into my room and settle down before my parents got home. That was an impossible task. The moment I closed the door and sat there in the quiet of my own room, everything Karen had told me came rushing back. I saw the most horrible images and knew I would probably have my own nightmares about it now. She was right to warn me away, to tell me I'd be better off not being her best friend. I wasn't just sharing her pain and suffering.

Because we were so close, it was easy to imagine it happening to me, too.

How horrible, I thought, and imagined her lying there too terrified to raise her voice in protest, too terrified to tell her mother. She was trapped and at the mercy of someone who was . . . who was what? The story she told me about Mr. Pearson having conversations with his dead mother and now going into her old apartment to sleep was even more frightening in some ways. Did he see a ghost?

How would this all end? There had to be something we could do. I sat there feeling so helpless and trapped myself until my gaze fell on my bookcase, and a collection of short stories popped out at me. It really wasn't meant for me. It was Jesse's book, but it had gotten mixed up and put in my room. From time to time, I read some of it. The collection was called *Campfire Chills*. It was supposed to be a collection of scary stories told around a campfire. Most of them were silly to me, but there was one that sprang to mind as if it had been written on springs.

I jumped up and pulled the book off the shelf, turning to the story quickly and rereading it with the speed of someone looking for a word clue.

Yes, I thought. Why not? It was easy to substitute Mr. Pearson for the character in the story and easy to substitute Karen and myself for another. We would do the same thing. I practically lunged at my phone to call her.

Her mother answered.

"You were just here, weren't you?" she asked me.

"Yes, Mrs. Pearson, but there was one important thing about the schoolwork I forgot to tell Karen."

"Oh," she said. "Just a moment."

I waited, knowing Karen would have to come down the stairs to talk to me unless her mother permitted her to pick up the phone in her and Mr. Pearson's bedroom. She apparently didn't, because it took a while for Karen to pick up.

"What?" she finally said.

"I have an idea, a solution to your problem," I said. "It could really work."

She was silent.

"And what would that be?" she finally asked.

"I have something for you to read tomorrow, and then we'll talk about it, okay?"

"I see. Yes, thanks for calling. I'll see you on the bus," she said, and hung up.

That's all right, I told myself. I wasn't upset at all at how abruptly she had ended our conversation. It didn't mean she was angry or upset at me for still talking and thinking about the things she had told me. It probably just meant her mother was standing close by and listening to our conversation.

I put the short story collection into my school bag so there would be no chance of my forgetting it in the morning.

She'll like this idea, I thought. After all, she was the one who called her home Pretend Central, wasn't she?

I felt relieved, excited. I fit the definition of a best friend, after all.

I could help her.

5

All Alone at the
Bates Motel

"**I** understand what you're suggesting," she told me on the bus after school. I had given her the book in the morning, and she had read the story during a study hall period. "I think it's dangerous."

She looked out the window. When I had awoken in the morning, it was the first thing that came into my mind, and the light of morning, the beginning of a new day, had a way of making exciting ideas a lot less exciting. It's as if the sunlight illuminates all the obstacles you missed in the darkness.

And, as she said, the dangers.

"I know," I said in a loud whisper. "I'm sorry. I just hate seeing you upset and frightened and when this came to mind, I had to call you."

She spun around, her eyes narrow and cold.

"I didn't say I wouldn't do it. I just said it's dangerous. It might not be a bad idea."

She looked out again.

I could feel the blood rushing into my face. She would actually consider doing it? Of course, I would help in any way I could, but now that I had proposed it and she was actually considering it, fear and terror were like leeches on my body, sucking out my courage.

"Really?"

"We'll talk about it later. Can you come to my house tonight?"

"Absolutely," I said. "I'll come over right after dinner."

"Good," she said, and continued to look out the window. "Good," I heard her whisper.

What have I done? I suddenly wondered. Maybe I was giving her false hope. Maybe I was getting myself into deep trouble. If it all went wrong, my parents would be devastated. My brother would hate me, too. A part of me wanted to pull back, to say it was really just a silly idea, we couldn't do this, but another part of me was truly impressed that I had come up with something that might actually help Karen. I had to firm up my nerve, be brave. This was no time to be a child or even a teenager. What was happening to Karen wasn't meant to happen to children and teenagers. It wasn't meant to happen to anyone, but adults were better equipped to handle it than we were, I thought.

Whether we liked it or not, Mr. Pearson had seized us by the neck and ripped us out of our youth. We would still laugh, we would have fun, but there would always be that quiet moment, that look between us that reminded us where we had been. Funny, I was already thinking in terms of we when it was all really happening to Karen and not to me. I am her real friend, her sister, after all, I thought.

She rose when the bus pulled in front of the stop in Sandburg.

"See you later," she said. She patted the short story

collection. "I'll hold on to this and keep thinking about it and how we could apply it."

"Okay."

She started away and then paused and returned.

"When you come over, Zipporah, you have to be sure you don't look strangely at Harry or talk to him any differently from the way you did before. We mustn't give him even a hint that I told you anything, understand?"

"Yes."

"If it's too hard, just ignore him, pretend he's not there. That's what I do half the time."

"Okay," I said.

Now I was really nervous again. I wanted to suggest she just come to my house, but I knew why she wanted me at hers. We had to plan and think of ways to do what we had to do. It was as if we were looking over a prospective battlefield.

She flashed a smile and started away. I watched her get off the bus and walk in the direction of her house. The bus continued toward Church Road. I didn't realize that I was trembling until the bus stopped in front of my house and I rose to get off. My legs wobbled. I sucked in my breath and hurried down the aisle.

I couldn't remember if my mother was on the day shift or the night shift that day. I was so distracted by Karen's problems that I didn't listen when she had told me, so I entered the house quietly in case she was sleeping. My parents' bedroom door was open, and I could see she wasn't home yet. She probably was doing the late afternoon shift, which wouldn't end until eleven p.m. I checked the kitchen and, sure enough, found instructions for preparing my father's dinner. She had already made a meat loaf. I just had to warm it up along with the mashed potatoes and vegetables. I'd make my father and me a nice salad, too. There was still half of my father's favorite pie in the refrigerator, chocolate cream.

I looked forward to these dinners with just my father and me. I had been doing the dinner warm-ups and preparations ever since I was ten. Most of the time, Jesse was there, too, but sometimes he was at a practice or at an away game or even on a date. I know that these dinners with only the two of us brought my father and me closer. He would ask me questions about school, and he would even tell me about his legal work, why a case was interesting and what he intended to accomplish. It was at these special dinners when he would tell me more about his own youth.

What worried me tonight was whether or not he would see the turmoil inside me. He wasn't as good at reading my feelings and thoughts as my mother was, but when there were only the two of us, he could focus sharper attention on me and see right through any false face. If he had even an inkling of what Karen and I were planning, he would surely go through the roof. I had seen him when he was very angry because of something one of his law partners had done or something a judge had decided. He could swell up and look pretty intimidating. Fortunately for me, I could count on the fingers of one hand how many times in my life he had been more than just a little irritated at something I had done, and the same was true for Jesse. I could sense that he hated being angry at either of us more than we hated it.

That didn't mean he would let either of us get away

with anything. Jesse and I were certainly not spoiled. Our parents were firm and far from doting. Anything they gave us, they gave us after careful consideration, and we were always made to appreciate it. Nothing was to be taken for granted. My father, especially, was always keen on us understanding the value of a dollar, as he put it. That, he said, was the way his father had put it to him.

"Show me you're responsible, and I'll give you more responsibilities," he always told us.

For most of our lives, it seemed, we were always proving ourselves to our parents.

I was already setting the table and getting everything ready for dinner when my father came home.

"Little Mama's at it again," he sang to me when he stopped at the kitchen doorway. "Be right down."

The debate began to rage in me. One side of me said I should tell my father everything and ask him to keep it a secret but do what had to be done to protect Karen and her mother. The other side of me came roaring back, the voice screaming about how I would hurt my best friend so deeply even the other students at school would hate and distrust me. I would have to move away as well.

"So, how's it going?" Daddy asked, slipping into his chair.

"Good," I said, and quickly turned to the food. I could feel his eyes on me as I worked.

"Everything looks good," he said. "And I'm hungry. I had one of those working lunches where you don't know what you're eating after a while. I'm not sure I ate anything."

He started to eat.

"Everything okay?" he asked. I knew why he asked. I was being too quiet.

"Yes, Daddy. I have this test to study for, so I'm going over to Karen's after I clean up."

"Oh. How is Karen? Your mother mentioned she was having some sort of a health problem?"

"No, it's nothing," I said quickly. "She had a headache one day in school, that's all."

"Glad she's feeling better. She's a nice kid," he said. "When I was your age, I palled around with one guy most of the time, Bobby Mallen. We were inseparable."

"I never hear you talk about him."

"That's because when I went off to college, he went into the army, and we lost touch. I made other close friends, and I'm sure he did, too. It's natural. You go off in different directions. Not many people remain close friends with the friends they had in high school. That's true even with college friends, for that matter. Jobs, careers, travel, change it."

"That sounds sad to me," I said.

He shrugged.

"Sometimes it is sad. It's all part of . . ."

"Growing up. I know," I said, and he laughed.

"I wasn't going to say that. I was going to say something bigger, part of life. We zigzag through the years, turning this way and that. I went to one high-school reunion, but Bobby didn't show, and I had trouble even recognizing some of the other classmates. One of these days, you'll read that novel by Thomas Wolfe, *You Can't Go Home Again*."

"What's that mean?"

"You can't recover the past. It's something that is

gone forever, despite albums and yearbooks and old letters. We're just not who we were, honey. It's foolish to try to be. Be comfortable with who you are now and later. But you're too young for any of this talk, so don't worry about it," he said, waving his hand as if the words and thoughts were annoying flies. "When you're my age . . ."

"I'll forget Karen and all our days together?"

"You won't forget. It will just be different. Everything is so intense right now. Time has a way of making what you think is terrible now not so terrible and what you think is wonderful not so wonderful. There are things, Zipporah, older people can tell you but you just can't appreciate or even understand until you go through them yourself. Then you wish you could go back and do so much differently.

"Hey," he suddenly cried, "why are we being so heavy here? I want to talk about my new golf clubs. You should have seen me on the third hole at the Monster golf course last Sunday. I won ten bucks, too."

I laughed. It felt good. It felt like a cool breeze on a terribly hot and muggy afternoon.

How lucky I was to have parents like mine, I thought, and how horrible it was for Karen to be where she was. It made me even more determined to do what I could to help her.

My father went into his home office after dinner to finish up some work. He heard me shout to him that I was off to Karen's, and he called back not to be too late. I promised I wouldn't and left after putting my bundle of books and notebooks in the bike bag. At least, we had to make it look as if studying was what we were doing, I thought.

Everything Karen had told me had changed my whole view of her home and her mother and Harry Pearson. The house looked ominous to me as I pedaled up the driveway. Shadows seemed painted forever over the front. The tree branches were as still and luminescent as skeletons caught in the moonlight. I saw the lights were on in Karen's room. I was sure she had told her mother I was coming. It was already past seven, so Harry was probably home. Karen came to the door so quickly when I rang the bell I suspected she had been waiting on the stairway.

"They're eating," she said, nodding toward the dining room. "It's just Zipporah!" she shouted in that direction.

"Hi, Zipporah," I heard her mother call back. Harry said nothing. I was happy I didn't have to face him right off. We practically ran up the stairway to her room and closed the door. She plopped onto her bed. The book of short stories was open to the right one.

"Tell me exactly what you think is going to happen and what you were thinking we should do," she said.

I hadn't thought up any details. It was just the concept. I stared at her and shook my head.

"I don't really know exactly how we should do it."

She looked disappointed.

"But when the character in the story believed the ghost was telling him to kill his brother-in-law, he went ahead without any hesitation," I added quickly. "People who believe in ghosts believe that ghosts see everything, know everything, I suppose, and when you told me how he talks to his mother and even seems to hear her talk to him, I thought of this story. Maybe he thinks he sees her ghost."

She nodded.

"It's a pretty nasty story. I'm surprised your parents let you read it."

"They don't know the book was in my room. It's Jesse's book, but it was moved with another carton of stuff."

"So you think if we can get Harry to believe his dead mother knows what he's done, that he's come in here, and that she disapproves, he'll be sorry and stop?"

I shrugged.

"That was sort of my idea. What do you think?"

"I think it's worth a try. What's he going to do to me that he hasn't already?" she muttered. She picked up the book and turned the pages. "I really don't know what we should do specifically, either. It was just the idea that excited me," she said.

"Maybe it's stupid, after all."

"No, no. It was good thinking. To do anything like this, I think we have to get into the apartment."

"The apartment?"

"There are two ways to get into the apartment, through the door that leads from the kitchen and the outside door. It has a separate entrance. Both are locked, but I know where Harry keeps his keys. We'd have to get one, probably to the outside door, and have a copy made while he's at the drugstore, so we can go in and out anytime we want. We can do it Saturday," she said. "As soon as he and my mother leave for the store, I'll get the key. We should not have it made here at Heckman's Hardware, though. We should go at least to Monticello or Liberty."

"Perfect!" I cried. "Remember, I have to go see my

grandmother in Liberty. I'll ask my parents to let you come along, and while they're visiting, we'll ask to take a walk and go to the hardware store there."

"That's a very good idea."

"Once we get in there, what are we going to do to convince him that his mother knows and disapproves?"

She looked thoughtful.

"We have until Saturday or so to figure that out. We'll come up with something," she said. She looked at the book again. "In the story, the man's sister forged their mother's handwriting."

"The perfumed stationery really got him."

"We can't use anything like that. I told you Harry's mother had all these allergies. She didn't wear any perfume. Besides, a mere note in what looks like her handwriting wouldn't be enough. No, we've got to find a better way."

"What if when he came to your room, you were wearing his mother's nightgowns or something else of hers? He wouldn't know we got into the apartment, and he would be shocked enough to turn around and leave."

She looked at me and smiled.

"That's very good, Zipporah. I must be rubbing off on you. Maybe that would work." She looked at me hard. "Of course, if he did find out what we had done, found out you were part of this, you could get into very bad trouble, Zipporah. He might be so angry. Perhaps I should go into the apartment myself and get what I need."

"I'm not afraid. I want to help you," I said firmly. "No matter what."

"No matter what?"

"Bird Oath. We'll be friends forever and ever, and we swear to protect and help each other as much as we would ourselves," I recited, and added, "no matter what."

"Maybe we will be friends forever and ever," she said, as if the possibility had just occurred to her.

Daddy's wrong, I thought. We'll never make turns, take different paths, and forget each other. This would bind us in a way that could never be unraveled or untied. For us, there would always be a way home again, home to each other.

"Okay. Let's take it one step at a time, and then later we'll decide just how much I need you to do with me. Saturday, then, the key gets made."

"Saturday," I said. I had the feeling we should be writing it in blood or something.

"I was thinking of running away, you know," she confessed.

"You were?"

"Yes. I was going to steal as much money as I could from Harry and just run off. I'm afraid of something he could do to me."

"What?" I asked, nearly breathless.

"Well, he is a pharmacist. He could slip something into my food or drink and . . ."

"Poison you?"

"Drug me so he could have his way with me, maybe, and then maybe cause me to have a heart attack or something."

"Nobody would believe that. You're too young to have a heart attack."

"A lot of good it would do me, then," she said.

I nodded. She was right, of course.

"Maybe we shouldn't wait until Saturday."

"No, that's perfect. I'll be all right. Don't worry," she said.

We did try to do some homework, but neither of us could concentrate well enough. I decided I would do as much as I could on the bus and in study hall.

I was hoping that I would be able to leave her house without seeing Mr. Pearson, but when I descended the stairway to go home, he stepped out of his living room and looked up at the two of us. I was surprised to see he still wore his pharmacist's coat.

"Well, hi there, Zipporah," he said, smiling. "How are your parents?"

"Fine, thanks," I said. I couldn't help shifting my eyes and hoped he didn't notice.

"And your brother? He's enjoying college?"

"Very much, Mr. Pearson."

"Good. I'm sure you're all proud of him. You tell your mother and father hello for me," he said, and kept walking down the hallway.

"I will," I called to him.

Karen nodded toward the front door. We hurried to it and stepped out.

"Did you see that? He doesn't even look at me if he can help it," she said. "I do my best to avoid him."

"Your mother has to notice something's not right."

"She doesn't."

"How can . . ."

"She doesn't want to notice," Karen answered before I could ask the question. It was what I had feared myself. "Forget about that. I'll see you tomorrow," she said. She turned to go back in, stopped, and turned back to give me a hug. "Thanks for being there for me," she said, and went back inside.

I got on my bike and then turned when I heard a door open and close.

Mr. Pearson came out of the house and walked toward the rear, where Karen said the apartment was located. He didn't look my way. He looked as if he was talking to himself.

I got onto my bike and shot off down the road, my heart pounding as if I had been riding for hours. My father was watching television when I arrived.

"All studied up?" he called from the living room when he heard me enter.

"Yes," I said.

"This is a pretty good show," he told me.

"I have to do some more reading for English class," I said. I really did, and I couldn't do that and the homework I planned to do in the morning and in study hall.

"Go ahead. I'm going to bed after this. Big day tomorrow, two depositions and a court procedure. Your mother has the same shift as she had today. I might not be back for dinner. I'll let you know. You all right with it?"

"Yes. Maybe I'll invite Karen over."

"Good idea," he said. "Sleep tight, princess."

It brought tears to my eyes to hear him call me princess, because I was lying to him, or at least not confiding in him, and he trusted and loved me so. I wasn't his princess right now. Was that terrible, or was it okay to be loyal to a friend in need?

Lately, I was inundated with concerns. I felt as if I was in a downpour of question marks, rushing from the cover of one answer to another. I lay there thinking about what we had decided. Somehow, some way, we were going to try to get Harry Pearson to believe his dead mother disapproved of what he had been doing to Karen. That was a good thing, and if his mother were alive, she would disapprove for sure, anyway, I thought.

However, in my heart of hearts, I suspected from what Karen had described that Harry Pearson had a very special relationship with his mother's memory. If he found out what we were planning to do or realized we had done something that violated that memory and relationship, he could become so angry he would do something terrible, maybe poison Karen, just as she feared. And we would have been the cause of it! I truly felt as if we were juggling dynamite sticks. And lit ones to boot.

In the morning, we looked at each other like two conspirators, dying to talk about what we were planning but afraid of being overheard.

"I've been thinking and thinking about it all," Karen told me on the bus. "You hit on a good idea. His mother was big on wigs, and I'm sure they're still in the apartment."

"Wigs?"

"She hated that her hair was thinning. She was actually getting bald, like a man gets bald. I saw her without her wig a few times, and she looked worse than a woman on chemotherapy. Even her eyebrows looked almost gone. Although she was allergic to lots of things, she was heavy with what makeup she put on. Her cheeks were always too red, clownish. Her lipstick was on so thick it made her lips twice the size. That's not hard to copy."

"But . . ."

"I'll look through the window into the apartment to see what's there, what we can utilize."

I nodded, but just the idea of sneaking into that apartment made me shiver now. Maybe I shouldn't have pushed so hard to go along with her.

That night, with my parents both gone, I prepared dinner for Karen and myself. I had spoken to my mother, and she told me to prepare one of my favorite things, lamb chops. She told me she had bought a rack and would have it ready to bake. Karen had to go to the drugstore to tell her mother she was coming to my house for dinner and studying.

While I waited for her, my father called to say he wouldn't be home for dinner, after all. My mother called to see if everything was all right, and then Jesse called.

"Daddy's away at a deposition," I told him, "and Mama's got an evening shift tonight."

"All by yourself in the Bates Motel?" he teased, and hummed the background music from *Psycho*.

I knew he was referring to the notorious Doral story, but that was exactly the wrong thing for him to be telling me at this moment.

"Very funny. Thanks."

"You can handle it," he said. "So, what are you up to?"

I told him I was preparing dinner for myself and Karen, and he asked after her.

"She have a boyfriend yet?" he wanted to know.

"No. She doesn't like any of the boys at school. They're all dorks."

"I don't see how they can all be dorks, but that's

okay. Karen probably needs an older guy," he said. "She's too sophisticated for the boys there."

Did my brother think he would become Karen's boyfriend someday? Wasn't she too young for him? What about the girls at his college?

"What about you? Did you find a new girlfriend?"

"I'm working on it," he said. "Am I still the best-looking guy you know?"

"No, you're the best-looking guy you know," I said, and he laughed.

I suddenly missed him more than ever. I longed to hear him strutting through our home, whistling or calling out something silly to me. Occasionally, he and I would have a very serious conversation about other kids we knew or plans we had for ourselves. There were nearly four years between us, but I couldn't remember him ever treating me like an annoying young sister. Somewhere I once read that it was usually in houses where there was a great deal of turmoil and conflict between parents that there were animosities between the children as well. I remembered the line, "The table was set for misery to flourish." That table's not set in our house, I thought.

"What are you doing for fun these days?" Jesse asked.

"Nothing special. Karen and I do a lot together."

"Be careful."

"Of what?" I asked quickly. He made my heart thump.

"Of getting a crush on the same boy. Nothing breaks up a friendship between two girls faster."

"What makes you such an expert about girls?"

"Male instinct. Why, is something like that happening?"

"No worries there. I told you, Karen doesn't like anyone at our school."

"I can't believe it. Karen likes boys, doesn't she?"

"Of course."

Why was he pushing so hard to find out about her crushes?

"And you do, I think."

"Stop it, Jesse."

"All right," he said, laughing. "I got to go. Tell Mom and Dad I'll call on Sunday. I'm starting on third base, too," he added, as if it was nothing.

"Wow. Daddy will be excited."

"You're not?"

"Stop it, Jesse. Of course, I am." After a long enough pause, to kid him back, I asked, "What's third base?"

He laughed. "Bye, Zipper," he said. That had been his nickname for me as long as I could remember.

"Bye."

I hung up but stood there by the phone as if I could still hold on to his voice and keep his face in my eyes. He would surely be angry if he knew what Karen and I were up to, I thought. The doorbell rang. I knew it was Karen.

"You're not going to believe this," she said, rushing past me and into my house as soon as I opened the door. She turned in the entryway. Her face was flushed with excitement.

"What?"

"As I said I would do, I went around to the apartment. Usually, the curtains are drawn and the shade is down on both windows, so it's impossible to see into the place, but the shade was up a good four or five inches, so I was able to kneel down and look into the place."

"And?"

"I could look into the bedroom. It's really not much more than a studio apartment."

"Weren't you ever in there?"

"No. I told you, his mother wasn't happy Harry married my mother and took me into their home. I don't think I ever looked at her without her looking back at me with an expression full of disapproval. I avoided her. She was just an older version of a zero."

"What did you see in the apartment?" I asked.

"On the bed, on the pillow, was one of his mother's wigs with one of those manikin heads people use to keep their wigs on."

"Really?"

"The head had as much makeup on its cheeks and lips as his mother used."

I couldn't speak or swallow. I just shook my head.

"That's not all."

"What else?" I managed.

"Under the blankets, there must be more pillows or something. It looks like . . ."

"What?" I practically screamed.

"Like someone is under the blanket. You know. Bunched up like a body. There was a chair beside the bed, which I imagined is where he sits when he goes in there."

I stared at her.

"What are you saying?" I finally asked, because she just stood there with a half-smile on her face. "Are you saying he's deliberately making it seem as if his dead mother is in that bed?"

"That's what I'm saying. Only, he doesn't think of her as dead."

I brought my hand to the base of my throat and stared at her with my mouth open. She smiled.

"Why are you so happy about this?"

"Don't you see? He is nuts. He will believe his mother is moving about. He really thinks she's still there!"

6

Nightmares

Where do nightmares come from? I wondered. Some people believe they're caused by something you eat that's disagreeable, but doesn't there have to be something scary and horrible already in your head, stuck in your brain, something dormant that gets nudged and comes gleefully up, rising like some dark sea creature?

"The first nightmare for everyone is being born," Jesse once told me after I had suffered a bad dream and cried. I think I was eleven.

"That's stupid, Jesse," I said.

"No, really. Just think about it. Here you are, happy, content, well fed, warm, and comfortable floating around in your mother's womb, and suddenly, for no reason, you get shoved and pushed, squeezed and pulled, until you're out in this bright, noisy place called the world. That's why babies cry as soon as they're born."

"Don't tell her things like that," our mother chastised, but she smiled at him and shook her head. "Spreading that story will hurt the feelings of everyone in the maternity ward in my hospital."

I remember wondering if Jesse were right.

Right at the moment, listening to what Karen was telling me about what went on in her stepfather's mother's apartment, I felt as if I could crawl back into the safety of my mother's womb. Who wanted to be in a world where such things were happening?

"My guess," Karen continued, obviously still very excited about her discovery, "is that Harry crawls into that bed just the way he did when he was a little boy and something frightened him. He wanted to be with his mommy.

"And he still does!" she added. Her face turned angry, sour. "Wait until his mommy finds out what he's been doing to me. She'll throw him out of the bed."

"Are you sure you don't want to tell your mother about all this?" I asked. "I mean, she can go in and see it for herself." I was actually trembling.

"Oh, absolutely not. She would go ape wild if she knew I was spying on Harry."

"But . . . it's so weird, Karen. She couldn't be upset with you."

"Don't tell me what she'll be and not be," she snapped back at me. Then she smiled. "Look, Zipporah, don't you think I've tried in little ways to get my mother to see what Harry is really like? She's comfortable in the life she has now. There are no money problems. She can go and buy whatever clothes she wants. She has her own expensive car. The work in the drugstore is easy. She can flirt with other men, and Harry doesn't get upset. I have everything I need, and I'll have college tuition, which takes worrying about me off her back. We live in the village's nicest home. And now," she said after a pause, "you want me to go to her and tell her the man who is providing all this is a nutcase pervert, and we should pack and leave?"

"The bad things are happening to you, not her. She's your mother first, whether she likes it or not."

"My mother," she said, her eyes steely cold, "is not your mother, Zipporah. I told you. I was a blunder. If she believed in abortion, I'd be nothing more than an inconvenience, but she pretends to be religious, even though the last time we went to church was my real father's funeral. Not everyone has this . . ." She looked around. "This perfect world you live in. "

"My world is not perfect," I said defensively, but after hearing what she was telling me, it surely was.

"Okay. Anyway, don't you see why I'm telling you all this? This makes your idea even better and more possible."

I wasn't sure now that I liked it to be called my idea. Wasn't it our idea?

"Hmmm," she said, looking toward the kitchen. "Something smells yummy. I wish I was as good a cook as you are, but Harry wouldn't eat anything I made, even warmed up."

"He wouldn't?"

"No. Only mommies can feed Baby Harry."

I shook my head. "Who would think these things of him? People have no idea what he's like at home. I know you couldn't meet a more pleasant man when you talk to him in his drugstore. My parents think he's very nice."

"He smiles at everyone until they smile back. Remember that line Mr. Potter used in English class when he yelled at adorable little Bobby Sandow? 'The devil hath a pleasing face'? Something from a Shake-speare play."

"Yes."

"Well, that's Harry." She paused and looked around. "Where's your father, by the way?"

"He's tied up in some legal matter and won't be here until later."

"Just the two of us?"

"Yes."

"Great. Let's eat soon. I'm starving," she said.

How she could have an appetite under these circumstances amazed me. I had just lost mine but pushed ahead. She set the table, jabbering away about Alice Bucci and Toby Sacks smoking a cigarette in the girls' room.

"You'd think they were the first ones ever to do it. They took two puffs each and flushed it down the toilet. Now they think they're big deals. I swear the girls in this school are as lightheaded as foam on an ice cream soda. Did you see what Abby Jacobs was wearing today? That pleated skirt she wore was so short you could see what she had for breakfast when she bent over. I was so embarrassed for her."

On and on she went, as if we were living in a television show, her voice not revealing any of the deeper tensions or the events she was living through at home. Anyone listening to us would surely think we were typical teenagers. They would never dream we were planning to confront a sexual abuser and save Karen from the horrors that occurred in her own bedroom.

She paused and looked at me and saw what I was thinking. "Stop worrying so much, Zipporah. If you walk around with that gloomy face all day, someone is going to wonder why, especially your parents. We don't have to dwell on it. It will only make us nervous and afraid, and then we'll fail, and things will be worse."

I nodded. She was right of course. I had to admire her strength.

I smiled.

"I made us some chocolate-drop peanut butter cookies."

"You did?"

"It was just a mix. Nothing special."

"I don't even know how to open the box," she said, and we laughed.

She rattled on and on, talking more about what life would be like once "the Harry thing," as she called it, was over.

"I'm always worried about developing a relationship with any boy at school," she said. "It's all because of Harry."

"I don't understand."

This was the first I heard she would even consider any of the boys we knew as a boyfriend. It made me think of my recent phone conversation with Jesse.

"I feel . . . dirty," she said.

We had eaten our dinner, and I had just put out the cookies. She took one and nibbled on it the way a rabbit would.

"I feel like they, anyone, would know the moment he touched me, kissed me, even held my hand."

"That's silly."

She looked up quickly. "No, it's not, Zipporah. You have no idea what it's like. Don't say that it's silly."

"I didn't mean it that way. I meant . . . I meant you

shouldn't feel . . . that way," I stumbled. "No one could look at you and know anything. I don't know anyone who can hide trouble or worry better than you can. I'm always wishing I was more like you."

She looked at me and smiled as if she could turn off one emotion and turn on another with the ease of changing channels on a television set.

"Yes, you're right. It's just a psychological problem right now. It will go away soon, as soon as the Harry thing is over."

"Whom do you like at school?"

She shrugged. "Hey, I wouldn't throw Dana Martin out of the house," she said, and laughed.

Dana Martin was the school's basketball star. At six-foot-two, with a shock of light brown hair and cerulean eyes that practically beamed when he smiled, he was what any girl would call a dreamboat. He had a steady girlfriend, Lois Morris, but he did like to flirt.

"What about you?" she asked.

"I don't know."

"You should know, Zipporah. You would like to go to the junior prom next year, wouldn't you?"

"I suppose." This was the first time we had talked about it.

"Well, after the Harry thing, let's you and I start working on it," she said. "It's time we broke out of our little cocoon and invaded the world the zeros think they own. We're just teenagers!"

To think of our lives as becoming normal after all this was not easy, but I didn't want to say anything or do anything that would upset her. Perhaps this was the way she dealt with her terrible situation.

After we cleaned up the kitchen, we went to my

room to do some homework. Every once in a while, I would pause and think again how we were going along with life as if nothing was unusual, when looming behind every look, in every pause and quiet moment, was the Harry thing.

My father came home and stopped in to speak to us.

"How are you, Karen?" he asked.

She gave him one of her best Karen Stoker smiles, looking as if she might just get up and do a little dance of joy.

"I'm fine, Mr. Stein. How are you?"

"I'm overworked," he complained, and then laughed. "How I wish I was a teenager again," he sang.

"Jesse called and said he'd call on Sunday," I told him.

"Oh. Great. How's he doing?"

"Starting at third base."

"Really? I guess we'll have to attend a game or two. Maybe you can come along, Karen."

"I'd like that, Mr. Stein," she said.

"Okay, I'll leave you guys to your plotting and scheming," he said.

I felt myself blush. If he only knew how true that was, I thought.

Karen didn't even blink. She smiled back at him and looked at the science text again.

"I just love your father," she said, her eyes on the textbook page. "My real dad was a good guy, too." She rarely talked about him, so I didn't breathe. "If he knew what was happening to me now . . ." She looked up at me, her eyes glassy with tears. "There is nothing better than having someone to protect you, Zipporah."

I nodded, tears coming to my eyes as well.

Then she smiled. "We're going to do it, though, aren't we? We're going to make it all right. We're going to protect ourselves."

"Yes," I said. "Bird Oath."

She reached for my hand, and we held each other's hand for a long moment. Then she sucked back her tears, took a deep breath, and said, "Mrs. Lotha is absolutely sadistic to give us this much homework. Let's start calling her Mrs. Loathing."

I laughed. Karen was really the wittiest girl I knew.

Afterward, I stood outside in the dark and watched her get on her bike to ride back to the village. When she had gone to say good-bye to my father in the living room, he had offered to drive her and put her bike in the car trunk, but she said she wanted to ride through the darkness.

"It's kind of exciting in a way, Mr. Stein," she said. "It's not pitch dark. I can see where I'm going all right, but with the stars and all, it's just nice."

My father smiled at her and nodded. "Yes, sir," he said, "I wish I was a teenager again."

The way he said it and continued to look at Karen made me think he wished he was a teenager just so he could pursue her. It put a cold and then hot surge through my heart, and I looked at her with a new sense of envy. I was even a little angry. First Jesse expressed admiration for her, and now my father looked as if he was doing the same thing. Of course, I couldn't imagine him lusting after any woman other than my mother. I didn't want to hear even a reference to any of his former girlfriends.

"You must have been quite a teenager in your day, Mr. Stein," she told him, and he beamed.

"I had my fun," he admitted.

"You'd better get going," I told Karen, "before your mother starts worrying about you."

She looked at me and nodded.

"Night, Mr. Stein. Say hello to Mrs. Stein."

"Will do," Daddy called to her.

I followed her out. We stood on the stoop for a few moments. Neither of us said anything. She looked as if she had frozen. Her eyes didn't move, and her jaw was taut.

"Karen?" I said.

"I hate him," she said suddenly, with such vehemence I felt chilled. She looked at me. "I hate what he's done to me. I hate going back there."

She got on her bike.

"Maybe you should talk to your mother, Karen."

She spun on me and glared. Then she shook her head and started to pedal away.

"Karen. I'm just worried about it. Karen," I called, "I'm still going to help you. Karen!" I screamed, but she didn't stop, and a few moments later, she was lost in the darkness.

That darkness was thicker than I could ever imagine. Later, I would think it was as if it had actually absorbed her, sucked her into it, until she had become part of it and would never escape from it.

"Everything all right?" my father asked when I re-entered the house.

"Yes," I said. "I'm tired," I added quickly, and ran up to my room.

I sat there for a while, thinking about everything, and then I got ready for bed, said a prayer, and put out the lights. I was asleep faster than I imagined I could be, but I was grateful for that and for the sound of my alarm clock telling me I had slept through the night and had somehow dodged all the nightmares floating about and looking for a way into my dreamland.

My mother was up and preparing some breakfast for herself and for me.

"How are you, honey?" she asked. "I hate not seeing you for a few days like that."

"I'm okay."

"Daddy told me what a great job you did on his dinner the other night. You and Karen had a nice dinner last night?"

"Yes."

"Everything all right with her? Those headaches gone?"

"Yes, Mama," I lied.

"Good," she said, and started to talk about the hospital, how busy they were, and what some of the nurses were complaining about. I listened as attentively as I could. She was so absorbed in what she was saying that she didn't notice how nervous I was. For once, I was happy to be ignored or to be second to her work-related problems.

My father came down and called to me as I was heading out to meet the school bus. "I'm having breakfast with Jeffery Zimmer in Centerville this morning, Zipporah. I'll drop you off at school."

What student wouldn't want to be driven to school rather than ride the bus? But I was looking forward to meeting and talking to Karen this morning. How could I tell my father that?

"Okay," I called back, and waited while he spoke to my mother about their plans for the day.

He and I got into his car in the garage.

"This year is flying by," he said. "Soon you'll be a high school junior, and I can remember like it was yesterday taking you to kindergarten. I had to do it because your mother was on duty, remember?"

"Yep. Yes."

"Your teacher was amazed at how grown-up you were about it. Jesse cried the first day he was taken to school, you know."

"No, I didn't know that."

"He did. Your mother had some time of it. I started to think you were happy to get away from me."

"I was not," I said, laughing.

"Giving any thought to what you want to do career-wise?" he asked.

"Teach, maybe," I said. "Jesse still wants to be a lawyer?"

"We breed them like rabbits," Daddy said, smiling. "Yes, I'm having him work with the firm this summer. Learn some of the ropes, so to speak. What do you want to do with yourself this summer?"

"I don't know."

"Maybe Karen's stepfather needs someone in the drugstore. You should ask."

I didn't say anything.

"Of course, he would have her work for him, I guess. It gets busy, though. He might need both of you." He looked at me because I didn't say anything. "You don't have to work, but it's good to keep busy," he said.

We didn't catch up with the school bus until we were nearly halfway to Centerville. I tried to see if I could spot Karen looking out the window from the rear seat, but when we passed the bus, I couldn't see through the windows because of the glaring sunlight reflecting off the glass.

When we arrived at school, I stood by the doorway and waited for the bus. It unloaded nearly completely, and I didn't see her, but I thought that was because she always sat in the rear. I stood and waited and watched. The bus driver closed the door, however, and she hadn't come out. Where was she? I wondered.

The first warning bell for homeroom rang, but I didn't move from the doorway.

How could she not come to school? Had something happened again the night before? I hurried to my homeroom, but I was too troubled to pay attention to anything all day. I couldn't wait to get on the bus at the end of the day and stop off at her house. I fidgeted in all my classes and nearly got into trouble and put on detention when I annoyed Mr. Kasofsky in social studies by not hearing him ask me a question twice.

Toward the end of the day, I noticed the teachers coming out into the hallways and talking to each other quietly. The moment any student drew close, they all stopped.

"Something's up," Alice Bucci practically shouted across the classroom when our last period teacher, Mrs. Shannon, went to the doorway, spoke to someone in the hallway, and then told us to read our math assignment while she stepped out.

For no reason I could think of, my heart started to go like a jackhammer.

Mrs. Shannon came into the room, looking very disturbed. She said nothing, went to the front of the room, glanced at us, and took a deep breath. The bell rang, and we rose quietly and started out. I immediately sensed a heavy, almost funereal atmosphere in the building. Glancing at the principal's office, I saw the door was closed, but through the window in the door, I could see people buzzing around the secretary's desk.

I stepped out into the warm, partly sunny day along with the other students who would be riding buses home, but when I looked at the parking lot, I saw my mother standing by her car and waving toward me. I could feel my heart stop and then start. She beckoned, and I started toward her quickly.

"What's going on?" I asked. "Weren't you going into work at three today?"

"I pushed it back to five. Someone's covering for me. I wanted to pick you up, Zipporah. Get into the car," she said.

"Why?"

"Just get in. I'll take you home," she said.

I got in, and almost before I closed my door, she was backing out of the parking spot. She took a deep breath and looked at me.

"You haven't heard the news" she asked.

"What news?"

"Harry Pearson is dead," she told me, and then, to be sure I understood, she added, "Karen's stepfather is dead."

I felt the blood drain from my face.

"Is that why Karen isn't in school?"

"Oh, yes," my mother said, shaking her head, "that's why Karen isn't in school."

She looked as if she was going to laugh.

"What do you mean, Mama? When did he die? How did he die?"

"It's not pleasant, Zipporah. I can barely form the words to tell you," she said.

"Tell me!" I shouted.

"Calm down," she said, even though she was the one who looked as if she needed calming down. "He was stabbed to death. It looks . . ." She started to cry and had to slow down and pull the car to the side of the road.

"Mama?"

"It looks like Karen did it, honey. It looks that way. She's run off."

I actually tried to speak but couldn't. My throat had closed up.

"Oh, Zipporah," my mother said. "I'm so sorry. I know how close you two were. Did you have any idea such a thing might happen?"

How could I answer that question? As soon as I told her yes and told her why, she would be angry that I hadn't come to her. And what would she think now if I told her about our plan?

I just stared to cry.

"Oh, honey, I'm so sorry for you. That's why I knew I had to pick you up. I really am surprised you didn't hear about it before you left the school. The news is flying through the community faster than electricity. I'll get you home. You had better rest," she said, and started driving again.

I felt my body shudder and seem to sink lower and lower in the seat. I kept my eyes closed.

"I know Karen wasn't particularly fond of her stepfather. I know she didn't want to be adopted and give up her name. There was that, but what on earth . . ."

I kept my eyes closed, my head against the window.

"Do you have any idea where she might have gone? Is there someone she knew? It's better she doesn't stay out there, running, hiding."

I shook my head. I didn't know. I couldn't even imagine.

"Her mother is in shock. Dr. Bloom had to give her a sedative. You can just imagine the commotion around the house," she said.

"Where . . . did it happen?" I asked.

"From what I understand, Darlene found his body just inside Karen's bedroom doorway. She had been down to Middletown shopping, and by the time she returned, Harry had closed the drugstore and gone home."

When we drove into town, I saw all the police cars still parked in front. There were village, town, and state police vehicles and officers standing around talking. Another policeman was out in the street moving traffic along. I glanced at the house and closed my eyes again.

After we pulled into our driveway, I practically jumped out of the car before my mother brought it to a stop. I ran for the house.

"Zipporah!" she called to me, but I went inside and ran up the stairs to my room.

I closed the door quickly behind me and folded myself into a sitting position on the floor beside my bed. I heard my mother coming up the stairs. She knocked on the door.

"Zipporah?"

"Leave me alone for a while. Please!" I cried.

"I want to be sure you're all right before I go to work, honey."

"I'm all right. I'm all right."

"Daddy will try to be home for dinner."

"I'm all right," I said again. "Tell him it's okay."

She didn't move for a few moments, and then she said she would call from the hospital. I heard her walk back to the stairway, descend, and leave the house. I rose, went to my window, and looked out to see her car going down the road. The silence in the air around me was so heavy I had trouble breathing.

Why did this happen? Why didn't she wait for us to put our plan into action? I sat there sulking. The house was so quiet I felt it was sulking along with me.

Then I suddenly heard a methodical gentle rapping from above. It was like Morse code or something. I listened. It stopped and started again. Daddy was always worrying about rats or field mice getting into the rafters. We had pest-control people service the house periodically, and there were traps set in every dark and dank corner. I had yet to see a rodent in the house.

There it was again, gentle rapping, too much in a pattern to be the random noise of any rodent. I rose slowly, listened, and then walked out of my room and looked at the short stairway that led up to the attic. Slowly, I approached and listened and started up the stairs. I opened the attic door and gazed into the long, wide room. Afternoon sunshine flowed freely through the uncovered windows, capturing the dust particles that resembled golden flies floating aimlessly in the shaft of light.

Nothing moved. The rapping had stopped. I stood there thinking, remembering so many happy afternoons up there with Karen in our nest, and I had turned to leave, when I heard her call my name.

It was almost as if a ghost had whispered it. I saw no one when I turned back. Perhaps I had imagined it, but then a shadow suddenly came to life and took her form. She stepped out into the better-lit area, and my heart seemed to bounce under my breast along with a rush of ice water through my veins.

"Karen?"

"Yes, it's me. I'm sorry," she said. "I had nowhere else to go."

7

Confession in the Attic

"**I** climbed up the fire escape on your house and through the window," Karen said before I could ask.

Our house was practically the only residence in Sandburg that had a fire escape. All the tourist houses and hotels were required to have them.

"What happened?"

She walked to the leather sofa and sat with her elbows on her knees and her head in her hands, staring down at the floor. I closed the attic door and joined her.

"I was unable to wait to put our plan into action," she said, looking up at me. "I knew my mother was going to be shopping and having dinner with one of her friends in Middletown. She wouldn't be home until at least nine, maybe even ten. Your idea was too good to delay, and I knew with my mother away, Harry was surely coming to my room last night."

"What did you do?"

"Exactly what we planned. I went into the apartment, got Harry's mother's wig and one of her dresses, put her makeup on my face just the way she did it, and waited for him, trembling so much I nearly passed out before he came to my door."

"What did he do when he saw you?"

"He stopped and looked at me in disbelief at first, and then his shock changed quickly to outrage. I could see his anger bubbling in his eyes and around his mouth. It was as if his skin erupted with tiny volcanic explosions. I couldn't move, and for a moment, he couldn't, either. Then he roared with such power I thought I was blown back into the wall. 'How dare you?' he screamed. 'How dare you make a mockery of my mother?' "

As Karen described this, I couldn't move. It was as if I had been in the room with her, as if I were there right now. She wasn't looking at me. She was looking ahead, with her eyes so wide I felt she was truly reliving it all. I actually glanced in the same direction, thinking I might see Harry Pearson there in front of us right at that moment.

"He took a step toward me," she continued after another deep, painful breath. "I whipped off the wig and threw it at him and shouted, 'Keep away from me!' The wig hit him in the face and fell to his feet. He paused and looked down at it, and then he picked it up gently and with such loving care my blood turned cold. He was crying and petting it as if it was his mother's real hair."

"Crying?"

"Tears streamed down his cheeks, and he looked at me as if I had killed his mother. I was never so afraid."

"I can't imagine . . ."

She rose and turned toward me, her face in imitation of what Harry's face had been like.

"He took another step toward me, now clutching

the wig in his fist," she said, her right hand in a fist. "I had nowhere to run, but I even considered opening the window and leaping out."

She stepped toward me, and I sat on the sofa and looked up at her as she continued. "I backed up until I hit my night table. He continued to come forward, his lips stretched so tight and thin they looked like they would snap like a rubber band. And they were as white as milk, bloodless. My hands went down to my drawer."

She reached to her right as if the drawer were there.

"I opened it and reached in for my knife."

She held her hand up the way she would have held the knife.

"I thought I might frighten him away, but when he saw it, he grew even angrier. He tossed his mother's wig to the bed and reached out for me. I ducked under his hand and lunged to go around him and through the bedroom doorway, but he managed to grab onto the back of the skirt of his mother's dress that I was wearing and tugged so hard I fell back, slamming down on my rear end."

She paused to take a breath. I couldn't move, couldn't swallow, couldn't stop staring at her and waiting.

"At first, all he wanted to do was get his mother's dress off me. He groped and pulled, tearing it but managing to rip it off me, practically lifting me completely off the floor when it got caught on my arms. The knife fell out of my hands and landed in front of me. I fell forward, too. Instantly, his fingers were around the back of my bra, pulling at me to keep me from going any farther forward. I resisted, and the bra unsnapped.

He fell back, and I rose. Maybe if I hadn't stopped to pick up my knife, I could have gotten out of the room and out of the house, but when I did that, he embraced my legs. He was on his knees, and I couldn't pull myself free.

"I looked down at him," she said, gazing at the floor, "and saw he was mumbling and crying as if he were trying to get his mother to forgive him for something. I knew he wasn't ever going to let go of me, and when his hands began to move up my legs, I brought the knife down and caught him in his neck, in his throat. I was just as surprised as he was. I was doing it only to drive him away. He let go of me and grabbed at the knife and then fell to his side.

"I didn't wait to see how he was or anything. I hurried to my closet, pulled a dress off the hanger, and put it on in the hallway as I went out and down the stairs. I didn't know what to do, but I was crying so hard and gasping for breath, so I hurried out the door and then just crouched behind our hedges. I was there for a while, calming myself. Then I got up, and as inconspicuously as I could, I walked down the sidewalk.

"I headed into the woods behind Echerts' garage and just walked and walked until I recognized some of the places you and I had been behind your house and realized how far I had come and how I had instinctively headed in this direction. There was no one home in your house, so it was easy to climb the fire escape and climb in through the attic window. I hid up here as quietly as I could until I knew you were home with your mother. I saw her leave the house and thought you might be alone. That's when I started to knock on the floor. I could have yelled for you, but I wasn't positive your father wasn't here."

She closed her eyes and sat again, leaning back to let her head rest against the cushion, exhausted from the effort to describe it all to me.

"You've been here all day?"

"Yes, sleeping most of it. He's dead, isn't he?" she asked without opening her eyes.

"Yes. According to what I heard, your mother found him on the floor of your bedroom, near the door, just as you described."

"She hated me when I was born, and she'll hate me forever now," Karen said.

"No, she won't. We're going to take you right to the police, and you'll tell your story."

She looked at me and grimaced. "Are you crazy? They're not going to believe me. No one in this community is going to believe Harry Pearson would have done such a thing, and everyone knows how I feel about him. I haven't exactly kept it a secret. On many occasions, especially before you moved here, I had arguments with him openly in the drugstore. I can't count how many times I shouted at him in front of his customers, 'You're not my father. You'll never be my father. I hate you.' And he always wore this terribly hurt look on his face, like he was doing everything he could to make a home for me, to be a father to me, and I wasn't letting him. He played it up so well for his audience. You know people believed him, felt that I was the one who was ungrateful and felt sympathy for him. How many times have you told me yourself about the way his customers look at me when he talks to me nicely and I don't respond or I answer him without respect?"

"But after what he's done to you . . . especially when they find all that out concerning . . ."

"The police will take my mother into a separate room, and they'll question her. They'll ask her if she knew it was going on. They'll ask her if I ever told her anything, and she'll say no, because she won't know how to describe any of it, when it occurred, how it occurred. She wouldn't listen to me; she wouldn't hear of it, remember?"

"You can tell them. You can give them as much detail as they need."

She shook her head. "It's just my word against hers." She looked down. "How many stories have you heard about me in school, Zipporah, stories some of the boys told, fabricated? Didn't you tell me what they wrote about me in the boys' room?"

"Yes, but . . ."

"No one will believe I lost my virginity to a perverted, crazy stepfather," she said, her eyes cold with the hard truth. "I can't even claim that."

"No boy in school would dare testify that he . . ."

"Can you even imagine such an interrogation, all those boys brought in to answer whether or not they did it with me? Will the police believe any of them, whatever they say? One or two of them might even lie and say yes to make himself look like some kind of big shot."

"How can they?"

She stared at me, and then she smiled in such a chilling way it made my heart stop and start.

"Didn't you tell me you were coming over to my house the other night to warn me about the things your mother had warned you about? You know, how sex can be dangerous?"

"Yes, but only because of Harry, because of what you told me about Harry."

"You're my best friend in all the world, and your face, which you admit is like a window pane, shows some doubt, Zipporah. If I can see it, the police will. Oh, that's right." she continued. "Don't think the police won't call you in for questioning, lots of questioning. You're going to bear witness to my claims, aren't you?"

"Of course, I will."

"But you never saw any of it happen to me. You have only my word for it."

"That's okay. I'll tell them how desperate you were, and I'll tell them about our plan. When they hear about the wig, the dress, they'll believe us. I'll show them the book of short stories to prove where we got the idea."

"You'll admit to conspiring with me to rid me of Harry? You'll admit to never telling your parents about it? They'll be so hurt. Your father is an attorney. It might even affect his career here. Maybe he'll lose his job. Do you really want to be part of all this?"

I didn't speak. She had injected a quart of terror into my blood, and it congealed around my heart, freezing it in my chest.

"Well, what can we do, I do?"

"I warned you that day. I told you that you don't want to be my best friend. I pleaded with you to stay out, but you insisted, and you vowed we would be friends forever. Bird Oath, remember?"

"We will be friends forever," I said, but weakly.

"Sure, we will," she muttered.

We were both quiet, wallowing in our muddled

thoughts. How had all this happened so fast? I gazed around the attic. Was it all just a terrible nightmare? Would I wake up and be so happy it was only a dream? Would I hurry over to her house to warn her about what could happen? Could I change the course of the events? Could I go to my mother and my father and ask them for help as I should have done? Could I have a phone conversation with Jesse and get him to help as well, even if it were only to talk to our parents for me?

Oh, Fate, give us another chance, please, I pleaded in my secret thoughts. *We'll be good. We'll do the right things. Don't let this all be true, all be happening to us.*

The attic creaked with the gust of wind coming in from the northeast, snapping at the leaves, forcing thin branches to nod in respect. The great house that had survived so many different kinds of weather seemed to groan as if it were having a bellyache because of us. Surely, it was thinking, *Oh, no, not another dark and horrid story to attach to the rafters and cladding, not another notorious legend to inhabit the rooms and cling to the walls to make it harder, if not impossible, for another warm and loving family to live here.* Abandoned, it would rot away and slowly disintegrate into nothing more than an empty shell to be pummeled by teenagers on some Halloween rampage, smashing out all the windows and splashing imitation blood on its outside walls and walks, until some merciful vagrant set it on fire and sent its memory up in smoke to be carried away in the same wind that visited us right now.

"Well, what are we going to do, Karen?" I asked, struggling to control my panic.

"I'm not sure yet." She stared a moment longer at the floor and then turned to me. "For now, I want to stay up here, hide up here."

"Here? In the attic?"

"Remember *The Diary of Anne Frank,* and how adults as well as children stayed safely in an attic to hide from the Nazis? They were there for years. If all those people were able to do it, we can do it. I can do it. I'll be dead quiet when your family is here, too. During the day, when everyone is at work and you're at school, I'll do what I have to do and move around undetected."

"But . . ."

"Don't you want to help me? Help us?"

"Of course, but how can you stay up here by yourself so long and be so quiet no one will know?"

"I can do it. I've actually got it easier than Anne Frank. I can leave the attic sometimes, most of the time, thanks to both your parents working. I could go out when no one is here and get some air. You and I are practically the same size. I can wear some of your things, use some of your things. When no one is here, I'll shower and bathe in your bathroom. It will be okay. At least, until we come up with a better plan," she said.

"Everyone is looking for you. They'll probably make up those wanted posters with your face on them and put them in post offices."

"I know. That's what makes this so smart," she said, holding her hands out and looking around the attic. "It's big. I have a place to sleep. I'll be fine for a while. As long as you want to help me, that is."

"I want to help you. Of course, I want to help you."

"So? Just now, neither you nor your mother knew I was here until I decided to let you know, right? We can do this. You'll see. It will be a lot easier than you think, and besides, I'll be the one who's doing any sort of suffering, not you."

"Don't you want to talk to your mother, ask her to help you?"

Her face turned hard, her eyes as dead as marbles. "She didn't help me when I needed her the most. All she's doing right now is mourning what she lost, the life she lost, but she'll find a way to fix it without me, believe me." She looked away a moment and then turned back to me. "I always believed she drove my father to his death. I never told you the things I remembered about them, how my mother aggravated him about our not having enough money, how she belittled him and tried to get me to think less of him."

"No, you never said anything about that," I said, now amazed and shocked at her new revelations. It was truly as if what had happened, what she had done, had stripped away any pretense. Nothing could be hidden from me any longer, no matter how terrible it was.

"Yes, well, besides it being so painful to think about, I was ashamed of it as well. My mother is . . . what's the word . . . an exploiter. She knows how to milk everything to her own advantage. She's actually the most selfish person I know. Her favorite words are *me, myself,* and *I.*"

I hated hearing her talk about her own mother that way. It brought tears to my eyes, for I could never in a million years imagine myself talking like that about my mother.

"You'll see," she continued. "After a while, it will be like I never existed. Oh, she'll put on a good act in the beginning. She's probably at home right now, bawling her eyes out for the police and friends, accepting sympathy like some pauper on the street filling her hands with charity. I'm sure it's already 'poor Darlene, poor, poor Darlene.' First she loses a young husband to a freaky heart attack, and then she loses her new wonderful provider to the evil and viciousness of a self-centered, miserable daughter who never showed any appreciation for her wonderful gifts and loving stepfather. I could write the gossip and hand it out for the people of this village to recite," she said bitterly. "You know I could, and you know in your heart that I'm right about all of it."

I took a deep breath. Yes, everything she was saying was surely true, I thought.

"Look," she said reaching for my hand. "You're going to be questioned by the police. You were practically the only friend I had at school, and we spent so much time together. You better practice in front of a mirror or in front of me, so you don't give anything away or break down."

I shook my head. Just the thought of such a thing put the tremors in me.

"Are you sure the police will be asking me questions?"

"Yes, Zipporah. Be real. We couldn't be closer friends, could we? All right," she said, letting go of my hand and standing. She walked about for a few moments with her hands behind her and then turned and glared down at me. "Zipporah, when was the last time you saw Karen Stoker?"

"The last time?"

"Don't repeat the questions. It looks like you're trying to come up with a lie. Just answer them. When was the last time?"

"Um . . . when I was over at your house talking about the short story and . . ."

"Oh, Zipporah. Are you crazy? Think before you speak." She walked over to a table and picked up the book of short stories. "I had the sense to bring this back to you for you to put back on the bookshelves. No one must ever know we read and used the story in here. If anything makes you an accomplice to all this, it's the book. See? Even in my most dreadful moment, I was thinking more of you."

She tossed it into my lap.

"Let's return to the question. When did you last see Karen Stoker?"

I took a breath, looked down at the book and then up at her. "At her house, when I went over to do homework with her."

"Good. And at that time or any time before, did she indicate or say anything about wanting to hurt her stepfather? Well?"

"No, nothing," I said quickly.

"Nothing? Not even a wishful thought?"

"She . . ."

"Yes?"

"Wished her real father was still alive. She cried a lot about him, about losing him."

"Good. Do you have any idea why she would want to kill her stepfather?"

"What should I say?" I asked her.

"Just say no, Zipporah. If you tell them anything,

you'll have to tell them everything. You were my friend, but you had no idea about anything that happened in my house. Leave it that way."

"They won't believe me," I moaned.

"Get them to believe you for your own benefit," she advised. "All this is just as much a shock to you as anyone. Cry a lot. That will put a quick end to it."

"I won't have any trouble doing that."

"Good." She looked around and smiled. "It'll be fine. We'll do fine," she said. "I'm hungry. I'd go down with you, but your father's surely coming home soon. I'm sure your mother's called him. Be careful not to get caught gathering food to bring up. I'll need water, too. Fill up a few quarts."

She laughed and walked toward one of the dressers, bending over to pick up something beside it. She showed it to me. "Remember when we didn't know what this was, this chamber pot?"

"Yes."

"Looks like I'm going back to the nineteenth century in a hurry," she said. "Don't worry. I'll take care of all that."

"It will be so unpleasant for you, Karen."

"Not anywhere nearly as unpleasant as it has been in my own home. You know that."

I rose. "Okay. I'll get the food and water."

"And books . . . start thinking of other books for me to read. I'd like to keep my mind off things for a while," she said.

"Right."

"And magazines, too. Lots of magazines," she called as I walked toward the attic door.

"Right."

"I'll stay up all night and sleep most of the day. I'll be like a vampire."

I nodded and hurried down the stairs and to the kitchen to get what she needed before my father did come home. She was probably right about my mother calling him and both of them worrying about me. I fumbled about because I was so nervous and I was rushing so much, but I managed to put together a platter of cold chicken, some salad and bread, and a piece of cake. I found a carton and put everything in it along with two quarts of water, using empty milk bottles.

Hurrying up the stairs, I nearly tripped. She was waiting in the doorway and took the carton from me.

"Great," she said, looking at it all. "Perfect. This is going to be fun. You'll see."

Fun? How could this possibly be any fun?

We both heard what sounded like a car pulling into our driveway and the garage door going up.

"My father!" I said, practically choking on the words.

"Calm down. He won't know I'm here unless you do something very stupid. Go on back to your room."

I nodded and moved quickly down the short stairway. I got into my room just as my father entered the house. He called my name and started up the stairs. I plopped onto my bed and held my breath. He knocked on my door.

"Come in," I said.

He opened the door slowly.

"Hey, kid-o," he said, smiling. "How are you doing?"

"Okay," I said.

"A real shocker," he said, shaking his head and coming farther into my room. He blew some air between his lips and sat on the bed. "I can appreciate how difficult all this is for you to process."

I didn't say anything. I kept my eyes toward the ceiling, nervous that Karen might drop something or do something that made enough noise to attract my father's attention. I was literally holding my breath. I saw him glance at me and then look away.

"Your mother is worried about you, and since she's a nurse as well as a mother, I thought I'd better get just as worried real quickly," he said, trying to insert some humor.

Instead of smiling, I closed my eyes.

"So tell me, honey, did you have any idea, any inkling, that such a thing might happen?" he asked.

I let out my breath. I was about to take my first step into the world of deception and lies, hiding the truth from the people I loved the most in the world, betraying their trust, and risking their deep-seated disappointment and anger forever and ever. This was the crossroads I had feared approaching the moment I heard what Karen had done.

Few of us get to know and understand the moment when our childhood ends and our adulthood begins. In childhood, all our feelings are simple and easy. Nothing is really very complicated. We want this; we can't have that. We love this person; we don't love or even like that one. We're excused from responsibilities or agree to our little chores. Our decisions are about things so trivial that later on, it makes us laugh at how much weight and importance we put on them. There is, after all, no greater dispensation, no excusing and forgiving coming from anything as much as from our youth. We are protected by the simple phrase, *too young to know or appreciate the full extent of her actions.*

A fifteen-year-old girl can commit an act as terrible and as significant as what a twenty-one-year-old could do, and she will be known as a juvenile. It doesn't matter how bright she is or how sophisticated. Her age is all that matters.

Here I go, I thought again. In my heart, I knew that someday I would regret and struggle to explain myself to the people I loved, but for now, there was nothing to do but remain a juvenile on the surface while making a major adult decision.

"No, Daddy," I said. "I had no idea."

He nodded and wore that face that my mother said made him so successful in a courtroom. Why couldn't I have inherited his ability to look so unrevealing or what my mother called "poker-faced"?

"No wonder he wins at cards. He's good at bluffing," she said. "Half the time, I can't tell if he means what he says or not."

"Well, honey," he said now, "because everyone knows you and Karen were close friends, the police want to talk to you as soon as they can. I got a call from the township police chief just a little while ago. They'd like to come here or have me take you to the station. Which would you prefer?"

"The station," I said quickly. It was terrifying to think of the police in the house with Karen up in the attic.

"Okay. I'll be right there with you the whole time. You just answer their questions truthfully, and that will be that." He glanced at his watch. "Why don't we say we'll leave here in about fifteen minutes? I've got a few calls to make to the office. Don't worry about putting on any different sort of clothing or anything. We go there, get it over with, and then how about the two of us going to Carnesi's for pizza? I'm in the mood, if you are."

"Okay," I said. At the moment, the more time we were out of the house, the better I thought it would be for Karen. I wished there were some way I could tell her what was happening. I could take a chance and run up the stairs to the attic, but if my father heard me, he would wonder why, and I could give it all away.

He leaned over to kiss me and then left. I heard him go downstairs. I went into the bathroom, threw cold water on my face, and ran a brush through my hair. Then I left, gazing up the stairway toward the attic door. I was tempted, but I resisted and instead went downstairs to meet him.

"Ready?" he said, coming out of his home office.

"Yes."

"Don't worry about it. They just have their job to do. We'll be in and out in no time."

It wasn't until we were in his car and backing out of the driveway that he turned and asked me if I had any idea where Karen might have gone. I know my eyes shifted, and I looked up at one of the attic windows, but luckily, he was looking at the road and didn't see.

"She always wanted to live in a big city," I said, which was true. "She wished she would grow older faster so she could leave and be on her own."

"Really? Well, unless she has some money, she's going to find that living in a city is much more difficult than she thinks. They'll know if she boarded one of the buses heading to New York. There aren't too many people traveling back and forth yet. Do you think that's what she did?"

"That's what she would have liked to do," I said. That wasn't a lie.

He nodded. "Wherever she is, she's got to be a very frightened young lady."

She didn't seem as frightened as he thought. Was that only an act?

"What would make her do such a terrible, terrible thing? I never realized she had that sort of desperation, anger, in her. You never did either, huh?" he asked.

"She didn't like having him as her father. She never called him her father. She's very sad about her real father dying so young. She's always been angry about that, and she never liked that her mother married Harry Pearson." It was all true.

"Understandable," my father said. He smiled at me and shook his head. "Only, that's no reason to take such a violent action against Harry Pearson. No, my guess is there was something else going on there, something so well hidden not even you, her best friend, knew it. I'm sure it will all come out in the end. It always does. Keeping truth down isn't easy. It has a way of showing up sometime or another." He laughed. "It's like trying to keep a beach ball underwater. Somehow, it slips around your hands and pops up."

We drove to the township police station. Just the sight of it made me tremble. I hoped I didn't look as shaky as I felt when I got out of the car. Before we reached the front door, my father seized my wrist and gently turned me to him.

"You want to help Karen, don't you, Zipporah?"

"Yes," I said.

"Then tell the truth in there, Zipporah. You can't help her any better than by doing that," he said. "You understand? Don't hold anything back, no matter what. In the end, it's only worse for everyone. Okay?"

His inscrutable grayish blue eyes fixed themselves on me. I swallowed back the lumps that had come into my throat and nodded.

Then we walked in.

8

Interrogation

I could always tell from the way other people looked at my father and addressed him that he commanded great respect. Just in the relatively short time we had lived in this community, he had been in the newspapers often enough. A feature piece had been done on him after his last court victory, because it involved a lawsuit against the county over some environmental issues. He had taken the case and charged only expenses, because he believed in the importance of protecting the environment. There was already some talk about asking him to run for a political office, but he loved what he did too much to do anything else.

Never having been inside a police station before, I did not know what to expect. From watching old movies and television, I thought I would see prisoners in cells, but it looked more like a government office, with secretaries and office machinery. Even the woman who I learned later served as a police dispatcher wasn't in a uniform.

There were two detectives waiting with the chief of police when we arrived. My father explained that they came out from state law enforcement agency called the

Bureau of Criminal Investigations and were the ones usually called upon when there was a capital crime.

Chairs had been set up for my father and me. One of the detectives, a tall, thin man with light brown hair and unusually dark brown eyes that reminded me of shoe polish, sat across from us. His long, lanky legs were crossed, which made his upper torso look lower in the seat. He introduced himself as Lieutenant Cooper and the other detective as Detective Simon. Simon was considerably shorter, stouter, and less good-looking because of his oversized facial features and somewhat balding head of thin black hair. His forehead looked as if someone had drawn permanent crease lines in it with a thin stick of charcoal, too.

The chief was a kindly looking fifty-some-year-old man with what I called grandfather eyes and a pleasant, soft smile. His face was angular, with a firm mouth and a strong, taut jaw. He was about my father's size but broader in the shoulders. His name tag read "Chief Keiser." He rose after the detectives were introduced and offered my father his hand.

"Thanks for bringing her down so fast, Mr. Stein."

"No problem. She's obviously very upset, and I think it's best we do this now and quickly."

"Oh, I couldn't agree more," Chief Keiser said. "Just a terrible thing. Terrible." He smiled at me again and indicated we should sit.

It didn't come as any surprise that the police would have found out so quickly how close Karen and I were. In our small school, everyone knew everyone else's relationships, friends, and family. Besides, Karen and I were together every opportunity we had during the school day. As Karen had said many times, we were birds of a feather. Of course, now I had to wonder just how close my feathers really were to hers.

"When something like this happens," Lieutenant Cooper began, turning his attention directly to me, "we like to find out why as quickly as we can. It helps us understand more about it all. We've been speaking with a number of people about it, and we have some ideas, but from what we've been told . . . Zipporah, is it?"

"Yes, sir," I said.

"Zipporah. From what we've been told, no one would have a better idea, perhaps, than you."

"Her mother would," I said quickly.

The two detectives exchanged a quick look, and Lieutenant Cooper turned back to me.

"Why do you say that, Zipporah?"

"Because she's her mother," I replied. The answer was so obvious it brought a smile to my father's face and even the chief of police's face, but the two detectives didn't even move their lips.

"Okay," Lieutenant Cooper said. "If you were Karen's mother, what would you know?"

"I don't know what her mother knew and didn't know, sir. I was just her friend. I didn't live in the same house. I never even had dinner with them."

"Boy, you can tell this is the daughter of an attorney," Lieutenant Cooper remarked.

I could feel Daddy bristle beside me.

"I don't think that's called for," he said. "She's trying to be as accurate as she can be. Maybe you should phrase your questions better, be more specific, Lieutenant."

"Right, sorry. Do you know where Karen Stoker is right now?" he asked sharply.

"No," I said. I told myself it wasn't a lie. I knew where she was before we left the house, but I didn't know where she was at that moment. Maybe she had left the attic. Maybe she was outside. Maybe she was in my room.

"Did she tell you she was thinking of doing this terrible thing?"

"Oh, no." Again, that was no lie. She hadn't ever said anything about killing her stepfather.

"We've heard she was upset about her mother marrying Mr. Pearson, and we know she never wanted him to adopt her, but did you ever witness anything in their home that would upset her enough to do this?" Detective Simon asked.

"I didn't witness anything that would give me such an idea, no."

"You never saw them argue?"

"I never saw Karen and Mr. Pearson argue when I was in the house."

"Did you see them argue anywhere else?" Lieutenant Cooper asked with a deep sigh of annoyance.

I shrugged. "They didn't argue so much, but Karen was upset with things he said when she was at the drugstore sometimes."

"According to her mother," Detective Simon said, some frustration in his voice, "you were with her more than she was."

"I don't know how that could be true. We rode the school bus together back and forth. We were together when we could be in school. I went to her house occasionally, and she came to mine to study and stuff. A few times, my father took us to the movies and out to eat. We went to some school ballgames together. I never slept over at her house," I said. "She has slept over at mine, but she's been with her mother all her life."

"I didn't mean that literally," Detective Simon said, closing and opening his eyes. "I meant, and I'm sure her mother meant, that you were with her more than any other person, friend."

"Yes. We were *les oiseaux d'une plume,*" I said, smiling.

"What?"

"I think that means 'birds of a feather' in French," my father said. "No one denies they were inseparable, Detective, as girlfriends. That's why you asked to see her right away, isn't it?"

"Okay," he said. He looked at me again. "Was her father too strict with her?"

"Her father died about four years ago," I said.

"Her stepfather, he means," Lieutenant Cooper said, and glared at my father.

"She told me he wouldn't let her talk on the phone for more than two minutes, and he wouldn't put a phone in her room."

"Oh, how cruel. So she killed him," Detective Simon muttered.

"Easy," Chief Keiser said. He flashed a smile at Daddy and then at me.

"Did she talk about that and about other things he wouldn't let her do?" Lieutenant Cooper asked me.

"Sometimes, but not that much," I said.

"What else, then?"

"She told me he wouldn't let her serve him any food, meals."

"How come?" Detective Simon asked.

"I don't know."

"Did she act strange, stranger than ever, this past week or so? Was anything in particular bothering her?" Lieutenant Cooper followed before I could respond to the first question.

"She had some headaches."

"Headaches?" They looked at each other. "What kind of headaches?"

"She went to the nurse at school. You could ask her what kind they were. I don't know much about headaches," I said, and I heard my father grunt a chuckle.

"Did you ever see a knife in her room?" Detective Simon asked me, so suddenly I couldn't respond for a moment.

"Yes, I saw a knife."

"Did you ask her why she had it there?"

"No." I hadn't asked. "I have a knife in my room," I recalled. "My brother gave it to me as a present. It's a real Boy Scout knife, I think. It has . . ."

"All right. You have a knife," Lieutenant Cooper said.

He sat back. Everyone was quiet, and they were all looking at me.

"You know it's against the law to hold back any information that relates to this case," Lieutenant Cooper finally said. "You could get into big trouble."

"You have no reason to threaten her," my father said. "She came down here, and she's answering your questions. She's just trying to be as accurate as possible."

He looked at my father, nodded, and turned back to me.

"Did she ever talk about a place she would go, somewhere she wanted to go?"

"The city," I said.

"The city?" He looked at Detective Simon as though I had given them a brilliant lead.

"New York City?" Simon asked.

"That's the only city people up here mean when they say 'the city,' " Chief Keiser said.

"All right. If you think of anything that might help us understand this situation more, you call the police station here, and ask for Chief Keiser. He'll get to us right away, especially if Karen Stoker calls you, understand?" Lieutenant Cooper asked me.

"If she calls me, I'll call you right away," I promised. She would never call me in my own house.

"Thank you, Mr. Stein," the chief said, standing and offering his hand.

Daddy rose to shake it, and I stood.

"No problem," Daddy said. "Good luck with the investigation," he told the detectives, and then he led me out of the police station. He didn't speak until we were in the car. He inserted the ignition key and started the engine first. Then he turned to me. "You did real well, honey. Don't let the detectives upset you."

"I'm not upset," I said.

I was actually a little proud of myself. Somehow, I felt I had escaped telling an out-and-out terrible lie. As silly as it might sound to someone else, I felt Karen would be proud of me, and I was happy about it.

"Good. Let's go get some pizza," he declared, and we were off.

I felt guilty about having a good time with my father at dinner while Karen sat upstairs in the darkness trying to keep as quiet as she could. Of course, she didn't have to worry until my mother or we were home, but still, she had to eat leftovers and had to eat by herself. I wondered how I could get to see her. Since my mother would be on duty into the evening and then sleep late in the morning, I would have to leave the house for school before I could get up to the attic. My first opportunity wouldn't be until after school.

Daddy decided that at dinner, we would not talk about Karen and what was going on, but he did talk about what he now thought was my need to get myself more involved with traditional school activities.

"You need to make more friends. You could join the chorus. You sing so well, Zipporah. I'm sure they'll want you. And what about drama club? I was in drama club, you know," he said, and told me about the plays he had been in and the parts he had acted. I had never known that.

It occurred to me that we get to know even the people we love in little ways over a long period of time. Just because someone is your father or your mother doesn't mean you know everything about him or her. Everyone reveals things about himself or herself carefully, slowly, sometimes because he or she didn't remember these things until something stirred up the remembrance. Maybe we go through our whole lives and never really get to know the people we love or think we love. Look at how much I had learned about Karen in just the last few months.

My father mistook my deep thinking for sadness.

"We'll try to do something this weekend," he promised after we left the restaurant. "Maybe we'll take a ride to the city and see a show. I think your mother gets this weekend off. That'll be fun, won't it?"

"Yes," I said. I juggled my sadness about Karen

missing all the fun with the realization that she would have the house to herself and wouldn't be so restricted in her movements. She could even watch television, play music, anything, if she was just careful about not leaving any traces. We'd have to go over that, I thought. We'd have to be sure that was followed strictly.

There was so much preparation to do and so little time to do it. An idea occurred to me.

"Daddy, I'd like to stay home from school tomorrow."

"You would? Why?"

"It's going to be terrible for me to go back right after all this. They'll gang up on me to tell them everything I know, and they won't leave me alone all day. I need a little time. Please," I pleaded.

"Sure, I understand," he said. "I'll call your mother at the hospital and let her know. No problem, honey."

"Good," I said. Good, I told myself. The moment my mother left for her shift, I'd be able to get upstairs and be with Karen.

Pretty smart thinking, Zipporah, I heard myself think. It was as if Karen had just said it, too.

The phone was ringing almost as soon as we entered the house, which gave support to my theory and reason to stay home. Suddenly, girls at school who would barely nod at me wanted to speak to me. I told my father to say I was unable to speak on the phone. I was asleep. They all understood, but I was sure all that did was make me more desirable. They were all hoping for the same thing: exclusive information that they could then spread through their gossip mill.

My mother called to see how I was doing, and I went to the phone to speak with her.

"Daddy told me about the police, Zipporah. I guess they weren't as nice to you as they should have been. Are you all right?"

"I'm okay," I said, "but I want to stay home tomorrow."

"Yes, he explained that, too. I agree you should. Get a good night's rest. We'll talk in the morning."

"Okay," I said, and went up to my room. My father was on the phone, so I shouted good night, and he shouted back, "Sleep tight!"

I was tempted once again to go up to the attic. He would probably stay downstairs and watch television or read or do both, as he often did. The risk remained too great, so I opted to be patient. When I went into my bathroom to wash and brush my teeth, however, I found a note on the sink.

Hey, I'm doing fine. Don't worry. I got something to read and I found a box of Cracker Jacks in the pantry. You know I love Cracker Jacks. I'll save the surprise for you. Have a good day in school. I can't wait to hear the gossip. Destroy this right away. K.

I did just that, and then I brushed my teeth and went to bed.

As I lay there in my bed and looked up at the ceiling, I tried listening hard to see if I could hear Karen's movements. Except for the usual creaks and moans in the old house, I heard nothing new. *She's probably asleep herself,* I thought. *She has to be totally exhausted.* It would be a nice surprise for her tomorrow when she found out I didn't go to school. We'd have lots of time to spend together.

I didn't think I could fall asleep after the events of this day, but I surprised myself. Minutes after I closed my eyes, I spun into a dark tunnel and fell into such a deep sleep I didn't hear my father get up in the morning or anything. Since I had turned off my alarm clock the night before, by the time I opened my eyes, it was nearly nine o'clock. I had slept through my normal breakfast and the school bus pickup. Now I wondered if Karen knew and was worried that something was going to happen any minute.

My mother came to my room and saw I was awake.

"Hey, how are you, honey?"

"Okay," I said.

"What do you want for breakfast?"

"Scrambled eggs," I said. She made the best, with cheese. My appetite put a smile on her face, and she went down to make breakfast. I rose, washed, and dressed quickly, putting on a pair of old jeans and a short-sleeved blouse. Before I went downstairs, I looked up at the attic. I half expected she would be peering out.

I started toward it, thinking I would just open the door and tell her quickly not to worry, but the moment my foot touched the first step, it creaked so loudly I was sure I had alerted my mother below. I froze, listened, then turned quickly and hurried down the stairs, thinking there was no sense in taking any risk when I would be free to move about in a short while.

"I'm glad you wanted to stay home today," my mother told me when we both sat at the table. "I was worried about not having time to spend with you after all this. It's good for you to catch your breath before going back into the fish bowl. That's what it's going to feel like for a while. Once your classmates realize you don't know all that much more about it than they do, they'll stop talking to you about it. The one thing you don't want to do, however, is be so closed-mouth and secretive that they think you do know more. Understand?"

"Yes."

"Daddy told me the questions you were asked and how you answered them. Was there anything else, something you didn't tell them that might shed some light on all this?"

How ironic, I thought. My mother, who was a nurse and not a police detective, got right to the heart of it. How would I squirm out of it without telling a bald-faced lie?

"I wasn't sure what they wanted to know," I said. "I thought I told them everything they wanted to know."

My mother's eyes narrowed a bit.

"Your father said they called you a lawyer's daughter, something like that."

I kept eating.

"Karen's mother, I heard, told the authorities she has no idea what would drive Karen to do such a thing. Should she have an idea, Zipporah?"

"She's her mother," I replied. "Sure she should."

"But you don't know why she did what she did?"

"I wasn't there," I said. I stopped eating and looked as I felt, upset, even getting nauseated. "I knew she had a knife in her room, but I never thought she would . . . she would . . ." I started to gag.

"Okay, okay. I just want you to be comfortable with what you told the police. Let's not talk about it anymore. What are you going to do today?"

"I'll catch up on some of my studying and do some reading and rest," I said.

"Good. I've got to do some shopping before I return to the hospital today, so I'm going to leave in about an hour. I'd take you with me, only I don't think it would look so good, your not going to school but shopping instead."

"It's all right. I want to stay here."

"Fine. You call Daddy if you don't feel well or anything," she said. "Call him especially if Karen gets in touch with you, Zipporah. If she does, tell her to go to her mother immediately."

"I will." I had already told her that. I held my breath. Would my mother see through me? I could see she believed my being on the verge of tears was solely because of what Karen had done and had nothing to do with my raging conscience.

"And we'll hold your father to his promise to take us to see a show in the city this weekend, okay?"

"Yes," I said, smiling.

I helped clean up the kitchen and then went up to my room to wait. She stopped by again to tell me she was going and again told me to stay in touch with my father. I knew they were both expecting Karen would be in touch with me, and they both feared I wouldn't do the right thing.

As soon as I looked out the window and saw her drive off, I headed up to the attic. Karen was standing by the window facing the front, too, and knew my mother was gone. She was dressed in one of the antique dresses we put on when we sat up in the attic and pretended. For a moment, seeing her like that took me by such surprise I couldn't move or speak. It was as if she had turned back time to a point when we were up there amusing ourselves and nothing more.

"What are you doing home?" she asked quickly. She looked angry about it instead of happy. "You could give it all away."

"I thought you'd be alone too long, so I got my parents to let me stay. I didn't want to face all those *petite bourgeoisie,* anyway."

"You should have gone to school," she said, instead of showing appreciation and gratitude. "The faster you get rid of their suspicions, the better. The police might even be watching this house now. The trick is not to do anything that detours from your normal routine. Every detective story we've read teaches us that."

"I don't think the police are watching the house. I've already spoken to them. You were right. My father had to take me to the police last night."

"What?" She went to the sofa. "What happened? Tell me everything."

I described my session with the detectives, relating their questions and my answers as accurately as I could. She listened attentively, her eyes narrow and cold. Then she nodded.

"Good. I like that part about the headaches. They'll think I went nuts or something."

"What will the school nurse tell them?"

"That she couldn't find any reason for my having a headache, no fever. She thought I was behaving strangely, especially when I pleaded not to be sent home. I kept promising I would be better soon, and she got busy with other students and forgot all about me."

"I'm pretty sure your mother told them she didn't know why you would have done what you did."

"Didn't I say she would?" she asked, and rose. She

paced, her arms extended firmly, her hands clenched into fists. "She'll never admit to anything now. She'll just wring her hands and cry."

"Why are you so sure?"

She stopped and turned on me. "Don't you see? Don't you get it? Stop being so thick. I gave her a perfect way out of everything. She'll collect on some life insurance or something. Or she'll sell the drugstore and move away to live like a wealthy woman and find herself another well-to-do man. I did what she couldn't get herself to do."

"But I thought you said she didn't care about being married to Harry. You said she didn't even mind making love to him."

"That was earlier. She was getting disgusted, too. Why do you think she spent so much time away, shopping, meeting other women? She wanted to avoid being home, even though she was leaving me with him." She laughed. "She didn't know why I would do it? That's just the beginning. You wait and see. She'll start talking about the strange things I did and how she couldn't talk to me or how I wouldn't let her get close. She'll make up tons of stuff until I look like . . . like some Lizzie Borden or something. Forget her. She'll never help me. We've only got each other," she said. "*Les oiseaux d'une plume.* So where did you go with your father? I was afraid to go downstairs. I thought you'd be back any moment, but you stayed out so long."

"He took me for pizza."

"Pizza? Oh, when will I have pizza again?" she cried.

"We can have it today. My parents are both gone.

You and I will make our special homemade pizza, just like we've done many times."

"That's right." She smiled. "Let's pretend none of this happened. Let's pretend it's a weekend, and we're together, and we're just doing what we want. C'mon," she said, heading for the attic door. "I'll find something of yours I can wear and get out of this old dress. We'll go into your father's office and play Parcheesi, just as we've done a hundred times. But I want to shower first and wash my hair and put on some makeup and perfume. I want to feel normal and happy again."

She charged down the stairs ahead of me. If she could get herself to forget it all, I should be able to, I thought, and quickly followed. I waited for her to shower. We talked while she dried her hair with a towel. She wanted to know everything I had said to my father and mother and all the questions they had asked. I explained how I answered everything so carefully.

"You were great," she said. "I couldn't have done any better if the roles were reversed."

Roles reversed? I would have a better chance walking on the moon. There was no way the roles could have ever been reversed. I wanted to tell her that, to be sure she understood that we were birds of a feather only in some ways. No matter how many half-truths or clever answers I came up with, I was not standing in the same shoes and never would.

As I watched her brush her hair and do her makeup, I thought how weird it was that she could still be so beautiful and care so much about her looks under these circumstances and after what had happened. It was truly as if she could step out of the person she had been the day before and become someone else today. Did that come from inner strength or inner madness?

She chatted on, planning our days and nights as if she believed we would go on like this for months and months, maybe even years.

"After a while, the police will stop running all over the place looking for me," she said. "People will forget or want to forget, especially after my mother moves away."

"How can you be so sure she will?"

She smiled. "I know my mother. Believe me, she's not going to be happy wallowing in this too long. She's very aware of how people, especially men, look at her. What available unmarried man is going to want to get seriously involved with a woman whose daughter is being hunted by the police for killing her husband? Someday, years and years from now, I'll ring her doorbell wherever she is and give her a heart attack," she said.

"You mean it?"

"Not really a heart attack. She'll be so shocked she might faint, but that's all. She'll have to take me in, give me money, do whatever I want her to do to help me, or I'll tell her new husband everything. I'm sure whomever she meets will not know the story. My mother is an expert when it comes to hiding the truth. You know that."

"I don't know that."

"What do you mean, you don't?" she snapped at me. "I've told you everything, how she's buried her head in the sand, how she did the same thing with my real father. I've told you."

"Oh, yes, you have," I said.

She relaxed, looked at herself in the mirror, and then glanced at me. "You know, if we had gone through with our plan exactly as you suggested, you might have been in that room, too. Did you ever think of that?"

I felt my jaw weaken and my mouth fall open. She laughed.

"I can't even imagine how you would have acted. You probably would have frozen, and I would have done everything, anyway. Maybe we would have buried his body in the backyard," she said.

I shook my head. "I couldn't have done that."

"Don't worry. You could have if you had to, but you didn't have to. I've done it all now, done it all for both of us. You sure you have enough cheese for our pizza?" she asked, almost in the same breath.

"Yes, I'm sure."

"Good. Well, how do I look?" she asked, spinning around and smiling.

"Great," I said. She really did.

"You have to do better with your own makeup now, Zipporah. I'm going to show you stuff I learned from my mother. After all," she cried, as if she had just made a tremendous discovery, "for a while, you've got to have all the romance for both of us!"

9

A Daily Dose of Poison

"**R**omance for both of us?"

"Sure. While I'm trapped up here, I'll live vicariously through you, through every kiss you get, every touch, everything. So don't hold back on a single juicy detail when I ask you to tell me exactly what happened."

She played with my hair, pushing my bangs this way and that, just as my mother often did. What she suggested made me think about myself and recall the conversation I had had with my mother in the sitting room.

"Actually," she continued, "I've planted some seeds for you already."

"What does that mean?"

"You'll see," she said. "Stop looking at me that way. What are friends supposed to do for friends? They look after each other, Zipporah. You're looking after me right now, aren't you?"

"Yes, but . . ."

"No buts. I decided it's time we both had experiences we'll never forget. Little romances are important at our age. You don't just dive into a major love affair, you know. That always turns out to be a disaster. You need to get some battlefield experience. That's how my mother always referred to her early dating when she was our age—battlefield experience. She personifies that expression, all is fair in love and war."

"Whom would I go out with now?"

She shrugged and said, "You could go after Dana Martin."

"What? When you mentioned him before, I reminded you he's a senior, and he's going with Lois Morris."

"Everyone's going to want to talk to you, even him, I bet. Play it up. Take advantage of the situation, silly. Don't be thick."

She sat back. "I don't like any of your bras. They're like training bras. Don't you have any that give you some more lift?"

"No. I'm not as big as you and don't have as much to lift."

"You can make it look that way. There's all sorts of little tricks. I'll show them to you, don't worry. I learned a lot from my mother just watching her prepare to go out with someone. Actresses don't prepare as much to walk out on a Broadway stage. You know what she calls it, the coiffeur, the makeup, the perfumes, dresses, bras, jewelry, all of it?"

"What?"

"JFD, justifiable feminine deception. In her way of thinking, women trap men. Harry's mother wasn't all wrong about her, but even if we don't think exactly the same way, why shouldn't we benefit from her knowledge? Most of the boys in our school are too thick to realize they've been deceived, not that you're all deception or I am. We're both pretty good-looking girls. Any boy in that school should be happy to be with either of us."

She smiled at herself in the mirror and then at me. "Remember when I told you that day that I had deeper cleavage?"

"Yes."

"I was really talking about a new bra."

How could we be talking about all this? I wondered. Less than forty-eight hours ago, she was attacked by and killed her stepfather. Was she in some form of shock? Was I?

"Stop looking at me as if I were crazy," she said. She sat back.

"Well, you're saying silly things. Dana Martin. Why would he even think about talking to me? When he looks my way, he makes me feel invisible."

"Okay, I'm going to tell you something, a secret I kept even from you."

"What?" I held my breath. What else could she have kept secret?

"I've had a crush on Dana Martin for a long time."

"You have?"

She shrugged. "And every chance I had, I flirted with him so he would know."

"You did? Where was I?"

"You weren't with me every breathing moment, Zipporah. Don't be so thick." She paused and smiled.

"What?"

"He came down to Sandburg in his car some nights recently, and I met him."

"Really?"

"We just sat in his car talking the first time. Then he came down again. He really isn't all that crazy about

Lois Morris anymore. He wanted me to be his girl-friend, but I wouldn't, so I'm sure he's going to come asking you questions about me."

I stared at her. "What did you do when he came to see you?"

"We took a ride to Echo Lake and parked."

"You did?" I couldn't believe all this had gone on without my knowing.

"Remember when I told you how hard it was for me even to think about having a relationship with a boy because Harry made me feel so dirty?"

"Yes."

"Well, that was part of the reason I agreed to see him like that. I wanted to see if I could be with a boy after what Harry was doing to me. I wanted to see if I could forget it."

"What happened?"

"I could," she said. "And I enjoyed it, too," she added quickly, and pressed her lips together as if she had just confessed to a priest.

"I don't believe you," I said.

"It's okay. I don't mind your doubting me."

"Why wouldn't you have told me after all this time?"

"I shouldn't have told you now. I see you're getting upset that I kept it so secret. Maybe you're not ready for all this yet."

"I'm not getting upset. I'm just so surprised. How could you keep such a secret from me?"

"I'm sure I don't know everything about you. I'm sure there are things about your brother you haven't told me, for example," she said with a note of annoy-ance.

"No, there aren't."

"There are things we both don't talk about, because they're so private, so much a part of us, it would be like betraying the people we love. It's not a terrible thing to keep some things to yourself. Anyway," she said, looking at her watch, "let's go work on the pizza for lunch. I want to watch *Heart of a Woman.* It's my favorite soap opera to watch whenever I'm home. I'll bet you anything my mother's watching it today, too. She used to talk about it as if they were real people, and she was spying on their love lives."

"I can't even imagine how she could be sitting and watching a soap opera today, Karen." I really meant her, as well.

"When it comes to my mother, I can. C'mon," she said, getting up, grabbing my hand, and leading me out of my bathroom. "Afterward, we'll play some Parcheesi and talk more about the boys at school. I know more about many of them, thanks to Dana." She stopped on the stairway and turned to me. "We've got to live as if nothing's happened, Zipporah. Otherwise, we'll go mad."

She continued down.

Maybe we had gone mad already, I thought.

Our chatter in the kitchen was built around the same topics we had discussed before the Harry thing. We were doing it so well that at one point, when we were laughing and giggling, I had to stop to ask myself again if any of it had really happened. Then the phone rang, and reality came crashing back. It was my father, asking if I was all right.

"I could come home for lunch," he said. "It's not a problem."

"I'm fine, Daddy. You don't have to come home to have lunch with me," I said, looking at Karen as I spoke.

"All right. Call if you need anything." He paused and then added, "You haven't had any other calls, have you, Zipporah?"

"No, Daddy. No one else has called."

"Good. There's still no sign of her," he told me. "Apparently, from what I've learned from a friend of mine over at the district attorney's office, there is no proof she got on a bus, either. Of course, she could have hitchhiked her way out of here, or," he said, "she could be hiding somewhere here."

I couldn't speak or even swallow to let me grunt an answer. I felt terrible letting him go on and on about her while she was standing right in front of me in his own house.

"Whatever," he said, realizing I wasn't going to say anything. "Talk to you later. Oh, I have bought our tickets for the New York show, and we'll be staying overnight at a hotel."

"Great."

"Bye. See you soon," he said.

"Bye."

"What?" Karen asked immediately. "Well? What did he say about me? I know he said something."

"They know you didn't get on a bus. They think you might have hitched a ride out of here, but he said you could also still be hiding somewhere."

She lowered herself to a kitchen chair and looked very thoughtful and unhappy.

"My father said he bought the New York show tickets. We'll be going to the city on Saturday and staying overnight, so you'll have lots of freedom here. Just be very, very careful not to leave any clues or be seen outside."

She nodded, and then she looked up, smiling. "I have a great idea."

"What?"

"Come on," she said, rising and reaching for my hand. She tugged me along and led me back up the stairs to my room. We had spent so much time in my room together that she knew as much about my things as I did. She opened the closet, knelt down, and took out my tape recorder. It was very small and ran on batteries.

"What are we going to do with that?"

She tried it, and it didn't work.

"Oh, no. The batteries are dead."

"So?"

"Do you have any others?"

"Maybe in the pantry. Why?"

"Let's get them first, and I'll show you," she said.

We returned to the kitchen and went into the pantry, where I did find two unused batteries. After she installed them and tested the tape recorder, she sat at the kitchen table.

"Okay, I'm going to record something on here. You're going to put this in your suitcase, and when you are able to get away for a few minutes in New York, you're going to go to a pay phone and call my mother collect, using my name. Then you'll play what I record now and immediately hang up."

"Why?"

"She'll tell the police I called, and they'll be able to find out I called from New York City when they check with the phone company. That's why I want you to call her collect. They'll stop looking for me here."

"What if I can't get away? I've never been by myself in New York City."

"You've got to get away. You've got to do this. It's too good an opportunity for us, Zipporah. Be creative. Tell them you're going to the magazine store or something. Don't fail," she warned. Then she gestured for me to be quiet.

She sat forward, her expression slowly turning angrier, and angrier as if she could work herself up into any mood she wanted just like a good actress. Finally, she pressed the record button.

"Hi, Darlene," she began. "Don't say anything. Just listen. I guess you never expected to hear from me again or so soon, but I just wanted you to know I was all right and you didn't have to risk a wrinkle by worrying about me, not that you would. I'm not coming back to Sandburg. I'm off to see the big wide world. You know I hated that place and living in that house with that man. Everything that's happened is more your fault than mine, so when you sit down to write your confessions, be sure to include it. I can't say any more. I have a train to catch at Grand Central. Have a good new life without me."

She let the tape keep running without saying anything, clicked it off, rewound it, and played it back.

"Perfect," she said, clicking it off again. "You just put the receiver close to the little speaker, and be sure to hang up before it goes off, so she doesn't know it's a tape recording, okay?"

"I don't know if I can do that."

"Yes, you do!" she cried, her eyes wide. "You know

you can do it, Zipporah. Don't act thick now. It's too good an opportunity for us. Well? We can't lose this chance. It means a great deal to me, to us."

"Okay, okay," I said.

She handed it to me gingerly.

"Let's go hide it in your suitcase now, so you don't forget it, and be sure you pad around it well, so it doesn't get broken or anything stupid, okay?"

"Yes," I said, and headed back upstairs. She followed to be sure I did everything she had suggested.

"Now," she said when I was finished, "let's have a game of Parcheesi. I need some fun."

We played until we were both hungry, and I made the pizza. While we ate, we talked about our plans, thinking of ways to ensure that Karen's living up in the attic would remain undetected by my family.

"My brother's coming home soon," I reminded her. "It's going to be harder and harder."

I brought that up because she sounded as if she had no intention of ever leaving.

"We'll cross that brother when we come to him," she replied, and laughed. Once again, I was amazed at how casual she could be about it all. If I were living upstairs in her home secretly, I would be on constant pins and needles.

"What are you planning on wearing to school tomorrow?" she suddenly asked.

"I don't know. Nothing special. Why?"

"You have to wear something special, silly. First, I want you to look bright and happy and more mature, somehow. You're going to be the center of attention. The worst thing you can do is look dreary and depressed. People, especially boys, will stay away from you. If you play your cards right, you can enjoy this."

"You're making me so nervous about going to school again."

"You'll get over it."

"I don't see how I can enjoy this, Karen."

"You will. You have to think of it that way, or you'll do something stupid. Let's check your wardrobe and think about tomorrow," she said.

"Wait!" I cried. "The dishes, everything first. My father could walk in here and see all this and wonder why, if I was alone, I needed two plates, two sets of silverware . . ."

"Okay, okay. You are the worrywart. I wouldn't have forgotten."

We cleaned the kitchen and put everything away so well it looked unused. I caught every crumb.

"I don't know," Karen said, looking it over when we were finished. "It looks suspicious. It's too clean. It looks like a coverup."

"No, it doesn't. I clean it this well all the time when my mother's at work."

"Mama's goody girl. I forgot," she said, looking angry at me for being so. Then she smiled again. "Okay, to the closet," she cried, and we headed for the stairway.

While we were picking out something for me to wear to school, she chose a few things to wear herself while she was up in the attic. I gave her fresh panties and socks. She didn't mind not having a bra.

"I don't want to take too much. It could raise suspicion if your mother noticed so many things were missing, unless she's like my mother and has no idea what I have."

"She doesn't?"

"One of the privileges I was given when she went to work at Harry's drugstore was the right to take care of my own clothes and be responsible for them. Wasn't that wonderful?" she asked with a smirk. "Once in a while, I went shopping with her and bought some new things, but she was very conscious of what she spent on me so Harry wouldn't complain."

"He would complain about that?"

"Of course, he would. He was like his mother. He knew just how many matches there were at the stove. Believe me, he died with his first dollar still in his bottom dresser drawer. Well, not all of it. I took some before I left. Forgot to mention it."

"But he made so much money, and the house is so nice. Why would he be such a miser?"

"Some people make money to spend it and buy things, and some make it to accumulate it and stare at numbers in bank books. With what she'll inherit, my mother won't lack for anything for a while, but only for a while. Her taste has gotten considerably richer since she's been married to Harry. She never hesitated spending on herself."

"Why didn't he complain about that?"

"He did, but she had ways of hiding things from him. I know she stole from him at the drugstore," she added casually.

"Really? She stole from her own husband? I can't believe it."

"Everything I tell you, Zipporah, is true. See what I mean about holding back some secrets sometimes? I wasn't exactly eager to brag about all this."

"I guess not," I said.

"Forget about it. It's all in the past," she said, waving her hand as if she easily could wipe away everything that had happened.

We both heard the sound of the garage door going up.

"Who is that, your father or mother?"

"I don't know. I didn't expect either one, but I'm glad we got the kitchen cleaned up. Hurry," I said.

She gathered everything she was going to take upstairs with her and went out.

"Oh, I've got to get something for your dinner," I moaned.

"Don't worry about it right now. When you get a chance, you'll do it," she said, and tiptoed up the stairs. I watched her enter the attic and close the door softly. Then I went downstairs to see who had come home and why.

It was my mother, and she didn't look happy.

"Why are you home so early?" I asked.

She looked at me without speaking and then took a deep breath and put her purse on the kitchen counter.

"I had a terrible to-do with Beverly Bucci."

"Alice Bucci's mother?"

Alice's mother worked in the radiology department at the hospital.

"Yes. In the cafeteria. Apparently, her daughter and her friends have done a lot of gossiping about you and Karen lately, and Beverly Bucci got an earful. She cross-examined me as if she was one of the detectives who interviewed you. She was very loud about it, and a crowd developed around us. I told her how upset you were and how you didn't know all that much more about it than anyone else, and she actually challenged

me, wagging her head and saying she couldn't understand that. 'How could your daughter be practically
her sister and not know what was going on?' I let her
have it between the eyes and . . ."

"What?" I said when she hesitated.

"Some doctors and my supervisor had to break it
up. My supervisor told me to take the rest of the day
off. I'm glad about it. I didn't feel comfortable leaving you here by yourself all day after what happened,
anyway."

"I'm all right, Mama."

"Of course, you are, but you don't know how these
things will affect you or are affecting you, believe me.
The nerve of some people. She practically accused you
of being an accomplice. If that daughter of hers gives
you even the slightest trouble tomorrow, I want you to
call me immediately. I won't stand for it," she vowed.

"I can handle Alice Bucci," I said with as brave a
face as I could put on. The word *accomplice* made me
shudder.

"Sure you can." She smiled. She looked around.
"Smells like you baked a pizza."

My heart started to thump. I had cleaned up the
kitchen well, but I didn't air it out.

"Yes," I said. "I made a small one. I had to keep
busy," I said, hoping she would be satisfied with that.

She kept her smile, but it turned into a little smile
of curiosity.

"But you had pizza last night with Daddy."

"I didn't even think of it, but you know me and
pizza. I guess I could eat it every night."

"I guess so. Okay." She looked at the time. "I have
an idea. Let's go for a ride. I don't think it's healthy

for you to be shut up here all day. I don't care about anyone talking about it, either. There are too many busybodies."

"Where will we go?"

"Down to that little shop in Wurtsboro where they sell those pretty and unique things for the house. We don't spend enough time together," she added. "It's my fault. I give too much of myself to this job. Pretty soon, you'll be off to college like your brother."

"I like to be with you, Mama, but you don't have to do this. I'm not complaining."

"I know you're not." She hugged me. "You're too sweet. I'm going up to change into something comfortable, and then we'll be off." She started out and then paused in the doorway.

"You would tell me if she called you, wouldn't you, Zipporah?"

"I would tell you if she called me," I recited back to her.

She held her gaze on me for a few moments, scrutinizing my face. Some alarm had been triggered inside her. There it was again, I thought, that extraordinary sensitivity a mother has with her children. Maybe I was good at being as poker-faced as my father when it came to speaking to the police, but my mother surely honed in on my nervousness. She was just unsure whether it came from being in the spotlight because of Karen or something else.

"Okay. I'll call your father to let him know where we are, so he doesn't worry if he calls or gets home before we do."

"He's going to be upset when he hears what happened at the hospital."

"That's all right. It's not your fault, Zipporah. I know you're thinking that, but none of this is your fault, understand?"

"Yes," I said.

She flashed another smile and headed for the stairs.

I felt my legs soften, and I plopped down onto a kitchen chair and listened to her footsteps on the stairway. If she ever discovered Karen, she would be devastated by my withholding the truth. She would surely feel betrayed. It would never be the same between us. I was risking so much. I felt like running after her and crying, "Mama, please listen. Karen's in the attic, hiding. I had to help her. She is my best friend, and when you hear why she had to do what she did, you won't be angry."

Why not?

I should do that, I thought, and started to rise, but then another voice inside me asked, "What will your mother feel like after she learns it all, even now? She's been defending you. Your father's been defending you. It won't make that much difference, and you'll lose Karen forever. Besides, maybe you really will be accused of being an accomplice, especially after holding back information. That detective made it very clear."

I stopped and sat again.

It's too late, I thought. I've got to go through with it and wait for Karen to leave on her own.

A short time later, as my mother and I were driving off, I looked up at the attic window. Karen would see us go and know she could go downstairs and get herself water and something to eat for dinner. I hoped and prayed she would leave no clues behind. Every minute of every day, I would feel like someone walking a tightrope, I thought.

I knew my mother expected that our drive together and our fun shopping would bring us both some desperately needed relaxation and divergence. I had to do my best to get her to believe it was happening. I've got to be more like Karen, I thought, and move smoothly from one emotion to the next. Concentrate on it, I ordered myself.

My father was home before we returned. Despite my mother's reassurances, it was obvious that he was upset about her incident in the hospital when he heard about it.

"I'm not going to put up with this," he declared. "You tell me if anyone makes even the slightest accusation."

I wasn't sure if he was directing that solely to my mother or to both of us.

"People can be very nasty," my mother said. "What about the funeral, Michael? Are you going to be free to attend it with me?"

"I'll make myself free," he said. "I'm taking the morning off, anyway. I have to get up to see Mom and explain why we didn't visit on Saturday. I'll get to the funeral right after that."

"When is it?" I asked.

"Tomorrow, eleven a.m.," my mother told me. "I'm sure there'll be people from other areas who are just too curious to stay home. What they expect they'll see, I don't know, but it's the first murder victim in a long time."

"Chief Keiser tells me that aside from a few suspicious hobo deaths during the summer, there have been none since the one that occurred in this house."

"Allegedly occurred," my mother reminded him, and he laughed.

"Whoa. Who's the attorney in this family?"

They both smiled at me, worried that the talk of Harry Pearson's funeral would upset me even more.

"Lawyering is contagious," my mother said. I laughed at that, and everyone relaxed.

"What's for supper?" my father asked, and my mother went to prepare our dinner.

"Hey," she called from the kitchen. "You've been nibbling, Michael Stein."

"I have not," my father said.

My heart skipped a beat as he walked to the kitchen.

"Well, when I left this morning, this box of graham crackers wasn't opened."

"I had some," I quickly confessed.

"I thought you didn't like them," my mother said.

"Someone told me they were good with some jelly on them, so I tried it," I added. Karen had once told me that.

"Well, is it?" my father asked.

I nodded. "It's not my favorite thing, but it's okay."

"Nerves make us nibble and munch on things almost unconsciously," my mother explained, but it looked as if she was explaining more for herself and my father than for me.

"Eileen, let's get her calmed down before she eats us out of house and home," my father joked, which again broke the tension.

Our happier mood lasted through dinner. The phone rang a few times as the story of my mother's argument in the hospital cafeteria was circulated through the gossip network. Karen and I were always amazed at how quickly news like that spread. She thought it might be the birds that lighted on telephone wires.

"They fly around depositing the gossip on different telephone lines."

It was a funny idea. I'd miss those silly little conversations, I thought, conversations we didn't have to hide from the world and conversations we could hold without a dark shadow hovering over us.

Once again, after dinner, I lay quietly in my room and listened to see if I could hear her moving about above me, giving herself away. She was remarkably quiet, so much so that I actually wondered if she had left. She would at least put a note in my bathroom, I thought. Where would she go, anyway? How would this end?

I had a harder time falling asleep this night than the one before, because I kept anticipating what it was going to be like in school. I couldn't stay away another day. My absence would attract even more attention and interest.

The following morning, my father decided he would drive me to school. He didn't want me riding the bus. I knew he was hoping to prolong any confrontations or unpleasant discussions for as long as possible, and he also thought I'd have more insulation against them when I was actually in the building and under the supervision of the teachers. He gave me advice all the way there.

"Don't be like your mother and react to anything. Try to shrug it off. In time, it will all go away, believe me. The girls who disliked Karen will probably be the nastiest," he told me. "Speaking of that, how come she didn't have more friends, Zipporah?"

"I don't know," I said. Was he going to ask me why I didn't, either?

"Kids in school can be so clannish. It's hard to be a real individual sometimes. If someone is really annoying, don't hesitate to go to your teacher and ask for help. Don't think you have to carry it all on your shoulders. Karen took the easy way out, running away," he added. "For now, it seems easier, but it won't be easier later on, believe me. If she had any reason to do what she did, she should have gone to people who could have helped her."

He glanced at me to see how I would react. I looked out the window. I knew what he was doing. He was giving me every opportunity to tell him more, to tell him what I really knew.

"I know you feel sorry for her. That's all right. You should. She was your friend," he continued. "But Harry Pearson was well liked. No one can say anything bad about him. His customers thought he was compassionate and considerate, and as far as anyone could tell, he was providing a nice home for Karen and her mother. That's all true, isn't it, Zipporah?"

I closed my eyes. "I thought you didn't want me to talk about it for a while," I said. "You keep talking about it. You're making me so nervous I don't want to go back to school." My voice got so shrill it even surprised me.

"Yes, you're right. You're right. Sorry. I'm just as guilty as everyone else around here. Damn."

He leaned over to give me a kiss when we drove into the school parking lot. He held me a moment longer.

"I'm proud of you, Zipporah," he said. "Proud of the way you're holding up under all this."

It nearly brought me to tears, tears of happiness and tears of guilt. One again, I was on the verge of confessing it all and asking for his help and forgiveness. He turned away before I could.

"Thanks, Daddy," I said, and got out quickly. If I remained a moment longer, I was sure I would confess it all.

I didn't look back, but I sensed he was sitting there watching me walk toward the school entrance to be sure I was all right. I passed through the front door. It didn't occur to me until then that Karen wouldn't be inside. We wouldn't hang out at our lockers and enjoy making comments about some of the other girls who buzzed around us like frantic bees. What I was actually afraid of facing were not the questions that would come my way but the little silences that Karen and I filled for each other to make each other comfortable and secure.

I suddenly felt as if I were entering the school for the first time, with a first-time student's anxieties. I was alone once more, searching for a friendly smile.

Who would become my new friend?

Whom could I trust with my friendship?

And who would want to trust me with theirs?

Especially now.

In a few hours, Karen's stepfather would be buried but hardly forgotten. Her name would be on everyone's lips. All this would be happening while she moved in the shadows and behind the curtains of my house, because I was keeping her secret, a secret like a daily dose of poison that could make me sicker and sicker.

10

Back to School

I saw from the way the girls clumped around Alice Bucci while they looked my way that the story about her mother and mine arguing in the hospital was already old news. She led them toward me the moment I went to my locker. They all wore gleeful smiles, their eyes dazzling with anticipation. The show was about to begin. The curtain they had expected to go up yesterday was finally being lifted. They gathered in a semicircle, trapping me against the bank of lockers. I felt myself stiffen and tighten all over, but then I imagined that Karen was right beside me. Together, we could stand against any and all.

One thing was certain: I couldn't show any fear, not even nervousness.

"So, what do you think of your friend now?" Alice asked.

"I still prefer her to you," I said, and her face turned traffic-light red so fast it looked as if a fire had started in her nose and mouth. Her friends all groaned and laughed.

"Well, you're just . . . a . . . you're just a . . ."

I stepped closer to her. We were practically nose to nose, my eyes drilling into hers.

"Don't spit it out, Alice. Swallow it!" I shouted.

Her eyes nearly exploded with fear and surprise at my strength and aggression in the face of her and all her friends.

When I shifted my gaze to the others, I saw they were looking at me with similar expressions of terror, and I suddenly realized that because I was Karen's best friend and because of what she had done, I wore a new cloak of invincibility. It was as if they believed I might be capable of the same violent actions and was therefore someone too dangerous to confront. They were already stepping back. Alice spun around and retreated. Her friends froze for a moment and then followed her down the hall, waddling behind like baby ducks.

I let out a trapped breath. I had met my first test and held up. *Karen's going to be proud of me. Wait until I describe this to her,* I thought, and smiled to myself. Head high, I sauntered down the hallway to my homeroom before the first warning bell sounded. Mrs. Cassidy, my homeroom teacher, gave me a friendly and comforting smile, and I felt my body soften and relax while we all listened to the morning announcements.

All day, I sensed the eyes of my fellow students following me, watching my every gesture, my every expression, and listening to me whenever I was called on to answer a question. My voice never cracked. I didn't stumble. I was just as prepared as I ever was, not that I was any genius. Some looked surprised; many were disappointed. Sally Bruckner, a mousy-looking girl in our class who was more often alone than not, was the nicest to me. Loneliness made us birds of a feather.

"I'm sure you're upset about Karen," she said. "It's very sad."

"It is," I told her, and she left it at that. Later, I sat with her in the cafeteria.

To my utter astonishment, Dana Martin came over to sit with us. Apparently, Karen was a wizard when it came to predicting what the other students, especially boys, would do.

"Mind if I join you?" he asked, putting his tray on the table and sliding into a chair.

"Anyone is free to sit anywhere he or she wants," I said.

He smiled, sat, and shook a container of milk. Sally looked down at her food. When he started to eat his sandwich, I saw how almost everyone else in the cafeteria was watching us. My heart began to pound, despite my brave front.

"Did you know I saw her the night before all this happened?" he asked, taking another bite of his sandwich.

"Saw who?"

"Very funny," he said, smiling.

"If you're referring to Karen Stoker, the answer is no. The night before all this happened, as you put it, I was with her at her house."

"All night?

"No."

"I imagined you two shared everything. She didn't tell you how she snuck out to meet me once before?"

I looked at Sally and then at him. Karen had told me about meeting him, of course, but I had no idea she had done so the night before her confrontation with her stepfather.

"No, she never told me such a thing."

"I guess she wanted to keep it a big secret. I just thought she would have told you, if she told anyone."

"Well, she didn't. Maybe you're imagining it, fantasizing."

He laughed and continued to eat. I saw the way he was looking across the cafeteria at his usual gang of friends. I suspected he had bet on what he would or would not find out from me. He probably claimed he could get any girl in school to do anything he wanted her to do.

"So, where is she?"

"If I knew, I wouldn't tell you, would I?"

He laughed again. "I had no idea she was capable of such a thing, did you?"

"Capable of what thing?"

"C'mon," he said. "Don't play dumb."

"What do you want me to say? I'm just as upset and surprised about it as everyone else. If you're here to tease me or anything, to show off for your friends, you're wasting your time. Go back to your fan club," I snapped at him. It was precisely how Karen would say it, I thought.

"Relax. I'm not here to do anything of the sort. She told me how close you two were. She said you were as close as sisters and were interested in the same things. She said you were a lot more mature than people knew, just like she was. In fact, she wanted me to arrange a double date for this coming weekend, so that's how I know whatever happened was unplanned. I might even be a witness or something if the police find out what I know."

"So, why don't you just go and tell them?"

He shrugged. "I'm not crazy about getting myself involved. Of course, we now have another witness."

Sally looked up at him and then at me.

"Sally's not a gossip," I said. "She's a lot more intelligent than the rats who follow you like the Pied Piper."

"So, Sally here is going to be your new buddy?"

"She's not only more intelligent, but she happens to be nicer than most of the girls in this school."

"Probably true," he said, smiling at Sally. She immediately blushed from ear to ear. "You and I should get together and talk," he said, folding up his wax paper and bag. "Compare notes, so to speak. I'll give you a call."

"Why?" I asked as he stood up.

He shrugged. "I'm sure it's as hard for you to live with it as it is for me. Maybe together, we can help each other understand it. I know you need someone to talk to," he added. "We can comfort each other. There are ways."

He winked at me and started toward his friends.

Sally looked at me, her face the picture of envy.

How did Karen know this would happen? I wondered. What had she told him about me, about us? Was this what she meant by planting seeds? Could it be true about the double date idea? What would I do if he did call me?

I was so anxious to hear the bell ending the school day, I couldn't stop squirming and turning in my seat. When it finally did ring, I rushed out of the classroom and down the hallway, keeping my eyes fixed on the exit and not looking either right or left at any other students. The moment I charged out of the building, I was shocked to see my father waiting in the parking lot.

I hurried over to him.

"What are you doing here, Daddy?"

"How'd it go?" he asked instead of answering.

"Okay," I said.

"I had an hour before I need to be somewhere, so I thought I'd stop by and give you a ride home."

"You don't have to do this, Daddy. I'm fine," I said. I looked at the other students making their way to their buses and cars. To me, it seemed they were all looking my way and smirking. "They'll all think I need to be babied or something. It just makes it worse," I said. I knew Karen would surely be wondering why I needed to be taken to and from school like this, and it would cut down on the time we could spend together.

I saw from the way his lips tightened that I had hurt him with my sharp tone.

"I only mean to help you, honey."

"I know. I'm sorry, but I can't expect you to be here to pick me up every day, and I've got to be able to do it, don't I?"

"You're right again, of course. Parents just can't help being overprotective, especially in light of something like this. Go on. Take the bus, just as you normally would. I'll head back to my office."

"Okay, thanks," I said.

He nodded and got into his car. Feeling terrible, as if I had swallowed a pile of pebbles, I turned and hurried to the bus. I made my way down the aisle to the rear seat, as usual, and plopped down, pulling my legs up and turning my body so I didn't have to see any other student, just the way Karen always did. I looked out the window, but I wasn't looking at anything. When the bus started away, the noise around me grew louder and louder. The chatter sounded like electric motors humming away. I wasn't listening to anyone in particular. Words ran into words until they were indistinguishable. A kaleidoscope of emotions twisted and turned under my breast. The great secret of Karen in our nest bore a hole in my heart because of how I was deceiving my parents. I couldn't stop thinking about handsome Dana Martin, either, and the tension of the day. Anticipating more confrontations kept me on such edge I felt as if I had been running for hours.

I closed my eyes and bounced along with the bus as it went around turns, made stops, and continued. I was actually feeling quite nauseated. Nervousness had twisted my insides as if I were made of rubber bands. Why did I turn my father's offer down? I could have been home already and comfortable. Why was I afraid of frightening Karen? She didn't seem capable of fear, at least the fear I felt. I looked up at the attic window as I stepped off the bus, but I didn't see her peeking out. Maybe she was downstairs, I thought, and hurried to the front door.

Just as I was about to shout for her, the phone rang. I debated letting it ring but decided it might be my mother calling from the hospital to be sure I was doing okay.

"Hello," I said, gazing around in expectation of Karen appearing out of one of the rooms.

"Zipper," I heard, and knew it was Jesse. "I can't believe what Mom told me. I've been calling every minute for the last twenty, hoping to catch you as soon as you got home from school before I have to attend my next class. What happened? Why did she do it?"

How strange, I thought, that lying to my parents was easier than lying to Jesse. I started to say, "I don't know," and stopped.

"She hated him."

"I knew she wasn't fond of him or the marriage, just from what I picked up in her sarcasm, but this . . ."

"I don't know everything, Jesse," I said. It wasn't a lie. I didn't. "No matter how close you are with someone, you don't know everything." Karen's words and wisdom seemed quite appropriate at the moment.

"I guess not. How are you doing?"

"Okay," I said.

"It's hard for you at school, I bet. Everyone had to know how close you two were."

"Yes." I wondered if he had heard of my mother's argument with Mrs. Bucci at the hospital. I wasn't going to be the one to tell him.

"Well, I wish I was there to help, but . . ."

"I'll be fine."

"Listen," he said, taking on the voice of a big brother, "if she calls you, Zipporah, you let Dad know, okay? Promise?"

"I already have promised him, Jesse."

"Good. You'll be helping her, too. Okay, I'll call you in a few days."

"Don't worry about me," I said. "Just do well in school."

He laughed. "I never thought she was capable of such a thing," he said. "Funny, how you think someone who's so pretty and so dainty can't be dangerous."

I didn't say anything. The silence was roaring through the phone at both of us.

"Speak to you soon," he said, and hung up.

"Hey," I heard, and looked up the stairway. Karen was standing there, wearing one of my bathrobes. It was the heavier one, a light pink terry cloth. "Who was it?"

"My brother."

"Oh, great. Did he ask about me?"

"Of course, he did."

"What did you say?"

"I didn't tell him you were here, if that's what you mean."

"Good."

"I didn't have a pleasant day," I said.

She smiled. "Come on up to the nest, and tell me all about it, and don't leave out a single detail, no matter how unimportant it might seem. I've been going crazy here imagining it all."

I started up the stairs. The phone rang again just as I reached the top, so I went into my room to answer. It was my mother, as I had expected. I reassured her that I was fine and school had gone okay. Then I told her Jesse had called.

"Yes, I thought I had better tell him before he heard from someone else. He was very upset for you."

"It's okay. He's fine," I said.

"He's fine?" She laughed. "We weren't worrying about him, Zipporah. We were worrying about you. All right. I'll see you at dinner tonight, and so will Daddy."

"I wish everyone would stop worrying so much about me," I complained. I heard her audible sigh. "I mean, I'm grateful, but . . ."

"Okay. The funeral was gigantic," she said. "Did Daddy tell you?"

"No."

I felt terrible not even asking about it.

"He didn't?"

"I didn't let him drive me home, Mama. I came home on the bus."

"Oh."

"I've got to be able to do things on my own."

"Sure you do."

"What was the funeral like?"

"Darlene Pearson was so sedated she could hardly stand. I had forgotten she had a younger sister, Jackie Nelson. She came from Dallas, Texas, with her husband, Brady. Your father and I didn't go to the house afterward. I had to get to work, and so did he. It was the biggest funeral in Sandburg. The church overflowed into the street. Anyway, I'll see you later."

"Right," I said.

Karen waited impatiently in the hallway. As soon as I hung up, she started for the attic stairway. Why did we have to go up there now? I wondered, but I followed her. She went right to the leather sofa and sat, pulling her legs up and under herself. Her face was lit with anticipation.

"That was my mother," I said. "She and my father went to the funeral. My mother said your mother was so sedated she could barely stand, and your aunt and uncle from Texas were there."

"I don't want to hear about it," she said immediately, and covered her ears to emphasize it. Then she smiled. "Tell me about your day. That's far more interesting for me than my mother putting on an act for the community."

I began by describing my confrontation with Alice Bucci and worked my way to lunch and Dana Martin.

"I knew it. I knew it," she said. "Didn't I tell you he'd be interested in you now?"

"He told me about his coming to Sandburg at night to see you secretly."

"So?"

"He said you met him the night before . . . before it all happened."

She shrugged.

"Did he?"

"Yes, it's true. I saw him for a little while after you left the house."

"You did? How could you? I mean, considering what we were planning and everything."

"I wasn't planning on all this happening, Zipporah. I was still trying to have a normal teenage girl's life in this town. You knew that. You knew that was why we were coming up with a solution."

I nodded. "He wants to talk about you, about it all. He said he was going to call me."

"I bet he will."

"What should I say if he does? He wants to see me."

"Of course, he does. You'll meet him. I'll tell you exactly how to act and what to do."

"I don't want to meet him."

"Why not? Is there someone better-looking at school?"

"No, that's not it. I'm sure he just wants to talk about you, but it will make me uncomfortable, and I'm liable to slip and say something."

"You won't. You'll get him to change the subject, believe me. Don't underestimate yourself. He won't just want to see you to talk about me. He mentioned you enough when we were together."

"He did?"

"Yes, Zipporah. You can be so thick sometimes. With a little work, you're going to look pretty damn sexy, sexy enough for Dana Martin, believe me."

"But I'm not sure . . ."

"We need these experiences, Zipporah."

We again? I thought.

She had a very strange smile on her face.

"Speaking of experiences, guess what I discovered today," she said.

"What?"

She reached down under the sofa and came up with a black-and-white notepad.

"Your brother's diary or journal, whatever boys call it. *Diary*'s too feminine-sounding to them, I suppose."

"What? Where did you find that?"

"In his room."

"You went into my brother's room?"

"What's the big deal? It's just another room, and I got bored. I didn't expect to find it. He had it hidden under a box full of stamp albums. I started to look at the stamps and moved the box, and voilà!"

She held out the notebook.

"I don't want to read it. It's his personal thing. You shouldn't have read it."

"It's not a classified government document, Zipporah. It's just your brother's journal. There's all sorts of good stuff in it. He's kept it for some time. It goes back to when he had his first sexual experience. Of course, it was with himself." She laughed.

"Stop it!" I screamed, and pulled the notebook out of her hands.

She looked at me askance and then smiled. "You're embarrassed. I can see we have a lot to do, a lot to catch up on, before you meet Dana Martin."

"I'm not meeting him," I said.

"Why not?"

"We can't keep you secret much longer. My mother almost discovered you yesterday when she smelled the pizza and wondered why I had made it for myself, and then she found you had opened the new box of graham crackers. I had to lie about that, think of something quickly. She knew I didn't like them and wouldn't have eaten them. I told you to be more careful. I told you."

She started to nod her head slowly and glared at me. "So, you're going to betray me, too."

"I didn't say that. I'm just . . . how can we do this much longer, Karen?"

"After I confided in you and told you about all the disgusting things that were happening to me and you came up with the plan, you do this now?"

"I didn't come up with the plan to kill him."

She looked as if I had slapped her across the face. Again, she nodded, but this time, she said nothing. She rose and went to her own clothes hidden behind the big cushion chair. She dropped my robe from her body. I was surprised to see she was naked. She kept her back to me as she started to dress.

"What are you doing?" I asked.

"What am I doing? Well, it's pretty obvious you

don't want me around anymore, so I'm going to leave."

"Where are you going to go? Are you going to the police?"

"And do what, go to prison? With Darlene not supporting me, I'll be convicted of some terrible crime. It's all right. I had no one before; I have no one now."

"Stop it. I didn't say you had to leave immediately. I'm just saying it's going to get harder and harder to keep you secretly up here."

"It hasn't been too hard until now, has it? I've been quieter than a butterfly."

"But how long can we do this?"

"As long as we have to. We came up with the New York idea, didn't we? It will keep them from looking too hard for me around here."

Again, *we*. It had been her idea entirely to record the message and have me pretend to be her and call her mother.

"Things will calm down, and we'll come up with another plan, a bigger one," she said. "We're pretty good at it, aren't we? We're a team, birds of a feather. At least, we were," she said, and returned to her clothes. "Bird Oath," she muttered under her breath.

"All right," I said. "Maybe you're right. I'm sorry. We'll keep going."

She smiled. "I knew you would stand by me. You know I would stand by you."

I looked at her and then down at my brother's notebook.

"You shouldn't have taken this, Karen."

"Don't make a big thing of it, Zipporah. We'll put it back where it was, and no one will be the worse for it.

But," she said, "there are some very interesting things in there about you, too."

I looked up at her. "Me?"

"I think you'll be pleased with what you read. Toward the end of what he's written so far, there are some interesting things about me as well. Maybe you should know about that. I felt myself blushing as I read it, in fact, and it takes a lot to make me blush, as you know."

I stood there, thinking and looking at my brother's secret journal. I imagined this must have been the way Eve felt in the Garden of Eden, so tempted to do something so forbidden. I shook my head.

"You know," she continued, "if it was the other way around, he finding your diary, he wouldn't hesitate to read it. Boys are like that, and then they love to tease their sisters afterward."

"How do you know that? You don't have a brother."

"I know. I've heard some of the other girls at school complaining about their brothers, younger and older, doing just that or something similar."

I sat on the sofa. She reached down, picked up my robe, and put it on again.

"Jesse wouldn't do that," I insisted.

"Oh, boy. When you read the journal, you'll have a more informed opinion."

"I'm not reading it."

"Suit yourself," she said, and shrugged. "*Celui qui vous satisfasse, mon cher.* Whatever pleases you, my dear, but you're making a dreadful mistake."

"I would just feel so sneaky, Karen."

"I know what we'll do," she said, bursting with an

idea. "I'll read it aloud to you. That way, you're not really reading it. You're just listening."

"It's the same thing. Isn't it?" I asked.

"Not really, but the choice is yours."

I thought it would be worse having her read it. It was bad enough that she had read it already. Here I was, betraying another member of my family. All that was left was for me to betray myself, if I hadn't already.

"I'll think about it," I said. "For now, I want to put it back."

She shrugged. "Suit yourself. You'll change your mind," she predicted. "Okay. Let's talk about Dana Martin. When did he say he would call you?"

"He didn't say exactly when."

"He'll call soon, maybe even tonight. You have to be prepared."

"What do I have to prepare?"

"For starters, would your parents let you go on a date with him?"

"Why wouldn't they?"

"Have you gone on a date, a date meaning a boy picks you up in his car at night? Well?"

"You know I haven't."

"So, you don't know if they will. You'll find out soon enough, I suppose, but what are you going to do if they say no?"

"I won't go."

"Dumb," she sang. "Come to think of it, why even bother asking permission? You'll go, but you'll do it a different way. You'll meet him in the village secretly, as I did."

"How can I do that?"

"You'll take a bike ride, supposedly to get some ice cream or something. Be creative."

I shook my head. "Why is it so important for me to be with Dana Martin, anyway?"

"You want to be a virgin forever?"

"What?"

"One thing I did learn from my mother that makes sense, Zipporah, is that we have the opportunity to decide with whom and when we want to have our first full sexual experience. Too many girls have it sponta- neously, get swept into it or talked into it, or just are too stupid to realize what's happening. Not us, not you and me," she vowed.

"Now," she continued, taking my hands into hers and looking directly into my face. "Can you think of a better-looking, more exciting boy to be with this first time than Dana Martin? It's something you'll have for- ever. Imagine," she said, "having the experience with some oaf or some ordinary boy who just happens to ring the right bells."

I started to shake my head again, memories of my mother and my conversation in the sitting room re- turning.

"It's too dangerous even to consider," I said.

"Dangerous?" She laughed. "No, it isn't. That's what adults, mothers and fathers, are supposed to tell you, even though they didn't live that way themselves. It's the crowning hypocrisy of parenthood. We'll be different sorts of mothers, won't we? We'll be honest with our children."

"But weren't you afraid of becoming pregnant?"

"Dana is sophisticated, Zipporah. He comes pre- pared. You know what that means?"

"Yes," I said. "Stop talking to me as if I were a child, Karen."

"Good. So, you know what to do, then."

"I'm not saying I know everything I need to know. I know about that, at least. Why is my sexual progress so important to you now, anyway?"

She smiled and sat back. "Because I want us to be together, silly. I want us to share everything. We're closer than sisters. We're practically two parts of the same person. *Les oiseaux d'une plume,* remember? Well? Are we, or are we not?" she demanded.

"Yes, of course, we are," I said.

"So, then? You've got to catch up. I can't go flying higher and higher and leave you behind and below. I love you too much," she said. She held her gaze on my face. I felt the tears come into my eyes. "I hope you love me too much, too."

"I do," I said.

"Then remember the Bird Oath. We're friends forever and ever, sworn to protect and help each other as much as we would ourselves. Isn't that still true?"

I nodded, and we hugged.

She looked at Jesse's journal in my hands.

"Go on and put it back," she said. "I understand and respect your feelings about it."

I smiled. That was the right decision. Ironically, however, I resented the fact that she knew what was written in it, and I didn't. Would that eventually get me to read it?

We heard the phone ringing below.

"I'd better answer it. It might be my father," I said, and leaped up. I nearly fell down the stairs rushing to my room, but I got to the phone on the fourth ring.

"Hello," I said.

Karen had followed slowly and stood in the doorway. She saw my eyes widen.

I covered the mouthpiece and whispered, "It's Dana Martin."

She nodded, smiling.

"Tonight? I don't know. I have so much homework. My parents don't like me going out on a school night, anyway."

Karen smirked and shook her head.

"No," I said. "Not this weekend. My parents and I are going to New York City to see a show. We'll see," I said. "I'll talk to you tomorrow. Bye."

I hung up before he could say another word.

"Actually," Karen said, tilting her head a bit and leaning against the door frame, "that's good."

"What do you mean? What's good?"

"Your reluctance. It makes you more desirable when you play harder to get. I like it," she said. "I wish I had been that way, but I didn't exactly have the benefit you have."

"What benefit is that?"

"Me, silly. Don't be thick. You have the benefit of my experience. By the time I'm finished with you, you'll seem as sophisticated as any girl he's been with. Boys like to think that they're using you, getting the better of you, but by the time we're finished with Dana Martin, he'll be the one who will feel he's been used, believe me. C'mon," she urged. "Let's go back up to the nest. We have lots and lots to talk about now."

She turned and headed for the stairway.

Somehow, I thought, some way, all that was terrible

that had happened, even the fact that today was her stepfather's funeral, was forgotten.

We really were like two small birds in our own nest, totally unaware that the woods were on fire around us. Upstairs, we could shut it all out.

I hoped we wouldn't be shaken out and fall too soon.

11
Another Orphan in the Nest of Orphans

My parents hoped our upcoming weekend in the city would put a smile back on my face. I tried to be as upbeat as I could about it, but I was nervous about making the phone call to Karen's mother. There was still a great deal of chatter about her and what was going on as a result of what had happened. A parade of Pearson customers, even those who didn't particularly care for Darlene Pearson, visited her after the funeral, and everyone who left was pleased to leave with some sort of news, some information or discovery. Karen's gossip birds were very busy flitting from wire to wire to spread the chatter over telephone lines.

It was quickly known that instead of trying to sell out and perhaps even move away, Darlene Pearson had immediately begun advertising for a pharmacist. She told people she wanted to hold on to the drugstore, keep her beautiful home, and remain in the community. Everyone, even her detractors, remarked about how well she was holding up. She wasn't avoiding anyone or anything, instead taking on all her problems head-on. Before we left for the weekend trip, I was even more surprised to learn that Karen's mother had called my father and asked if she could see me. He broke the news to me on Thursday night right after dinner. My mother obviously knew already.

Karen and I had devised what she called our postal service, because neither of us was comfortable with her leaving notes in my bathroom. I might miss one, and my mother might find it. Karen decided she would leave a note for me in my copy of *The Diary of Anne Frank,* and I would respond and leave my answer in the book, just in case we had little or no opportunity to meet in the attic because my mother would be home when I returned from school and my father would be home before she headed off to the hospital for a late shift.

"What do you mean, she would like to see me?" I asked my father when he made the announcement concerning Karen's mother's request.

He had sat back and begun by telling me he had received a phone call at his office that afternoon from Darlene Pearson.

"She asked how you were doing. She was concerned about you," he said.

My mother stood off by the sink, quietly putting dishes into the dishwasher but keeping her eyes on my face as my father spoke. I didn't say anything.

"It's rather generous of her to be worried about you with all that's on her head," he told me. I saw my mother nod. "I think she had expected you would come around to see her on your own. I know she was a little disappointed about that, but I explained how hard it has been for you at school and such, and she understood. However," he continued, fingering a coffee spoon, "she would very much like to see you, and I think it would be a nice gesture, don't you?"

He looked up quickly for my reaction.

"What does she want?" I asked.

"Just to talk. These last few months, she felt as if she had two daughters," he added. "At least, that's what she says, honey. Eventually, you're going to run into her, anyway. There's no point in avoiding it, is there?"

I shook my head. "I'm not avoiding it. I just don't know what I will say to her," I said.

"You'll think of something. Why don't I pick you up after school tomorrow and we go over to her house together?" he suggested.

I looked away quickly. The house? Returning to it, returning to where it had happened, where it had all been developing, was suddenly quite terrifying to me.

"I'll be there with you the whole time," my father said, sensing the need to reassure me.

"I could change a shift with Sue Cohen and be there, too," my mother offered. "We should probably all be together, don't you think, Michael?"

"I guess. But I don't want to make it look like we're afraid to have her question Zipporah," he said.

I shifted my eyes back to him quickly. "Question me about what?"

My father smiled. "I don't know, honey. I'm sure she's as confused and troubled by it all as anyone can be. Maybe she thinks you'll be able to help her get through it, understand it better. It would only be a kindness, even if you add nothing to her search for answers."

He looked at my mother. "Her sister and brother-in-law left a few days ago. It can't be easy remaining in that house alone now."

My mother shook her head and clicked her lips. "To lose two husbands," she said. "It's a wonder she can function."

It's a wonder she can function? If they only knew what I knew, what Karen had been telling me about her mother, they wouldn't be so sympathetic, but I could hardly say anything about all that now. What was Karen going to say about all this? I wondered. I shouldn't go over there until I had a chance to speak with her.

"Can we wait?" I asked. "Can we do it next week? It makes me nervous to think about it."

My father just stared at me a moment and then turned to my mother to see what she thought.

"It is very fresh, Michael. She's just getting steady on her own feet again."

"Hmm," he said, but his suspicious eyes made me more nervous. Perhaps I was only stirring up the pot. Perhaps I should just do it and get it over with.

"I mean, I'll go if you want me to."

"Michael?"

"Okay, I'll call her and explain. How about we all go see her on Sunday evening, after we return from New York? Maybe after being away, you'll feel better."

I tried not to look too relieved.

"That's a better idea. We could know more about Karen's whereabouts by then," my mother suggested.

"Yes, that could be. Right now, it's as if she disappeared off the face of the earth. According to Darlene, not a relative, not a family acquaintance, has heard from her. I did learn that she took some money, so she might just be holed up somewhere, some cheap motel or something. Her picture has been well circulated. She can't walk into any bus station or hail some taxi driver without being recognized," my father said.

To me, it seemed he was saying it all for my benefit.

"She's only making things worse by hiding like this," my mother added. "No one gets a chance to hear her side of things."

"If there is a side," my father said. Again, he focused on me.

"Okay, that's enough," my mother declared. I had the distinct feeling they had rehearsed the entire dialogue and agreed on what each would say. "You can go do your homework, Zipporah. I'll clean up."

I nodded and rose. Could they tell from the way I stood and ambled out of the dining room that I was on the verge of confessing everything and leading them up the stairs to the attic?

The moment I left, I heard them start talking about me.

"Actually, I would have thought she'd want to go over there on her own," my father said.

"She's very fragile at the moment, Michael. She's under so much pressure at school, from the police, the community, and now us. You shouldn't have agreed you'd bring her over to see Darlene yet."

My father didn't respond, and I didn't want to remain there eavesdropping. I hurried up the stairs to my room to construct a letter to Karen that I would leave in the book. My mother was on an early shift in preparation for our trip to New York the day after, so I wouldn't have much time to see Karen before we left, and here my father was suggesting our going over to see her mother as soon as we returned.

As I wrote the letter describing what was going to occur, I considered sneaking up the stairs to the attic after my parents had gone to bed. However, the risk now seemed even greater than it had been. If I did wait until they were asleep, I could try, but the way everything in the house creaked under our weight, especially the attic stairway, would surely sound an alarm. Nothing seemed worse than being caught now, and every passing day that I kept this great secret made it more and more impossible to confess it.

Falling asleep seemed an impossibility this particular night. Every time I closed my eyes, I was sure I heard something, some noise Karen had made above, and I held my breath, waiting to see if my father or mother had heard it, too. After a while, I felt I was imagining it, but that didn't make it any easier, and in fact, when I did finally fall asleep, I had a vivid dream about Karen being discovered. In my dream, my father was screaming, and my mother was crying so hard, her tears were tears of blood. I woke up in a sweat, my heart pounding, and sat up in bed, listening to see if it had indeed happened. There was just the usual heavy silence interrupted by a creak or a moan in the house, making it seem as though the house were still complaining.

I tossed and turned throughout the night and slept past the time to rise and get ready for school. I had forgotten to set my alarm clock. Maybe I subconsciously wanted to be late for school. My mother was suspicious of the silence coming from my room and actually had to come in and shake me to wake me.

"Are you all right?" she asked when I moaned and batted my eyelashes open.

"What? Oh. Yes," I said. "Thanks," I told her when I looked at my clock.

She remained there, looking at me with her face twisted in worry.

"I had a hard time falling asleep," I admitted. "And I forgot to set my alarm."

"Your father shouldn't have promised Darlene Pearson anything," she said. "Or at least told you before you were going to bed."

I was afraid they'd argue about it.

"No, that's okay. I should go see her. He's right. I will," I said.

"We'll see how you are on Sunday," she decided. "You need some oatmeal for breakfast, soothe your stomach."

I smiled at how she prescribed things, how she was always the nurse.

"Okay."

I rose quickly, showered, and dressed. My father was reading a brief at the breakfast table, but I could see and feel the tension in the air. They had obviously continued a sharp discussion about me and the prospective visit to Darlene Pearson. They barely spoke to each other before my father rose and said he had to get going. He gave my mother a halfhearted kiss, as if he thought he'd burn his lips on her cheek, and then he left, grunting a "See you later."

"I have a nurses' meeting today," my mother told me, still looking in his direction. "I'll be home about five instead of three, but you call the hospital if you need anything."

"I'm fine, Mama. Really," I said.

"Sure you are," she told me. She smiled and brushed

my hair. "What a terrible thing to have your best friend involved in something like this. No one can or should blame you for being upset."

Oh, God, I heard myself cry inside. My heart was shattering in my chest. My mother's love for me and her desire to protect me made what Karen and I were doing seem that much more terrible. My guilt, my nervousness and fear, was being misinterpreted, and I was letting it be. All the sympathy and affection my mother had for me at this moment was being accepted under false pretenses. It made me feel dirty.

"I can't help it that I liked Karen so much," I said. It was the closest I could come to a confession.

"You shouldn't feel guilty about it. You can't feel you're responsible for what happened, honey, just because you were good friends. Of course, you should be very sad. If you weren't, I'd worry more about you," she concluded, and kissed me on the forehead, both to show me how much she loved me and to check to be sure I had no fever. I knew her little tricks.

"I've got to get myself going," she declared, and hurried out. "I'd take you to school, but I'm running late."

"I'm okay with the bus. Don't worry."

I had barely enough time to get myself together and out to meet it. She left just before the bus arrived, and for those few moments, I seriously considered turning around and going back inside. Could I get away with cutting school? Normally, I might have tried it, but considering the way everyone was centering attention on me, I didn't dare risk it. There was a strong possibility my parents had asked the principal to request that my teachers keep a close eye on me, and if I weren't in school, the principal might just call either my mother or my father to see how I was. He might even suspect I had cut.

Karen would read my letter, anyway, I thought, and she would be prepared to talk during the hour or so we would have before my mother returned from the hospital. When the bus pulled up, I looked up at the attic window and saw the curtain parting. I had just a glimpse of her face, but it was enough to tell me how sad and trapped she felt. She was a bird in a cage. I had to help her. I had to help find a way to set her free—and, in doing so, set myself free as well.

My school day was remarkably normal. It amazed me to see how quickly everyone had slipped back into the normal interests and concerns. There was a lot of chatter about an upcoming school musical and an important baseball game, as well as the end-of-the-year school party. The student government held three big parties, one on Halloween, one right before the Christmas holidays, and one in the spring right before the school year ended. The day was peppered with announcements, banners going up on the corridor walls, and much louder chatter and laughter between classes. I wished I could be part of it, just submerge myself in everything and be like the zeros Karen called mindless teenyboppers.

To be sure, there were still questions and curiosity about Karen and what was happening, but it wasn't on everyone's front burner anymore. She was as good as dead and forgotten to most of the girls who disliked her, anyway. Only Dana Martin pursued me with vigor about it. Once again, he sat with me at lunch. If his old girlfriend's eyes could launch the darts in them, I'd be punctured with so many holes I'd look like someone who had broken out with the measles. She sat with her friends two tables away, aiming her fury at me.

"Too bad you're going to the city this weekend," Dana began.

"I don't think it's too bad. I'm very excited about it."

"I could come by your way tonight," he suggested. "You're not going to the city until tomorrow, right?"

"We're leaving early. My parents would rather I stay home," I said, even though I hadn't brought up the subject with them.

"Okay. You're back Sunday. How about I come by Sunday night?"

"I don't know what time we're coming home, and I have to be somewhere Sunday night. Actually," I said, thinking this might discourage him, "we're paying Karen's mother a visit."

"I heard a rumor last night," he said, undaunted by my excuses and reasons not to see him.

"I'm sure there are lots of rumors."

"This one came from a reliable source in the police department. They think Karen's mother knows where she is but isn't telling."

"That's stupid. Why wouldn't she tell them?"

He leaned toward me as if he were afraid someone was listening nearby. No one could hear what we were saying, especially in this noisy place. He was just trying to be dramatic.

"They think Karen and her mother were in cahoots."

"What?" I smirked and squeezed my nose up so hard it actually hurt for a moment. "That's the dumbest . . ."

"Look at what she has now. Look at what she's inherited. Look at what she was married to before, or stuck in," he offered confidently. He nodded. "They'll come up with some good excuse for what she's done. You'll see. Wherever Karen is, her mother knows," he insisted. "You and I had better get together soon and compare notes. Who knows? Maybe they'll find a way to involve us and spread the blame just because we knew her better than the rest of the kids here."

"That's ridiculous. How can they do that? You're just making it all up to come up with some excuse to meet."

He shrugged and smiled at me. "Do I really need an excuse to meet you?"

The warning bell rang.

"I don't know what you need," I said, gathering up my books.

"Yes, you do," he called to me as I started away. "You need the same thing."

I glanced back and saw him still smiling.

Can someone be so handsome that he scares you as much as someone who's so ugly? I wondered. What frightened me was how much I wanted him to come around, and how inadequate and unprepared I felt I was for such a rendezvous. All I could think was that I needed Karen now more than ever to give me advice and guide me through this.

She was waiting for me as soon as I got off the bus and opened the front door of my house. Wearing one of my skirts and blouses, she stood by the stairway. In her hand was the letter I had left in the book. Her hair looked as if she had been running her hands through it for hours. I was sure that after reading what I had written, she had been frustrated having to wait for me to come home.

I closed the door quickly. "Anyone driving by who glanced our way could have seen you through the doorway standing there, Karen. Why are you being so careless?"

She waved the letter at me instead of answering. "This is just like her," she said, turned, and started up the stairway. About midway, she paused and looked down at me. "Well, don't just stand there. Come on up."

I hurried after her. She went directly up into the attic and flopped onto the sofa, her arms folded under her breasts. I glanced at my watch and entered.

"Before we start, Karen, my mother's coming home in less than an hour. Do you have everything you need for tonight? We'll be leaving early in the morning, but . . ."

"Oh, forget all that. I have everything I need. When did she call your father?"

"Yesterday, I think."

I moved in slowly, set my books down on an old dresser, and looked at her.

"She's going to put on some act for you and your parents. You sure they're going, too?"

"My mother said so. I didn't write it in my note to you, but we've heard that she is not going to sell the drugstore. She has already started to advertise for a pharmacist, and she's telling people she would never want to leave here."

"Oh, don't worry about that. She's pretty smart. She's going to get the drugstore up and running again as quickly as she can before she puts it up for sale.

The money is made on the drugs, not the toys and ice cream, cards, and sundries. She was always right there when Harry did his books. She knows exactly what's what when it comes to that place."

"I guess I never realized how much you dislike her," I said. I didn't intend to, but it just slipped out because of how bitter and venomous she sounded.

She looked at me strangely for a moment and then smiled, but it was an icy smile, her eyes more like frost-covered marbles.

"You didn't? How would you like a mother who ignored all that I described happening to me? Well?" she asked before I could breathe. "How would you?"

"Of course, I wouldn't."

"You're darn right, of course, you wouldn't. I don't dislike her," she added after a moment. "I just don't like her as much as I should. Actually, I'll probably become just like her as I get older. Harry was always saying the apple doesn't fall far from the tree unless the tree is on the top of a hill, whatever that means."

"Rolls down."

"What?"

"The apple falls and then rolls down."

"Brilliant. I knew what he meant, but it was just another one of the stupid things he would say to me. He was always trying to make me think I would amount to nothing if I didn't listen to him and obey him. He made it sound as if he provided the very air I breathed. But I've told you about all that, or most of it."

She shook herself as if to shake off a chill.

"Okay," she said, pulling her legs up and under as she often did, "let's think about it. My mother might grill you about me, about what I might have told you.

She'll probably want to see if you know the truth. She might not come right out and say it, but she'll make suggestions. She's probably worried it will get out, and people will know how she neglected me. Then she'll try to discover if you know where I am. Be careful, because she can be very tricky, very subtle. She'll seem so hurt and in so much pain, and then she'll slip in a question like that, and you'll blurt something out. Soooo," she added, smiling, "what you'll do is turn the tables on her right from the start."

"How?"

"You'll be the one who is full of pain and hurt and be unable to talk, even to sit in that house. Outact her."

"I *am* full of pain and hurt and unable to talk. I don't have to act."

"Good. Cry, and look down, and keep shaking your head. Your parents won't let it go on too long once they see how disturbed you're getting. Of course," she added, "by then, you'll have made the call from New York, and she'll be thrown off course, anyway. Things will settle down even more, and then I want to sneak back into the house."

"What? Why?"

"There are things I want that I shouldn't have left behind, but I wasn't exactly taking my time about it. There's jewelry and more money."

"But won't that be very dangerous?"

"Not if we do it carefully. I know how to get into the house even if it's all locked up. Harry has a rusted lock on the exterior basement door. It just looks locked, but it's not. My mother doesn't even know. We can get in through the basement and up into the house."

We? I thought.

"Okay," she said, waving away the whole idea. "That's for later. For now, tell me about your day. Did you see Dana?"

"He tried to get my attention in the hallway all morning, but I didn't stop to talk to him. Then he sat at my table again in the cafeteria at lunchtime."

"Brilliant. I couldn't have teased him any better."

"I wasn't teasing him, Karen. I was too nervous."

"If the result is the same, it's all right," she said. "You'll get over that quickly, anyway, as soon as you see he's like any other boy with feet of clay. It's our own fault for romanticizing them so much. The truth is, they're all so predictable."

"What do you mean by predictable?"

"They all want the same thing, to get to the same place. Some take one route, and some take another, that's all. There are those who will talk so much about everything else you'll forget what it is they're after, and, voilà, find yourself trapped and wonder how you got there. And then there are those who will tease and torment you like a cat teases and torments a mouse, until you're the one who's pushing toward that moment."

"How do you know all this?" I asked, amazed. Until now, our talk was so much fantasy and so little reality when it came to romance.

"I've had some experiences, and I've read a lot and don't forget. I've been brought up in the shadow of a real pro, my mother." She sat back, smiling. "I remember how she fished in Harry, the little things she would do in the drugstore to get him hooked. I was there, watching her accidentally brush her body past him, pressing her breasts against his arm, his shoulder, bringing her lips so close to his neck he surely felt the warmth of her breath. And those little smiles and movements with her eyes she gave him. I think he had orgasms preparing antibiotics for customers."

"Karen!"

"Don't be so thick. And you don't have to be modest with me, Zipporah. We've told each other too much about our own orgasms," she reminded me.

Still, it made me blush and catch my breath to hear her talk about her mother and Harry Pearson that way.

"Besides, you can get a real education about boys if you just read your brother's journal."

"I told you . . ."

"All right, all right. I'm just teasing you. Let's get back to Dana. After the phone call and your visit, short visit, with my mother, the coast will be clearer. Pedal your rear into town on Monday night. Tell him to meet you in front of the post office. Your bike will be safe there. He'll pick you up and drive you up the hill, maybe to the lake, ostensibly to talk about me, but he'll really be doing it because he's interested in you, so you don't have to do much more than say you don't want to talk about me. It's too disturbing. Something like that. Even get yourself to cry a few real tears. He'll want to comfort you. Let him, and that's how it will start."

"How can you be so sure of all this? You make it sound as if you've written the script," I said.

She smiled. "In a way, I have, I guess. Look, there's no reason for you to be moping about and suffering forever, is there? Besides, I told you. I'll be sharing your experience, and it will give me something while I'm holed up here."

"How long are you going to do this, Karen? Someday, my parents are bound to find out. My mother will come up here, or you'll make some noise or something."

"I told you. After a while, I'll just leave. I might not even tell you. I'll just be gone. Don't worry."

"I'm not worrying for myself as much as for you," I said. It was true.

"I know. I appreciate it. I need some more time to pass, and there are things I still have to do. I can't leave you behind in such a state of innocence. What kind of a friend would I have been?"

"Jesse's home in two weeks," I reminded her.

She stared at me a moment and then stood up, her arms extended and her hands clenched in fists. She paced a moment and turned on me, her face full of rage.

"You just won't stop. You just won't stop reminding me about how horrible my situation is. No matter what I do to forget for a while, to make things like they were, to keep us happy and birds of a feather, you just harp and harp and harp on my being holed up here!"

Her voice reverberated in the attic. I held my breath. She was crying, too.

"I'm sorry, Karen. I'm sorry."

"You're supposed to be helping me at my time of greatest need. We have a plan. Let's follow it."

What plan? I thought but didn't ask.

"Okay. Sorry. I can't help being nervous about it. I'm trying. Really, I am."

She started to calm down and returned to the sofa. She sat quietly for a moment, gathering her thoughts and nodding.

"The next few days are all set, then. You're off to-

morrow for New York. You'll make the call. You'll do
the stupid visit to my mother. You'll see Dana. We'll
have much to talk about and do, as much as we ever
would have. Right?"

"Yes," I said.

She smiled again, and then she hugged me. I looked
at my watch, and she pulled back as if I had slapped
her.

"Go on down before your mother drives in. You're
worthless to me when you sit there on pins and needles."

I rose, grateful for permission to go.

"You sure you have everything you need for tonight? I won't be able to come back up here."

"I'm fine. I have everything I need in the trunk behind the sofa," she said, nodding at it.

I looked around the attic. As big as it was, it still
seemed confining and dark to me. I always enjoyed
our times up there, but we always knew we could
throw open the window and shout or leave whenever
we wanted to leave. Once, it had been magical for
us. Could it be that way ever again? Was it still that
way for Karen? Was that what sustained her during all
those long and lonely hours alone?

"What do you do up here in the dark?"

"I use that little flashlight to read, but I put the blanket over me so the light can't be seen in the window,
not even a tiny glow, and then I just go to sleep. I'm
fine. I'm managing. I've done a lot more exploring of
the things up here, too."

"What if my mother came up here one day while I
was at school, and I wasn't here to give you any warning?"

"No problem. You know how those stairs announce visitors. I'd hear her, and guess what?"

"What?"

"I fit very well in that armoire in the corner. I've already tried it. I can breathe all right in it and watch through the cracks until I see her leave. I'm fine," she reassured me. "We'll be fine. In fact," she continued, "I have a lot to show you about the things up here and tell you about when we can spend more time together without worry. I've spent hours and hours looking at things we've never touched. You don't even know about the old journals and newspapers, I'm sure.

"And of course, I think about you and how you're living for both of us at the moment," she added. "That's why you can't fail. You won't be just failing yourself."

"I'm doing the best I can. It's hard lying to my parents and to everyone else, Karen."

"I know. Don't forget, I've been doing just that for most of my life," she said.

She smiled and hugged me again. I walked to the attic door, paused, and looked back at her.

"I could become like everything else up here," she said. "Another orphan in the nest of orphans if you desert me."

"I won't," I promised, and I left, closing the door behind me.

The tears I cried for her and myself all fell behind my eyes, like tiny hailstones pounding on my fractured heart.

12

A Collect Call

My parents prepared for our trip to New York as
if we were going to another country. They carefully
planned the travel schedule, how and when we would
get to our hotel, where we would eat dinner before
the show so we would be close enough to walk to the
theater and, if we wanted, to walk back to the hotel.
Since we had moved up to Sandburg, none of us had
been to New York. Because we had lived so close to
the city, we never stayed overnight in a hotel there,
either. My mother was excited about it, because my
father, through a friend, had gotten us a great deal on
a suite in a very fancy Manhattan hotel, the St. Regis.
I didn't know it before we left, but my bedroom in the
suite had its own phone. When we arrived and I saw
what our accommodations were like, I thought my
opportunity to make the phone call Karen wanted was
that much better and easier for me to accomplish, but
I underestimated how hard my mother would work at
having me do things with her in the city every minute,
and it occurred to me that it would be unwise to have
the call traced to our suite.

Almost as soon as we checked in, my mother

plotted out our every move, and from there until we
returned, I was never out of her sight. Together, we
would walk up Fifth Avenue and go from one wonderful department store to another. She was eager to see
and to show me the new fashions and buy me some
new clothes. She wanted us to have lunch at a restaurant that looked out at the skating rink in Rockefeller
Center. Our jaunt was to be girls only. My father was
happy about that. He was meeting some old lawyer
friends for lunch, anyway, and said he would then look
for a new suit and some new shirts and shoes on his
own, "without anyone looking over my shoulder."

I began to worry that I would have no opportunity
whatsoever to make the call, but after we had walked
and shopped and had our lunch and shopped some
more, my mother decided it was time to go back to the
hotel, rest, shower, and spoil ourselves with bubble
baths and facial creams she had bought in a beauty shop
on Madison Avenue. She was doing so many things she
normally did not do. I sensed she wanted to splurge and
be extravagant and carefree to help us all forget, especially me, what she called the Pearson tragedy.

We had two full bathrooms in the suite. I waited for
her to step into hers to take her bath, and then I took
the tape recorder out of my suitcase. It was nearly
four-thirty. I was afraid Karen's mother might not be
home, of course. What would I do if that happened?
We were to go to dinner and then the show. My parents
would be with me all the time, and afterward, back in
the suite, I couldn't risk playing the tape. They'd hear
it for sure. I'd have to sneak out somehow and get to a
pay phone, preferably outside the hotel. I did see one
about half a block down near a magazine stand.

I hurried out to the elevator and was lucky enough to have it right there and waiting. Moments later, I was out of the hotel, charging down the sidewalk. I got into the phone booth quickly, my hands trembling so much I nearly dropped the recorder, too, but I finally got myself together enough to dial the long-distance operator and request the collect call using Karen's name. My heart was thundering in my ears as I waited for the connection and heard the ringing. I held my breath until Darlene Pearson said, "Hello." The operator announced the caller and the request. Karen's mother was quiet so long the operator had to repeat it.

"Yes, operator, I accept the charges. Karen?" she cried into the receiver.

I pushed the button on the recorder, and it played back Karen's message. Then, as she had instructed, I started to hang up before turning off the tape recorder. As I brought the receiver back to its cradle, I heard Darlene Pearson screaming, "Karen! You come home!"

My heart was pounding even harder. I believed Karen knew what she was doing when she asked me to do this. I could understand how it would take the pressure off us, especially off me, in the community, but I felt terrible about hurting her mother. She must be in a frantic state of mind now, I thought. However, there was nothing I could do. The deed was done, and as my father was fond of saying, the die was cast.

I hurried back to the hotel. This time, I had to wait for the elevator and felt my insides tumbling around with tension. After all, I had done something else that would stun my parents when and if they ever found out. When I got to my floor and to our suite, I took a deep breath and then entered, praying my mother was still in her bath. She was. I hurriedly went to mine and ran the water. Then I hid the tape recorder in my suitcase. My chest still felt like a tight-skinned drum upon which my thumping heart pounded.

Even soaking in a tub full of soothing bubbles didn't calm me or stop the quivering under my breast. Fortunately, my mother was too absorbed in everything she had done and everything we had bought. She didn't notice the tightness in my lips and the abject fear in my eyes as we both started to dress. She did distract me for a while when she shared some of her makeup with me and talked about dressing up our faces. This was also something we had rarely done together.

Shortly after, my father arrived and showed us all the things he had bought, too. We had to rush a bit to get to our early dinner and make the show. No one had any time to think about anyone else. We ate at one of my father's favorite New York restaurants, where both my mother and I feasted on lobster. My father insisted we all share a mud pie, which was really chocolate and coffee ice cream in a pie shell. I know I ate much more than my share. I saw how they were both smiling at me, happy I had an appetite, but I was eating to keep from crying and to stop the bees buzzing in my stomach.

The show we went to see was, according to my father, "the hottest ticket in town," *Silk Stockings*. I did enjoy it and watching the performances and seeing the glamour of a Broadway show took my attention completely away from everything that was happening around the Pearson tragedy. While I was in that theater, I even forgot Karen was back at our house, hiding in the attic. As we came out of the theater into the crowds pouring out of other theaters, seeing the women in fashionable dresses, men in suits and tuxedos, taxicabs everywhere, and more limousines on the street than I had seen in a year, the excitement remained with me and my parents. We held hands and walked all the way back to our hotel, and when I looked up at the lights and the great billboards and saw all the people and the traffic, I understood what Karen had meant when she talked about living in a city that never slept.

Would she ever really sleep again?

Would I?

It wasn't until we were back in the suite that the three of us realized just how tired we were. My big four-poster bed with its lusciously soft pillows appeared so inviting that I felt like diving onto it. I was undressed and ready for it in record time. The music from the show was still ringing in my ears. I cuddled up and wrapped the comforter about myself just as my mother came in to say good night.

"Did you have fun today, Zipporah?"

"Yes, very much."

"So did I. We've got to do more of this sort of thing. With your brother, too," she added. "When he is generous enough to give us some of his precious time, that is. You know he's not coming directly home from college?"

"No, I didn't know. Why not?"

"He's visiting with his roommate's family for a week. They're all going to one of the Michigan lakes to a large cabin they have there. He was so excited about it I couldn't complain."

"That's nice," I said. I wanted Jesse home, but I

was very, very nervous about him coming back before Karen left. This, at least, gave us more breathing space to prepare for that.

"We'll have a nice breakfast tomorrow and then take a slow ride back. Your father wants to look at a new car in Jersey. It's just a small detour, but one of his friends has a friend who has a dealership. You know your father and his influential friends," she said.

We smiled. She kissed me good night and left. I cuddled the blanket and pressed my face into the pillow. I wanted to soak into the softness and disappear like a cherry sinking into whipped cream. I begged sleep to come, to take me away from my thoughts, but before it did, I conjured Karen back at our house, maybe watching television in my room or maybe even venturing outside in the darkness to get some air and feel less trapped, even though, for now, she was tethered to our house.

Where would she go when it was time to leave? I imagined her growing old in the attic, fading into a ghost herself, until I was no longer sure if she were there. She would dwindle like an old experience, harder and harder to recall, the details of it falling away until there was nothing left but a vague remembrance, something like my father's best friend in high school. He and his friend could pass each other on a street in this city and not know it. Something might be stirred for a moment. They would both pause and try to think what it was, but the noise, all that competed for their attention in the present, would drive it away quickly, and that would be that. Gone forever.

Heaven forgive me, I thought, but right now, I longed for that. Even thinking such a thing made me feel like a terrible traitor, like some bird leaving the nest but leaving her broken-winged sibling behind to stare out at the world she would never touch until she fell out and tumbled to the earth. In my dreams, the overcast sky rained feathers.

My parents were up before I was. My mother wouldn't let my father wake me, but he made as much noise as he could, because he was anxious to get under way. I was deliberately slow to get myself moving. I knew that sometime toward the end of this day, I would have to face Karen's mother. When I finally did get up and dressed, my father hurried us along to breakfast. The appetite I had the night before was gone. I barely nibbled on a toasted bagel, and I know I looked half-asleep.

"I guess Zipporah can't take the fast life," my father joked.

"We'll stop at a really nice place for lunch," my mother promised.

I tried to be upbeat, but I couldn't put aside thinking about all that awaited me at home. When we stopped in New Jersey on the way back up to Sandburg, I was surprised to see the car my father was considering. It was a red convertible sports car that sat only two people. We had three cars in the family already, counting Jesse's car, but if we traded in either my mother's car or my father's for this, how could we three fit if we wanted to use it for a family trip?

My father decided to take a test drive and asked me to go with him instead of my mother.

"It's all right," she said. "Go on. I'll ride in it later."

I got in, and we sped off with the top down. It accelerated so fast the wind whipped through my hair. I shrieked when my ribbon went flying. My father was driving it as he would a race car, careening around corners and trying the funny-sounding horn.

"Don't you dare drive it this fast," he told me.

"Me?"

"This will be your car eventually," he said. "Of course, I'll buy it now so I can break it in for you."

"My car?"

"Mostly. Your brother will try to steal it, of course, but we won't let him," he said.

I ran my hand over the soft, luxurious black leather seats. He turned on the radio and laughed with delight at the rock and roll. It was as if the car was magical and could turn him or anyone his age back into a teenager.

He slowed down for the return to the dealership.

"What do you think?"

"It's beautiful."

"And not hard to drive, as long as you keep within the speed limit. The day you get your first speeding ticket is the day I sell it," he warned.

"I don't even have my license. I have to wait to take driver's education, Daddy."

"It's all right. Years pass so quickly, you wake up one morning and think you've been in some time machine. Take my word for it. It seems like I was just eighteen."

He looked at me, his face taking on that dark seriousness he could muster in seconds, especially in court.

"The thing is, Zipporah, you have a lot to look forward to. These should be and will be your best years. I want you to enjoy them, enjoy your youth. I don't want what's happened with the Pearsons to ruin things for you so much that you let it all pass you by, understand?"

I nodded. My heart felt as if it were bubbling instead of beating. The words were bunching up in my mouth, pressing at my lips, urging my tongue to move and deliver. *Tell him!* the voice inside me screamed. *Tell him about Karen. End it before it becomes too late, before your parents are so disgusted with you they'll wish you were never born.*

"Daddy," I was sure I began, but he was so absorbed in driving the car and listening to the music he didn't hear me. He turned into the dealership and pumped the horn to bring my mother out.

"How do we look in it?" he asked her, beaming and sitting back with his arm over the back of my seat.

"Like it was made for you," she said, looking mainly at me.

Daddy rubbed the steering wheel and nodded.

"I'm going in there and make the deal. We'll have it for the summer," he said. He turned to me. "I'll sneak you onto some side roads and begin teaching you to drive it. Farmer's kids drive at fifteen."

"One little problem, Michael. She's not a farmer's kid."

"So we'll plant some vegetables in the backyard and have her tend them," he said, getting out.

We watched him walk into the dealership.

"You can take the man out of the boy, but you can't take the boy out of the man," she told me, shaking her head.

"He said he was buying it for me."

"Well, he is, in a way. For now, it's a good excuse to

buy it for himself," she said, laughing. "I have to admit that it is beautiful."

Who could deny that? I thought. How much fun it would have been for Karen and me to be riding in this to school. What would she feel like when she saw it parked in our driveway and found out it was going to become my car someday? I decided for now I wouldn't tell her.

"It will be delivered by next weekend," my father told us when he finished with the salesman. "I'll take you to school in it," he promised me.

"Your father is determined to spoil himself by spoiling you," my mother declared.

They kidded each other about it until we stopped for lunch. I did have a better appetite, which pleased them both. Just after we got the waitress to give us the check, my father looked at his watch and said, "We can get home early enough for us to go see Karen's mother first. I think that will be better than going there after dinner, don't you, Eileen?"

My mother glanced at me and nodded.

Moments later, we were off again, and I sat in the rear, looking out the window but seeing nothing. I hated the idea of going to Karen's house and seeing her mother like this, but now, after what I had done on the phone, I hated it even more. Was I capable of putting on the act Karen had told me to put on? Would I simply fall apart and confess everything right then and there? Was there still time for me to rescue myself? Was I terrible for thinking only of myself?

I couldn't help but also imagine Karen sitting up in the attic, gazing out the window, waiting anxiously for my return, and then waiting with frustration for the opportunity for us to communicate. All my emotions were twisting around inside me. My whole body felt as if it had been turned into a knot. I might not be able to get out of the car and walk to the Pearson front door. I might just faint or something the moment I stepped out.

"Don't worry, honey. Everything will be fine," my mother said.

She had been looking back at me periodically.

"Sure. This will go really fast," my father said. "We'll do what's right and go home. You'll feel better about it, Zipporah, believe me."

"I'm okay," I said, or thought I said. I wasn't sure if I just thought it.

As soon as we drove into Sandburg, I felt the blood drain from my face. I took a few deep breaths and then pressed my lips together as if I wanted to keep words from spilling out, just the way Karen often did. My father drove right up to the Pearson house and stopped. There was a police car in the driveway.

"Hey, something's happening," he said.

"Maybe we shouldn't go in, then, Michael," my mother said.

He nodded, thoughtful. My hopes rose. I might be able to avoid this now, after all.

"Let me see," he said, disappointing me, and got out. My mother and I waited in the car while he went to the front door and rang the doorbell. Karen's mother opened it. They spoke for a few moments, and then he turned and beckoned to us to come.

"Ready?" my mother asked.

I didn't answer. I just opened the door. I felt as if I were floating down to the sidewalk to stand. My mother reached for my hand. I kept my head down as we walked to the Pearsons' front entrance. Karen's mother had gone back into the living room, where Chief Keiser and the two detectives who had questioned me were also sitting.

"Karen called her mother yesterday," my father told us. He looked at me. "The police were going to call you anyway, Zipporah, to ask you about it."

"Me? Why?" I asked, my heart thumping. My lungs felt as if they would explode.

"Just to see what you know about her travels," he said.

I released some air and shook my head. "I already told them what I knew."

"Tell them again. Let's go," my father said, stepping aside for my mother and me to enter.

This wasn't fair, I thought. I was supposed to meet only her mother. I wasn't supposed to meet her in front of the police. This was different. *Karen and I didn't plan for this. I'll make a mistake.* The tears I was supposed to force were now coming to my eyes willingly. There was no need even to think about putting on any act.

To me and, I was sure, my mother, Darlene Pearson looked even more beautiful in the role of a mourning wife. She had her hair pinned back, but she had a face attractive enough not to fear its being emphasized. Her eyes, although unadorned with eye shadow and eye liner, somehow looked larger, more stunning in their sadness. In fact, I thought she held herself elegantly, her lips firm, her chin without quiver, and her posture as correct as ever.

She wore a short-sleeved black blouse and a black

skirt. The blouse was opened at her throat, and her thin gold necklace glittered in the late-afternoon sunshine streaming through the living-room windows. The blouse looked just a little tight around her full bosom. Two small diamonds in gold settings filled her pierced earlobes. She wore a pair of black flats with no stockings.

She turned to me and held out her hands. "Zipporah, dear," she said.

I took her hands, and she pulled me to her to hug me. I hugged back, but without any enthusiasm. She kissed me on the cheek and held me a moment longer.

"What you must be going through, too," she said, holding me at arm's length and looking into my eyes. I shifted my gaze to the floor quickly, and she let go of me. Instantly, I stepped back. "Please, everyone, sit," she told my parents.

Chief Keiser rose to give his seat to my mother. The two detectives were on the sofa. I saw that Karen's mother had given them all coffee. There was a small plate of cookies on the table as well.

"Michael, Eileen, would you like some coffee?" Darlene Pearson asked.

"No, thank you, Darlene. We're fine. We've just driven back from New York City."

"New York City?" Lieutenant Cooper said, perking up.

"Yes. I took my wife and daughter to a show, *Silk Stockings*," my father said.

"You were there overnight?"

"Yes. I had a suite at the St. Regis," my father said.

"Then I'll get right to it," Lieutenant Cooper said. "Karen Pearson called Mrs. Pearson yesterday at about four-thirty from New York City."

"Oh, dear," my mother said.

Lieutenant Cooper turned to me.

"Did you see or meet with her while you were in New York City, Zipporah?"

"She couldn't have," my mother said quickly. "She was with me all day, and at the time you mention, she and I were back in our suite preparing to dress to go to dinner and the theater."

"At no time was your daughter out of your sight?"

"At no time," my mother said firmly, forgetting about when she was in her bath. She simply assumed I had been soaking in mine, which only made me feel even more terrible. I was causing my mother to tell a lie unknowingly.

Lieutenant Cooper sat back, obviously looking disappointed. He had been hoping for a big breakthrough. He glanced at Detective Simon, who just nodded.

"Well," Chief Keiser said, "it does look like Karen's gotten herself to New York."

"She took money, a good deal of money, when she left," her mother said, and sank back into her chair. "Still, I can't imagine where she's gone or what she's doing. We don't have any family in New York City, nor does Karen have any friends who live there. She's never been there on her own. She's never been on a subway or ridden a city bus. Children her age don't just check into hotels."

"Into decent hotels," Lieutenant Cooper corrected. "There are fleabag places a leper with half his face missing could check into in New York," he muttered.

"Or she could be sleeping in the park. Lots of homeless people do that," Detective Simon added.

Karen's mother moaned and rocked a little in her

chair. She had her arms around herself as if she were trying to stop her body from falling apart. What a wonderful performance, I thought, but then I thought that no matter what she had done or ignored, she might now be drowning in regret.

She stopped rocking abruptly and looked so sharply at me I caught my breath and held it.

"Zipporah, do you have any idea where she might have gone in New York City? Did she tell you anything that would help us find her and bring her home? I can't imagine her out there by herself. She's going to get hurt for sure. You wouldn't be a good friend if you knew something about her going to New York and didn't tell us."

I glanced at my father. His eyes were fixed intensely on me the way I saw he could fix them on a witness in court. The detectives were staring at me as well, and Chief Keiser moved down so he could look directly at me.

Would my voice fail me? I actually thought I would start to speak but be unable to make a sound.

"She always talked about New York City and had some brochures about it," I began. "Karen wanted to live in a big city where there was excitement and always something to do."

Her mother smiled and shook her head. "She was so full of fantasy," she told the detectives, both of whom nodded as if they had known her as well as her mother had. "Sometimes, I felt as if I were pulling her down to reality as you would pull a kite back down to earth."

She turned back to me. "You two were as close as sisters, Zipporah. Surely, you had some idea something terrible like this might happen."

"No," I said quickly. That was so true. I wanted to
shout back at her that I never thought this would happen. We were only planning to scare him off, to stop
him from abusing her. Visions of all that returned,
especially the way Karen had first described it to me.
What was Darlene Pearson trying to do now, find a
way to blame me? Was she trying to say I should have
told someone so that it wouldn't have happened?

Was that true? Should I have done that? Was I really
partly, maybe significantly, at fault? Was Mr. Pearson
dead because of me as well as Karen?

I felt the first tears escape my lids and begin to
trickle down my cheeks.

"You're making her feel as if it's her fault," my
mother softly told Darlene. "She's had difficulty sleeping and functioning as it is."

"Oh, no, I don't mean that. I don't mean it's in any
way your fault. Of course not. It can't possibly be
your fault, Zipporah. What we're all trying to do is
find Karen first and try to understand what happened
and why. That's all. You know she and I were not as
close as I would have liked us to be. Teenagers are so
difficult these days," she explained to the detectives.
"Especially teenage girls. Karen was always moody.
Wasn't she, Zipporah?"

I shrugged. We're all moody, I thought, but didn't
say so. Karen's mother continued as if once she had
begun, she could never stop.

"I know she and Harry weren't getting along, but
she and I weren't getting along all that well these days,
either," she continued. "It's more difficult for a man
to be raising and caring for another man's child, especially another man's teenage daughter, but Harry was

a generous man. You know he bought her whatever she wanted, Zipporah. She never lacked for anything. She had her own room, clothes, everything she would need."

"Not her own phone," Detective Simon muttered, looking at me.

"What?"

"She complained about not having her phone. According to Zipporah," he explained, nodding at me. Darlene Pearson looked at me as if I had betrayed a deeply held family secret.

"She never asked either of us for her own phone," she said.

"But she wasn't permitted to talk for more than two minutes," I blurted.

"What?"

"Wait a minute," my father said. "No one kills anyone because she didn't get her own phone in her room. Let's move on here."

"I don't know what this talk about a phone is about. Harry was a generous man," Darlene Pearson recited as if it had become her mantra. "He created her college fund, too. You knew that," she told me sharply, as if I had suddenly been chosen to be Karen's attorney in court.

I was afraid of this, afraid I'd be cast in opposition to her mother and things would quickly get out of hand.

I shook my head. "She never told me about any college fund." She had never mentioned anything specific. She never used those words.

"Well, it's there. Probably never to be used now," she added. She took a deep breath.

"During this phone call from New York City," Lieutenant Cooper said, "Karen said she was going away, going down to the train station and leaving. Did she mention any other place she might like to go to?"

Again, I shrugged, and then I thought about our afternoons in the nest pretending we were in my car.

"We talked about lots of places. We thought when we had our licences and I had a car, we would take wonderful trips. We sent away for travel brochures."

"To where?"

"Everywhere," I said. "Florida, Michigan, California, Texas, even Canada."

"Canada?" her mother said, as if that was it. She looked at the detectives.

"If she tries that, it will be easier to catch her," Lieutenant Cooper assured her.

Why wasn't anyone wondering why Harry was in her room? Had they gone through the house? Did the detectives discover what was in the apartment Harry's mother had occupied? Should I suggest it, I wondered, or was I better off not saying another word?

"I think we had better be going," my father said, rising. "Even a fun trip is tiring, and we've all got to get ourselves ready for the work week. You know we're available to help you in any way we possibly can, Darlene," he told Karen's mother.

My mother stood up, too, and then walked to her to take her hands and embrace her.

"I'm sure I can't fully understand or appreciate how difficult all this is for you, Darlene, but if I can help you in any way, please call me."

"Yes, thank you," Karen's mother said. She looked at me again. "I'm sorry you're being put through the grinder, Zipporah. People are always saying you can't help who you have as relatives. You don't choose them, but in this case, it was unfortunate for you to have Karen as a friend, I guess."

"No, it wasn't," I said so sharply I surprised even myself.

No one spoke.

No one moved a muscle.

"She's not bad. She's not mean. This wasn't her fault," I said, and then, realizing I had said too much, I turned and rushed toward the door.

"I'm sorry," I heard my mother say. "It's a very emotional time for her, too."

No one said anything. My parents followed me out quietly. We all got into our car, and my father drove off. My parents remained strangely quiet the remainder of the trip to our house. After we pulled into the driveway and the garage, my father stood by the car and kept the garage door open. My mother paused to look at him, curious about why he was just standing there waiting for me to come around.

"Go on inside," he told her. "Zipporah," he said. "Take a walk with me."

"Why?" I asked, unable to hide my fear.

"Just do," he said firmly.

"Michael?" my mother asked.

"It's all right. We'll be in the house in a moment," he told her.

He walked to me. I turned and walked out of the garage with him. We kept walking down the driveway. Where were we going? What did he want? He paused at the road. When he looked back at the house, I held my breath. Was he looking up toward the attic? Could he possibly know? Nervously, I searched the windows. Karen wasn't peeping out. It was all dark and closed.

"What do you know about Karen's relationship with Harry Pearson that you're not telling us or anyone, for that matter, Zipporah?"

I started to shake my head.

"Why were you so sharp with Darlene Pearson in there?"

My tears were returning in force. I couldn't stand up against my father's cross-examination, and I did feel as if I were in court.

"I know you've held back on it, but you'd better tell me now, Zipporah."

I sucked in my breath.

"Well?"

"He was coming into her room at night," I said.

I could almost feel the tightness take hold in his body as he stood beside me.

"Coming into her room? You mean, to do things he shouldn't?"

"Yes."

"She told you this?"

"Yes," I said.

"Did her mother know?"

"I don't know for sure. I think so," I said. "Karen said she did."

"Why didn't Karen tell anyone else?"

"She had no one else," I said. "And she was ashamed of it. She didn't know what to do. She was afraid Harry would be arrested, and they'd lose everything, and her mother would hate her more."

"More? She thought her mother hated her?"

I nodded.

"How long has that business in the bedroom been going on?"

"A while. It got worse and worse."

I was sobbing openly now, my shoulders shaking hard. I turned away from him. He put his arm around me.

"Okay," he said. "It's not a bad thing to want to protect and defend someone you love. Believe me, as I've said many times, in the end, the truth will find a way to show itself. It always does. I'm only sorry you have had to bear this secret in your heart, bear it all alone."

I couldn't stop it now. I was crying harder. He kissed away my tears and held me tighter. Then we turned toward the house.

"I'll do what I can," he promised. "Don't you worry anymore."

I looked up quickly and thought I saw the curtains in the attic move.

I don't know how my legs carried me the rest of the way into the house, but they did. When we entered, my mother was right there, waiting. She looked at my father and then at me and moved quickly to embrace me.

"What happened, Michael? Is she okay?" she asked my father.

"She'll be fine," he said. "Everything will be fine," he assured us both.

My mother kissed me, too, and then I started up the stairs to my room.

I can't do this anymore, I thought, when I reached the landing and looked at the attic stairway. It's got to end. Besides, my father will help Karen now; he'll help us both. I walked to the stairway and up to the attic door, where I took a deep breath before opening it.

I entered. "Karen?" I called.

She wasn't sitting on the sofa or waiting by the window, nor was she hiding in any dark corner. Nothing was out, not an old dress or an old hat. The attic was just the way it was before she had come.

"Karen?"

I walked in farther and then started to move around the attic. She didn't appear, step out from behind any furniture now that she knew it was only me.

"Karen?"

I stood there, looking into the shadows and waiting, but I didn't see her or hear her.

For a moment, I thought I had imagined it all. She was never there. Then I remembered what she had told me about how she could hide herself in the armoire in the corner. I went to it, paused, and opened it abruptly.

It was empty.

I spun around, looking at everything again, and then I hurried out, down the stairs and to my room. I went quickly to my copy of *The Diary of Anne Frank* and rifled through the pages, but there were no notes, no letters, no explanations at all.

My mother came up and then to my doorway. She knocked on the open door to get my attention. I turned quickly, expecting to see Karen.

"Zipporah? Were you just up in the attic?"

"Yes."

She turned and looked at the stairway. "Why?"

"It was our place, our secret place, where we confided in each other, where we became close friends."

"Oh. Yes, of course. You poor dear. Are you all right, honey?" my mother asked.

I looked at her, at the book, then back at her, and nodded.

"Yes," I said. "I'm okay now," I told her, even though I had no idea if I was or wasn't and wondered if I ever would be again.

13

Too Late to Fix the Mess

At breakfast, neither of my parents said anything more about what I had told my father after we had returned from Darlene Pearson's house. He had gotten up quickly, spoke little to me, and then left earlier than he usually did. From the way he and my mother exchanged secret glances, I suspected it was because he was off to do something as a result of what I had told him. My mother was home and didn't have to go to work until three. She volunteered to take me to school, but I told her I would be fine on the bus. I didn't want her chasing around and thought she would need to rest for her hospital shift.

When I arrived at school, I put my things in my locker as usual and set out for homeroom. I was moving in a daze and didn't realize that as I was walking through the hall, Dana Martin had come up beside me.

"Wake up," he said, nudging me.

I paused to look at him and then kept walking.

"You and I definitely need to meet tonight," he said when we approached my homeroom door.

"Oh? And why is that?" I asked. I wasn't in the

mood for him, despite his good looks and the way all the other girls were eyeing me jealously every time he took a step in my direction. The truth was, I felt like wrapping myself up in some cocoon and sleeping away the whole day.

He leaned so close his lips actually touched my ear.

"Because Karen called me last night," he whispered, and then he kept walking toward his own homeroom. I felt the blood drain from my face.

Did that mean he knew she was still in the area, or had she called him, pretending she was in New York City? Why would she risk calling him after all this, anyway? Where was she? I stood there in the doorway in such a dumbfounded state I didn't feel the other students nudging me aside to get into the room. In fact, I didn't move until the bell rang and our teacher clapped his hands sharply to get my attention.

"Zipporah, take your seat, please," he ordered, and I hurried to it.

Everyone was looking at me. Did they all know how deeply I was involved with Karen's situation? Had they heard about the police interrogations? My visit to her mother? One way or another, I was still the center of attention. When would that stop? I didn't want to look at anyone or do anything that would suggest I wanted anyone to talk to me. I dreaded all their questions, comments, and accusations. Moving through my school morning was like paint-by-numbers for me. I could have had my eyes closed the whole time, and it wouldn't have made any difference. However, every time I heard a noise in the hallway or a door was opened, my heart stopped and started. I anticipated one of the detectives looking for me or my father coming to take me out of school. I even imagined Karen returning, opening the door, and taking her seat with a smile on her face, as if nothing at all had ever happened. I actually dreaded going to lunch, not only because of how the other students would look at me and treat me but because I was afraid of talking to Dana now, afraid of hearing anything more. Didn't Karen realize the tight spot she had put me in? I had to be careful of every word I spoke, every look and gesture.

Impulsively, when the bell rang, I headed outside instead of toward the cafeteria.

From what everyone who had lived in Sandburg most of their lives had told my parents and me, we were having a warmer than usual spring. They all said it meant a hot, humid summer. The last weeks of school were uncomfortable, because the school had no air conditioning, and some of the rooms were stifling. By midafternoon, it put the students into a stupor. Even the teachers looked drained. As soon as they had a free period, they rushed to the faculty room to bathe in the electric fans. There were fans set up in the cafeteria, so it was the coolest place for the students.

I found a shady place under a sprawling oak tree just to the right of the building. I could look out at the ballfields. No one was there, and because of the heat, no one else had decided to spend lunch hour outside. There wasn't even a breeze. I leaned back against the tree and closed my eyes. How was all this going to end? What exactly would my father do with the information I had given him? Where was Karen? Had she really run off to New York? What did Dana Martin really know? How much trouble was I about to be in? My nerves were like stripped electric wires, sizzling.

Sensing him standing there before he spoke, I opened my eyes and looked up at Dana.

"I wondered where you had gone to hide," he said. "Alice Bucci saw you leave the building."

"Figures she would be the one to tell. She'll play Brutus in the school production of *Julius Caesar.*"

He laughed and squatted beside me, pulling up a blade of grass and clenching it between his teeth.

"Karen told me last night that she wants us to get together," he said.

"Where is she?"

"You don't know?"

"Would I ask you if I did? Well?"

He shrugged. "I don't know for sure. She wouldn't tell me. I know she called from a pay phone some-where, because she had to put more change in, and I heard the coins dropping."

"Why does she want us to get together?"

"She said we were her best friends, and we should talk about how we could help her."

"How can you be one of her best friends?"

He shrugged. "Beggars can't be choosers," he said. "Anyway, she suggested I tell you that I would come by the post office tonight. She said you could ride your bike there about seven-thirty, so your parents wouldn't know you were meeting me. Was she right?"

"It doesn't matter. I can't do that. I can't lie to my parents anymore."

"What do you mean, anymore?"

"I mean, I can't lie to them."

He shrugged. "You won't. You just won't tell them everything. That's not a lie."

I looked away, and he lay back on the grass beside me, his hands behind his head, gazing up at the pale blue sky, with its wispy clouds so still they looked dabbed on the celestial canvas. Even the birds around us were too hot to fly. They stared out angrily from where they perched on tree branches, as if they thought Nature had betrayed them by imposing this blanket of humidity and heat.

"It wouldn't surprise me to learn that she's gone somewhere, probably somewhere far away. You know, of course, that Karen was always planning on running away from home," he said. "She was saving her money. She told me she wanted to go to California and become a movie star."

I didn't say anything. Karen and I had talked about many things, but she had never told me she was planning to run off without me, and I couldn't imagine her doing anything like that without telling me first.

"She said a lot of things. So what?" I muttered. "I'm sure you tell people you're going to be a sports star or something, don't you?"

He laughed. "I am."

"Yeah, right," I said.

He sat upright and leaned toward me. "Don't be so cynical," he said. "It's not attractive, and you can be very attractive."

I looked at him askance. "Yeah, right," I repeated, but not with the same enthusiasm. Whether he was being truthful or not, I liked hearing it.

"I noticed how you've changed, improved your looks. You have a good teacher."

"What's that's supposed to mean?"

"What is it Karen always says? Don't be thick? I know you've been talking to her all this time. Don't deny it," he added quickly, his hand up with the palm toward me. "You know a lot more than people think. You must have lied to the police."

"I didn't lie. I just . . ."

"Didn't tell them everything? See? You can do it."

I looked at him, at his impish smile. His eyes were beautiful. He's the one who could be a movie star, I thought. Maybe he would be. Maybe he was one of those people who would become what he dreamed of becoming. Karen always talked about some people being touched by an angel.

"Just one touch will do it," she said. "The luckier ones are kissed on the forehead while they sleep. They feel it, but they think it was a dream."

I didn't realize I was staring at him, but he did. He smiled and reached for my hand.

"Well?" he said, toying with my fingers. "Are you going to be there?"

"I don't know," I said weakly.

He pulled his hand from mine. "I'll be there at seven-thirty. Be there, or be square," he said, standing.

I didn't answer. He started away. I watched him saunter back to the school door, pause, look back at me to flash a smile, and then go inside. I didn't move until the bell rang to return to class. It didn't matter that I had nothing for lunch, either. I didn't think I could hold down a piece of bread. My stomach was in just that much turmoil. I thought every organ in my body was twitching the remainder of the school day.

When the final bell rang, I sighed with relief and hurried out, anxious to get home.

I knew that by the time I arrived at my house, my mother would be at her shift in the hospital, and my father would still be at work, so I would have time alone to think. I practically leaped out of the bus when it pulled up to my driveway. Head down, I charged up the walkway and unlocked the front door. I was on my way to the kitchen to get myself a cold drink. I thought maybe some milk would settle my stomach.

"Hi," I heard as I started past the living room. I paused and looked in to see Karen sitting on the sofa, looking relaxed and casual. She had one of my mother's recent movie magazines in her lap and a glass of lemonade in her hand. Anyone looking at her would think there was absolutely nothing wrong, nothing different about her or me.

"Karen!"

"Herself," she said, smiling.

"Where have you been?"

"I understand you did a good job with the tape recorder," she replied, instead of answering.

I entered the living room. She was wearing one of her own skirts and one of her own blouses. She had neither when she had come here.

"Where were you last night?"

She set the glass of lemonade on the coffee table and picked up a key to show me.

"Harry's mother's apartment," she said. "I had to apologize to his mother," she said, smiling.

"What?"

I sat, or rather flopped, on my father's recliner and clutched my books against my body.

"Just kidding, but I did spend the night there, and I can report there was no ghost. So, you went up to the nest looking for me after you came home from New York City and discovered I was gone? Is that it?"

"Yes."

"You went up to the nest with your parents in the house? Weren't you concerned they'd ask why you went up there? Weren't you worried they'd hear you go up? Weren't you afraid your mother or father might follow you up and find me? Well?" she asked, running her questions together so quickly there was no time to answer one before the other.

"As soon as we returned from New York City, we stopped to see your mother," I began.

"What's that got to do with it? I knew that you were going to visit her. Remember?"

"Yes, but the police were there because of the phone call I had made."

"It worked. I know. I expected it would, and she would call them to tell them. Thanks, but why did you go up to the nest? Why did you take such a chance, Zipporah? Especially after doing such a good job with the tape recorder, huh?"

"I got angry at your mother," I said. "I defended you, and I guess I blurted out and suggested things."

"I told you how to act, how to behave. I told you she'd get you to slip up. I warned you. Why didn't you listen?"

"I tried, but when she apologized for you, when she said I was unfortunate to have you for a best friend, I couldn't stand it anymore. Everyone was feeling so sorry for her for having a daughter like you. I had to speak up and tell them it wasn't your fault. But that's all I said before running out crying."

"It was enough. Oh, she is clever," she said, smiling and shaking her head. "Turning the whole thing around so you and she would seem to be the ones who should be pitied. What happened then? What did the police do? Did they come after you?"

"No. We left before they could ask me another thing, but when we got home, my father pulled me aside. He suspected you had a good reason to do what you did to Harry. He made me tell him."

Her eyes narrowed, and she leaned forward. "I know. I watched you talk to him."

"You were still up there?"

"Uh-huh."

"Where were you when I went up to the attic looking for you?"

"I had already left, out the window and down the fire escape. You told him what, exactly?"

"That Harry had been coming into your room at night and doing things he shouldn't have been doing. My father was upset for you, and he said he would do something. He's going to help you, Karen. You'll see. It's good that he knows. We should have told him right from the start, just as I had wanted. He'll make things all right."

"Things can never be all right. Not like that. You're such a little idiot," she said.

"I am not!"

"Oh, please, Zipporah." She looked away. "So now I know for sure why you went up to the nest looking for me. You wanted them to know about us, know that I've been up there all this time. You were going to betray me after all, right? Wasn't that it?"

"No, not betray you. I was going up to tell you that

you didn't have to hide anymore. I went up to tell you my father is going to help you."

"I thought I could trust you with my life. I thought we were birds of a feather."

"We are. I'm just trying to do what's best for you."

She shook her head, sat back, and looked as if she was going to cry. "Best for me? Why do you think I'm really not in New York City, Zipporah? Why do you think I'm still here? I could be long gone by now. I'm not afraid of being on my own. I've been on my own all my life, or at least since my father's death. But I'm here for you. Yes, that's right, you. You're right in the middle of this mess, and I couldn't just up and leave the nest and you behind to face the music alone. And besides, I know you've made sacrifices for me ever since we became friends and that you could have had many more friends, been more popular, had some boyfriends, but chose instead to be my best friend. I owe you for being so loyal to me," she said. "And now you've gone and done this. I don't know." She shook her head. "It might be too late to fix the mess you've made. I don't know."

"Why? I don't understand why you call it a mess."

She sighed and stared at me a moment, as if I were the one to be pitied here and not her, as if I were the one in all this trouble.

"I guess I shouldn't be mad at you. You're just too naive, too trusting. After all, you've been protected all your life." She held her arms up. "You've grown up in a loving family and always had a mother and father who truly cared for you. How many nights when I was only eleven, twelve, did I spend alone? All night, in fact, terrified of every sound."

"Why were you alone?"

She laughed as if I had asked the silliest question.

"Why was I alone? You think my mother's some sort of angel because she puts on that pained or hurt face all the time? You think Harry's been her only male experience since my father died? Late at night, she would slip out of the house and go to bars on the other side of the county, pick up someone, and often not come home until the wee hours of the morning or the next day."

"You never told me that."

"Oh, Zipporah. Don't you get tired of saying that? You want me to tell you every little grisly detail about my miserable life? Should I tell you about the night I spent in a motel in another bed while my mother and a man she met were in the next bed making love like two monkeys? Should I tell you how I put the blanket and the pillow over my ears to block out the moaning and groaning?"

I shook my head. "When?"

"All this happened before we met, but I couldn't tell you about it or tell you other stuff. I was afraid you'd think poorly of me and not want to be my friend."

"I would have been your friend no matter what, Karen."

"I know that now, but not back then, and I wasn't eager to revive the nasty memories."

I nodded. It wasn't hard for me to understand that. I felt even sorrier for her. I understood why she was so nervous about getting anyone to take her side, to believe her. Her own mother betrayed her and put her through such nasty things just to please herself.

"But what made you run off and sneak into Harry's mother's apartment to stay last night?"

"Instinct."

"What do you mean, instinct?"

She smiled. "When I watched you with your father out there and saw you sobbing, I had a feeling you might do something dumb like want to turn me in, let your parents know about me. I was also afraid your parents might have seen or heard the recorder or you might have broken down and confessed it all when you were with them in New York City. I just thought it was wise to be cautious and not take any chances. I thought there might have been a problem when you met my mother, too. Actually, I confirmed that last night."

"How?"

"When I was in the apartment, I put my ear to the wall. I could hear my mother on the telephone. She was telling someone about my phone call from New York and the police and then you. I didn't hear details, but I had the sense you had done something disturbing."

"Who was she talking to?"

"I don't know," she said. "She used that sweet, flirtatious voice of hers. I've always suspected she had a boyfriend on the side while she was married to Harry and some of these shopping trips were phony. Of course, it would be dreadful, disastrous for her, if that got out now. She has to be the mournful widow for a decent period of time. But, she went out to do something, and I snuck into my room and got some of my things, the jewelry I could sell, and some more money I remembered I had hidden. Don't worry. I was very careful. She'd never know I was there, and I waited until she was gone this morning before sneaking out and back here through the woods. So you see, you nearly destroyed everything."

She sipped some more lemonade. I looked down, wondering what to do, wondering if she were right.

"I'm sorry," I said. "I only meant to do whatever would help you."

"I believe you. You know what's going to happen next, though, don't you?"

I shook my head.

"After your father tells the police what you told him, they'll call you in again, and this time, they'll be grilling you like a hot dog on a spit. I'm not sure, but they might even have you face my mother and force you to make all those accusations about Harry. It could get very, very ugly for you."

"What should I do?"

"Nothing else, that's for sure. Just wait to see. We'll talk about it, prepare just as we had prepared last time. Oh, I can't stand all this!" she suddenly cried, and put her hands over her ears. She was pressing on her head so hard, she looked as if she would crack it like an egg. Her face reddened with the agony and the anger. "I want to drown it out just the way I used to drown out the sounds of my mother making love to some new boyfriend. She didn't wait all that long after my father died, either, to dip into her pool of lust."

She relaxed and took her hands from her ears. After a moment, she sighed and looked at me sadly. "We were doing so well, Zipporah," she continued, shaking her head at me. "I wanted us to have some fun, at least, as a distraction, but also for your sake. That's why I wanted you to meet Dana Martin. I've been working hard on that to keep my mind off things. Have you any idea what it's been like for me, sitting up there in silence, trying not to think of the terrible things that have happened to me? You can't imagine the pins and needles I was on while you were in New York and I was wondering if you would mess up the call or maybe not make it. It was good therapy for me to think about Dana."

"He said you called him last night. He said you told him we should get together to decide how to help you. He said you told him that he and I were your best and only friends now."

"Hook, line, and sinker," she said, smiling.

"What?"

"He thinks he's so smooth, so sophisticated, the Don Juan of our school, but he's just as easy to twist and turn as any of them. He fell for my story hook, line, and sinker. He wants to meet you tonight, right?"

"Yes."

"Good," she said, standing.

"When did you call him? He said you were on a pay phone."

"Before I went to the apartment. I called from the pay phone by Echert's garage. I took a big chance for you."

"For me?"

"Of course, for you. Haven't you been listening to anything I've said?"

"But why are we thinking about Dana Martin and me now, Karen?"

"I just explained it. What do you want us to do, think only about my problems, dwell on it night and day, let it kill us both?" she cried, her face reddening. "Do you want me to keep remembering what happened, to see that horrible scene again and again until I go mad? Is that what you want?"

She seized her hair as if she would rip it out of her head, and her eyes looked as if they would explode.

"No, of course not. I want it all to be forgotten, too. I want you to be able to go on with your life. I want both of us to do all the things we dreamed we would do," I said, feeling myself on the verge of tears.

Her shoulders relaxed. "Okay, then. Okay," she said, calming. Then she smiled. "We have a lot to do. C'mon. We'll start with what you should wear, and then I'll take you through the whole scenario as if we were rehearsing for a school play. It's that simple. Tonight is your night, Zipporah Stein," she announced, and moved her hand through the air as if she were lighting up a theater or movie marquee.

She lunged forward and reached for my hand to pull me up and out of the chair. We were charging out and up the stairs just the way we used to. It was as if we were switching channels on a television set. One moment, we were watching a tragedy, and the next, we were not only watching but becoming part of some show about teenagers full of music and laughter and great excitement. I was spinning around so fast I had to hold on to Karen's hand tightly and hope she wasn't pulling me into some disaster from which I could never hope to recover.

She sifted through my closet and moved my clothes around as someone who knew exactly what she was looking for would.

"Ah," she said, taking a blouse off the hanger. It was a light pink pullover with a zipper that traveled nearly down to my navel. "I like this on you. The material clings like a second skin."

She handed it to me.

"So don't wear a bra tonight," she added.

"What? Why not?"

"Your nipples will show. You'll move the zipper down, and when he gets a glimpse of your perky breasts, he'll melt like he's made of butter. You'll see. You'll see how quickly you can be in control. You should wear this skirt," she said, referring to her own. "It's a good length. I brought you something else because you don't have any."

"What?"

"Bikini panties." She smiled. "He might even remember them," she said, and smiled licentiously. I had no need to ask why he would.

I wasn't sure how I felt about Karen's revelations about her secret sexual adventures. A part of me was envious. I didn't like being the inexperienced little girl. We weren't that far apart in age, yet she spoke and acted as if we were. Despite how good-looking and popular Dana Martin was, I was also unsure about how pleased I was about her setting me up with him for some secret, passionate rendezvous.

When I fantasized about my love life, I saw myself finding my own Prince Charming. I imagined we would look at each other and something would happen to him as well as to me, something magical and wonderful. Maybe that was only the stuff of movies and romance novels, and maybe Karen had a better understanding about how things really were between young women and young men, but I still didn't like the feeling of being pushed and dragged along into what was to be a sophisticated love affair. To me, it still seemed sneaky, but I didn't want to say anything. After all I had done, I didn't want to upset her any more. This had obviously become so important to her that she'd take risks with her own future for me.

"C'mon," she said. "Now that we have decided on what you're wearing, let's talk about what you're doing. We had better do that up in the nest."

I followed her out and up the attic stairs. When she opened the door and we stepped in, I stopped in surprise. She had changed some of the furniture around so that it looked cozier, more like an actual living room. It wasn't haphazard. Whatever matched was brought to bear. She had even found a small rug and placed it in front of the sofa.

"I had nothing to do all day waiting for you after your mother left, so I started doing this. What do you think?" she asked. "We should have done this long ago, made it more like a room instead of some messy big closet. I'm organizing everything, I decided. The old books and papers and magazines will be like our library. There's even a small area I call the bathroom, the place where I put the chamber pot," she said, lowering her voice. "Of course, we don't refer to it as a bathroom. In those days, they called it a powder room or a water closet. Look," she said, pointing down the wall to our right. "I hung that old painting of the creek. I don't know why your mother hasn't brought it downstairs. Well? What do you think so far?"

I forced a smile, because inside I was trembling again. She was behaving as if she thought this would be a permanent home, or at least a very long residence. Why didn't she want to think more about a way out of all this?

"Nice," I said, but not as enthusiastically as she would have liked. She smirked.

"Stop worrying, Zipporah. If your mother sees it, just tell her you and I did it a while ago, when we called it our clubhouse or something."

I nodded. That could work, because my mother rarely came up here.

"Okay," she said, and began to take off her skirt. "Let's get you dressed for tonight and rehearse. Come on. Don't just stand there like a zero. Put on the blouse," she said, throwing it to me. "Take off your bra first," she reminded me.

I unbuttoned my blouse and took it off. She stood waiting in her panties while I reached back and undid my bra. Then she handed me the bikini panties she had brought for me.

"Let's get the show on the road," she said, and went to the sofa to sit and wait for me to finish putting on the blouse, panties, and skirt.

She clapped. "You look very good," she said. She laughed. She patted the place beside her on the sofa. "Come here."

I moved obediently and sat. "Now what?" I asked.

"I'm going to prepare you. You're not walking into any traps. You're the trapper."

"Why is this so important that we have to do it right now, tonight?" I asked, holding my breath.

She smiled instead of smirking and shook her head.

"Why put it off when there's a good opportunity? Silly girl. We've done everything together for so long. I've shared almost all my secrets with you. I told you. We can't be birds of a feather if we're not completely even, and we can't be completely even if one of us hasn't had the life-changing experience the other has had. Well, can we?" she asked when I didn't respond.

"I guess not."

"You guess right. I couldn't leave you here in this sleepy town without first making sure of all that, and that's why," she said, taking my hand into hers and pressing her lips to my cheek, "that's why," she whispered, "the virgin dies tonight."

14

In Dana Martin's Car

Karen and I had talked about losing our virginity. Until recently, she had me believe she was a virgin as I was, although she always did belittle its importance and value.

"Women like to think they're saving themselves for that one special man, while that one special man has been harvesting sex all along. I know my mother acted so innocent and pure when she first met and married my real father. Some men, most men, let themselves be fooled. They'd rather live in the fantasy that their precious love has saved herself just for him. It's damn one-sided, if you ask me. Right?"

"I suppose," I said. She sounded right, and I had never had a conversation with any other girl or my mother like the one we were having.

"And then there are those girls who convince themselves they don't really want or need to go all the way. They want affection and consideration and respect, while they sit home and read about real sex in some corner under some lamp while no one is watching. They're merely afraid of it and find every excuse in the book to avoid it."

She did get me thinking more and more about it. We used to review the girls in school, deciding who had lost her virginity and who had not. She said she could tell by the way the "completed" girls, as she called them, carried themselves and related to boys. "They have that *je ne sais pas,* that quality the French recognize."

She did have me wishing I had it, whatever it was.

"The virgin dies tonight?" I said.

She laughed. "Don't look so worried, Zipporah. You're not exactly a country bumpkin. Remember when you told me what happened when you were dancing with that boy back in your old school? I think you said his name was Barry Hasler. You said you were in tenth grade?"

"Yes," I said. I had forgotten I had told her about that. It amazed me that she remembered the boy's name, too. She and I had been talking about our secret little sexual encounters. It wasn't that long after we had become friends, and we had played the usual "You go first" game. After one had, the other felt obligated to reveal something. It was titillating fun. That was when Karen said, "We undress ourselves in many ways when we become close friends."

I had told her that this boy, Barry Hasler, had asked me to dance, and while we were dancing, I had felt his growing excitement when he brought his hips closer. I told her I had moved back quickly, but then I admitted to this unrelenting curiosity that brought me close to him again. Karen compared it to being drawn to a candle flame and putting your finger so close you either burn yourself or nearly do.

I confessed that just for a moment or two, Barry

looked into my eyes and saw that I knew what was happening to him. The fact that I didn't pull out of his embrace and hurry away put an even greater light and excitement into his eyes. I wondered what I had done to cause it. He held me closer, and when the dance ended, he smiled at me and tried to get me to dance with him again, but I was suddenly afraid, made excuses, and left the party before it was over. Nevertheless, he pursued me in school until he saw I wasn't going to be his girlfriend, and he gave up to pursue someone else.

"But you never forgot it. It's like an experience that's imprinted in your soul forever and ever. Even when you're an old lady, you'll think back to that first time, Zipporah, and it will make you wish you were young again."

"How do you know all this?" I asked. What I really meant was, how come she knew it and I didn't?

She shrugged. "From what I read, what I hear, what I see. There have been some real mother-daughter times for me and my mother, too," she said. "Unfortunately, they usually occurred after she had drunk too much or had a bad man experience, as she called it. She would sit ranting about this or that, not realizing half the time what she was telling me, but I didn't interrupt her with any silly, childish questions that would make her aware of it, so she went on and on, supposedly to help prevent me from becoming the victim she had become. That was her excuse, but she was and is a victim of herself. She just likes to blame others, including me. But forget about that," she added quickly. "I don't want any of that to ruin our good times."

She smiled again. "I'm bringing up your memory

and what you told me so you'll realize what power you do have, we have. I hate all these girls who pretend to be so helpless. They're such . . . zeros, phonies, dishonest . . . we're not going to be like them. When you drew closer to Barry again, you kept him excited, even more excited. You could have led him all around that dance floor. He might as well have had a collar and a leash. Dana Martin's not going to be any different."

"Dana's not in the ninth grade. He's a senior, and he's been with lots of girls, I bet."

"It doesn't matter. As my mother always says, 'They're boys forever.' As I said, when you get into his car, he's going to drive you to a safe spot so you can talk," she said, making quotation marks in the air with her index and forefingers when she said "safe." "Little innocent you will go along, of course. When you get there, he'll turn off the engine and the lights. The moon will be nearly full tonight. It will be quite romantic, actually. He'll begin talking about me, about how sorry he feels for me, and how wonderful a friend you've been to me and how he respects that more than anything. He'll knock all the other girls in school as self-centered, busybodies, even his old girlfriend, in order to make you feel very special in his eyes, and then he'll say something like he hopes you think of him as someone special, too. He won't wait for the answer. He'll put his arm around your shoulders and kiss you and try to convince you that's why he wants to be with you now, why you should want to be with him, why this is so right and good."

She paused, and I sat there unable to move, afraid to speak and stop her. I felt as if I were watching it happen to someone else.

"His hands will start their exploration of your body. He'll be on those perky breasts of yours like a fly on fly paper, but," she said, smiling, "this is where you take control of him."

"How?" I asked. My heart was already thumping with anticipation.

"You're not going to be the passive little limp rag in any boy's hands, Zipporah. I won't be, and you won't be. Before he moves that hand of his off your shoulder to get to your breasts, you put your hand right here," she said, and put her hand on the inside of my right thigh. "You order, command, and direct his excitement as a lion tamer in a circus orders, commands, and directs the king of the jungle."

I started to shake my head. "I've never . . ."

"Oh, you can do it. It's easier than you think," she said. "You're not going to wimp out on me, on yourself, now, are you? Not after all I've done, all the preparation, the setup. It's my gift, my chance to pay you back for all this," she said, indicating the attic. "Look at how much you've helped me, how much you've risked for me. Don't let me down now."

"I'm not helping you in order to get you to do something for me, Karen."

"I know that, but you've got to do this. In a real sense, you'll be doing this for me almost as much as you're doing it for yourself," she insisted. "Remember when I said you had to have a love life for both of us right now? Let's get back to it. You won't be frightened. You won't let yourself be disappointed. You're more like me than you think. Am I right to believe in you? Well, am I?"

"Yes," I said. I didn't know if I really was like her

or not in this respect, but I knew at the moment, I wanted to be. She sounded like a love coach, if there ever was such a thing.

"Good. He'll turn to you to try to take control again. Let him kiss you, but this time, when he touches your breasts, you push him back and say it's awkward in the front seat. He'll practically claw the seat to get into the rear. That's when you tell him to prepare so neither you nor he can get into trouble. See? You're ordering everything. He won't even realize it right away, but you've turned him into your sex slave, and not vice versa."

She looked at the sofa.

"This is about the length and width of Dana's backseat," she said. "Get up a minute."

I did, and she sprawled on her back and looked up at me.

"I'm Dana, practically with my tongue hanging out by now," she said, and stuck out her tongue. I started to laugh, but she shook her head. "No, no, let's stay serious. We'll have plenty of time later to laugh about it."

I was really laughing more out of nervousness than anything. "How come you think we'll laugh afterward? You think it will be funny?"

"You're so serious all the time, Zipporah. I have to work hard at getting you to enjoy yourself. Of course, it will be funny, too, but I want you to get more out of it than he does, and I want him to believe that."

"Why?"

"Because they always think they're so superior," she practically shouted at me. "It's just good to bring them down a peg or two. Now, you start to climb over the seat and stop and take off those panties."

"Take them off?"

"It will be quite difficult to do anything with them on, Zipporah. Hold them up. He'll be so excited he'll be begging you to hurry. Make sure he's done what he was supposed to. He uses the lubricated ones, which you need, this being your first time. He'll be impressed that you're making sure. He'll think you might even be more experienced than he is. He'll say something like, 'See for yourself.' You say, 'I will, and you'd better not be lying to me, or I'll leave you lying there to suffer.' Say that," she said.

I did feel as if she were writing this whole scenario right here and now, just as she had predicted she would.

"Reach down and check."

My heart was pounding with the thought of doing what she said.

"Then lower yourself slowly over him. We talked about orgasms before. You know what you're expecting to happen. Even if it hurts, don't let him know. You'll get past it. You'll see. When it's over, you'll recuperate faster. Climb over the seat, and tell him you have to get back quickly. He'll be moaning in the backseat. Tell him he's a wimp if he doesn't get moving. When he drops you off back at the post office, he'll beg for another date. Tell him you'll think about it. Make it seem as if he wasn't quite as good as you expected or hoped. Now, do you have any questions?"

"I don't know if I can do it all exactly as you described," I said.

She sat up. "Damn it, Zipporah, you can, and you will. Am I right? Well, am I?"

She looked furious. I nodded quickly. "Yes," I said. "Um, my father might wonder about this skirt."

"He knows your clothes that well?" she asked, grimacing.

"I've never worn it before. He might ask," I said. "I just want to be careful."

"So take it off for now, and put it on before you get to town," she said with some annoyance. "You can stop anywhere in the darkness and do it."

"I have other skirts."

"No, wear mine. Just like we were doing before," she said, "we're sharing everything. You should have this experience in my skirt. Promise me you will. Promise. Otherwise, it just won't mean the same to me, to us. Promise."

"Okay, okay, I promise," I said, even though I really didn't understand why it would matter so much.

"Good," she said, lying back. "Good." She smiled up at the ceiling.

"When you return tonight, we'll be closer than ever, because we'll have something new to share. I couldn't describe my experiences well to you, being you were such a virgin, but that will be different now." She reached up for my hand and pulled me a little closer. "Let's recite the Bird Oath," she said. "I need to hear it. It gives me comfort." We did, and she looked very pleased and at ease again.

"I've got to go down to prepare what my mother left for my father's and my dinner," I said. "He should be home soon, anyway."

"Fine," she said. She walked me to the attic door, where she reached for my hand again and then hugged me. "I'm so excited for you," she said.

I could see in her eyes that she really was, but I couldn't help still wishing she would worry more about herself and what would happen to her, more than she was about my having crucial life experiences.

"Stop thinking so hard," she said. "Everything will be just fine soon. Besides, let your emotions and feelings take over for a change. Give that overworked brain of yours a rest."

I forced a smile, nodded, and left her. Nothing she would say or I would do would stop the trembling inside me, however. Now that it was drawing close to the time my father would arrive, I was even more anxious. Then the phone rang.

"Hey, honey," I heard him say. "How are you doing?"

"Okay," I said. "Mom left us a roast chicken, and I'm putting up some wild rice and . . ."

"Well, I'm calling because I won't be home for dinner. Sorry. I can't get out of this meeting with a pretty important business client of ours."

"Oh?"

"Yes, it's something I have to do, or I wouldn't, especially tonight, believe me."

"It's all right, Daddy," I said.

"I'll be tied up until about nine-thirty or ten."

"Don't worry about me."

"I had a chance to talk to the district attorney today, Zipporah. They're going to speak to Karen's mother about the thing you told me, and later this week, maybe as soon as tomorrow, they'll want to speak to you again. Are you up to doing it? It would really help Karen."

"I'll do my best," I said.

"Good. You're a tough kid. Your mother will probably be calling to check on you soon, too. You're sure you're okay by yourself? "

"I'm sure," I said, and hung up.

I ran up to the attic to tell Karen she could come down and have dinner with me.

"See?" she said, after she heard my father wasn't coming home until later. "It's all working out as if it was meant to. You don't have to bother taking off the skirt and stopping on the road in the darkness to put it on. You'll be home before your father gets home."

"Yes, it's just as you said it would be. He also told me the police want to speak with me again."

"When?"

"Maybe tomorrow, maybe the day after. They're going to speak with your mother first."

"They are?" She looked thoughtful for a moment and then smiled. "Good. Maybe they'll catch her in a lie. Don't worry. I'll think about what you should say and do. You'll be fine."

"If they believe us, you'll be able to come out of hiding," I said. "My father might even be your lawyer and everything. He'll have you out on bail, and you can live with us without it being a secret."

"Sure," she said. "Let's just do it right. You don't tell them anything about me until I say so. Swear. Hand on your heart. Go on."

"I swear," I said, my hand over my breast.

"Good. I'm starving. Let's eat," she cried.

Why was she so much less intense about all these things than I was? I envied her for her calmness.

My mother called soon after, just as my father had

predicted. Karen stood off to the side, listening to me reassure her that I was fine.

"You're doing really well, Zipporah," Karen told me after I hung up. "I'm proud of you. I just knew you'd be the right person to invest my hope and trust in. I'm so lucky to have you as a friend," she told me, and I felt the tears come to my eyes.

"I'm lucky to have you, too," I said.

"Even after all the trouble I've made for you?"

"That's when friends are most important."

She smiled. "You know what I like about you the most?"

I shook my head, but I was eager to hear.

"I like your optimism. You don't know it, but the truth is, I wish all the time that I could be more like you. You really believe good things are going to happen. That's nice. Your days will be full of joy, I'm sure."

Now, she looked as if she was the one who would soon cry.

"I want you to be happy and safe, too, Karen. My days won't be full of joy if you're not."

"Thanks. All this has made us closer, but I still feel bad that you're doing so much for me. That's why I want so much for things to go well for you tonight. We've been teenagers together, and now we're going to be young women together. Imagine. We'll be sharing the same guy. We'll compare real notes later, so don't keep your eyes closed the whole time," she said, laughing.

Sharing the same guy, I thought, and remembered what Jesse had told me on the phone about the dangers of two girlfriends having the same guy. It couldn't be good. If Dana liked me more after this, she wouldn't be happy, and if I was a failure in his eyes compared to Karen, I wouldn't be happy. Jesse was right, I thought, but there was no turning back now.

At dinner, I thought we'd continue to talk about my rendezvous with Dana Martin, but she wanted to hear more about school and especially the other girls. When I spoke about our classes and teachers, there were some moments when Karen looked as if she really missed everything. She talked about the teachers she liked. She spoke in the past tense, as if she were already long gone.

Both of us watched the clock. I thought I should leave when it was just a little past seven, but she told me to wait a little longer.

"It's better if he thinks you might not come. Show him you're not dying to be with him."

I couldn't stop having the feeling I had swallowed a hive of bees. Finally, she turned to me and said, "Okay, you should set out. I'm sure he'll be there waiting."

She followed me out in the darkness to get my bike.

"Good luck," she said. "I know it's going to be wonderful."

I started away and stopped to look back at her. "Was Dana Martin your first, too?" I asked her.

"No, Zipporah, Harry was my first, and it wasn't very nice, remember? Remember I told you I went with Dana to feel good about myself again? You don't have that problem. This is just going to be a special experience for you. You don't have the baggage I had. You don't hate yourself."

I stared at her. I never thought of her as someone

who hated herself. Why should she? "You shouldn't hate yourself," I said.

"Let's not talk about me. It's hard for you to understand, I'm sure. You're a lot luckier than me. You've always been," she said.

I think she realized the way she sounded, the resonant note of bitterness under her words, because she quickly added, "But I'm happy for you. I really am. I'm happy for us both!" she said.

I nodded and started away.

"Don't you see? This really is like my first time, too. So don't let me down," she cried, as I rolled down the driveway. "You look like me in my skirt!" she shouted.

When I looked back, she was gone to return to the attic, or else she had simply stepped deeper into the shadows to watch me ride off.

Months ago, what she had just said would have made me very, very happy. I wanted us to be as close as two people could ever be, friends forever and ever, but now I wasn't comfortable about her living her life through me, even if it were to be for only a short while.

I had enough trouble living for myself, I thought. The added responsibility weighed heavily on my mind and my heart. I pedaled through the glow of the moonlight mechanically, as if my body were truly no longer mine, as if I had indeed fallen under a spell Karen had cast like a net over me. I was rushing downhill, unable to put on the brakes very effectively, and completely unable from to change direction.

The sight of Dana Martin's car in front of the post office sent a chill up my spine. I slowed my pedaling and hesitated. In a few moments, it would really be too late to turn back, I thought. How could I even think of turning back now, anyway, after all the promises I had made? I got off my bike and walked the remainder of the way. I could see him watching me in his rearview mirror. I put my bike on the side of the post office building and approached his car. He leaned over in his front seat and opened the door.

"Hop in," he said.

I looked back at the center of the hamlet. George's was closing. The lights were being flicked off in the front windows. The rest of the village was dark, except that the bar and grill was still open, and Sparky was out in front as usual, looking up the street. He was the only witness seeing me get into Dana Martin's car, I thought, and laughed to myself, recalling how Karen and I attributed so much possible testimony to Ron Black's dog.

"If he could speak, he could bring down most of the big shots," Karen had said. "My mother included."

The moment I closed the car door, Dana drove off.

"So," he said, turning and smiling at me, "have you spoken to Karen today? Did she warn you about me?"

"If she had, would I be here?" I answered.

He laughed. "Karen told me you were very special. She called you the school's biggest well-kept secret."

"Me? Why?"

He just smiled at me. "To be truthful, I've never heard any of the other guys talk about you except to say they wouldn't mind being with you."

"Why should they?"

Again, he just smiled.

"Where are we going? I can't stay out more than a half hour," I said.

"Okay," he said, whipping the car suddenly to the left to go down a side drive. He turned to the right and into a cleared area. I saw what looked like the start of a house construction. There was a foundation built and lumber piled on the side. "My cousin is general contractor for this house," he said, and turned off the engine.

"So," he said, "what are we going to do to help Karen?"

"What can we do?" I asked.

He moved closer.

"I don't know, but we should think about it. I'm sure you have. I've never seen two girls who were closer or better friends than you two. I guess you know as much about each other as any two people could know about each other," he said, running his fingers through my hair. "I know this . . . I'd rather have you for a friend than any other girl at that school. Most of the other girls are stuck on themselves, but not you. You're responsible, reliable, someone to be trusted."

"How do you know that?" I asked. He was doing just what Karen predicted he would do, saying the things she said he would say. How did she know?

"Give me some credit for being bright enough to see through the phony crap, will you? There's something real about you, something sincere. I've been watching you for a long time, even when I was going steady."

"Watching me? What about Karen?"

"Oh, sure, but that was just my way of finding out more about you."

"Huh?" I pulled my head back and my hair away from his fingers.

He shrugged. "Karen was flirting with me, so I paid attention to her, but after I was with her, I realized you were really who I wanted to be with. All we did was talk about you all the time."

"Talk about me?"

"Exactly. She told me about how you two pretended to go on trips, even a honeymoon."

"She told you we pretended to go on a honeymoon?"

We had talked about the places we thought were right for a honeymoon, but we never pretended to go on one.

"Well, something like that," he said, laughing. He edged closer again. "Whatever, I feel like I've known you a long, long time. I'd like to know you a long, long time," he added, and then he kissed me.

There was something about the moment, about what was happening, that made me suspicious, and it had nothing to do with what I had come to do. It wasn't because of his warm lips on my face or his hands moving up my arms and around to my breasts. It was all just a bit too perfect. An image flashed through my mind. Karen, my love coach, was coaching him, but on how to be with me. Was that ridiculous or not?

"What else did Karen tell you about me?" I asked, pushing him back.

"Nothing terrible. She told me you were the warmest, most loving friend she had, ever had, ever could have. She said she learned a lot from you."

"She said she learned a lot from me?"

"Sure. She said that was what was most interesting about you, how quiet you were and modest, but how much you already knew about life, about relationships, about . . . love," he said, and was at me again.

This time, he pressed his lips harder. He put the tip of his tongue to mine. His hands were under my blouse and his fingers on my breasts, moving over my nipples, lifting the blouse so he could bring his lips to them.

"You want to go into the backseat?" he asked. That was supposed to be my demand, but I was too deep in thought. Anyway, this was no longer happening the way Karen envisioned it would.

"I thought we were going to talk about Karen," I said, "talk about what we could do to help her."

"What can we do? She's gone. Running off. She just wanted to be sure you and I were together before she left us. She cared about you."

His hands were under Karen's skirt. He lifted it a bit and looked.

"Wearing your bikini panties?" he asked, continuing to explore with his fingers. "I guess she was telling the truth. You guys did share everything."

"Wait," I said, pushing on his chest. I moved enough to the right to get out from under him and pull myself back into a sitting position.

"What?"

"Why did you say *your* bikini panties?"

"Because they're yours, right? What's the difference?" he asked, moving toward me again and bringing his lips to my neck. "I've got what we need. I know you are concerned about it. Let's get into the backseat. C'mon. You said you didn't have much time."

This wasn't right. None of this felt right, and it wasn't because I was frightened or because I believed virginity was something to save. Karen couldn't accuse me of having those reasons to be reluctant. I didn't like the way he was rushing us, acting as if I had come solely for one purpose. It made me feel cheap and him a hypocrite. He wasn't with me because he felt I was special. He was with me because he believed I was easy.

"No, Dana," I said. "Just take me back to the post office now."

"What? Why?" he whined. "We've only been gone a few minutes."

"Just take me back," I said.

"I don't get it. I'm not good enough for you or something? Why did you change your mind?"

"Please, just take me back."

He sat back and slapped the steering wheel in frustration, so hard it made me wince.

"There are words for girls like you," he said.

"I don't need to hear them. Let's just go back, Dana. Please."

He didn't start the car. He turned to me again and just stared. I could see his eyes in the moonlight. They looked like two small balls of fire.

"So, why did you meet me, huh? Why did you tell Karen I was the best-looking boy in school, your dream lover? Why did you get me to come to Sandburg, anyway? What is this, some kind of game you two play?" he asked, raising his voice with each question.

"I didn't get you to come here. You said you were going to be here and told me if I didn't show up I was square."

"Because Karen told me you would meet me, that you wanted to meet me. Did you or didn't you? Well? Why would she lie about it? And you put on your famous red bikini panties," he added. "Why?"

I bit down on my lower lip. What could I say? They're not mine? I was still wearing them, wasn't I? And Karen's skirt, too.

I started to cry. I couldn't help it.

"Cut out the act," he snapped.

"I'm not acting."

"You want to know something? I think you're sick. You're both sick. What was it she would tell the other girls, that you're spiritual sisters? You're sisters, all right, but it's not spiritual. It's weirdness that makes you sisters. I guess she got some kind of perverted kick getting me all lathered up about you, making you sound like you were more sophisticated and even I would learn new things, things I never imagined in my best fantasy."

"What did she say?"

"Forget about all that. You know when a girl meets a guy like this, it's as good as making a promise. It's an unwritten agreement, a contract. Your father's a lawyer. You should know that."

"What?"

"What, what, what are you, a light bulb?" he cried, and then just threw open his door and got out.

My heart was thumping. He was really in a rage. Should I just get out and walk away or maybe run away? We hadn't traveled that far, but it was far enough to take me some time to get back to my bike and then home. My father was surely going to be back home by then.

"Dana!" I called, but I didn't see him. I turned and looked back and then in front of the car. Where was he? What was he doing?

Suddenly, the passenger side door was jerked open,

and there he was, but my heart stopped and seemed to drop to my stomach. He was standing there, naked from the waist down, and in the moonlight, I could see he had put on his protection. I was so stunned that I couldn't move. He reached in and pulled me out. I screamed, but he opened the rear door and forced me back into the car, lying over me quickly and forcing me back against the seat. There was no room to maneuver.

"Let's get those red panties off once and for all," he muttered.

I pushed at his shoulders, but his body was too heavy. His hands were on my thighs, tugging at my waist until he had the panties down below my knees.

"Stop!" I screamed. "Please don't do this, Dana. Please," I begged.

He grunted with the effort to have his way. What once had the potential to be romantic and beautiful had turned into something bestial and ugly. This wasn't going to be a memory to call up in our old age, as Karen had promised. It was going to be a memory to bury and struggle forever to forget. How could I stop it?

I don't know where the words came from, but I dipped deeply into some treasured place and drew them up. I spoke calmly, so calmly I even surprised myself, because the calmness gave what I said more authority and strength.

"You don't want to do this. You don't want to be this kind of person, Dana. It will haunt you the rest of your life. You won't be proud of yourself. You'll hate yourself, and you'll think of it every time you're with another girl, even the girl you eventually love and marry. I'm a virgin!" I moaned. "Karen didn't tell you the truth about me."

I felt his body soften and his grip on me loosen, but he kept the side of his head against mine and fought to slow his breathing. After another moment, he rose and backed out of the car. He slammed the door closed. I fixed my clothing and sat back to catch my own breath. Would he return, or was this over?

I heard him come around to the driver's side and open the door. He got in and started the engine. He didn't say anything, and neither did I. I just sat there until he pulled around and drove out to the road and back to the village, stopping at the post office.

"I don't know where she is," he said, without looking back at me. "But you tell her if she calls me again, I'll go to the police. And don't you talk to me or even look at me in school. I want to pretend this never happened, understand?"

"Not any more than I do," I said.

I got out, and he pulled away quickly, his tires squealing as he rounded the turn in the center of the village and then disappeared. I got on my bike and started for home.

And I cried all the way.

15

Harry Pearsons at Heart

As I approached the house, I saw it was dimly lit, just as I had left it, which meant my father was not home yet. My legs were tight from my frantic pedaling, and my heart felt as if it were flopping about madly under my breast. I had to stop and just stand a moment to catch my breath. I suddenly noticed all the stars and the moon. It had been as if I had ridden with blinders on, my head down, fleeing from the disaster with Dana. I didn't know how I had made it home without going off the road. I took some more deep breaths and then walked my bike up the driveway and pulled up the garage door.

After I put on the garage lights, I stowed my bike and closed the garage door behind me. I was happy my father was not home yet, because I knew I looked a mess, and there was just no way to avoid some kind of explosion if he ever found out what had just happened to me. I entered the house, half expecting to see Karen standing there anxiously waiting to greet me. She wasn't, and it was quiet, so quiet that for a moment I wondered if she had gone off again to stay in Harry's mother's apartment or someplace else.

I glanced at my watch. I had been gone a little less than an hour. There was probably still plenty of time before my father would be home. I started up the attic stairway and slowly opened the door. Of course, it was pitch dark, but the moonlight was still bright enough to illuminate the large room and at least silhouette most of the furniture.

"Karen?" I called in a loud whisper.

"Back so soon?" I heard her respond.

At first, I didn't see her, so I opened the door a little wider to let in more light and saw her lying on the sofa, naked.

"What are you doing?" I asked.

She sat up and brushed back her hair. "I was just thinking about you, imagining what you were doing, trying to feel what you were feeling."

"Oh?" How odd, I thought.

"Don't sound so surprised. It helped me pass the time. But why are you back already?"

She reached for her clothes and quickly started to dress.

"It was terrible," I said. "It wasn't the way you thought it would be."

She stopped dressing. "Why? What happened?"

"He tried to rape me," I said, my chin quivering.

"What? Why? Why would he have to do that? What did you do?" she asked, sounding as if she were accusing me, as if it had to be my fault.

"It wasn't what I did," I said. "It's what he did!"

"Tell me everything. Start at the beginning, and don't leave out a syllable," she said, patting the sofa.

I sat, and she finished dressing.

"Well?" she said when I hesitated.

I took a deep breath and began. "I biked to the post office and got into his car. We drove off, and he pulled into a driveway not far away, where he said his cousin was building a house for someone. There was a house being built, but I have no way of knowing if his cousin is involved."

"Oh, c'mon, Zipporah. I don't need those kinds of details. Stop babbling like an idiot. What did he say to you? What did he do?"

"I can't help it. I'm still shaking," I said. My tears felt hot as they ran down my cheeks.

She put her arm around me. "Okay, okay. Relax. You're here now, safe with me in our nest. Take a deep breath, and tell me exactly what happened."

"He started to talk about you and me and compared me to other girls at school, just as you said he would, complimenting me, saying how sincere a person I was. What a good friend. Reliable."

"Good. So?"

"But then he suggested I had been with other boys."

"Other boys?"

"Lots of other boys!"

"Pretending he knew you weren't such a goody-goody and therefore you shouldn't be one with him," she said, nodding. "Another male trick. I call it setting the sexual table for their feast."

"He said you told him I was the school's biggest well-kept secret."

"He said I did? What a liar."

"Then he saw the red bikini panties and talked about how we shared everything. He said you told him they were mine."

"Another lie. He probably thought he was stroking your ego or something."

"I started to get a bad feeling. Everything was moving so fast. There was nothing romantic about it. The moon could have been behind a wall of clouds. He was the one who demanded we go into the backseat."

"He got ahead of you. I was afraid of that. What did you do?"

"I wasn't comfortable with him anymore. I told him to take me back, and he became very angry and said you and I were just weird. He didn't call me any names, but I knew he thought I was just a tease."

"That's just his way of dealing with rejection. Any girl who doesn't just roll over for a boy is a tease in their eyes," she said.

"He said you had told him I was so sexually sophisticated I could teach him things."

"Exaggeration, exaggeration, exaggeration. In his dreams, maybe. Of course, I made you sound desirable, but he filled in the blanks himself. That's what boys do, Zipporah, fantasize. But you said he tried to rape you."

"He got out of the car, furious. I was going to get out, too, and just run back to the post office, when he opened the door on my side. He was standing there naked from the waist down."

"Really? What happened then?"

"He pulled me out and shoved me into the rear. He was on me before I could resist, and then he practically ripped off the panties."

"And?"

"And then I stopped him."

"How?"

"I told him he would hate himself forever."

"That was enough to stop him?"

"I said a little more and added I was a virgin, and he stopped, got dressed, took me back, and told me to tell you that if you ever call him again, he'll go to the police."

"Like I ever would," she said. "Boys and men are all the same. Selfish, wanting to please themselves at any cost. They're all Harry Pearsons at heart."

"Did you say any of those things about me? Did you tell him I liked him, thought he was the best-looking boy in school?"

"Of course, I told him you thought he was good-looking. Which he is, but I never made you out to be some tramp. Why do men try to turn every girl they meet into a tramp? When they get married, they hate the thought of anyone thinking that about their wives. I know Harry hated it, but look what he did with me. I'm sorry things didn't work out the way I wanted them to work out for you. It was supposed to be a great experience, so we would have more to share. There'll be other opportunities. Don't worry about it."

"I'm not worried about that. It was a horrible experience. He was like Dr. Jekyll and Mr. Hyde. I can't imagine how you were ever with him."

"I had the experience to handle him. He didn't dare try anything like that with me. I had him eating out of my hand, anyway. Let's forget about Dana. Let's not even mention his name."

"I can't just forget about it that easily, Karen. I'm still shaking."

"Yes, I can see that. I'm sorry," she said, and put her arm around me to hold me again. She kissed me on the forehead the way my mother often did. "Maybe I'll think of a way to get even with him."

"No. I don't want to have anything more to do with him," I said quickly. "Besides, we have other, more important things to think about now. We shouldn't have spent all this time and energy on Dana Martin, anyway. It was crazy to try to live normally and be like any other girl our age. We're not," I said, feeling the hysteria creeping into my voice. My episode with Dana made me feel as if my bones had been rattled and were still vibrating through my spine and my ribs. Even my legs were still trembling.

"Yes, yes, you're right. You're always so sensible. We really are like two parts of the same person, me the wild one and you the sensible one. Passion and thought, that's what we are, but without those two, you're not a complete person. What we do is complete each other. That's why we're so close."

"Maybe," I said, "but I think we should lean more toward thought for now."

"Exactly."

We heard the sound of the garage door going up.

"My father's back," I said, rising.

"Get yourself together, Zipporah. Calm yourself. Wash your face with cold water before greeting him," she advised. "You don't want him to know about Dana. It will just make all that worse and blow every-thing out of proportion."

"Everything is out of proportion," I said, with a little more anger and disgust than I had intended. I lowered my head as I walked to the doorway.

"You want me to leave again? Is that what you're saying? You blame what happened between you and

Dana on me, and now you want me to leave? You think I'm getting you deeper and deeper into trouble."

"No, no, of course not. I'm sorry. I'm still shaken up, but I'll be all right," I said, and left quickly, hurrying down the short stairway to the bathroom, where I did what she said. I washed my face in cold water, fixed my clothes, and brushed my hair. I heard my father calling to me from below.

"I'm in the bathroom," I shouted, after opening the door to stick my head out.

"Okay," he said from the bottom of the stairs. "I'm just checking. Come down when you can," he said. "I need to talk to you."

I sat on the covered toilet and kept taking deep breaths until I felt I was calm enough to face him.

"Hey," he said, looking up from where he was sitting in his chair in the living room when I entered. "Is everything all right?"

"Yes."

"No one called? I was expecting Jesse to call," he added quickly.

"No," I said.

He grimaced and then looked very suspicious. "That's not like him."

Oh, no, I thought the moment he rose from his chair. He walked past me to the kitchen and went to the phone. I heard him dialing. "Hey, big shot. I thought you were calling to let us know your exact schedule. What do you mean? Zipporah was home."

I stood there listening to the silence, imagining what my brother was telling him. He must have called while I was in the village meeting Dana. What would

I say? Making up lies to cover myself did not come easily to me, and I always had this fear that because my father was a trial attorney who was skilled in cross-examining people, he would see through any lie I told.

"Okay. So, let me get that down for your mother. Sounds good."

What? Well, it's not easy for her." He listened again. "Couldn't hurt," he added. "Okay. Have a good time. Bye."

I waited, my heart thumping.

"That's funny," my father said, returning to the living room. "Jesse said he called about a half hour, forty minutes ago, and you didn't answer."

"I was up in the attic," I said. "I guess I didn't hear it ring."

"The attic? Why?"

I sat and stared at the floor. "Karen and I made that our special place. I just like to go up there and think, be by myself."

"Oh, I see. Helps you to feel closer to her, huh?"

I looked up sharply. If he only knew how true that was.

"Yes," I said.

"Look. You have to stop beating yourself to death about this, Zipporah. There's no way anyone could or would think you had any blame. She was your best friend. She didn't want you to tell anyone what was going on in her house, and you respected her wishes. Friends are precious. The famous English novelist E. M. Forster wrote, 'If I had to choose between betraying my country and betraying my friend, I hope I should have the guts to betray my country.' "

"Really?"

"Yes," my father said, smiling. "Friendship is valuable. Your country is important, but loyalty to someone you love or who loves you is harder to betray."

He kissed my cheek.

"Oh," he said, returning to his chair. "There was a message back at the office for me from that detective, Simon. It just said to call tomorrow. I suspect it has something to do with what we talked about yesterday. I gave the information to the right people at the district attorney's office to get things under way. Don't worry. I'll set the ground rules for any more discussions between them and you," he said firmly. "They'll treat you with respect, or else."

"Okay, Daddy. Thanks. I'm going up to finish my homework," I said.

"By the way, your brother just told me he's cutting his visit with his roommate's family short. He'll be back next Sunday."

"Why?"

"He's worried about you," he said. "That's nice," he added. "Of course, he'll see the new car. Let him be surprised. Since he's being so nice and worrying about you, we'll let him take a ride in it, huh?"

I smiled, but my thoughts weren't about gratitude. They were about Karen and what I had to tell her to do. She had to leave before Jesse returned. It wouldn't be easy hiding her from him.

I started up the stairs and stopped.

She was standing there, just in the shadows.

"I heard everything," she whispered.

I looked back quickly to be sure my father was nowhere in sight and couldn't hear. Then I hurried up. She went directly into my room, and I followed. I couldn't believe that she had decided to take such a risk at this time.

"Why did you come down from the attic while my father's here?" I asked in whisper.

"I thought after all that's just happened, I had better hear everything I can firsthand," she said. "Don't worry. I'll get back up there without him hearing me. He usually watches television for a while this time in the evening." She smiled. "I know his routine."

"How?"

"There were times I came down and spied on your parents without you or them knowing."

"You did what?"

"Don't worry. I'm a trained church mouse."

She sat on my bed. Hearing her tell me this added to my sense of guilt and made me feel like more of a traitor to my own family. I had made it possible for her to snoop on my parents. What else had she observed?

"What do you mean, you spied on them? When, exactly?"

"Oh, there were times when you were gone but your mother was home before going off to her shift, and there were times when your father appeared unexpectedly," she added.

"Unexpectedly?"

She smiled. "What do they call that, afternoon delight? It's nice to see people married that long still have great passion for each other."

I felt the blood rush into my face. "What are you telling me, Karen?"

"Don't be thick. There's nothing wrong or dirty about it. They're married."

"You watched them?"

"Well, not exactly watched. I listened," she said. "I was bored sick! It helped me pass the time," she said, raising her voice.

I looked back at the door.

"Quiet," I snapped in a loud whisper.

"He's already got the television on." She looked at her watch. "I can even tell you what he's probably watching. Don't look so shocked, Zipporah. I always paid a lot of attention to what your parents did and said when I was here. They've always been . . . fascinating to me. All I've known, especially these past few years, is a mother who was so into herself she could examine her own kidneys. Besides, we're sisters," she added. "Do you think I would tell anyone anything I heard or saw in this house? It's become our house. Whether your parents know it or not, they've adopted me."

She smiled.

"Right?"

I shook my head. What was she saying? She was scaring me more and more.

"Adopted you?"

"You know what I mean. Not literally, legally adopted me, although you know I always wish they could. What I mean is, right now, thanks to you, they're providing me food and shelter. Don't blame me for imagining that they provide love as well. Or do you think they hate me now?"

"No, they don't hate you. Of course not. My father and mother are very concerned about you. That's all I hear from them."

"So?" She raised her arms. "That's why I say they've adopted me." Her expression hardened. "No one else but you and your parents really cares about me, least of all my own mother. Look at what she let happen."

I nodded. She was right. How could I be angry at her for anything? I might not have acted any differently if I were in her place, not that I ever could be.

"Okay. If you were listening, you heard what my father said about the detective. I'm worried about being questioned again by the police. I guess you were right. I should have kept my trap shut. Now I have to be in the spotlight again."

"Don't worry. We'll work it out," she said. She rose. "Let's think about it. What can you tell them? What do you actually know?"

"Just what you told me," I said.

"Exactly. What did I tell you? Be specific. Go on. Imagine you're in the police station. What did Karen Stoker tell you about her stepfather?"

"That he came into your room at night."

"Her room," she corrected.

"Her room. That he groped her and then he forced himself on her, especially when her mother wasn't around."

"Didn't she tell her mother about all this?"

"She said she tried, but her mother wouldn't listen, and she was afraid the more she pushed it, the more her mother would think she was only trying to turn her against Harry. She said her mother even ignored him being violent. I did see a bruise on her arm one morning, and she wouldn't talk about it. She acted as if she was ashamed about it. Oh. That's when you told me about your headaches . . ."

"She told you."

"She told me, and she even went to the nurse because of them. I already told them that, but now I'm telling them why."

"Exactly. Perfect. So, there it is. Simple. You can't give any more detail than that, Zipporah. Nothing to it, really. Just tell it like you just told it to me, and that's it. It will be my mother's problem after that. She'll be the one under suspicion. They won't accept her denials and her see-no-evil, hear-no-evil routine. The nurse will confirm I was in her office. The right amount of suspicion will be raised. And if I know this town, it will leak out eventually, and the chatterboxes will be open. Darlene will speed up her departure, believe me," she added. "It's just a matter of a little more time."

She did make it sound so simple, so matter-of-fact and predictable. From where did she get such confidence? She should be more frightened and nervous than I was. She smiled, and then she yawned and stretched.

"I'm tired," she said. "It's been a long day. You must be exhausted, too, considering what you've been through. Let's both get some sleep."

She started for the door and stopped. "I heard your father say your brother was coming home earlier than expected. What was that bit about a new car?"

"My father's bought a sports car."

"That you'll be able to drive, too, after you have your license?"

"Yes."

She stood there, thinking. I could see the envy washing through her face.

"And your brother will be here soon," she said, almost in a whisper to herself.

"Yes, he will. What will we do about that?"

She snapped back to attention. "Nothing. If we kept it all from your parents, why shouldn't we be able to keep it from him? Besides, he's not going to lie around the house, is he? He's supposed to go to work with your father's agency, right?"

"Right," I said.

"So there," she said, and opened the door.

"But how much longer can we do this, risk your being discovered?" I asked.

She thought a moment. "The house will protect me," she said.

"What?"

"Remember? Lucy Doral killed her husband in this house, and the house kept the secret."

She laughed silently and then slipped out the door. I watched her practically float up the stairway to the attic. She was that quiet. She opened and closed the door with as much noise as a breeze blowing through, and moments later, she was one with the darkness above and gone just like a dream.

Below, my father was laughing at something he had heard and seen on television. I didn't know what he was watching. I never paid much attention to it.

But Karen knew.

She was more of a member of this family than I had ever imagined she could be.

Fatigued and drowning in many emotions, I prepared for bed and cuddled my pillow. All I wanted to do was escape into that world of dreams where everything real was excluded and everything unpleasant was soon forgotten. A little while later, I vaguely sensed my father had come up to bed himself and peeked in to see me. He turned off a light I had forgotten to turn off, fixed my blanket the way he used to when I was a little girl, and then just touched my cheek as if he wanted to be sure I was really still there. I didn't open my eyes, but I could see him standing there, gazing down at me, a soft, somewhat sad smile written on his face.

All parents knew that someday, their children wouldn't be there; they'd be gone to become parents themselves or to find their way in the world, and what was once real to our fathers and mothers would be like a dream to them. We'd all become ghost children.

Could Karen's mother really be happy now? Was there a degree of selfishness so high that she or anyone like her could tolerate the absence of her child, her daughter? For people like that, children were only burdens. They didn't come from within, but in their minds, they were rained down upon them in a storm of divine wrath, perhaps as punishment for past sins or lust.

I couldn't imagine what it was like to be Karen now, to think of yourself as a form of punishment, never to be appreciated. She used her bitterness and anger to cloak her sadness. I imagined her alone, sobbing in the darkness above me, now that I couldn't see. Instead of cuddling with a pillow and hoping for candy dreams, she was clinging to herself, afraid to let go all night, afraid she would merely come apart and become like the artifacts and antiques stored away and forgotten in the attic.

What could be more pathetic than a nest without eggs, without birds?

Either I imagined it, or my father whispered, "Good night, Zipper."

That made me think of Jesse, and suddenly, I was no longer afraid or troubled by his homecoming. Maybe I would confide in him. He would find a solution, I thought. After all, he was my big brother, and somehow, because we were closer in age than I was with my parents, I now felt I could have a greater reliance on him. He would be more understanding, compassionate, and forgiving.

My father slipped out of my room and closed the door softly.

Darkness took me, a willing prisoner, and morning came like an uninvited rescuer, but I could do little about it. Sunshine unraveled the day as if it were rolling out a rug of fire upon which I had to walk. I feared so much that awaited me: Dana Martin at school whispering to his friends while they looked my way, the police detective waiting for me in the police station, Karen's mother looking at me with anger and distaste, and my own parents wondering just how much more entangled in all this I really was and, therefore, they really were.

I searched my mirror for the proper mask, a face to put on that would hide my tension and guilt.

But all I could see was the face I had as a little girl, alone and desperate, full of worry, searching, reaching, depending on the strong hands of my parents and waiting to be grasped.

Too soon, I feared, I had let go.

16

She Can't Hide Forever

My father decided to take me to school the next morning, and during the ride, he tried very hard to keep the conversation between us happy and light, talking about the new car, Jesse's impending return, the upcoming summer months, some ideas he had for little excursions to lakes and even to New England, maybe Cape Cod, before the summer ended. Listening to him go on and on about the things we could do as a family, I almost did forget all that had happened.

Unfortunately, the moment we pulled up to a stop in the school parking lot, I saw Dana Martin getting out of his car. He barely glanced my way, however, and a moment later was trading playful punches with some of his buddies. Before he reached the building, he joined his most recent girlfriend, Lois Morris, and put his arm around her shoulders. She didn't push him away. Instead, she laid her head against his shoulder. It was as if they had never stopped being together. For a split second, I felt like some sort of time traveler who was now thrown back to an earlier period. I'd find

Karen inside, and everything that had happened would dissolve like a bad dream.

Just before I stepped out of the car, my father touched my arm to turn me back.

"I might be busy today, Zipporah, and if I can't make it back early enough, I'm putting off your interview with the police. They know I insist on being there. It might not happen today. I know you'd like to get it over with quickly, but my court schedule is such that . . ."

"That's all right. Whenever," I tossed back at him, as if it was of very little concern.

He smiled. "That's great. That's my girl. Take it all in stride. It will all be over sooner than you think."

I gave him the best smile of confidence I could manage and headed for the building. Just as I hoped and anticipated, Dana continued to ignore me the rest of the day. For one second, I thought I caught him glaring angrily my way, but he waved to someone behind me, and that was that. I kept to myself the entire day. Even Sally was off talking with someone else at lunch, and for a while, I felt not only alone but invisible. What would happen now, after Karen? I wondered. Eventually, she would have to come out of hiding, and that would be that. Would I make any new friends here? Would I be forever alone, stained by my friendship with her, a friendship I had once cherished more than anything?

I did the best I could in school, but for long periods, I found myself drifting, not so much daydreaming as just staring blankly, like someone whose brain had just turned off. I barely heard anything or noticed anything around me. Bells to end classes and move us all along were practically the only sound to which I paid any attention. I boarded the school bus at the end of the day and made my way back to my seat to stare aimlessly out the window.

In fact, I was in such a daze I didn't realize the bus had arrived at my house. Mr. Tooey called my name, and I felt myself snap back to reality.

"Oh," I muttered, and hurriedly walked down the aisle. He looked at me oddly as I passed him and went down the steps. The door closed, and the bus went along, leaving me standing alone in the afternoon sun, the breeze gently lifting leaves and moving the blades of wild grass in what looked like a quiet ballet of Mother Nature. Head down, I started for the front door and then jerked my eyes upward when I heard it open.

I spun around to look behind me and up and down the road.

Was she mad? Insane? Appearing in broad daylight? My words of reprimand for Karen were lunging toward the tip of my tongue when I turned back. I stopped in utter amazement.

Jesse was standing there, looking out at me, that big impish grin carved around his firm, strong mouth, his light blue eyes twinkling with amusement.

"Hey, Zipper," he said.

Still disbelieving what I saw, I shook my head. He laughed harder.

"You're not supposed to be here until Sunday," I finally managed.

He shrugged. "I made a spontaneous decision. I wasn't enjoying myself knowing what you were all going through back here. Mom can try to hide it, but her voice betrays her, and I've learned how to read between Dad's sentences."

"Do they know you're here?"

"Not yet," he said. "Just arrived about two hours ago. I drove my car around behind the garage to surprise them."

I remained standing there, looking up at him. Two hours ago? What about Karen? Did she realize someone was in the house? Did she do anything to give herself away? Did she hear him drive up? Did he hear anything? I held my breath, expecting the second shoe to drop, but he continued smiling.

"You coming in, or are you planning on camping out tonight?"

"What? Oh."

I walked up the steps, and he stood there until he could reach out to hug me. It came as such a surprise that I almost dropped my books. I couldn't remember him ever hugging me like that.

"Sorry about what you're going through," he said. Then, feeling embarrassed by his show of emotion himself, he released me quickly and went into the house.

I followed, my confused heart thumping from fear and from joy.

"So?" Jesse said, folding his arms across his chest and standing in the living-room doorway. "How are you doing?"

"Okay," I said.

"Come on," he urged, leading me into the living room. I followed. He sat on the sofa and looked up at me. "Tell me about it."

"What do you want to know?"

"You must have had some idea, some inkling, it had gotten so bad. What happened?"

I sat in Daddy's chair but held on to my books. I had no doubt my father would tell him what I had revealed, so I had no reason to keep any of that secret anymore.

"I told Daddy everything I knew."

"Which is what?"

"Her stepfather was coming into her room at night."

His eyes widened. "You mean, to have sex with her?"

I nodded.

"Holy smokes." He sat back, shaking his head. "I didn't know Harry Pearson much at all, but what I saw of him, I'd never have thought it. He was always such a pleasant guy. He seemed to be trying very hard to get Karen to like him, to accept him as her father."

I just sat there staring at him.

"She told you all about it?" he asked.

"Yes," I said.

"Wow. So, what about her mother?"

I explained it the way Karen had explained it to me. He listened, shaking his head.

"Boy, she had it real tough," he said. "I feel sorry for her now. Before, I just thought . . . but now. She should come forward and tell the police. It would make a difference, especially if she were fighting him off at the time."

"She doesn't think anyone would believe her, because her mother won't or hasn't said anything about it and would deny it. It would be her word against her mother's, and if your own mother doesn't support you . . ."

His eyes narrowed as he looked at me, nodding slowly. "You sound as if you've spoken to her since, Zipporah. Have you? Well?" he followed quickly.

"I meant she didn't think anyone would believe her. That's why she never told anyone but me," I quickly corrected.

"Dad told me the police believe she went to New York City. Something about a phone call."

I nodded. The police did believe that. How I hated lying to everyone, but if I were careful with my words, I could skate on the border between falsehood and the truth, and my conscience wouldn't bother me as much. I wasn't ready to confide fully in Jesse. I wasn't yet sure it was wise to do it. I wanted to. I needed an ally, but I was still too afraid.

"Where could she go in New York? Did she have any friends in New York?"

"I don't know of any."

"She couldn't go to any relatives, that's for sure."

I nodded in agreement and breathed easier. At least, there was no question that Karen had made noise after Jesse arrived.

"What's it like for you at school?"

I described it to him, leaving out all the business with Dana Martin, of course.

"Yeah, well, at least you'll find out who could be a real friend and who couldn't," he said. "I better finish getting my stuff unpacked, clothes for washing and all," he said, rising. "I saw from Mom's schedule on the bulletin board that she'll be home by four today. What about Dad?"

"He said he might be working late. Otherwise, he was going to take me to see the police before dinner."

"To see the police again? Why?"

"He told them what I told him, and they want to talk to me about it."

"Oh. Right. Good," he said. "You do that, no matter what Karen's mother says or does. I'll go along, too," he offered. "If Dad says okay, that is."

"Thanks, Jesse."

"You'll be all right," he said. "I brought you something from college."

"You did?"

"Come on up to my room, and I'll show you," he said, and I followed him up the stairs, gazing toward the attic door as I turned into his room. It remained shut tight.

Jesse went to his suitcase and took out a sweatshirt from his college.

"Should fit," he said. "College girls like them to be a little large."

"Thanks," I said. "I'll wear it to school tomorrow."

"Good. I'll finish up here and meet you downstairs to greet Mom. I'll pop out from behind a door or something."

I laughed. It was so good having him home that I didn't care about Karen being hidden upstairs. She'd have to figure out how to handle it herself or go. Maybe this was all for the best. Finally, something would bring it to an end. I went to my room to change into more comfortable things and then went down to wait for my mother. I started to set the table for dinner. That would be her first clue, the extra plate, I thought, and laughed to myself at what her reaction was going to be.

The phone rang. It was my father telling me what he feared happening had happened. He would be delayed and might not even make dinner. It was on the tip of my tongue to tell him Jesse was home, but I thought Jesse wanted to surprise him.

"In any case, I've spoken with the police, and our interview with them is tomorrow after school. I'll be picking you up at school, and we're going right to the township police office," he told me. "Don't worry about it. You'll just tell them what you know, what you were told, and that will be that."

"Okay," I said.

"See you as soon as I can. Tell your mother for me."

"I will."

Not twenty minutes later, my mother drove in. She shouted for me as soon as she came in from the garage. Jesse was still upstairs.

"In here," I called back from the dining room.

She stood in the doorway, looking in.

"How's my roast? Did you get it started in time?"

"Yes," I said. "Daddy might not make dinner. He called a little while ago. He said he'll let us know."

"He's working harder than ever. Did you find the corn on the cob?"

"Peeled and ready. The water is in the pot. The string beans are set. I put the bread in the warmer."

"Good. How was your day?"

"Okay," I said, without any enthusiasm.

"It'll get better," she promised. I thought she was just going to turn and go upstairs to shower and change out of her uniform without noticing anything. She actually started away from the dining room and then stopped and slowly turned back. "Why are there four plates?" she asked. "Who's coming to dinner?"

The expression on her face told me she didn't think of Jesse. She was thinking of Karen. It made my heart stop and start, and for a moment, I couldn't respond. Then, Jesse called out to her from the stairway.

"Jesse! What are you doing here?"

"I found out I live here," he said.

"Where's your car?"

"Hidden. I wanted to surprise you and Dad."

"You did that, you little devil."

I stepped up to the doorway and watched them hug and kiss. He explained again why he felt more comfortable coming back early, and she smiled at him and looked at me with an expression that clearly told me how much she loved him. Jesse was always perfect in my mother's eyes. I used to be jealous, but now, I thought he deserved being loved more. After all, he wasn't hiding anything as terrible as I was. He was being a good son. When would I be a good daughter again?

We had to start dinner without Daddy, but Jesse kept us so entertained by his stories about his college experiences that we didn't realize how much time had gone by until we heard the garage door opening.

"I'll start warming everything up," Mama said, rising from the table.

Jesse sat back, a wide smile of anticipation on his face.

"Sorry," we heard Daddy sing out as he came in from the garage.

"You should be," Jesse called back.

Daddy said nothing. He just walked into the dining room.

"What the . . . why are you here?"

"Everyone asks me the same question. I'm beginning to feel unwanted."

Daddy smiled. "So? What happened? You told me
you were coming home on Sunday."

"I figured you needed professional help back here,"
Jesse said.

"Yeah, right. You just wanted a good home-cooked
meal, I bet."

"That, too," Jesse said, and they hugged.

"Hey, where's your car?"

"Behind the garage."

"You little sneak," Daddy said, but he smiled.

Tears came to my eyes. Daddy needed Jesse more, I
thought, more than ever. He, too, needed the good son.
Jesse had gotten into what I called boys' trouble from
time to time, but it was all Huckleberry Finn trouble,
pranks and silliness. Nothing he ever did and no one
he ever had as a friend ever brought the sort of darkness I had brought into our home.

"Everything's getting warmed up for you, Michael,"
Mama told him.

"I'll be right down," he said. "I hope, there's something left," he added, winking at Jesse.

"He looks tired," Jesse said as soon as Daddy left
the room.

Mama just glanced at him. "He likes working hard,"
she muttered, but I knew and felt his fatigue was coming from some other source. Who knew what he had to
contend with at work because of the Pearson tragedy
and my involvement?

"I was thinking," Jesse told him when he returned
and sat at the table, "that I would go with you and Zipporah tomorrow to see the police."

Daddy looked up quickly.

"She told me all about it," Jesse added.

"I don't think so, Jesse. It will look like we're worried about something. I'd like to make it as short and sweet as possible for Zipporah, but thanks."

Jesse glanced at me. He looked disappointed, but he didn't argue.

After dinner, he and Daddy went into the home office to talk, and I went up to do my homework after I helped Mama with the dishes. She kept telling me to go, that it was fine, but I was stalling, mainly because I was afraid of confronting Karen. By now, she surely knew Jesse had returned. The attic door was still shut tight. I sat in my room and listened as hard as I could but heard nothing, not even a creak in the ceiling. The tension was driving me mad. Was she cowering in a dark corner, frightened so badly she couldn't move? Was she racking her brain, trying to figure out what to do? Had she been able to get herself enough water, something to eat, before Jesse had arrived?

I couldn't stand it. It was truly as if I were the one hidden in the attic, suffering, not Karen. As quietly as I could, I went out and stood at the top of the stairway, listening. Mama was still in the kitchen. The dishwasher had been started. Daddy and Jesse were still in the office. I had to take my chances now or spend the night worrying. I wouldn't sleep. That was for sure.

It was better just to hurry up the stairs the way someone might walk over hot coals. I was hoping not to give the steps a chance to moan. I stepped as close to the corners as I could, since they creaked less that way. Opening the attic door, I peered into the darkness. The moon was sheathed in a thick cloud, so there was no illumination spilling through the windows. It took a moment for my eyes to get used to the pitch darkness. I made out the usual silhouettes of furnishings, but I heard nothing.

"Karen?" I whispered. "Karen, do you know Jesse's back?"

I waited in the doorway, keeping one ear turned toward the downstairs to listen for any sign of Mama or Jesse coming up. I heard nothing in either ear.

"Karen, I just have a moment. Please. Do you know? Are you all right?"

I waited but still heard nothing. Was she too frightened even to speak to me? Did I chance going in further, maybe putting on the dim ceiling fixtures? Would that put her into a greater panic and then expose us both?

"Karen?" I tried one more time, listened, and then backed out and slowly, as quietly as I could, closed the attic door. She probably had all she needed for tonight, I thought. She had probably decided not to take the chance I was willing to take. Perhaps she was smarter. What could I do if she didn't have what she needed now, anyway?

I practically tiptoed down the stairway, but I didn't have to. Mama, Daddy, and Jesse were all talking at once now in the living room below. I heard their laughter, too. For a long moment, I just stood there at the top of the stairway, listening, a smile on my face. It sounded like old times. I wanted so much to be part of it, to descend those steps and dive into the warmth of their love, to turn my back on the attic and all it contained. I felt guilty about it. I had this raft in the middle of this sea of turmoil, and I could swim to it and be safe. However, it would be truly as if I were leaving Karen out there to drown, deserting her to save myself. No matter which way I turned, I felt terrible.

The best thing to do was throw myself at my homework. I had lots of reading to do and a theme paper to write. It worked. I lost track of time and didn't look up until I heard Jesse come to my doorway and tap on the jamb.

"You all right?" he asked.

"No. I hate Mr. Whittier. He expects us all to be Hemingways."

Jesse laughed and came over to my desk. He glanced at my paper.

"Can I?" he asked, picking up a pen.

"Go ahead," I said. "Have a ball."

He circled words, found grammatical errors and spelling mistakes, and made some quick suggestions.

"I'll never be good at this," I moaned.

"It's all right. Not so bad. You probably would have picked up most of it in proofreading, anyway. The trick is to do it early, first, and put it away. Whenever you look at something after time passes, you can see the mistakes clearly."

The way he was looking at me, I thought he meant a lot more than a school theme paper. I nodded, thanked him, and made the corrections.

"I'm going to do some chores around the house tomorrow. The back lawn is wild. Bushes need trimming, and I promised Mom I'd fix two shutters. Later, I'll ride your bike into the village for some exercise. Don't worry about the police thing. Dad's got it under control, I'm sure."

"Thanks," I said. I glanced at the ceiling. What

would Karen do now? She would have to wait for him to leave. His arrival meant she would be trapped up there for much longer periods of time, and our time together would be quite reduced.

It's over, I thought. This is coming to a fast end. It brought me a sense of relief but also a sense of deep sadness. I listened as hard as I could before I went to sleep, but there wasn't a creak that was unusual. She was probably asleep herself, I thought, and closed my eyes. The tension had driven me deeper into exhaustion than I had anticipated. In moments, I was drifting off, not waking until the first rays of morning light snuck through the curtains to twirl about my face and draw me back into reality.

Everyone was up early. Jesse was down before our parents, in fact, and had put up the coffee. He behaved like a starving student, preparing scrambled eggs, sliced fruit, some bacon, and a pile of toast. As if their laughter had been put on pause, Mama and Daddy broke into immediate hysterics watching him shovel the food into his mouth. I wished I had half his appetite.

Dad drove me to school again. All the way, he talked about Jesse and how proud he was of him because of his school grades.

"Despite his activities and being a freshman, he's doing better than I did. Don't tell him I told you," Daddy added. "No sense blowing his ego up any more than necessary. The truth is, I nearly flunked out after the first semester. My mind was on other things."

I shook my head in disbelief.

"You did?"

"Yes, Zipporah, we all make mistakes and perform

less than perfectly. Don't you think you have to live up to any legends here."

Was he making all this up to help me feel better about myself and about what I had kept secret concerning Karen's terrible experiences with her step-father?

"There is good reason for distinguishing between the actions of minors and the actions of adults," he added. "Not that it serves as a total excuse, mind you, but at least it helps us understand. Do you understand?" he asked.

"Yes," I said. I did. He was giving me an out, and I was eager to wrap myself around it as I would a teddy bear.

The school day went much the same as it had the day before for me, except that I was somewhat more alert in class. One of the other girls, a borderline zero in Karen's eyes, Jackie Forman, was actually very nice to me.

"It must be hard for you," she said between classes when we walked beside each other in the hallway. "You're probably in a bigger daze about it than anyone."

I nodded.

Later, she joined me at lunch, and then Sally and another girl, Terri Buckner, a friend of hers, joined us, too. No one talked about Karen. Our conversation was built around our classes, some upcoming activities at school, and the impending summer break, what everyone was planning on doing. For a little while, at least, I felt almost normal. I believed I could come back from all this and enjoy my high school years. What was it my grandmother, Daddy's mother, always said? "This too shall pass."

Everything does eventually, I thought.

Maybe I would be all right after all. Maybe even Karen would.

Daddy was there waiting for me in the parking lot. I had been so happy about making new friends and participating in school, I actually forgot about what awaited me. The sight of him filled my stomach with snowballs. I hurried to his car and got in.

"How are you doing?"

"Good," I said. "I got an A on my English paper. Mr. Whittier stopped me to tell me before I went to my last class. He had corrected the papers during his free period."

"Wow, that's great."

"Jesse helped me," I confessed.

Daddy smiled. "That's legal," he said. "Any familial assistance on a theme paper is okay. That's why they call it homework." We both laughed.

I don't deserve him, I thought. I don't deserve the family I have.

We pulled into the parking spot for visitors at the police station twenty minutes later. He shut the engine off but sat there.

"The big question they are going to have for you, Zipporah, is why didn't you tell them all this the first time? Have you thought about that?"

"I swore to Karen that I would never tell," I said. "I promised."

He nodded. "Okay. Let's go."

This time, when we entered the chief's office, there was a tape recorder on the chief's desk. The two detectives were in the seats they had been in, and the chief was behind his desk. Chairs had been set out for us.

"Do you have any objections to our recording this

interview?" Lieutenant Cooper asked Daddy immediately.

"No," Daddy said. He nodded at me, and we sat. "I'd like a copy of the transcription, however."

"Understood," Lieutenant Cooper said. He turned to me. "So, apparently there was some significant information that you withheld the last time we spoke."

"Great way to begin with a cooperative minor," Daddy muttered.

Lieutenant Cooper glanced at him and smirked.

"There were things you could have told us before but didn't," he corrected. "Why not?"

"I had promised Karen I wouldn't tell anyone," I said. "She was very embarrassed about it, ashamed. She told me it made her feel dirty."

"Okay, but now you know this is about as serious as things could be, and you are required to give us any information that pertains to the situation, right? You're not going to keep anything else secret?"

"She came to tell you what she was told," my father said very slowly. "Why don't you just get to that without all these dramatics?"

"Jesus," Detective Simon muttered. Daddy glanced at him.

"Go ahead, Cooper," Chief Keiser pressed.

"All right. Tell us what you told your father Karen said was happening."

I began, describing the first incident as detailed as I could manage without blushing and being embarrassed myself. As I spoke, they all stared at me, only Chief Keiser looking shocked.

"How many of these incidents occurred? To your knowledge, that is?"

"Nothing she has said so far is to her knowledge," my father corrected. "She is telling you what she was told, not what she witnessed. I just want to make that clear."

"Right. How many incidents like that did Karen Stoker describe?"

"I don't remember any number. She just said it was getting worse and worse, and when I asked her to explain, she was too embarrassed to get into any more detail about it. One time," I added, "I came into town to buy an ice cream, and I saw her walking and crying. She didn't want to talk then, but later, when I asked, she told me it was because of what was happening. She told me she was having headaches because of it, too. I already told you about the headaches."

"Right. Okay, let's get to what you claim she said about her mother's involvement or lack of involvement in all this. Did she tell you she told her mother about any of it?"

"No, she didn't tell me of any specific conversation, but she said her mother knew. She said her mother knew about her bruise, and she said her mother ignored it."

"What bruise?"'

"She had a bruise on her shoulder one morning. I asked her about it, but she was too ashamed to tell me about it then. Later, she told me Harry would often get violent, frustrated with her, and do things like push her or pinch her too hard."

"And her mother knew about this?"

"She said she did but ignored it."

"And the reason she ignored it? Did she tell you?"

"She said her mother thought that she was making things up because she just didn't like Harry or her marrying him. She said it was always worse when her mother was away and she was alone with Harry."

"To your knowledge, did she tell anyone else about these incidents?"

"No. I mean, I don't know if she did or didn't."

"You mentioned her telling you that she spied on Harry when he went to his mother's apartment, that she saw him talking to a manikin head in the bed with a wig on it?"

"Yes. Karen said his mother wore wigs because her hair was getting too thin," I said. I wondered now if they would think about the wig found with Harry's body in Karen's room, but they said nothing or asked nothing about it.

Instead, the detectives looked at each other for a moment before Lieutenant Cooper flipped open a small pad he had in his hands and read something. Then he looked up at me.

"We're kind of intrigued by the fact that Karen called her mother from New York City the same day you were in New York City. We've followed up on that with the phone company. Did you see her there?" he asked.

"No," I said. I looked at my father.

"She was with my wife all the time and never out of her sight. You were told that the other day."

"Remarkable coincidence," Lieutenant Cooper muttered.

"Still a coincidence."

"What makes it even more remarkable is that the

pay phone we traced back to is maybe a minute from the hotel you were at."

My father just stared at him for a moment and then looked at me. "Did Karen call you at the hotel, Zipporah?"

"No," I said.

"Did she come to the hotel?"

"No."

"Did you in any way know she was in New York at the time?"

"No."

My father sat back.

"Thanks," Lieutenant Cooper told him. "I'll send you part of my paycheck."

"When you get my bill, it might be a bigger part than you anticipated," my father responded, not waiting a beat.

Chief Keiser laughed.

"So, all you're telling us here about Mr. Pearson, you heard from Karen Stoker herself? You never witnessed anything, nor were you present when Karen spoke to her mother about it or tried to speak to her about it?"

"That's true," I said. "Correct," I added, trying to sound more like my father now. I caught a slight smile on his lips.

"Okay," Lieutenant Cooper said after a deep sigh. "More than likely, we'll be talking to you again, Zipporah. You'll probably be a major witness at a trial. For now, we would rather you don't discuss this interview or any of this information with anyone else besides your father."

"Anything new on Karen's whereabouts?" my father asked.

"We're working on it," Lieutenant Cooper replied. He looked at me for a long moment, his eyes narrowing, and added, "She can't hide forever."

After a pause, he added, "No matter who helps her."

17

Protecting Jesse

This time, after my interview with the police, Daddy was silent most of the ride home. If he were angry at me, I'd much rather he would show it, and if he were afraid of something, I wished he would tell me what it was. My brother and I knew that whenever Daddy was so pensive as to make you feel you weren't even there, he was worried about something very serious. We would tiptoe around him, stealing glances but avoiding his eyes, as if he were on the verge of some explosion and merely looking at him the wrong way would set it off.

Finally, just before we arrived at the house, he turned to me.

"The stuff about the pay phone is troubling, Zipporah. It's too much of a coincidence for Karen to be making that call so close to where we were, where you were. If you knew for sure she had gone to New York City, you should have told us, told me. That is technically holding back pertinent information."

I started to cry.

"Well, what's done is done, but if it comes up again, I want you to tell the absolute truth," he said. "Okay?"

I nodded, and we drove on.

Jesse was waiting for us in front of the house, where he was whitewashing the porch railing. He turned as soon as we pulled into the driveway. I got out before Daddy pulled into the garage and held my breath in anticipation. Had Jesse discovered anything?

"How did it go with the police?" he asked.

"They weren't too nice. They were angry I hadn't told them all this before."

"Not too nice? They should have been happy you came forward with the information. Most people never tell what they know, because they don't want to be involved."

"They didn't act grateful. That's for sure," I said. "I felt like I was the one going on trial, not Karen."

"Why? Didn't they believe you?" he asked me.

"I'm not sure," I said.

Daddy came out of the garage.

"What happened?" Jesse asked him. "Zipporah makes it sound like they weren't appreciative. Didn't they think what she had to say was important to the case? Aren't they going to use the information she gave them?"

"Well, she told it just as she heard it from Karen. They recorded her testimony."

"What do you think?"

"I think they have trouble with the story," Daddy said, glancing at me.

"Why? Why do they think it's untrue?" Jesse demanded, as if Karen were his sister and not me.

"For one thing, I imagine they've heard only good things about Harry Pearson from everyone they've interviewed so far, including Darlene Pearson. Other than Zipporah here, Karen apparently told no one, and Zipporah admitted she had never witnessed anything herself."

"That doesn't necessarily mean it wasn't true," Jesse said, with more passion than either Daddy or I expected.

"No, it doesn't mean that, but it does mean that it needs more collaboration. Also, according to what your sister said she was told, Harry Pearson starts to resemble Norman Bates in *Psycho*."

"Maybe he did," Jesse said, without hearing any details. "You didn't really know him that well, did you, Dad?"

"No, but you don't know the rest of it."

"Well, what was the rest of it? What about Harry Pearson?" Jesse asked.

My father glanced at me again. "This is very upsetting for Zipporah, Jess. I know she would like it all to end. She hasn't had an easy day since."

"It's okay," I said. I wanted the story out in the open now. I wanted the world to know what Karen had been facing and suffering.

"You want to tell him the rest of it?" my father asked me.

I nodded. "Fine, go ahead."

"Karen told me Harry Pearson wouldn't give up on his mother, wouldn't believe she was dead. He would go to her apartment at the rear of their house and sit by her bed and talk to her wig. It was on a head like they have for wigs. It was also made up like his mother made up her face, with lots of makeup, clownish."

Jesse nodded, his face thoughtful.

"So what do you think of all that?" Daddy asked him.

"Who knows? It could have been true. No one suspected Norman Bates, did they?"

"That's a movie, Jess."

"All I'm saying is, could be."

"Did you hear what she's saying . . . talked to a wig, made up a head, and who knows what else? We're talking about the pharmacist, a man who had contact with most of the village residents."

Jesse shrugged, as if he had heard similar stories all his life.

"I don't know what's with you kids today," Daddy said. "In my day, a story like that would turn my bones to ice. Anyway, let's put it aside." He checked his watch. "I'm taking us all out to Frankie's for dinner. I've already told your mother, so clean up," he added, nodding at the paint. "We're going shortly after she comes home." He gazed around. "Nice job on the lawn, by the way."

"Thanks," Jesse said. He looked at me, and I dropped my gaze to the walk. "You did the right thing," he said as soon as Daddy entered the house. "Whether the police appreciate you and believe you or not."

I glanced up at the attic window in front. There was no sign of Karen, but I felt her presence as I would if she had been standing right beside me.

"I hope so," I said, and walked into the house. My brain felt as if it was bubbling in my head. What had Karen done all day while Jesse was there? What was she doing now? Was it possible she had been unable to get herself food and water?

"Let's get ready to go out," Jesse said, passing me on the stairway. "Dad's right. We need a night out together," he added, and hurried up the stairs to his room. I followed slowly.

I felt drained, exhausted, and very worried about Karen, but at least when we all went out to dinner, she would have the house to herself, and she could fetch whatever she needed. I thought I would leave a note in *The Diary of Anne Frank* for her, not only about Jesse's earlier arrival but briefly what had occurred at the police station. Surely, she was on pins and needles about it. I made sure to tell her that Jesse supported her story, gave it credence. She needed cheering up as much as I did, if not more. I stuck the note in the book and placed it on the shelf, sticking out an inch or so as usual, so she would know something was in it for her.

While I was getting dressed, my mother came home and came directly to my room. I was just finishing brushing my hair but hadn't yet picked out what I would wear.

"Hi," she said, looking as if she had expected to find me brooding in the corner or something.

"Hi."

"Your father told me about the police today and how unpleasant it was for you."

"They were terrible. Even Daddy got angry."

"You should have told them it all the first time, Zipporah. It didn't do Karen any good. But," she quickly added, "I understand why you felt the need to keep it to yourself. It's just that . . . well, after what had happened, why worry about her being embarrassed or her feeling betrayed? It didn't help matters, as you saw."

I turned away, the tears burning at the rims of my

eyelids. What was I going to tell her? Karen's not gone; it's not over? I'm still her best and only friend? And what about what Daddy had told me about not betraying a friend? I didn't say anything in my own defense, however. If I were too adamant about it, she might suspect something more, I thought.

"Her mother should have been the one to tell them," was all I could think to say.

"Yes, she should have. You're certainly right there. What a horrible mess. Anyway, your involvement in it all is over. There isn't anything more you can do or tell them," she said, mostly for herself, it seemed. "It's up to them now. I'd better get changed," she added, and hurried out.

Later, at the restaurant, my parents did all they could to keep the Pearson tragedy out of our conversation, but unfortunately, there were people at the restaurant whom my father knew, and when they stopped to say hello, they had to make reference to the news in Sandburg. One man, another attorney named Clarence Hartwick, thought he was amusing telling my father he had picked the wrong small town to settle in, a town full of Lizzie Borden's relatives.

"He's a sick S.O.B.," my father muttered to us as soon as Hartwick walked away. "I never liked him in court or out."

"I don't think it's fair comparing Karen Stoker to Lizzie Borden anyway," Jesse said. "There's quite a difference in what motivated each."

"Let me give you a little advice," Daddy said, sitting back. "Be miserly when it comes to just how much faith you spend on your clients' honesty. You'll be far less disappointed in the end, even if you win your cases."

"What are you saying, Dad? Zipporah is lying about what happened to Karen?"

"No, of course not. Why should Zipporah lie? But we're going completely on hearsay, Jess. Don't fault the police for being skeptical. They won't do a good job if they're not skeptical."

"Yes, well, I just can't imagine a girl like that doing something like that out of the blue," Jesse insisted.

A girl like that? I had mixed feelings about his support for Karen. On the one hand, it made me feel better about myself and my own investment in her, but on the other, it made me uneasy, even a little jealous, to see him come so vehemently to her defense. He didn't know her as well as I did, and if he knew how she had found his journal and read it, he would not be so eager to come rushing to her aid. These contradictory feelings I had confused and disturbed me. I must have been showing it, too. I saw my mother staring at me, her face molding into an expression of deeper and deeper concern.

"Can we change the subject?" she asked. "I'm so tired of this. It's running away with our lives."

"Absolutely. So, Jesse, you're coming to the office tomorrow, right?" Daddy asked him. "I'd like you to meet everyone and work out how you're going to help out there this summer. I have an interesting case, too, and you'll be of real assistance with the research."

"Not tomorrow. How about the day after? I have a few more chores to do around the house."

"Chores? You keep surprising me, Jesse, but don't be a better handyman than your father. It makes him look bad," Daddy told him.

"I won't. No worries there."

"We might have a surprise or two in store for you before the week's out," Daddy told him, and winked at me.

"What surprise?"

"Wouldn't be a surprise if we told, would it, Zipporah?"

"No."

"You're finally going to break down and get us a dog, is that it, Dad?"

"No clues," Daddy said. "And don't try to trick your sister into telling you, either. She's sworn to secrecy, a blood oath."

The laughter and teasing helped us all ease out of the tension. By the time we were on our way home, we were all in a lighter mood, and once again, I felt as if I were back to a time before the Pearson tragedy. In the morning, I would get on the school bus and wait for Karen to board. We would play our mind games and laugh about some of the other students. Our conversation would be light and airy and full of silliness. Oh, how I wished that would be. Why couldn't we just close our eyes and wish really hard for good things? How easy it used to be to imagine and pretend. There wasn't anyplace Karen and I couldn't go, any world we couldn't enter through the magic of our own fantasies.

However, as we drove up to the house and into our driveway, the darkness of the attic windows brought me quickly back to reality. I hoped, Karen hadn't done anything to leave any traces of herself or any clues to her presence in our home. I rushed into the kitchen ahead of my mother to check the countertops and table, to be sure every cabinet door was closed and there were no crumbs or wrappers, anything that would draw attention and curiosity, as she had done the first time. Fortunately, the kitchen was as spotless as we had left it.

Daddy went to his home office for a while, and I went up to my room. Jesse remained below watching television with Mama. I felt so helpless just sitting there and, again, so guilty because of the good time I had just had with my family while Karen sat in the attic darkness. I just had to chance it. It had been too long, and too much had happened since Karen and I last spoke to each other. I had to know how she was doing. Once again, I tried to fly up those noisy attic steps unnoticed. I paused at the door and listened. The television was on below, and I could vaguely hear Mama and Jesse talking.

I opened the attic door and slipped in, closing it softly behind me. For a long moment, I stood there with my back against the door, panning the attic. The clearer night sky painted everything in a skeleton-white illumination. It looked like a room full of ghosts. The far wall creaked.

"Karen?" I called in a loud whisper. "Come out. Speak to me," I said. "It's all right. We have a few minutes. It's safe. Karen, where are you?" I demanded, more forcefully.

"Why did you come up? They're all in the house," I heard her say right beside me. She had pressed her back to the wall just behind a cabinet. She didn't move forward, however. She remained there as if she had been hung along with some of the old pictures and frames.

I stepped further into the attic.

"It's all right. My brother and my mother are watching television, and my father's working in his office. How are you? When did you realize Jesse was back? How have you managed with such little time?"

"Just go back out and down to your room," she said. "I'm fine."

"But . . . food, water. Did you get what you needed when we were out?"

She was silent, and then she stepped away from the wall and walked softly into the dim pool of light. She was wearing one of my nightgowns. Her hair was down. She had a smile on her face, a smile I didn't expect. She looked happier, comfortable, content. How could she be?

"No," she said, smiling at me. "I got it all before you left, way before you left."

"Oh. You mean when Jesse left the house?"

"No, Zipporah. I got everything I need for now from Jesse," she said.

"What? From Jesse? I don't understand. What are you saying?"

She seized my hand and pulled me toward the sofa. We both sat.

"Listen to me," she began, speaking quickly and excitedly. "I didn't know he had come home. I had fallen asleep and was still asleep when he drove in and parked his car behind the garage. He didn't make much noise after he entered the house, either. I woke up and went down the attic steps to get some fresh water and something to eat. He didn't hear me coming down the stairs, and I didn't know he was in his room, but the door was open and . . ."

"And what?"

"He was changing and standing there in his under-
wear when he turned and saw me in the hallway."

"Oh, no."

"Yes. Of course, like you, I thought this was the
end. I'm done for, and so are you."

"Jesse didn't say anything about it," I told her,
shaking my head. I was convinced she was making it
up. Maybe it was one of her fantasies. I started to feel
sick.

"Of course he didn't. A brilliant solution came to
me instantly. It was almost as if . . . as if Lucy Doral
was whispering in my ear," she added, which brought
even more chills sliding along my spine.

"What solution?"

"I pretended as if I had just arrived."

"Just arrived?"

"Yes, don't you see? I pretended that you didn't
know I was there yet. He didn't even bother putting on
his pants. He charged forward to the doorway. 'What
are you doing here?' he asked. I started to cry, standing there with my arms around myself and sobbing so
hard I imagine I looked like I might just crumble at his
feet. He thought so. He reached out to hold me, and I
pressed my face against his warm skin and let my tears
soak his chest. 'What are you doing here?' he asked
again. I cried harder, and he took me into his room and
sat me on his bed while he went for a warm, wet wash-
cloth to wipe my face. He squatted in front of me and
held my hand and waited for me to catch my breath. I
was so good, Zipporah. I wish you had seen me. Too
bad they don't give Academy Awards for everyday
real-life performances. I'd be making an acceptance
speech."

"What did you tell him? Why didn't he say anything to me, to my father, about any of this?"

"First, I told him I had been in New York. I figured I had better use our phone call, the call you made to my mother, in case he found out. I told him that it wasn't as easy as I had imagined to hide out there, to find a decent place to stay with the little money I had, but when I thought where I should go, I could think only of your house. I talked about our attic, our nest, and how it had been our world away from the world, how I had felt safe there always, even when I was living under terrible circumstances. I described how I came up the fire escape and into the attic but that I was hungry and had come down to get something to eat.

"He felt so sorry for me that he almost cried himself. He insisted he get me some food right away. That was when he put on his pants, but he didn't bother with shoes or socks or a shirt. He led me down to the kitchen and fixed me a pretty good toasted cheese sandwich with a tomato and a pickle and a cup of hot chocolate with whipped cream."

"How could you think about food?"

"I was pretty hungry, Zipporah. Anyway, while I sat and watched him make the sandwich, I began to put my story together. I described hitching to New York City. I put in this episode with an older man who tried to get me to go to a motel with him and how I jumped out of the car at the first red light. I told him how I wandered through the city streets, lost and afraid, and how I almost ended up in an alleyway. He kept shaking his head and saying, 'Damn, what you've gone through.' Then I told him how I made up my mind to chance returning but that I had hoped to hide out in the attic a while. He served me the sandwich, and while I ate, he asked me what had happened and why, and I told him everything, everything about Harry, including his madness over his dead mother."

"That explains it," I said, nodding.

"Explains what?"

"Why Jesse wasn't surprised about it when I told him and why he was so adamant about your having told me the truth. He had already heard it all from you."

She smiled. "He's very, very sweet," she said. "Anyway, I started to cry again when I got to the part about my mother and how she wasn't going to come to my defense or support my story. That made him angry. I threw myself on him, crying, 'What should I do, Jesse? You're so much smarter than I am. What should I do?' He thought for a moment and decided I should do just what I had intended for now."

"Meaning what?"

"You'll love this. Meaning I should remain hidden in the attic. He would take care of me, be sure I had what I needed, only he was insistent that no one find out, even you. So you're not supposed to know I'm here. Isn't that funny?"

"My brother wants to hide you in the attic?"

She nodded, smiling. "He thought I should stay here until he figured out something better for me. He said my mother should somehow be forced to come forward and tell the truth, so that when I appeared, turned myself in to the police, there would be a great deal of sympathy for me. He said he was going to think hard about it and come up with a plan. He made me promise that if I screwed up, made noise, gave myself away, I would not involve him, however. He said his parents would be devastated. If I did get caught or discovered, I was to say no one knew I was up there. He was especially insistent that you not know."

"Why?"

"He thought you would do something that would give me away. I almost laughed then. I was even tempted to tell him you already knew, but it was too late. You don't change your story in midstream," she said, as if she were giving me instructions for lying. "Of course, I agreed. It would be our little secret. So you see, you had better get downstairs quickly and not reveal in any way that you know I'm here."

I shook my head. "It's not like him to do something like this, to hide something like this from our parents."

"Why not? You did," she reminded me.

I looked at her. Yes, I did, I thought, but I always thought Jesse was better than I was. He was the good son, the perfect son, rarely disappointing our parents in any way, polite, responsible, and far more mature than most boys his age. My father trusted him with his work, was going to use him to help research his cases. He had brought home only trophies and honor roll status on his report cards.

"Jesse's different," I said.

"Sure, he's different, silly. He's a man, and remember, I know things about him that he doesn't know I know," she said.

"If he did, he wouldn't want to help you a bit," I fired back at her.

"Well, you're not going to tell on me now, are you?"

I was silent a moment. "I left you a note in the book," I said.

"I have it," she said. "I'm not surprised at how the police treated you. Now you know why I'm not so anxious to walk into the police station and cry, 'Here I am!'"

She stood up abruptly. "You'd better go down quickly and quietly, Zipporah. You don't want our Jesse to discover you found me. He'll be so embarrassed."

I rose slowly. *Our Jesse?* When did he become *our Jesse?*

"Hurry," she said in a loud whisper. "You've been here too long already."

I walked to the doorway and opened it slowly to listen. They were all still downstairs.

She stepped up to me, her body pressed against mine as she brought her lips close to my ear.

"I feel so much better knowing Jesse is trying to help me," she whispered.

I didn't say anything.

"You've got to be even more careful now, Zipporah," she continued. "You're not only protecting me. You're protecting Jesse."

Without replying, I walked out of the attic and closed the door behind me. Then I descended the dark steps quickly, not realizing I was crying until I got to my room and looked at myself in the vanity-table mirror. The tears were moving in little jerks down my cheeks and bubbling near the corners of my lips before falling forward to my chin.

Above me, a floorboard in the attic creaked. It was her way of reminding me how important silence was, her silence and my own.

And now Jesse's, too.

I didn't know why I was so sad, until I realized I wasn't sad for myself.

I was sad for Jesse.

Like me, he would soon realize whom he was betraying.

18

Naked on the Sofa

It was nearly impossible for me to get any sleep. I tossed and turned most of the night, listening for any sound, and then, just after midnight, I was positive I heard the attic steps creak. Jesse wasn't used to them, I thought. Karen wouldn't be coming down now. It had to be Jesse going up to her, chancing discovery. There was a deep silence and then another creak and another. I sat up, listening harder, and thought I heard the attic door open. I tiptoed to my bedroom door and looked up through the dim hallway illumination. Then I heard the distinct sound of steps above me. It grew very quiet quickly. I sat there in my bed, listening and waiting. They had become very quiet. Growing more and more tired, I finally relented and let my head rest on the pillow. I tried to keep my eyes open, but my eyelids were like magnets shutting down.

Some time before morning, I thought I heard the creak of the attic steps again, but I wasn't sure if I had really heard them or it had just been a dream. I overslept, and my alarm woke me. My mother heard it go off and came in to see if everything was all right.

"Jesse's already up and having breakfast," she added.

"Jesse's up?"

I recalled all I had heard the night before and hurried to shower and dress. By the time I got downstairs, my father was dressed and having coffee with him. My mother was going to continue her morning-to-afternoon shift for the rest of the week, so she was almost finished with breakfast, too.

"Hey, sleepyhead," Jesse said when I entered the kitchen. "What happened to our famous early riser?"

"When I was in college," Daddy said, "I cherished the mornings I didn't have to get up early. Your brother is scaring me with all this responsible and good behavior. He's up to something," he teased.

I shifted my eyes to Jesse to see how he would react. *Oh, yes,* I thought, *he's up to something.*

"It's easier to sleep in the dorm," he said. "I got used to the noise. It's too quiet here to sleep late."

Our parents laughed. Jesse glanced at me, and in that short look, I thought I saw him wondering if I knew anything, but it might have been wishful thinking on my part.

"Okay, so when are you going to be at the office, Jess?"

"I'll go with you tomorrow, as I said. Okay?"

"Fine," Daddy told him, and turned to me. "You all right with going to school on the bus, Zipporah? I can wait a few more minutes if you want."

"No, I'm fine, Daddy," I said.

I wasn't, of course. I couldn't imagine paying attention to anything at school. Mama was on her way out and gave both Jesse and me a kiss.

"I'll be home in time to prepare dinner tonight," she

told me. "Jesse has the list of groceries to get. Don't forget them," she warned him.

"Not a chance, Mom. I like eating too much."

She gave him a second kiss, and I felt myself cringe inside when I imagined her discovering what he was up to now concerning Karen. It occurred to me that I could play the innocent if that happened. Jesse was convinced I knew nothing, and Karen certainly wouldn't tell. I would suddenly become the better child, the good daughter. Could I live with it? How easily one deception gave birth to another.

Both our parents left before I went out to wait for the school bus. Jesse followed me, bringing out the paint he had been using to whitewash the railings. As he set things up behind me, I glanced up at the attic window and saw the curtain parting, but the morning light was too bright to reveal Karen's face. I turned to Jesse, who had begun his chore again.

Should I say something? I wondered. Wasn't I part of a new deceit? What would he do if he knew Karen had lied to him? Had read his journal? Would he throw down his paint brush and charge up to the attic to demand that she leave? Throw her out on the street? Would that satisfy me now?

And what would result from it? When the police found her, would she describe how she had been harbored in our house right above my parents? Would people in the community believe they didn't know? Did Jesse realize the danger our entire family was in? How couldn't he? What made him take such a risk?

He turned and smiled at me. "Don't worry," he said, as if he could read my thoughts. "Things will work out. It will be over soon. Try to forget about it for a while. I'll see you after school."

Again, I looked up at the attic window. She had opened it just enough to hear our conversation. I was sure she was worried that I would say the wrong thing.

I heard the bus coming and moved down to the side of the road. Jesse stood up to wave as I went around to get onto the bus. I hurried to the back and looked out at him as we pulled away. He returned to his painting but looked as if he was working faster.

He's going up to her again, I thought.

And who knew what else he would do today?

I should be sharing in this. I shouldn't be playing the innocent, unknowing little sister. I slumped in my seat and stared ahead. This was going to be the hardest day of all at school. I'd haunt that clock, trying desperately to move its hands around faster. It occurred to me that I should have pretended I was sick and stayed home, but I had used that excuse too recently.

It was too late now.

Or was it?

I could go to the nurse's office and complain about cramps. That always worked. Of course, I was afraid of the havoc and concern I could cause for my parents, but the idea lay just under the surface of my thoughts all morning. I was terrible in class, missing notes, failing to answer questions, and annoying my teachers with my restlessness. My nerve endings felt like guitar strings twanging, and I was paranoid, positive that the other students in my classes and in the hallways were looking at me and whispering. The whole world suspected something wrong was going on at my house.

This town was too small for such an embarrassing and devastating revelation. We were on the verge of being destroyed, my father's wonderful career irreparably damaged, and it would be all my and now Jesse's fault. We were greater failures as children than some of the young people who were always in trouble for misbehavior at school and elsewhere.

I made it to lunch, but I had no appetite. I sat staring at my food, the clatter of dishes, chatter, and laughter merging around me in a great cacophony of unintelligible noise. My head felt as if it were empty of everything but the echoing sounds.

"Did you tell Karen about our little episode?" I heard, and realized Dana Martin had put his hands on my table and was leaning toward me, his face only inches from my own. "Did you let her know you and she are in quicksand?"

I couldn't speak. I turned away, feeling my throat close.

When he laughed, I jumped up so abruptly he nearly fell over backward. Everyone in the cafeteria had stopped talking and was looking our way. I fluttered a moment, and then I charged out of the cafeteria and practically ran all the way to the nurse's office. Her door was locked, with the sign on it telling students she was at lunch, and anyone who needed her should go directly to the principal's office. I did. His secretary, Mrs. Schwartz, looked up at me and instantly knew something was very wrong.

"I need to go to the nurse's office," I said. "I have terrible cramps, and I feel like I might throw up."

"Okay, okay," she said, rising quickly and getting a set of keys from a side drawer. "Follow me."

She hurried out, her high-heeled shoes tapping like a pair of woodpeckers on a petrified tree. She fumbled with the door lock but got it open and saw to it that I had a cot in one of the small rooms. She gave me a blanket and then mumbled something about going to get the nurse. She gave me a pan in case I did vomit. Then she left, closing the nurse's office door. I closed my eyes and tried to calm my thumping heart.

A few minutes later, the nurse, Mrs. Miller, came into her office and hurried to my side. She asked me about the cramps and took my temperature.

"It's normal," she told me. "Your time of month?"

I nodded, even though it wasn't.

"You'll be fine," she said. "But you probably shouldn't try to attend any more classes today. I can't give you anything, but I'm sure your mother has what you need at home." She knew my mother was a nurse, too.

"She's at work at the hospital," I said.

"Well, I have to call either her or your father."

"My brother is home from college, too," I said.

"He's not your guardian. I have to call your parents," she told me. I felt terrible about it and now really did feel sick inside.

Daddy was in court and couldn't be reached for a few hours. My mother had been asked to assist in an operation and was also out of reach for now. Reluctantly, the nurse called my house to speak with my brother, but she returned to tell me no one had answered.

"I've left messages for your parents, but I can take you home," she said.

I struggled to my feet, and she led me out to her car in the parking lot.

"I used to have periods like you're having," she told me. "I used to hate Adam and Eve," she added, smiling.

"Why?"

"My grandmother told me God was so angry at Eve that he cursed us all with pain related to giving birth, which includes having periods." She laughed again. "My mother used to yell at my grandmother for putting all these thoughts in my head. Later, I had a girlfriend in school named Eve, and I used to wonder what her parents were thinking when they named her that. My father told me it wasn't Eve's fault entirely, anyway. It was the devil's, the snake, but he made the point clear to me that in the end, we have to be responsible for the things we do and the choices we make. You can always say no," she added.

I closed my eyes. It wasn't as easy as she made it seem, I thought, but she was probably right. I had my own Garden of Eden at my house. Actually, Jesse and I both had it now.

Was there a snake whispering in our ears?

"This is it, isn't it?" the nurse asked me as we drove up to my house.

"Yes. Thank you, Mrs. Miller."

"Is that your brother's car in the driveway?" she asked.

"Yes."

"Well, good. Someone's home. I'll be sure to let your parents know you've been brought home. Just rest for a while," she said. "You'll be fine."

"Thanks again," I said, getting out.

She nodded and backed out of the driveway. I looked at Jesse's car and then hurried into the house, taking care not to touch the recently painted railings.

The first thing that struck me was the silence. I stood in the entryway for a few moments listening. Then I went into the kitchen and saw Jesse had bought the bags of groceries Mama had asked him to buy. The empty bags rested on the counter. Everything had been put away. So that's where he was when the nurse had called, I thought.

"Jesse," I called, moving toward the living room. I listened again, but I didn't hear him anywhere downstairs. It occurred to me that he could be in the back, working on the grass or staining the wooden landing. I hurried to the rear door and stepped out.

Circles of maddening insects hovered above the recently cut grass, but Jesse was nowhere in sight. My heart sank. I knew where he was. I knew it the moment I had driven up with the school nurse, but I had gone through the motions, searching for him everywhere else, in hopes I was wrong. It was time to stop burying my head in the sand, time to stop the lying. If we were going to help Karen, we would do it together.

I returned to the stairway and ascended, glancing once into Jesse's room to be sure he wasn't there. The silence told me he was in the attic. Why was it so silent? If he didn't know I had come home or hadn't seen the nurse's car, there was no reason for him to be so quiet with Karen. Perhaps they had left together to carry out some sort of plan.

I hesitated at the attic door, listening hard. I thought I did hear some low murmuring, so I closed my eyes, sucked in my breath, and turned the knob. Once I entered the attic, I thought, it was over, the pretending was over. I stepped in softly, slowly, and for a moment, I thought the attic was empty. Then I saw them.

They were naked on the sofa, our sofa, the sofa where Karen and I had staged so many fantasies, imagined trips, and spun out so many dreams. It wasn't hard to see what they were doing. It was Karen who saw me first, turning her head to the right. I heard her say, "Oh," and then Jesse turned.

I couldn't stand there. I stepped back, shutting the door hard and fast, and then charged down the attic steps. It was as if I had sprouted wings. I flew down the main stairway and burst out the front door. All I could think to do was run, flee, escape from the sight and the memory that clung to me like the cans malicious young boys tied to the tail of a poor dog. Somehow, I thought if I ran harder, faster, I could block out the memory and the shock of it all, but it wasn't working, and my chest felt as if it was expanding to the point where my ribs would crack and I would just come apart on the road.

"Zipporah!" I heard. "Zipporah, wait!"

I stopped running and glanced back. Jesse was in his pants, barefoot and shirtless, charging after me. I just turned away and walked, holding my side to stop the pain. Fortunately, there were no cars, no one. The road looked as if it led to nowhere. The thickened forest was still, and I realized there wasn't even a slight breeze. It was as if the whole world had stopped turning for a moment to wait and to see.

"Zipporah," Jesse said, and reached out to grab my left arm at the elbow. I stopped, but I didn't turn. I kept my head down. "What are you doing home from school?" he asked as if all that I had seen and all that had happened was somehow my fault. I didn't reply. I simply stood there, staring at the road.

"I know this looks weird, frightening, but I can explain it," he said.

I took a deep breath. A crow came flying out of a tree ahead of us, swooped toward the road, and lifted itself over the tops of the pine and the birch. How I wished I could grab onto it and go wherever it was going.

"Yesterday, I discovered Karen had come to our house," Jesse continued.

I turned and looked at him.

"She was desperate. She had gone to New York and had a horrible time of it. She came to our house for help. I couldn't turn her out."

"I saw the help you were giving her," I said sharply.

My big brother, who had loomed somewhere near Mars in the celestial skies for me, had suddenly fallen to earth. In his pants, barefoot and shirtless, he seemed smaller, even embarrassing, to the point where I was worried someone would come along and see me with him. I pulled my arm from his grasp and started toward the house.

How would I play this? Would I go along with Karen's deception and enjoy the role of the violated, disappointed sister, or would I spin on him and tell him the whole truth and watch him shrink even more before my very eyes? How had Karen behaved after she saw me in the doorway? Did she cry and pretend they had hurt me by keeping her secret?

"Wait, Zipporah, please," he begged. I kept walking. "She's your best friend," he added in desperation.

I stopped and turned back to him.

"So? How does that make it any better, Jesse?"

"Look," he said, walking slowly to me, "I know it

wasn't nice for you to see that, but I've had a crush on Karen for a long time. I was writing to her from college. She never told you?"

"No," I said. "You were writing to her?"

Never once had he written to me.

"Yes, and I called her a few times. I guess she thought it was better to keep it a secret for a while, and then all this happened—exploded, I should say."

I shook my head, disbelieving. I thought I was the one deceiving everyone, especially my parents, and all this time, Jesse was in touch with Karen? He was actually deceiving me.

"I'm sorry I never told you, but I thought that after I started college, I'd be so involved in the social life there, I would forget her. I didn't, and then all this," he said. "I'm sorry."

My anger toward him shifted more toward Karen. All those times we shared our secrets, our sexual and romantic fantasies, she never revealed any of this.

"It's not so unusual for a guy my age to like a girl your age, Zipporah. There's nearly seven years' difference between Dad and Mom, you know."

"I don't care. You can run off and elope with her for all I care," I snapped back at him, and continued toward the house, walking quickly now. He ran to catch up.

"I'm not going to run off with her, but you have to feel sorry for her, for what's happened, don't you? We can't just throw her out now."

I spun on him again, this time so sharply he stopped and actually leaned back as if he expected me to swing at him.

"You know what, Jesse? I used to think you were

so smart, miles above me, but Karen is right about one thing. All you boys want the same thing and don't care how foolish you look or act, as long as you get it. I'm glad I saw you two. I'm glad you're not my big hero anymore. I'm glad I have both my feet on the ground, and at this moment, I feel sorrier for you than I do for her or myself or anyone."

"Zipporah . . ."

"Just shut up," I said. "I'm going up to the attic. I don't want you to follow. You wait in your room until I come down," I ordered. I had never used such an authoritative tone with him, but I was thrust into the role of the more mature, more responsible of the two of us.

He nodded and didn't follow me to the house until I reached the front door. He started after me, and I entered. I half expected Karen to be waiting down-stairs, but she wasn't there. I climbed the stairway and walked up to the attic door. She was standing by the window that faced the front of the house. She was wearing one of my skirts and blouses. I waited. I knew she knew I was there, but she wasn't turning around so quickly. Finally, she did and smiled.

"Sorry about that," she said. "Always knock before entering a room, my mother says." She walked toward me, still smiling. "In her case, it mattered even more. She slipped men into the house so quietly and easily. I used to think she pulled them in under the door. I'd be sitting there having breakfast the next morning, and some strange man would come into the kitchen, pour himself a cup of coffee, and smile at me. Half the time, they were in their briefs, and one guy even came in naked. I had to pretend it didn't bother me. I had to be cool, sophisticated. Sometimes my mother wouldn't even tell me their names or explain a thing. She would act as though it had been a dream of mine."

"Maybe it was," I said. "Maybe you're just giving me one lie after another."

"You're just mad right now. You shouldn't be."

"You never told me he was writing to you and calling you. Why not?"

"Look at you. Look at how angry you are. That's why. I knew it would bother you. What's that joke I told you about the little boy who learned how he was made by his parents? Remember? He looked at them and said, 'My mother, never. My father, I believe.'"

She laughed and then turned serious, even angry-looking herself. "You put him on too high a pedestal, Zipporah. He's just like any other boy. Remember when I told you to read his journal? I was trying to get you to discover things, but you were too goody-goody about it. Not you, not Zipporah Stein read someone's secret journal, especially Mr. Perfect's journal."

"Shut up," I said.

"So you're going to blame me for everything? You're going to continue to keep him on some pedestal?"

I looked away and then glanced at our sofa.

"Were you with him before this, too?"

"Once. I came to your house, and you were somewhere with your father. Your mother was at work, and Jesse was here. Look," she said, "if you were in my shoes, you would have done the same thing. And don't try to be Miss Perfect yourself. You did go with Dana

Martin that night, and it wasn't to talk about world events."

"You wanted me to be with him just so I'd be like you. That's what you said. You meant all of it. This especially," I said.

She shrugged. "It's hard when your girlfriend is so pure, and you're not. It's better when you're both . . . complete," she said.

I sat on the sofa. "You should tell him the truth now," I told her. "You should tell him you were here already, and I was helping you. Why didn't you?"

"It was more important to me to protect you. Even now, even though I'm the one in the big mess, I was thinking first about you," she said.

"It's not right. He should know it all."

"So we'll tell him, if you think that's best. He'll probably take it well and not blame you for anything. He's not mean. He's actually a sweetheart," she said. She sat beside me and took my hand. "C'mon, don't blame anyone for this. It happened. It happens. Someday, something like it will happen to you, too. It's not healthy to feel guilty and dirty afterward, Zipporah. There's no reason to, anyway. My mother certainly doesn't," she added.

I was silent. So many emotions and contradictory thoughts were entwining within me. I felt as if I might just start spinning like a top and never stop.

"Besides, it's better now that we have someone with Jesse's intelligence helping us. He'll find a solution, as long as you let him. If you pout and hate us both, I'll just leave, and that's that."

I almost said, "Just go," but then we heard Jesse call out.

"Hey! Can I come up?"

Karen looked at me.

"Come up," I shouted back to him.

Karen squeezed my hand, and we both looked at the open attic doorway. Jesse stepped in meekly. I saw his right foot was bleeding.

"What happened to your foot?" Karen asked first.

"I must have stepped on some glass or something out on the road. It looks worse than it is."

"Well, go wash it, stupid," she told him.

"Yeah, I will. How are you two doing?"

"Just peachy keen," she said. "Will you go wash that? If you tracked blood up the stairs, you'd better wash that away as well."

"Right." He looked at me.

"Go ahead, Jesse," I said. "We'll come downstairs."

He nodded and hopped out on one foot.

"Thanks," Karen said, and hugged me. I didn't hug her back. She didn't seem to notice. She was up and out the attic door, chasing after Jesse.

We joined him in the upstairs bathroom and watched him wash, disinfect, and bandage his foot.

"I told you to put on your shoes," Karen said.

Jesse nodded. "Don't worry about it. I'm fine. Let's not think about me now. Let's think about you. I'm going to try to find out if the police have questioned your mother and what she told them."

"How are you going to do that?" I asked him.

"I'll be at Dad's office tomorrow. He can make some calls. I'll get him to do it."

"How?" I pursued. He was no longer the miracle worker to me.

"I'll make him realize you feel alone out there with the story, and it's important you get some vindication, some support. Give me a chance. For now, just don't be happy about it."

"I look happy to you?"

"You know what I mean."

"What if they find out we're hiding her up in the attic, Jesse?"

"They won't if we're careful about it."

I looked at Karen. Was this the time to tell him the whole truth? She just held her soft smile, waiting to see what decision I would make. I didn't come right out with the truth. Instead, I skirted it by saying, "Both of us are deceiving them now, Jesse."

He smiled. "They won't find out if we do everything correctly. Karen won't make a sound, and we'll make sure she has what she needs. It's not for long, anyway. So, why did you come home from school?"

"I didn't feel well," I said. I wasn't going to tell him the reason, not now.

"Are you all right?"

"No, but I'll manage," I said petulantly.

He nodded. "Okay, let's get some stuff together for Karen. Dad might be home before Mom today."

We went down to the kitchen and put together Karen's dinner and breakfast and filled water bottles. While Jesse and I did that, Karen picked out some things to read. My mother called after she had spoken to the nurse, and I told her I was all right, that it was just a little stomach upset.

"I'm even hungry again," I added, to relieve her from worry.

"Okay, then. It's probably because of the tension you're under. If anything changes, let me know. I'll call your father at the office."

While I spoke to my mother, Karen and Jesse carried everything upstairs. When I went up, I saw she was settled in the attic again, looking cool and unaffected by anything that had just occurred.

"Are you sure you'll be all right up here like this?" Jesse asked her anyway.

"Oh, yes." She looked at me. "Thank you," she said. She stepped up to us both and put her arms around me and Jesse, burying her head in his shoulder but holding us both tightly. "You're my only family now," she said when she stepped back.

"Don't worry," Jesse said. "We'll bring this to a head and get it right."

She smiled and, after glancing at me, leaned over to kiss him on the cheek. We turned and started out, looking back once to see her standing in the dwindling light of the sun sinking behind the trees on the west.

The shadows looked eager to swallow her and imprison her in their darkness once again. Despite it all, I couldn't help but feel sorry for her. I wanted to hate her, but my heart drove those feelings deep down and away.

"I love you, Zipporah," she whispered loudly enough for me to hear.

"I love you, too," I heard myself say. It was truly as if someone else within me was saying it.

I saw the look in Jesse's eyes. He really and truly did admire us for our close friendship. He had his share of buddies and good friends, but nothing compared to how Karen and I were. Maybe it was just a girl thing.

I followed him out and closed the attic door. We descended the steps slowly, and at the base, he turned to me, looked up at the closed door, nodded, and said, "I have an idea. We're going someplace tonight after dinner."

"Where?"

"To the Bates Motel," he said. "You know where I mean?"

"Yes."

"Are you okay with it?"

"Yes," I said, but I was more frightened than I had ever been.

19

At the Bates Motel

That night Jesse started on his plan to get Daddy to make the calls to the district attorney. He made a reference to it at dinner and presented it in such a way that it did look as if he was thinking only of me. Daddy agreed he was right. That plus my mother obviously telling him I had stomach problems because I was so nervous and tense these days made him promise to try. As I was helping Mama with the dishes, Jesse returned to the kitchen and asked if I wanted to go with him to a department store outside Monticello. He said it was open for another hour, at least. Because Monticello was the county seat and the biggest village, that was credible.

However, Mama shook her head and smiled at him skeptically. "You're just asking her to go so you can try to pry out the surprise we're expecting tomorrow," she told him.

Jesse pretended that was the reason but added that he and I spent too little time together. I know my mother thought he was implying that he was going to talk to me about the Pearson tragedy and try to cheer me up.

"Your brother's right," she said. "Go ahead. I can finish here. There's not much left to do."

We hurried out to his car.

"That was close," Jesse said. "I thought she wasn't going to let you go."

"What exactly are we going to do, Jesse?" I asked as we backed out of the driveway.

"A little police work," he said. "Don't worry. We'll be extra careful."

I noticed he had a camera.

"What are we taking pictures of?"

"Not sure, but let's wait to see," he said cryptically.

The village was its characteristic sleepy self. There was nearly no traffic, and the only storefront light was from the bar and grill. Sparky was out in front, as usual, and raised his head when we paused at the blinker. The wind lifted some paper and made it dance on and off the walk until it settled on the street. Jesse shook his head at the empty streets and sidewalks.

"Reminds me of the movie *On the Beach*," he said. "The end of the world."

"It feels like that tonight," I said. For some reason, I was whispering. It did seem to fit what we were doing and where I expected we were going.

He nodded, and we drove on. A little ways past Karen's mother's house, Jesse pulled to the side and parked. He turned off the engine and the lights and just sat there quietly, gazing into the rearview mirror. For me, the silence was unnerving.

"Why are we doing this? What do you hope to accomplish, Jesse?" I asked.

"I could tell from the way Dad reacted, and I imagine the way the policemen you spoke to reacted, that the part of Karen's story involving Harry Pearson and his dead mother didn't fly," Jesse said. "My guess is they didn't even bother to check out that part, but we will."

"How?"

"C'mon," he said, grabbed his camera, and got out.

I followed, and we started back down Main Street, hovering close to the shadows along the sidewalk. Just before Karen's mother's house, Jesse stopped. There was a small light on in what I knew to be the living room, but other than that, the house was dark.

"Looks like no one's home," Jesse muttered. He paused and gazed around again.

"What are we doing?"

"Just follow me. Stay close," he said, and cut abruptly into Karen's mother's driveway. We walked quickly, still clinging to the cover of darkness and avoiding the illumination of the streetlights.

I followed him around the garage to where Karen had described the apartment Harry's mother had lived in until she passed away. Of course, it was pitch dark inside, and the window shades were drawn down.

"Does Karen know we're doing this?" I whispered.

"No," he said. "I started to mention it, and she became very agitated. She's very frightened she'll cause more trouble for us if we get caught here."

"She's right," I said.

"Shh."

He went to one of the windows and pressed on the frame.

"Seems like it was never opened, or it's locked."

"Of course, it's locked," I said. "Why shouldn't it be locked? There are probably . . ."

He went to a second window and pushed, and this time, the window moved. He paused and looked at me, and then we both froze and listened. It sounded as if someone was coming down the sidewalk in front of the house. The footsteps quickened, slowed, and then disappeared as the person walked past and toward the center of the village.

"I'm going in," Jesse said. "You stay out here and watch for anyone. If you hear anything, just whisper, and I'll come out quickly. Okay?"

"I'm scared, Jesse."

"I'm not exactly free from fear, but this could go a long way to helping Karen," he said. Then he climbed in through the window.

If my heart beat any faster, I would surely faint on the spot, I thought. It beat so hard I could hear the thumping reverberate through my bones and fill my ears. It was so loud that I wouldn't be able to hear anything else. He was so quiet inside. I was suddenly even more worried.

"Jesse," I whispered, drawing closer to the open window. "Are you all right?"

"Quiet," he returned.

I waited in anticipation of the camera flashing, but nothing happened. What was he doing? I could hear him moving around inside. Finally, he appeared in the dark opened window. I stepped back to watch him climb out.

"What are you doing? Did you take any pictures? What did you see?"

He didn't reply. "C'mon," he said, and walked quickly back the way we had come. I followed. He was walking with his shoulders hoisted as if he were trying to keep from getting a bad chill. He turned abruptly onto the sidewalk, not even stopping to look back to see if I were right behind him. Then he started to cross the street, practically running. I did run to catch up. He got into the car, and I went around to get in on the passenger side.

He didn't start the engine. He just sat there, staring ahead.

"What is it, Jesse? What's going on? Why did you come out without taking any pictures?" I asked.

He turned to me slowly. "There's nothing to take pictures of," he said.

"What do you mean, nothing?"

"Not a bed, no furniture, nothing. In fact," he added, "the room's never been completed."

"Not completed?"

"The walls are studded, but they were never sheet-rocked. The wiring is hanging out. It's an unfinished room, Zipporah. No one could have lived in it."

"But Karen said . . ."

He stared at me a moment, and then he started the engine. "I know what she said."

"What does it mean?"

"I don't know. Maybe, maybe, her mother just had the place ripped apart to do something else with it."

"Why?"

"She didn't want to remember any of it. Of course, that would be something we could easily prove or dis-prove. Just check with the builder remodeling it, but I think it's highly unlikely." He shook his head. "Highly unlikely," he repeated.

We rode around aimlessly to pass time so our parents would believe we had gone to the department store. Jesse said he would claim it closed before we arrived.

"I don't understand this, Jesse. Karen and I were going to go in there," I told him.

"What do you mean?"

"Didn't she explain what our plan was originally?"

He slowed down. "No, tell me."

I described it and told him how she said she wore Harry's mother's wig, made up her face to resemble the way his mother did hers, and wore one of her dresses.

"And she confronted him that way?"

"Yes. He came to her room when her mother was away, and that's how she wanted to greet him. She said she expected him to come, and she was trying to get him to stop."

"What about the wig, the dress?"

"She left it behind afterward," I said.

"That's great. The police would have found it there. Listen—" he said.

"But how can you explain the room, the apartment she said was there? She even told me she had slept there recently.

"I don't know just yet. Let's not say anything to her about this for now. I don't want to see her frightened or unnerved in any way at the moment. She's walking on hot coals as it is. Dad will get me the information about what the police did and didn't find."

"How will you get him to ask for that sort of de-tail?"

"Leave it to me," he said. "Dad and I have a good relationship, Zipporah. Sometimes we're more like brothers."

"Not if he finds out who's in the attic," I muttered.

"He won't," Jesse said confidently, but to me, it sounded more like a prayer.

He was silent now, and I settled back in my seat, feeling numb. Suddenly, he slowed down, stopped, and pulled to the side of the road.

"What's wrong?" I asked.

"I just realized something. How did you know all that about the actual incident and what she left behind? You spoke to Karen afterward? Did she call you?"

Lies give birth to lies, I thought, which have a way of leading you to the edge of a cliff. After you fall, the only parachute available is honesty.

"Yes," I said.

"When?"

"When she came to the house."

"I don't understand. You mean just now?"

"No, Jesse. Karen didn't tell you the truth. I've been hiding her in the attic all this time."

"What? You've been hiding her? But what about her trip to New York?"

"She never went to New York," I said, and described how she had prepared the tape recorder and I had made the call from a pay phone.

"But . . . why didn't she tell me the truth, tell me she was already there in our house for some time?"

"When I asked her that, she told me she was protecting me."

"Oh," he said. "Yes, I suppose that makes sense."

"Does it?"

"Sure. You're her best friend. Look at all you did for her. Why shouldn't she think of you, of protecting you?"

"There's more she didn't tell you, Jesse," I said. I couldn't hold back anything now.

"What more?"

"One day, she found your journal, and she read it. She wanted me to read it, but I wouldn't."

He was silent. I couldn't see his face well in the darkness, but I felt his confusion, his disappointment, even his embarrassment.

"Well," he finally said, "I'm sure she was bored sick. I probably would have done the same thing. I never noticed it had been taken," he said, sitting back again. "It was childish to keep a journal like that."

"There's no reason to find fault with yourself because of what she did, Jesse. That's stupid."

"Yeah, I know. I'm not blaming myself. It'll be all right. Somehow we'll bring it to a good end," he said. He sounded as if he were talking to himself now.

We drove the rest of the way home in silence, each of us trapped within our own terrors and fears and perhaps more bonded as brother and sister than we had ever been.

Mama quickly accepted Jesse's excuse for not having bought anything. She still believed his principal purpose was to have a heart-to-heart talk with me. We didn't linger. We both went up to our rooms. I saw he was still a little shaky from hearing the truth.

"Don't go up there tonight, Jesse. Those stairs make so much noise under you. I was surprised Mama and Daddy didn't hear you the other night."

He looked surprised that I knew, and a little guilty as well.

"Right," he said.

We both glanced at the closed attic door before retiring for the night.

I was determined to be stronger the next day and do well in school, so I wouldn't attract any more attention to myself. Jesse volunteered to take me to school on his way to Daddy's office. I knew he wanted the opportunity for us to talk again.

"I've given it all a great deal more thought," he began. "If I can, I'll come by for you at the end of the day. I think the two of us should meet with Karen to tell her what we found out last night and what I find out from Dad."

"What if you don't find anything out from Daddy?" I asked.

"We'll worry about that later. Just be sure to wait for me before you say anything about last night."

"I'm going to tell her I told you everything," I said. "She should know."

"That's fine," he said. "You can explain that I'm not angry. No sense in worrying her about it."

"Maybe she should be worrying a little more," I replied.

"Take it easy," Jesse said. "Don't condemn her yet."

Was he saying that because he had become her lover or because he wanted to be fair?

"Whatever," I said.

We drove into the school parking lot. He saw the way I was looking at the school, contemplating all I had to face inside.

"I know it's hard for you, Zipper, but try to think of other things. Dive into your schoolwork. That will help."

"Right," I said, and got out of his car. It was easy for him to say.

"I'll try to be back in time," he called.

I lifted my hand without turning back and kept walking toward the building entrance.

As it turned out, I had forgotten completely about the delivery of the sports car. Jesse had no idea why, but Daddy had arranged for both of them to cut the work day short. I had done what Jesse had suggested and concentrated hard on my classes, my lessons, and homework. It worked. I didn't feel under the microscope as much and the day passed quickly for me. Dana Martin left me alone as well, probably because of my dramatic reaction to him yesterday in the cafeteria.

I really didn't have high hopes for Jesse to be there when the final bell rang, but there he was, waiting in the parking lot. I hurried to his car, and he explained that Daddy had sprung him.

"And himself. Something's cooking," he said.

I reminded him about a surprise.

"So what is it?"

"I won't disappoint Daddy," I said, and thought to myself how hollow that sounded now. I wouldn't disappoint him with something like this, but I would disappoint him deeply with what Jesse and I were doing with Karen. "What did you learn?"

"Nothing yet. Dad was waiting for a return call. He might have gotten it before he left. I left first. I didn't want to pressure him too much about it. That could raise some suspicions."

Somehow, in my heart of hearts, I felt that suspicions had been swimming just under the surface of Daddy's thoughts from day one of all this. Jesse looked more troubled and worried to me as well.

However, when we drove up, Daddy was already home and standing next to the convertible, his face beaming.

"Holy cow!" Jesse cried. He pulled up beside it quickly and jumped out of his car.

Daddy started laughing.

"When did you get this?"

"A little while ago," Daddy replied. "It's going to become Zipporah's car eventually."

"Zipporah's car?"

"But if you're nice to her, I'm sure she'll let you use it from time to time. Should we let him take a ride in it now, Zipporah?"

"Sure," I said.

"How did she rate something like this?"

"Play your cards right, and we'll look into a trade-in for you, too," Daddy said. "Go on. Take her for a short spin, but don't dare speed on these roads."

Jesse walked around the car, his hands gliding over the sides and hood, as if he believed it could react to his appreciation. His eyes lit up with excitement.

"Girls and cars," Daddy told me. "The formula for male ecstasy."

"Get in," Jesse cried.

I did, and we drove off with Daddy standing there still beaming after us. Jesse didn't drive fast, but it felt fast with the wind blowing through my hair. It was a beautiful car, and for a few precious minutes, we both forgot all our troubles.

"He's a good guy," Jesse said, slowing down to cruise for a while. "We don't deserve him."

More than ever, I believed that now, but all that did was make me sadder. Daddy had gone into the house before we returned. He stepped out again when we drove in.

"Well?"

"I got a feeling you bought this for yourself, Dad," Jesse teased.

"Your mother accused me of the same thing, but someone has to break it in. We'll do it together this summer," he added. "Come on in. I want to talk to you both." It had an ominous ring to it. Jesse glanced at me, and we followed Daddy into the house and into the living room. He sat in his chair.

"What's up?" Jesse asked.

I sat on the sofa, and he followed.

"I received a phone call while you were taking the ride."

"Oh. And?"

"The police went to Karen's mother's house after Zipporah's second interview. There was no way Harry's mother could have been living in any apartment behind the house. There was an unfinished room, but there was no bathroom or any kitchen connections. Darlene Pearson said her mother-in-law had her own room in the house, the biggest bedroom, and never moved out. She had a stroke, and for a while there was a nurse. "I wondered if Karen meant Harry went to that bedroom, of course."

"Sure, she could have meant that, right, Zipporah?" Jesse asked me.

I didn't reply. There was no confusion about it in my mind. Karen was specific about there being an apartment. She even talked about listening at the door.

Jesse was disappointed by my silence but tried to ignore it. "Did you ask about the crime scene?"

"What is it you expected us to learn, Jesse?"

"I just wondered if there was anything to support the story," he said, and glanced at me.

"They found Harry Pearson's body. They found the knife. That was it, Jess."

"Maybe Darlene Pearson cleaned up the room before the police arrived," Jesse suggested. "Covering up what had happened, what she didn't prevent."

I felt how hard he was struggling to support what Karen had told me and him.

"Cover up? Like what? What was there to cover up? Harry was dead on the floor."

"Harry's mother's wig or something?"

"Why would Harry's mother's wig be in that room? Are you suggesting that Harry wore his mother's wig? You're taking the *Psycho* thing a bit far, aren't you? Isn't it a little on the incredible side to believe Darlene Pearson would tolerate such a state of affairs? Even if she wasn't worried for Karen, she would be worried for herself. Anyone would."

Jesse looked down.

"You guys know more than you're telling me," Daddy said.

Neither of us denied it.

Daddy leaned forward. "Holding back any information is a crime. You've been told that, Zipporah, and you know it, Jess. I'm not bothered by that as much as I am discovering you guys didn't trust me with the information."

Jesse couldn't raise his eyes. The silence was tearing at both our hearts.

"It's not his fault. It's mine," I blurted.

"What is?"

Jesse looked at me and shook his head, but I knew the time had come. Daddy had warned me that keeping the truth down wasn't easy.

"I spoke with Karen right after she stabbed her stepfather," I began.

"Where?" Daddy asked.

"Here," I said. "She came here, Daddy."

My throat was closing, and tears were burning at my eyelids. I tried to swallow. He was staring at me, the disappointment beginning to seep into his face, his eyes narrowing. He leaned forward, his hands on his knees.

"Here?"

"Yes, Daddy. I came home and found her here. She was in the attic."

He leaned back. "In the attic?"

"Yes. She had no place else to go."

"Where is she now, Zipporah?"

"She's in the attic," I said.

Daddy was quiet. He glanced at Jesse, who continued to look down at the floor.

"You're not telling me she's been upstairs in that attic all this time, are you, Zipporah?"

I nodded. "Except for one night or two."

He took a deep breath and gazed out the living-room window for a moment. Then he turned to Jesse.

"When did you know about this, Jesse?"

"The day after I came home," he said.

Daddy's face hardened. "What about the New York phone call, Zipporah?"

"I did it with my tape recorder. She recorded the message, and I played it over the phone. She didn't want the police looking for her around here anymore. I went to the pay phone while Mama was in her bath."

"My God," Daddy said. "You've been harboring a fugitive in our home. You assisted her in deceiving law enforcement. You caused your mother to tell a lie. Do you realize what you've done?"

"She was my best friend, Daddy," I cried through my tears. "You told me what E. M. Forster said about choosing between your friend and your country."

"That was something entirely different from this, Zipporah. I would have thought you understood. I've overestimated you, both of you," he said, looking at Jesse. "Okay. Go upstairs, and bring her down immediately. Go on!" he snapped. His lips were whitening in the corners with the flow of anger through his face.

I rose and walked out, glancing back at Jesse, who still hadn't raised his gaze from the floor. Tears were flowing freely down my cheeks now. I wasn't crying for myself or even for Jesse or Karen. I was crying for my father, who looked as if his heart had been torn into pieces.

Who knew how Karen would react to all this? I thought. I expected some hysterics. This was going to be a terrible scene. I took a deep breath and opened the attic door.

"Karen," I called.

I didn't see her anywhere.

"Karen, are you here?"

Silence was barely interrupted by the breeze whistling through the shutters. Not finding her waiting there stunned me. Daddy wouldn't believe me. He might want to come up to see for himself. I turned and hurried down the stairs. When I reentered the living room, I saw Jesse had his hands over his face. Daddy looked as if smoke could come flowing out of his ears any minute.

"Well?" Daddy asked.

Jesse took his hands away to look at me.

"Where's Karen?" he asked.

"Yes, where is she?" Daddy demanded.

I shook my head. "She's not there, Daddy. I'm not lying. She's not in the attic."

He sat there for a moment. Then he leaped to his feet. "Neither of you leave the house. If she comes back, call the police. Do you hear me, Jesse?"

"Yes sir," he said.

"Don't say a word to your mother if I don't get to her first," he added.

I wondered how we would manage that. One look at us would tell her something was terribly wrong. He looked at us, shook his head, and walked out of the living room. To me, it felt as if the air followed him. Jesse sat there staring at the wall. Then he turned to me slowly.

"You're not lying, are you? She's really not up there."

"I didn't see her, and she didn't respond when I called," I said, and then something came to mind, something that sent a chill through me.

"What is it?" he asked, seeing my face pale.

"I didn't look in one place, her hiding place, the old armoire. She once showed me how she could hide in it if anyone came up to the attic unexpectedly."

"But why wouldn't she come out when she heard you call her?"

I shook my head, rose, and walked slowly back to

the stairway. Jesse followed, and we went up the attic steps. I looked back at him, and then we continued up to the door, paused, and opened it.

She was standing by the window, looking down at the new sports car. She had been in the armoire.

"Karen," I said. It was barely a whisper.

She turned slowly, smiling. "You two have a wonderful life, you know that? Whenever I came over here, I would bathe in the love and affection. I would fantasize that it was my home, too, and they were my parents. I told you that before, didn't I, Zipporah?"

"Yes."

"I never told you, Jesse." She laughed. "I even felt a little incestuous being with you. That's how powerful my fantasy was."

"Jesse knows everything now, Karen," I said.

"That's good. I wish I did. Know everything, that is."

"There's no proof to support the story you told about Harry Pearson," Jesse said. "We mean the part about him and his dead mother. The apartment . . . there is no apartment."

"There was," she said.

"No, I was in it last night. It's an unfinished room. No one could live in it."

She kept shaking her head.

"And the police didn't find the wig you claimed you were wearing, or the dress," Jesse added.

Karen's eyes widened. "They're lying."

"Why would they lie about something like that, Karen?"

"Then my mother got rid of it all before they arrived."

"But why?" Jesse asked. "Why would she submit both of you to such madness?"

"You'll have to ask her. Maybe someday someone will, but probably not anyone in this one-horse town. You ever hear of *Gulliver's Travels*? Well, this is Gullible Travels, stories about the fools in Sandburg," she said, and laughed.

"My father knows everything, Karen."

"Everything again? Even what went on between us, Jesse?"

Jesse blushed.

"I didn't think so. I saw him rush out and drive off and figured as much. Well," she said, walking toward us and the door. "At least I'm getting out of here."

"Where are you going?" I asked her.

She paused in the doorway. "I'm going home," she said. "It's time to go home. Call me later. Maybe we'll do something. I just hate thinking about all the homework that's piled up, but you'll help me with it, won't you, Zipporah?"

I didn't know what to say. I just stared at her. She was making no sense.

She smiled.

We watched her walk out and down the attic steps.

"Jesse," I said, squeezing his arm. "Do something. She's in a daze. It's all been too much, finally too much."

"Hey," he called down to her. "Don't you want a ride?"

She turned at the base of the attic steps and looked up at us. She was smiling again.

"In the new car?"

"Yeah, sure," Jesse said.

She stared a moment, holding her smile, and then shook her head.

"I don't think so, Jesse. Maybe tomorrow. I'd like to walk. I've been shut up indoors too much, and that's not very healthy. But thanks."

She continued down the hallway, down the stairway, to the front door. Jesse and I followed slowly and watched her walk out. I started to cry as she went down the driveway, glanced back to wave at us, and continued on the road to the village. In moments, she was gone. How many times had I wished for that? Now it was breaking my heart.

Jesse went to the phone and made the call Daddy had asked us to make. He quickly explained who he was and what was now happening. I saw him wait until someone else took the phone, and he went through it again.

"She's just walking down the road toward town," he told whoever had taken the call. I imagined it to be Chief Keiser himself. "Just walking," he repeated, as if he had to convince himself as well.

Then he hung up and looked at me.

I turned and ran upstairs, ran all the way back to the attic and shut the door.

Epilogue

Somewhere I read that this world, everything that happens, even everything that happens in the whole universe, could be God's dream, and the bad things that happen are just his nightmares. We don't exist, at least not in the sense we think we do. I thought if that were true, then maybe nothing was our fault. We were as Jesse said Shakespeare wrote, merely players on a stage.

I certainly hoped so. God would then snap his fingers and wake up, and this dream would pop like a bubble. He would start dreaming again, and we'd have another chance to be young and carefree. Darkness would no longer seem like a disease creeping in over us, and rain wouldn't feel like tears.

Funny, but what I feared the most was not the eternal anger and disappointment of our parents but the loneliness that could result from it. When you deeply hurt people you love and who love you, you push away from everything just enough to be out of sync with it all. You can't look at people straight on anymore, and when you walk, you think the world itself has tipped a little. Nothing, not flowers or trees, blue skies or dazzling stars, not music or laughter, nothing, brings you the joy it once did. It's as if you lost the right to be happy.

Of course, our parents wanted to forgive us, and I never doubted they tried with all their heart and soul, but we knew that in the end, even though they could find a way to turn us back into a family, they couldn't find a way to forget. What made all this particularly difficult was what some people call the dropping of the second shoe. When it fell, it fell with thunder and lightning and seemed to tear the earth below our feet. How we didn't both fall into the chasm and disappear is a mystery or a miracle I would not fully understand.

Soon after Jesse called the police that day, a police cruiser came by, and they took Karen away. As it turned out, Daddy was at the police station at the time of Jesse's call. Whatever influence Daddy and his associates had with the powers that be was enough to keep me and Jesse from being charged with any crime. The district attorney took into consideration our youth and Jesse's having made the phone call. It didn't prevent the story from leaking out. Daddy always believed the two state detectives did much to make sure that it did. He told me it was part of the cost of being who he was. It was his nature to be a thorn in the side of bureaucrats.

For a while, our boat was rocking. We worried about the impact it would have on Daddy's career, and more than one night was taken up with a serious discussion about the wisdom of remaining in Sandburg. There were always other opportunities in other communities, and that was true for Mama and her nursing as well, if not more.

As it turned out, however, small towns proved to be more forgiving. The diminutive population, the nearly daily contact most inhabitants had with each other, made everyone a sort of extended family. All understood one another's struggle to make a living, survive, and do well, and most had empathy for the difficulties we all had.

Karen and I used to enjoy mocking the village and its inhabitants, but I began to see that all of the derision was mostly coming from her, from her own wounded self, her envy and longing to get off the emotional crutches and walk as proudly as any other girl her age, especially me.

When the older people in the village saw me, they would shake their heads, wag a finger of caution, and give me some sage advice, such as, "Remember, you are known by the friends you keep," or simply, "Make sure you help your parents."

The younger people had completely different reactions. At school, which was winding down to the end of the school year, I suddenly became infamous. Before, I was merely the friend of someone who had done a terrible thing, but now I was something of a folk hero. Everyone wanted to know how I had managed to keep such a secret. I began to feel as if I were a character in a movie who had suddenly stepped off the screen and started up the aisle. Invitations to parties, to sleepovers, and even for dates, started flowing my way. To some of the boys, I was dangerous, and that made me exciting. Even Dana Martin looked disappointed in himself for driving me away.

Of course, I did none of these things for a while. I could never get myself to ask my parents for anything and wondered if I ever would again. I worked hard to bring my final grades up, helped around the house more, and took great care not to get into any trouble. No teacher would even look at me with reproach, not that I was Miss Perfect or anything.

I think I floated most of the time. At least, that was how it felt. Right afterward, I actually ran a fever and felt so numb all over that Mama took me to see Dr. Bloom, who studied me carefully and concluded I had no infections. I was deeply depressed. He spoke softly to my mother privately about it, and I know one of the things she and my father considered was a therapist, but I rallied soon afterward, and the problem just went away.

Jesse took it all much harder. If he could, he would have gone out back and whipped himself. He was too ashamed to return to Daddy's offices, and for weeks, he remained at home, working on the house as if he wished he could embrace it and get some solace and comfort from it. He went at it all with a maddening drive of perfection. Not a shingle would be permitted out of line, not a spot of rust on any pipe, not a weed on the lawn. It was his idea to empty the attic of all the old things. One night at dinner, he suggested we donate most of it to thrift shops and give whatever else to a consignment store.

"Some of it is so dry and brittle. We have a fire hazard," he declared. "And besides, I'd like to clean up the place, repair and paint the walls. Maybe we can do something better with it."

I didn't oppose the idea. When Karen was taken away, I had gone up to the attic, but I hadn't been there since. I was afraid of the memories it would stir up.

Daddy agreed, and Jesse took on the task of emptying the attic. He did it mostly during the day, while I was at school. I was grateful, for I didn't even want to see any of the furniture, especially our magic sofa.

Sometimes, I imagined Karen was still up there. There were times at night, after I had gone to bed, when I thought I heard footsteps above me. One time, I was absolutely positive I did, and it put a chill under my breast and down my stomach. I rose and listened harder. Then I considered the possibility that it was Jesse. I went out to the hallway and saw that his bedroom door was ajar, so I peered in and saw his bed was empty. He was upstairs. I thought I would go up to see why, but I chose instead to return to my bed. He had his own demons to exorcize, I thought. He needed to be alone.

More than one girl at school, however, begged me to show her the attic, the scene of the fantastic story, or, as Karen had once said, "our own Anne Frank hideaway." I simply shook my head to indicate the mere idea was distasteful.

"It's been shut up," I told them. They believed it, because they imagined that would be exactly what their own parents would do. Lies were still useful, unfortunately.

I had one terrible confrontation with Karen's mother. She was so angry Daddy thought she might influence the district attorney or clamor for Jesse and me to suffer some punishment somehow. He also feared she or her attorney would find some way to initiate a civil suit, so when she called to come over to see us, he thought it would be wiser not to reject her.

"She has a right to this," Daddy explained.

Jesse and I sat in the living room like two errant children, waiting to be reprimanded. Fortunately, Mama was home. My parents greeted Darlene Pearson at the front door, and Mama hugged her, both she and Daddy stringing apologies, sympathies, and hope in their greetings. Then they brought her to the living room. We both looked up at her. She shook her head, and Mama asked her to sit in Daddy's chair, facing us.

"Would you like a cold drink, Darlene?"

"No, nothing, thanks," she said, her eyes burning through me. "I came here to hear from your own lips why you did such a thing," she said.

I thought I wouldn't be able to speak. My throat felt that tight.

Jesse chimed in quickly. "We didn't intend to hurt anyone. We thought we were helping her."

"Helping her?" She looked up at Daddy who was leaning against the living-room doorjamb, his arms folded. Mama was looking down and standing just to Darlene's right. She turned more to me. "You came to my home. You lied to the police. You lied to me to my face. You let me feel sorry for you, when all along, you were in cahoots with her, deceiving everyone. Can you imagine what my nights were like, my days, facing all those people and worrying about her, while all along, you two were playing house down the road?"

"That wasn't what we were doing," I said.

"You didn't do her any good delaying it all. Poor Harry," she said, and looked up at my parents again.

Mama nodded. Daddy glanced at us but said nothing. "I did my best," she said, the tears coming into her eyes now. "You have no idea what it's been like for me."

She looked up at Daddy. "There isn't anyone in this community who didn't know how hard it was for me with her after I married Harry."

Daddy nodded.

She turned back to me. "I thought you would be a good influence on her, Zipporah. She would do better in school. She would see how wonderful a family could be."

"I'm sorry," I said. "She was my best friend. I loved her like a sister."

Those words at least took the heat out of Darlene Pearson's face.

"Well." She sighed deeply and then rose. "I don't know what I'm doing anymore. I don't even know why I came here, what I expected from any of you," she said.

"Don't hesitate to call on me if you need anything, any help, legal or otherwise," Daddy told her.

She nodded and started out, pausing to look back at Jesse and me.

"I can only pray for her, pray for you all," she said, and left. Mama followed her out. Daddy stood there looking at us for a long moment and then left.

"I don't care what they say about Karen," Jesse told me. "That woman had something more to do with it all than she makes out. She's just trying to pass off her own guilt."

I was glad Daddy hadn't heard him.

Afterward, information about Karen's disposition trickled into our home. We knew that Daddy had the information way before but filtered it slowly, like someone who was trying to prevent arsenic poisoning. Too much at once would kill you. Of course, we knew Karen was placed in confinement, which we later found out was really a mental clinic. The district attorney had put everything on hold until a clear and concise diagnosis was made. It went on that way for nearly two months, and then, toward the end of the summer, that second shoe was heard.

Jesse had done a good job of cleaning out the attic. He deliberately painted it a bright blue to contrast with the faded gray walls it had. He and Daddy considered redoing the flooring as well. It was a large enough area to present all sorts of opportunities.

For a while, our lives seemed to be readjusting. The return to what was normal for us had come, and there was even some laughter in our home again. Jesse was preparing for his return to college, and Mama and I had done most of the shopping for my return to school—new clothes, shoes, and a new school briefcase. There were ripples of optimism.

And then Darlene Pearson drove up one evening just as we had sat down for dinner. She rang the doorbell.

"Who could that be?" Daddy asked.

"Only one way to find out," Mama said, rising.

"It better not be one of those religious fanatics come to preach the end of the world," Daddy shouted after her. "I just might believe him."

Jesse and I smiled at each other and waited.

"Oh! Darlene," we heard Mama exclaim. Moments later, she followed her into the dining room.

"Sorry to interrupt your dinner," she declared with

a smug smile that churned my stomach. I held my breath. "Late this afternoon, I learned the news, received confirmation that Karen is pregnant."

For a long moment, no one spoke. When I gazed at Jesse, I saw the explosion of pure terror and fear in his eyes. Daddy rose quickly and reached for the extra chair.

"Please, Darlene, have a seat."

She contemplated it as if it were on fire, and then she relented and sat, her lips drawn tightly, burying the corners in her cheeks.

"Apparently, Karen kept all the symptoms to herself," she continued.

"How far along is she?" Mama asked, slipping into her own seat.

"Ten weeks." She looked at Jesse. "Does anyone have any idea where Karen was ten weeks ago?"

"Jesse?" Daddy said.

Jesse nodded, the guilt pouring off his face.

"What do you intend to do about it, Darlene?" Daddy asked her.

"It's not what I intend to do, is it?"

"She's bringing the baby to term?"

"I certainly won't ask her to have an abortion. I am not a good Catholic. I don't attend church regularly, but there are certain sins I won't commit."

"Of course not," Mama said, even though I suspected she would have chosen differently. "Have you spoken to Karen?"

"Yes. She says she must have the baby, it was an immaculate conception, but we know otherwise, don't we?" she asked, again glaring at Jesse.

"Of course, we'll pay any expenses," Daddy said.

"For how long?" Darlene countered instantly, turning to him.

"For as long as necessary," he said.

"I can tell you this much," she said. "Karen obviously cannot be a mother, and I, at this point in my life, don't want the obligation and responsibility of rearing another child. I failed terribly with my one and only."

Again, there was a long, silent pause.

"Well, I'm sure you can give the baby up for adoption," Daddy said.

"Yes, I'm sure. Like cleaning up after spilt milk."

"I'll help you in any way I can," Daddy said. "Please, be assured of that, Darlene."

She nodded, her chin quivering. Mama rose and put her arm around her shoulders.

"It just doesn't end," Darlene moaned. "I don't even know what will be with Karen."

There was nothing to say. Jesse had his head down, and I looked away, biting my lower lip. Darlene rose slowly and, with Mama still embracing her, walked out. We heard the front door open and then close. Mama returned, shaking her head, her own face now crumpling. She turned and ran out. We heard her pound the stairs to her and Daddy's bedroom.

Daddy sat back.

"I'm sorry, Dad."

"Me, too. Go up and talk to your mother," he said. "I'm still hungry." He stabbed his fork into a piece of roast beef.

Jesse stood up, glanced at me, and walked out.

"My father used to say that when you made a big mistake, a real error in judgment, you placed yourself in the hands of unmerciful forces. Things have a way of spiraling out. I doubt that you'll forget any of this, Zipporah, but I hope you won't fall into those unmerciful hands, too," Daddy said. "Go on and eat. Your mother will feel even worse if she sees no one ate her dinner."

"I can't," I whined.

"It's not all your fault, Zipporah. It didn't start with your hiding her out or Jesse having an affair with her. We don't know what started it, but it's not all your fault. I don't want you to think I believe you're innocent of any wrongdoing, but you're not solely the bad guy here. Understand? Do you?"

"Yes."

"Then force yourself to eat something. You have to think of restoring yourself. We all do," he said.

Would I ever have his wisdom and strength? I wondered. Would Jesse?

Before Daddy and I were finished, Jesse returned with Mama, and they sat at the table.

No one spoke. Jesse helped me clean off the dishes and then clean up the kitchen, while Mama and Daddy talked softly in his home office. Afterward, Jesse and I went out and sat on the front porch, staring at the dark road. Only one vehicle went by.

"I think that's Mr. Bedick," I said. "He almost hit me one night when I was walking home from the village. It was my fault. I wish he had."

"Don't talk stupid," Jesse said. "I have the monopoly on that in this family."

I couldn't help but smile.

We heard the front door open. Daddy stood there looking out at us a moment.

"Come inside," he said. "In the living room." He

turned, leaving the door open, and we quickly followed. Mama was already seated on the sofa. We sat beside her. Daddy took his seat.

"We've made a decision," he began. "We're adopting the child."

"You are?" I asked, incredulous.

"Adopting might be the wrong word. I'm not sure. He or she is our grandchild," he said. "Your mother and I are somewhat old-fashioned when it comes to this sort of thing."

He looked at her, and she smiled at him. With that smile, she looked years younger to me.

"We believe in bearing responsibility. We believe in family, in blood."

"But what about your work?" Jesse asked Mama.

"I need a break. I'll go back when I can. Or maybe I won't. It seems the length of time and attention you should give your children might not be as short as one would think."

"But everyone will know," I said, not meaning to have it sound as if I were complaining.

"They'll know anyway. Some probably know already, considering Darlene Pearson's anger."

"What will you tell the baby when he or she is old enough to ask questions?" I asked.

"The truth, of course," Daddy said. "The last lie was told in this house months ago."

"Are you sure you really want to do this?" Jesse asked. "It's all my fault."

"It's not all your fault. Most of it, maybe, but what are you going to do about it, Jesse? Stop going to college? Take some menial job to pay for diapers and bottles? No, it's decided," Daddy added. "You return to college. You, Zipporah, return to school and, when you can, help out."

"Okay," I said.

"It's all right, Jesse," Mama told him. "I wouldn't do it if I didn't think it was right and if I didn't want to do it."

He nodded. He was crying, but he sucked back his tears, rose, and walked out. We heard him go upstairs to his room.

"We're going to be all right," Daddy told me. "We're going to take care of each other better from now on, too."

I left them. I was probably just as numb, as stunned and afraid, as Jesse was, but there was nothing more to say about it. I sensed they had made an irrevocable decision. Their firmness once they had made up their minds gave me pause and strength. It gave me hope as well. Maybe we would be all right.

Of course, as I lay there thinking. I wondered about Karen now, lying alone in some institution where there were bars on the windows. What was she thinking? Did she hate me? Hate Jesse, too? Maybe she was talking to herself or to an imaginary person like me, talking about traveling.

"When we get our licenses, we'll leave this hick town," she was saying. "We'll see America. We'll have adventures, so when we're older and stuck in some marriage, we won't regret it. We won't think we missed anything. We'll take your convertible. We'll ride with the wind in our hair, and we'll think of nothing but tomorrow.

"Will you do it? Will you come with me, Zipporah? Can we be together again and forever?"

"Yes," I whispered in the darkness of my own room. "Nothing but tomorrow."

Through my bedroom window, I saw the moon fool a cloud and slip free. It poured its golden light over the treetops like a promise.

Karen was returning, I thought. She was returning in her child. Ironically, she wanted us to adopt her. In a real sense, we would. What had bonded us before hadn't weakened, after all. It had tightened and strengthened and wrapped itself around me.

Around all of us, actually.

And what that would mean for all of us lay cloaked in the mystery of the same darkness that made ancient peoples hug each other. Like them, I wondered if we would be safe, if we would ever be safe again.

I could only wait to know.